PENGUIN CLASSICS

THE PENGUIN BOOK OF
MURDER MYSTERIES

MICHAEL SIMS is the author of *Arthur and Sherlock*, which was a finalist for the Edgar from the Mystery Writers of America, the Gold Dagger from the Crime Writers Association of Great Britain, and numerous other awards; *Adam's Navel*, which was a *New York Times* Notable Book and a *Library Journal* Best Science Book; *The Story of Charlotte's Web*, which was chosen by *The Washington Post* and several other venues as a Best Book of the Year; *In the Womb: Animals*, the companion book to a National Geographic Channel series; and other books. For Penguin Classics he has edited several anthologies, including *The Annotated Archy and Mehitabel*; *Arsène Lupin, Gentleman-Thief*; and *The Penguin Book of Victorian Women in Crime*. He writes regularly for *The New York Times* and other periodicals, and his books are widely translated around the world.

T0038559

The Penguin Book of Murder Mysteries

Edited with an Introduction by
MICHAEL SIMS

PENGUIN BOOKS

PENGUIN BOOKS

An imprint of Penguin Random House LLC
penguinrandomhouse.com

Introduction and selection copyright © 2023 by Michael Sims
Penguin Random House supports copyright. Copyright fuels creativity, encourages diverse voices,
promotes free speech, and creates a vibrant culture. Thank you for buying an authorized edition of
this book and for complying with copyright laws by not reproducing, scanning, or distributing any
part of it in any form without permission. You are supporting writers and allowing Penguin Random
House to continue to publish books for every reader.

LIBRARY OF CONGRESS CATALOGING-IN-PUBLICATION DATA
Names: Sims, Michael, 1958- editor.
Title: The Penguin book of murder mysteries / Michael Sims.
Description: New York : Penguin Classics, 2023.
Identifiers: LCCN 2023017202 (print) | LCCN 2023017203 (ebook) |
ISBN 9780143137535 (trade paperback) | ISBN 9780593511626 (ebook)
Subjects: LCSH: Detective and mystery stories, English. |
Detective and mystery stories, American. |
English fiction—19th century. | American fiction—19th century. |
LCGFT: Detective and mystery fiction. | Short stories.
Classification: LCC PR1309.D4 P44 2023 (print) |
LCC PR1309.D4 (ebook) | DDC 823/.087208—dc23/eng/20230809
LC record available at https://lccn.loc.gov/2023017202
LC ebook record available at https://lccn.loc.gov/2023017203

Printed in the United States of America
3rd Printing

Set in Sabon LT Pro

Contents

Introduction

The Society of Connoisseurs in Murder

"Thou shalt not kill," commands the King James Bible—without, as opponents of capital punishment like to point out, riders or qualifiers. Curiously, this translation of an injunction in the ancient Hebrew Torah did not lead the list of Yahweh's rules; it arrives after other warnings, such as no swearing and no bowing to the swarm of other gods out there. It is, however, blunt.

Murder is the most desperate act a human being can commit against another—-which is why, in its dramatic fertility, it has been a fruitful trope in the arts from the Mesopotamian epic of Gilgamesh to Attica Locke's recent detective series about Texas Ranger Darren Mathews, from Cain's murder of his brother Abel to the Hulu comedy *Only Murders in the Building.* Whether taxonomized narrowly or broadly, whether in the latest court case or prior to the ancient legal code attributed to the Babylonian king Hammurabi, murder is always with us.

The *Oxford English Dictionary*, a marginally less revered source than the Bible, defines "murder, *n.*" as "the most heinous kind of criminal homicide." This definition includes the adjective *criminal* because, technically, *homicide* describes the killing of another human being in any circumstance, whether deliberately in *murder* or negligently in *manslaughter*—both varieties of *unlawful killing.* Even suicide is sometimes defined in statistics as self-inflicted murder. It is still homicide when one kills during war or a state-sponsored execution; but, however tragic it may be, it is by definition not unlawful when state-approved.

Otherwise Jack Ketch, the infamous executioner under Charles II who became an eponym for *hangman*, would be remembered as a murderer himself.

In court, *murder* is a charge, characterized by degrees of premeditation and malice. The adjective *willful* implies intent and also that it is possible to commit murder during loss of control over oneself. The often-contested charge of *felony murder* points out that if someone dies as a result of your criminal action, you are liable for murder whether or not you intended it; many nations and some US states have removed it from their books.

"Stranger danger" is a favorite theme of people who claim that society's allegedly innocent citizens are better protected from its allegedly dangerous citizens by remaining in a kind of moral panic, a red alert of suspicion toward people they do not know. Of course, within reason we must be wary of strangers. For people of color, for women in general, and for those who visibly identify outside the traditional binary of sexual orientation, stranger danger is a daily possibility, especially in notoriously racist nations such as the United States. But people who work to address daily tragedies such as domestic violence and sexual assault point out that stranger-oriented paranoia ignores the sober reality that most victims are harmed by people they know—often by family members. And for centuries many people have had to remind themselves daily that they would find neither refuge nor justice from those whose job was to enforce the very laws that subjugated them.

Crime fiction is so popular nowadays that devotees of allegedly historical accounts must define their category as "*true* crime," a curious term like *nonfiction writer*. True-crime podcasts tirelessly speculate over what motivates heinous crimes, and the best fictional detective series—on page or screen—exploit how investigative procedure takes us behind the scenes of tragedy. Everybody seems to find murder fascinating. Nowadays, without the murderers and victims who draw tourists to its Chamber of Horrors, the Madame Tussauds waxworks in London would be limited to a hoodied Mark Zuckerberg peering over a laptop and Kate Middleton clutching a purse.

We are drawn to the horrific with good reason. We understand that, in our soft mammalian bodies, evolved from predatory primates, we are at risk of accident and violence. We know loss and grief. Even hamsters exhibit self-preservation, but presumably they lack our foreknowledge that all creatures tread the edge of the abyss. One of the quirks of *Homo sapiens*, however, is that we get a *thrill* from the abyss. Perhaps its proximity fires up our primordial synapses. In a world of stationary bicycles and decaffeinated coffee, of streetlights banishing the ancient night, do we miss that shiver down the spine?

The shiver is not new. *The Penguin Book of Murder Mysteries* celebrates how the nineteenth century added a modern twist to the ancient theme of bloody murder. Gradually, the suspenseful race of pursuers hot on the trail of a culprit began to entwine toward the denouement with a parallel story of how they gathered and deciphered clues. This narrative updating wed venerable kinds of epic stories, such as quest and vengeance, to the sense of mystery formerly limited to supernatural narratives. The Gothic cobwebbery festooning many early crime stories—much of which now looks as silly to us as a haunted fairground in *Scooby-Doo*—met the fresh new idea of legal justice. Although there are occasional earlier examples of crime-solving, the murder mystery as we think of it nowadays centered upon a detective figure interested at least in the conservative notion of the restoration of "order," and at best in the liberal ideal of justice. The genre could not have evolved before modern notions of a codified legal structure and organized police—ideally a commitment to evidence versus torture, clues versus accusation. In every society, of course, the evolving system has been structured to protect the dominant group, so corruption and bigotry polluted each system. But at least there was beginning to be a system.

The myriad approaches to murder mysteries keep us returning to this genre. For example, writers have expressed some curious notions about how guilt manifests itself. "Murder, though it hath no tongue," murmurs Hamlet to himself, "will speak with most miraculous organ." His father's ghost claims he was murdered by his brother, Claudius, but Hamlet cautiously plans to confirm this posthumous accusation by setting a trap for Claudius: a play about a man who murders his brother that would prompt Claudius to confess his guilt. Edgar Allan Poe also thought that shock would jolt a confession, as he demonstrates in his story "Thou Art the Man," and later Lieutenant Columbo tried it on TV. In one of the earlier stories herein (it would be a spoiler to tell you which), suspects are required to touch the victim's corpse.

Granted, many detective stories use a corpse only as Alfred Hitchcock employed what he called a MacGuffin—as a plot device to get the story moving. We do not lament the token death that motivates the lighthearted antics of Jessica Fletcher in *Murder, She Wrote*. But other murder mysteries break your heart with the everyday tragedies of grief, the cancerous gnaw of regret and guilt growing ever more deadly, the ways that people try not to get involved, the passions and fears of ordinary people living their extraordinary lives with all the tired grandeur of Lear on the heath.

And then, amid the poignant aspects of well-played melodrama, the murder mystery performs that magic that gives detective stories their unique aesthetic pleasure. It makes you entertain many successive provisional conclusions, and then it presents you with one last flourish. *Et voilà*, it makes you restructure all your tentative ideas, which have been forming and re-forming throughout this performance, and replaces them with What Really Happened. For examples of this kind of narrative reversal, I recommend stories in this anthology such as James McLevy's "The Dead Child's Leg" and Anna Katharine Green's "An Intangible Clue." I ought to mention that McLevy's tragic, gruesome tale will also break your heart.

The emotional satisfaction of this routine may indeed be a restoration of the forces of order—a kind of narrative reassurance. Perhaps that explains why mystery novels were so popular during World War II among the crowds hiding in the Underground from Nazis blitzing London. The aesthetic thrill, however, is separate. It's a magic show. The rabbit must emerge from a different hat than the one you are watching. A bit loony, this low art—artificial as a sonnet, simplistic as opera. Aristotle would classify most of it as mere spectacle. Yet at its best a murder mystery isn't quite like any other kind of literature. *The Penguin Book of Murder Mysteries* is for connoisseurs of murder.

The February 1827 issue of *Blackwood's* magazine included an outré essay (or story?) by Thomas De Quincey, "On Murder Considered as One of the Fine Arts." De Quincey claimed to include a paper delivered in London at an organization he called the Society of Connoisseurs in Murder. "They profess to be curious in homicide, amateurs and dilettanti in the various modes of carnage, and, in short, Murder-Fanciers," he wrote. "Every fresh atrocity of that class which the police annals of Europe bring up, they meet and criticize as they would a picture, statue, or other work of art."

By *police annals* De Quincey meant also the flourishing popular press devoted to sensational crime—especially bloody murder. For example, in De Quincey's time the *Examiner*, which was founded by essayist Leigh Hunt, featured a column entitled "Murders and Murderous Crimes." In the 1820s forty thousand people gawked at the hanging of murderer John Thurtell. In the vein of this already well-established form of grisly entertainment, De Quincey's narrator cites a number of real-life murders, applauding the artistry or decrying the lack thereof in their performance. He examines, for example, the killing of Mrs. Ruscombe and her maid in 1764, as well as the horrific Ratcliff Highway murders from 1811, whose victims included an entire family and their maid.

With the straight-faced tone employed by Jonathan Swift a century earlier in his *A Modest Proposal* that the children of the poor should be sold as food for the wealthy, De Quincey remarks casually, "People begin to see that something more goes to the composition of a fine murder than two blockheads to kill and be killed, a knife, a purse, and a dark lane." This described a common occurrence in an ill-lit London two years before the formation of an official police force, and not an unknown phenomenon nowadays. "Design, gentlemen, grouping, light and shade, poetry, sentiment, are now deemed indispensable to attempts of this nature." De Quincey was already known for his scandalous account of his own travails with laudanum, *Confessions of an English Opium-Eater*, and this new performance did not redeem his reputation. His status as a clever stylist, however, was secure.

I think he would have enjoyed the artistry with which authors in *The Penguin Book of Murder Mysteries* crafted their atrocities and carnage—the light and shade of their atmosphere, the design and composition of their clues and pursuit. This anthology is something of a historical tour of the genre, in chronological order, but it is aimed at twenty-first century murder-fanciers, connoisseurs who want to read about more than two blockheads, one to kill and one to be killed.

In planning a cocktail party or an anthology, I select the invitees based upon the likelihood that some may be even more interesting in juxtaposition than in my previous individual encounters with them. Like any host, I devise my guest list based upon my own preferences. For this anthology, for example, I omit the Dr. Thorndyke stories because I find R. Austin Freeman's numerous antisemitic portrayals offensive. I have been similarly arbitrary throughout. Thus some other usual suspects have not been invited to this party. You will not find here many of the celebrity detectives who make the rounds of every mystery-fan party like board members an executive director was afraid not to invite. No doubt Sherlock Holmes and Auguste Dupin kept checking their mailboxes for an invitation, but I left them off the list. The world does not need another reprint of "A Scandal in Bohemia" or "The Murders in the Rue Morgue."

I have already edited a fat anthology that follows and demonstrates the genre's origins and development (*The Dead Witness*), and smaller volumes that explored particular themes

(*The Penguin Book of Gaslight Crime, The Penguin Book of Victorian Women in Crime*). When Elda Rotor, the publisher of Penguin Classics, and I talked about my doing a new anthology with them, we agreed that I ought to seek the different, the unjustly forgotten, as well as crime fiction by writers not associated with the genre. There is a special flavor to nineteenth century literature. It inspires in me an archaeologist's thrill of unearthing the past. Or is it a time-traveler's frisson of witnessing the roots of my own era? I also love the antique cadence of the language, which is a kind of music to me. Victorian writers have replaced musicians as my companions for long drives.

Surprises within these pages include Gerald Griffin's "The Hand and Word," a dark Irish murder story published fourteen years before Poe's Dupin deduced the existence of a homicidal orangutan in the Rue Morgue—sixty years before young Sherlock Holmes peered through his magnifying glass at the word *Rache* scrawled on a wall in Lauriston Gardens. If you want to see the evolution of a genre during the nineteenth century encapsulated, contrast Griffin's almost medieval Gothic story with the sly urbanity of Anna Katharine Green's "An Intangible Clue," published eighty-eight years later.

At this party you will mingle with the humane novelist Charles W. Chesnutt, who, with majority white ancestry, could have passed as white but chose instead to identify and write as Black and became one of the earliest prominent writers about Black culture in the United States. I brought out of the shadows former stars in the crime field, such as the Austrian novelist Auguste Groner, whose star faded in the United States after Germany's role in World War I, and the prolific American Geraldine Bonner. Speaking of whom, half the guests of this anthology are female, including some writing about the rebellious early "lady detectives." Some of these stories have never been reprinted before *The Penguin Book of Murder Mysteries*.

In literary as in larger history, the establishment of "firsts" is a question of definition as much as chronology. Scholars of crime fiction, for example, debate the honor of the first detective and first detective story, but doing so requires more than ferreting out publication dates. What constitutes a detective story? Does it require a professional detective of some sort—police or private—to qualify? Many earlier tales featured crime, violence, pursuit, revenge. At what point did we begin to write stories about eagle-eyed detectives? For example, the "steady-looking, sharp-eyed" Inspector Bucket bloodhounds successfully through the pages of Dickens's 1852–1853 novel *Bleak House*, but it is not a detective story. Poe often gets credit for the first detective story because the snooping and theorizing of his smug dilettante Dupin form the center and point of "The Murders in the Rue Morgue." We don't witness the murders; Dupin re-creates them for us from clues.

One perennial question is, "Who was the first *female* detective?" Some commentators nominate a character named Ruth Trail, heroine (and also villain) of Edward Ellis's penny dreadful *Ruth the Betrayer; or, The Female Spy*. Its fifty-two weekly installments began in 1862 and ended the following year; the sole complete copy in the British Library bears a stamped arrival date of February 1863. Thus we can assign Trail a precise point on the timeline. More than two decades before women actually held any employment in the police force, Trail works with the police as, according to one male colleague, "a female detective—a sort of spy we use in the hanky-panky way when a man would be too clumsy."

But do we want her on this timeline? Rather than a detective story, *Ruth the Betrayer* is a serial saga that adds up to a long episodic novel about a criminal who happens to also be a crooked cop. For our purposes, this résumé handicaps Trail's eligibility for the title of first female detective. Two more worthy nominees for the title appeared almost simultaneously, soon after Ellis's book. One, known only as "Mrs. G.," narrates Andrew Forrester, Jr.'s "The Judgement of Conscience" herein. Mrs. G. proves a worthy ancestor to Sara Paretsky's V. I. Warshawsky and Ann Cleeves's Vera Stanhope. More of this fascinating background can be found in the introduction to "The Judgement of Conscience."

Let us glance briefly at an example of the appeal of grisly horrors to members of the Society of Connoisseurs in Murder.

"Nancy is no more," Charles Dickens wrote to his friend John Forster, in August 1838. Amid the inky pages of his ever-growing stack of manuscript, Dickens had just killed off one of the most sympathetic characters in *Oliver Twist*. This was the first work of fiction to be published under Dickens's own name, rather than the pseudonym Boz, and the first to draw entirely from his own inspiration. Its sunny predecessor, *The Posthumous Papers of the Pickwick Club*, had resulted from a confident young freelancer's willingness to write a text to accompany a series of sporting illustrations. Posterity has judged that the writer's contribution eclipsed that of the artist—whose name, once known in London but now merely a historical footnote, was Robert Seymour.

Dickens's dark saga of Oliver, the parish (charity) boy who falls into London's criminal underworld, could not have differed more from Pickwickian picnics and the wit of that quotable Cockney valet, Mr. Sam Weller. The orphaned Oliver's misfortunes include falling under the tutelage of Fagin, who dominates a gang of urchins he has forced into thievery, including the now-famous one nicknamed the Artful Dodger. Eventually one adult in Fagin's gang, a prostitute named Nancy, tries to help Oliver—after which her lover, Bill Sikes, murders her. It is a horrific scene. He strikes her twice in the face with his pistol and then bludgeons her with a club.

Three prolific decades later, in November 1868, Dickens was looking for a new sensation in his renowned public performances of his own work. Before a group of invited friends, he staged his first reading of this tragic scene from *Oliver Twist*. The attendees were gratifyingly shocked—aghast—thrilled. Some admonished him against reading such horror in public. "My dear Dickens," warned one prim doctor, "if only one woman cries out when you murder the girl, there will be a contagion of hysteria all over this place." Yet women seem to have survived this assault on their allegedly delicate sensibilities.

No riots were reported, nor even fainting, that now-extinct species of editorial.

Dickens got so caught up in acting out his own scene of Bill Sikes's murder of Nancy that his performance was said to cause his pulse to hammer and his breathing to falter. Often he had to be helped from the stage afterward to rest on a sofa, unable to speak. Dickens edited and shortened the passages from his books that he chose to read in public. A surviving reading script for this staple of his later tours includes notes to himself: "Point. . . . Shudder. . . . Look Round with Terror."

No doubt we are all civilized people here. We obey the law and wish each other well. Of course we do. And yet—here we are, preparing to enjoy stories about murder.

Although we don't have to wear out our hearts performing such tales before audiences, most of us know the pounding pulse that accompanies suspenseful literature. It is one of life's great quiet pleasures, disappearing into a book, losing yourself in the experiences of another. In lively, atmospheric stories such as those in the following pages, we identify with the protagonist, with the victim—at times even with the perpetrator. We get to play both hero and villain. Within the stories, where our out-of-body experience of literature takes us, we peer around for clues, look over our shoulders at sudden noise. For a moment we may lose track of where we are. Back in the allegedly real world, our corporeal bodies shudder. Like Dickens, we look round with terror.

Then, perhaps with a little anticipatory smile, we turn the page.

MICHAEL SIMS

A Note on the Text

Spelling and punctuation have been kept as in the original stories with obvious typos corrected, and a few works retain racist or otherwise objectionable terms, especially Charles W. Chesnutt's rigorously realistic 1889 story "The Sheriff's Children." Ancillary editorial materials have been Americanized.

The Penguin Book of
Murder Mysteries

GERALD GRIFFIN

(1803–1840)

But oft he thought, 'mid holy strains,
Upon that lovely woman;
For oh, the blood within his veins
Was warm, and young, and human.
He told his nightly beads in vain,
Sleep never came so slowly.
And all that night young Kevin's brain
Was filled with dreams unholy.

Gerald Griffin must have sympathized with the mixed feelings of poor Kevin, the tormented protagonist of his poem "The Fate of Cathleen: A Wicklow Story." Griffin's psyche seems to have been a cocktail of mixed feelings, tormented by his febrile religious views, especially by what he construed as a struggle between spirit and flesh.

Gearóid Ó Gríofa was born in Limerick, grew up by the banks of the Shannon, lived for several years in a house called Fairy Lawn, and died in Cork. He had thirteen siblings. Griffin lived only a busy thirty-six years, during which self-doubt prompted frequent new beginnings. He read slush-pile manuscripts at a publishing house and translated works from Spanish and French. He began attending law school. He tried his hand at all sorts of writing, from journalism to the stage. Like many beginning writers, however, he was ill-paid, not as lucky as he hoped to be, and perhaps not as talented as he imagined.

Disappointed by the struggles of life, he turned ever more toward religion. "His imagination," wrote Griffin's brother in a biography of him, had "a strong tendency to be affected by the supernatural." At the age of thirty-four he declared that literature had been a waste of time and a distraction from more useful contributions to society. "I do not know any station in life," Griffin wrote to his father, "in which a man can do so much good, both to others and to himself, as in that of a Catholic priest." He burned his unpublished manuscripts and joined, not the priesthood, but an associated lay clergy organization called the Institute of the Brothers of the Christian Schools. This group promoted the education of poor children, but throughout its history—already reported by Griffin's time and documented as recently as a 2014 British government inquiry—its mission was sabotaged by men who sexually abused boys they were meant to guard and teach.

Two years after joining the Brothers, Griffin died of typhus. He left behind quite an array of poetry and drama and fiction, from the story collection *Tales of the Jury-Room* to the novel *The Collegians,* the story of the investigation and trial following the murder of a young woman. Renowned actor and playwright Dion Boucicault adapted this novel as the successful play *The Colleen Bawn,* since filmed more than once and revived in Belfast theater as recently as 2018. In Ireland Gerald Griffin is remembered in literature, in street names, and in the names of some Irish football clubs. Considering his frustrations with his literary endeavors, he might have found these other connections to his name more satisfying, but they too are a byproduct of his writing.

"The Hand and Word" was published in Griffin's 1827 collection *"Holland-Tide"; or, Munster Popular Tales,* and was reprinted in a two-volume 1830 anthology (anonymously, like the other stories in it) entitled *The Storyteller.* Apparently it has not been reprinted anywhere else in the intervening two centuries. The following version, taken from Griffin's original, retains his curious punctuation, spelling, parenthetical definitions of Irish terms, and occasional footnotes. The story has its own atmospheric weirdness and melodrama of bloody murder. But it also demonstrates the impressive difference between the discursive, less structured stories of the early nineteenth century, which seem festooned with antique trappings as if barely fighting their way out of the Middle Ages—especially in this story of isolated islanders desperately clinging to cliffsides like the lesser black-backed gull called in these remote islands, as Griffin says, "horse gulls"—and the lighter touch, smoother pacing, and more realistic dialogue of the later stories herein.

THE HAND AND WORD

—Porque ninguno
De mi venganza tome
Vengarme de mi procuro
Buscando desde esa torre
En al ancho mar sepulchro

Calderon's *El Mayor Monstruo los Zelos*

Vengeance is here the right of none—
My punishment be mine alone!
In the broad waves that heave and boom
Beneath this tower I seek my tomb.

The village of Kilkee, on the south-western coast of Ireland, has been for many years to the city of Limerick (on a small scale) that which Brighton is to London. At the time, however, when the events which form the subject of the following little history took place, it had not yet begun to take precedence of a watering-place somewhat farther to the north on the same coast, called Miltown Malbay, which had been for a long time, and still was, a favourite summer resort with the fashionables of the county, such as they were. The village itself consists merely of six or eight streets, or straggling rows of houses, scattered irregularly enough over those waste banks of sand in which the land terminates as it approaches the Atlantic.

Those banks, or sandhills, as they are called, do not in this place slope gradually to the marge of the sea, but form a kind of abrupt barrier or natural terrace around the little bay, descending with such suddenness that the ledges on the extreme verge completely overhang the water, and with their snow-white fronts and neat green lattices, produce a sufficiently picturesque effect when the tide is at the full.

The little inlet which has been dignified with the title of a bay, opens to the north-west by a narrow mouth, rendered yet narrower in appearance by the Duggara rocks, which stretch more than half-way across from the southern extremity. A bed of fine hard sand reaches as far as low-water mark, and when the retiring waves have left it visible, affords a pleasant promenade to the bathers. Winding on either side toward the opening of the bay and along the line of coast, are seen a number of broken cliffs, which, rising to a considerable height, form to the north a precipitous headland called Corballagh, and to the southward they stretch away behind Duggara in a thousand fantastic shapes. Closest to the mouth or opening, on this side, is the Amphitheatre, which has been so named in later years, from the resemblance which instantly suggests itself to the beholder. Here the rocks lift themselves above the level of the sea in regular grades, bearing a kind of rude similitude to the benches of such a theatre as that above-named, to the height of two or three hundred feet. In the bathing season this place is seldom without a few groups or straggling figures, being turned to account in a great many different ways, whether as a resting-place to the wanderers on the cliffs, or a point of rendezvous to the numerous pic-nic parties who come here to enjoy a dinner *al fresco*, and luxuriate on the grand and boundless ocean-prospect which lies beneath and beyond them.

A waggish host of the village with whom I had the honour to domiciliate during a brief sojourn in the place a few years hence, informed me that a number of serious accidents had rendered the visitors to the Amphitheatre somewhat more cautious of suffering themselves to become entangled among the perils of the shelving and disjointed crags of which it was composed. Among many anecdotes of warning he mentioned one which occurred to a meditative guest of his own, for which I at first gave him credit for a poetical imagination, though I afterwards found he had spoken nothing more than a real fact.

"To take out his book" (he said in answer to a question from me, as to the manner of the occurrence), "and to sit down as it might be this way on a shelving rock, and the sea to be roaring, and he to be thinking of nothing, only what he was reading, when a swell riz and took him out a distins, as it might be good to give him a good sea-view of the cliffs and the place, and turning again the same way it came, laid him up on the same stone, where, I'll be your bail, he was mighty scarce in less than no time".

Beyond the Amphitheatre, the cliff rises to a still greater height, forming an eminence called the Look-out. Shocking as the tale may appear to modern readers, it has been asserted, and but too many evidences remain to give weight and colour to the supposition, that in those barbarous (though not very distant) times, this place was employed as an observatory by the wild fishermen of the coast and neighboring hamlets, the principal portion of whose livelihood was derived from the plunder of the unfortunate men who happened to be wrecked on this inhospitable shore; and it is even recorded, and generally believed, that fires were, on tempestuous nights, frequently lighted here, and in other dangerous parts of the coast, in order to allure the labouring vessel, already hardly set by the roar of winds and waves, to a more certain and immediate destruction on the rocks and shoals beneath, a practice, it is said, which was often successful to a fearful extent.

The most remarkable point of scenery about the place, and one with which we shall close our perhaps not un-needful sketch of the little district, is the Puffing-hole, a cavern near the base of the cliff last-mentioned, which vaults the enormous mass of crag to a considerable distance inland, where it has a narrow opening, appearing to the eyes of a stranger like a deep natural well. When the tremendous sea from abroad rolls into this cavern, the effect is precisely the same as if water were forced in an inverted tunnel, its impetus of course increasing as it ascends through the narrow neck, until at length reaching the perpendicular opening, or Puffing-hole, it jets frequently to an immense height into the air, and falls in rain on the mossy fields behind.

At a little distance from this singular phenomenon stood a rude cottage. It was tenanted by an aged woman on the place, the relict of one of the most daring plunderers of the coast, who was suspected to have been murdered by one of his own comrades a good many years before. The interior of the little building bore sufficient testimony to the unlawful habits of its former master. All, even the greater proportion of the domestic utensils, were formed of ship timbers: a rudder had been awkwardly hacked and hewed up into something bearing a resemblance to a table, which stood in the middle of the principal apartment; the rafters were made from the spars of boom, peek, and yard; a *settle-bed* at the further end had been constructed from the ruins of a gallant ship; and the little boarded parlour inside was furnished in part from the same materials. A number of planks carelessly fastened together by way of a dresser, stood against the wall, shining forth in all the glory of burnished pewter, wooden-platter, and gaudily painted earthenware the heir-looms of the house of Moran.

Terrified and shocked to the soul by the sudden fate of her late spouse, Mrs. Moran, the proprietress of the cottage, resolved that their boy, an only child, should not follow the dangerous courses of his father. In this she happened to be seconded by the youth's own disposition, which inclined to a quietude and gentleness of character. He was, at his sixteenth year, far beyond his compeers of the village in point of education, and not behind in beauty of person, and dexterity at all the manual exercises of *goal*, single-stick, etc., etc., accomplishments, however, which were doomed not to be wasted in the obscurity of his native wilderness, for before he had completed his seventeenth year, he was laid by the heels, one morning as he sat at breakfast, and pressed to sea.

One day was allowed him to take leave of old friends, and prepare to bid a long adieu to his native home. This day was a painful one, for more reasons than one.

Of course it is not to be supposed that so smart, handsome, clever, and well disposed a lad as Charlie Moran, would be unappreciated among the maidens of the district in which he vegetated. He had in short a lover; a fine flaxen-haired girl, with whom he had been intimate from infancy up to youth, when the wars (into the service of which he suspected he was betrayed by the agency of the girl's parent, a comfortable *Palatine* in the neighbourhood) called him away from his boyish sports to the exercise of a premature manhood. Their parting was by no means more agreeable to little Ellen Sparling than to

himself, seeing that they were more fondly and deeply attached
to one another, than is frequently the case with persons of their
age and rank in life, and moreover that it would not have been
the easiest matter possible to find a pair so well matched in
temper and habits, as well as in personal loveliness (just then
unfolding itself in each with a promise of perfect maturity)
anywhere about the country-side.

The father of the girl, however, who, to say the truth, was
indeed the contriver of Moran's impressment, looked forward
to his absence with a great deal of joy. The old Palatine, who
possessed all the prudence of parents in every soil and season,
and all the natural obstinacy of disposition inherent in the national character of the land of his forefathers, had on this occasion his prejudices doubly strengthened, and rendered at last
inveterate, by the differences of religion and education, as well
as by that eternal, reciprocal, and indomitable hatred which invariably divides the usurping and favoured immigrant from the
oppressed indigenous disinherited inheritor of the soil. Fond of
his little girl, yet hating her friend, he took the part of weaning
them asunder by long absence, a common mistake among more
enlightened parents than Mr. Sparling.

On the day preceding that of young Moran's departure, when
the weeping girl was hanging on his neck, and overwhelming
him with conjurations to "prove true", an advice, to follow
which, he assured her over and over again in his own way, he
needed no exhortations, her lover proposed her to walk (as it
might be for the last time) towards a spot which had been the
usual limit to their rambles, and their general rendezvous whenever her father thought proper to forbid their communing in his
house, which was only done at intervals, his vigilance being a
sort of chronic affection, sometimes rising to a height which
seemed dangerous to their hopes, sometimes relapsing into a
state of almost perfect indifference. To this spot the lovers now
repaired.

It was a recess in the cliff that beetled over the caverns, and
was so formed as to hold no more than three or four persons,
who, when they occupied the rude seats naturally formed in the
rock, were invisible to any human eye which might be directed

otherwhere than from the sea. The approach to it was by a narrow footway, in ascending or descending which, one seemed
almost to hang in air, so far did the cliff-head project over the
water, and so scanty was the path of the descent on either side.
Custom, however, had rendered it a secure footing to the inhabitants of the village, and the lovers speedily found themselves within the nook, secluded from every mortal eye.

It was a still autumn evening: there was no sunshine, but the
fixed splendour of the sky above and around them, on which
the lines, or rather waves, of thin vapour extending from the
north-west, and tinged on one side by the red light of the sun,
which had just gone down, presented the similitude of a sea
frozen into a brilliant mass in the act of undulation. Beyond
them lay Bishop's Island, a little spot of land, shooting up from
the waves in the form of a gigantic column, about three hundred feet in height, the sides barren and perpendicular, and the
plain above covered with verdure to the marge itself. Immediately above their heads was a blighted elder tree (one of the most
remarkable phenomena* of this woodless district) which now
hung, like a single gray hair, over the bare and barren brow of
the aged cliff.

The wanderers sat here in perfect security, although by a
step forward they might look upon a tremendous in-slanting
precipice beneath, against the base of which, at times, the sea
lashed itself with such fury, as to bound in huge masses over
the very summit, and to make the cliff itself shake and tremble
to a considerable distance inland.

"I have asked you to come here, Ellen", said her lover, as he
held her hand in one of his, while the other was passed round
her waist, "for a very solemn purpose. It is a belief amongst
us, and many have seen it come to pass, that those who pledge
themselves to any promise, whether of hate or love, and who,
with their hands clasped together as ours are now, plight their

---

*A sufficiently characteristic observation of Cromwell on the barrenness of
the country inland, is preserved among the peasantry, "There was," he observed, "neither a tree to hang a man from, fire to burn, nor water to drown
him".

faith and troth to perform that promise to one another—it is our belief, I say, that whether in the land of the living or the dead, they can never enjoy a quiet soul until that promise is made good. I must serve five years before I obtain my discharge; when I get that, Ellen, I will return to this place, and let you know, by a token, that I am in the neighborhood. Pledge me your hand and word, that when you receive the token, whether you are married or unmarried, whether it be dark, moon-light, or stormy, you will come out alone to meet me where I shall appoint, on the night when I shall send it".

Without much hesitation the young girl solemnly pledged herself to what he required. He then unbound from her hair a ribbon by which it was confined, kissed it, and placed it in his bosom, after which they ascended the cliff and separated.

After the departure of young Moran, his mother, to relieve her loneliness, opened a little place of entertainment for the *fish-jolters*, whose trade it was (and is) to carry the fish taken on the coast to the nearest market-town for sale, as also for the fishmen of the village and chance passengers. By this means she had accumulated a very considerable sum of money in a few years. Ellen Sparling observed this with satisfaction, as she felt it might remove the greatest bar that had hitherto opposed itself to her union with Charles Moran.

Five years and some months had rolled away since his departure, and he had not been heard of during that time in his native village. All things remained very nearly in the same state in which he had left them, with the exception of the increased prosperity of his mother's circumstances, and the matured beauty of Ellen, who was grown into a blooming woman, the admiration of all the men, and it is said, though I don't vouch for the fact, of all the women too, of her neighbourhood. There are limits of superiority beyond which envy cannot reach, and it might be said, perhaps, that Ellen was placed in this position of advantage above all her female acquaintances. It is not to be supposed that she was left untempted all this while, or at least unsought. On the contrary, a number of suitors had directly or indirectly presented themselves, with one of whom only, however, I have any business at present.

He was a young fisherman, and one of the most constant visitors at the elegant *soirées* of the widow Moran, where, however, he was by no means a very welcome guest, either to the good woman or her customers. He held, nevertheless, a high place at the board, and seemed to exercise a kind of dominion over the revellers, perhaps as much the consequence of his outward appearance, as of his life and habits. He was powerfully made, tall, and of a countenance which, even in his hours of comparative calmness and inaction, exhibited in the mere arrangement of its features, a brutal violence of expression which was exceedingly repugnant. The middle portion of his physiognomy was rather flat and sunken, and his mouth and forehead projecting much, rendered this deformity disgustingly apparent. Deep black, large glistening eyes glanced from beneath a pair of brows, which so nearly approached each other, as, on every movement of passion or impulse of suspicion, to form in all appearance one thick shaggy line across, and the unamiable effect of the countenance altogether was not improved by the temper of the man, who was feared throughout the neighbourhood, as well for his enormous strength, as for the violence, the suspicious tetchiness, and the habitual gloominess of his character, which was never more visible than when, as now, he affected the display of jollity and hearty good-fellowship. It was whispered, moreover, that he was visited, after some unusual excitement, with fits of wildness approaching to insanity, at the accession of which he was wont to conceal himself from all human intercourse for a period, until the evil influence (originating, as it was asserted privately among his old associates, in the remorse with which the recollection of his manifold crimes was accompanied) had passed away—a circumstance that seemed to augur a consciousness of this mental infirmity. At the end of those periods of retirement, he was wont to return to his companions with a haggard and jaded countenance, a dejected demeanour, and a sense of shame manifested in his address, which, for a short space only, served to temper the violence of his conduct. Robbers and murderers, as all of his associates were, this evil-conditioned man had gone so far beyond them in his total recklessness of crime, that he had obtained for himself the distinguished appellative (like most nicknames in Irish low life, ironically applied) of Yamon Macauntha, or Honest Ned; occasionally varied (after he had reached the estate of man-hood, and distinguished himself among the smugglers, over whom he acquired a speedy mastery, by his daring spirit, and almost invariable success in whatever he undertook) with that of Yamon Dhu, or Black Ned, a name which applied as well to his dark complexion, long, matted, coal-black hair and beard, as to the fierce and relentless energy of his disposition.

One anecdote, which was told with suppressed breath and in-voluntary shuddering, even among those who were by his side in all his deeds of blood, may serve to illustrate the terrific and sav-age cruelty of the man. A Dutch vessel had gone to pieces on the rocks beneath the Look-out. The waves rolled in like mountains, and lashed themselves with such fury against the cliffs, that very speedily nearly all those among the crew who clung to the drift-ing fragments of the wreck, were dashed to atoms on the project-ing granite. A few only, among whom was the captain of the vessel, who struggled with desperate vigour against the dreadful element, succeeded in securing themselves on a projecting rock, from whence, feeble and exhausted as they were, the poor mari-ners endeavoured to hail a number of people, who were looking out on the wreck from the cliff above them. They succeeded in attracting their attention, and the spectators prepared to lower a rope for their relief, which, as they were always provided against such accidents, they were not long in bringing to pass. It was first girded around the waist of the captain, and then fastened around that of his two companions, who, on giving a signal, were drawn into the air, the former holding in one hand a little casket, and with the other defending himself against the pointed projection of the cliff as he ascended. When very near the summit, which completely overhung the waves, he begged, in a faint tone, that some one would take the casket from his hands, as he feared it might be lost in the attempt to secure his own hold. Yamon was but too alert in acceding to the wretched man's request; he threw himself forward on the sand, with his breast across the rope, and took the casket from his uplifted hand.

"God's blessing on your souls, my deliverers—" cried the poor man, wringing his clasped hands, with a gesture and look of fervent gratitude, "the casket is safe, thank God! and my faith to my employers——" he was yet speaking, when the rope severed under Black Yamon's breast, and the three men were precipitated into the yawning waters beneath. They were hurried out by the retiring waves, and the next moment their mangled bodies were left in the recesses of the cliff.

A cry of horror and of compassion burst even from the savage hearts of a crew of smugglers, who had been touched by the courage and constancy which was displayed by the unfortunates. Yamon alone remained unmoved (and hard must the heart have been which even the voice of gratitude, unmerited though it was, could not soften or penetrate). He gave utterance to a burst of hoarse, grumbling laughter, as he waved the casket in triumph before the eyes of his comrades.

"Huh! huh!" he exclaimed, "she was a muthaun—why didn't she keep her casket till she drew her painther ashore?"

One of the men, as if doubting the possibility of the inhuman action, advanced to the edge of the cliff. He found the rope had been evidently divided by some sharp instrument; and observing something glittering where Yamon lay, he stepped forward and picked up an open clasp-knife, which was presently claimed by the unblushing monster. However shocked they might have been at the occurrence, it was no difficult matter for Yamon to persuade his companions that it would be nowise convenient to let the manner of it transpire in the neighbourhood; and in a very few minutes the fate of the Dutchmen seemed completely banished from their recollection (never very retentive of benevolent emotions), and the only question held regarded the division of the booty. They were disappointed, however, in their hopes of spoil, for the casket which the faithful shipman was so anxious to preserve, and to obtain which his murderer had made sacrifice of so many lives, contained nothing more than a few papers of bottomry and insurance, valueless to all but the owners of the vessel. This circumstance seemed to touch the villain more nearly than the wanton cruelty of which he had been guilty; and his gang, who were superstitious exactly in proportion to their want of honesty and all moral principle, looked upon it as a supernatural occurrence, in which the judgment of an offended Deity was made manifest.

This amiable person had a sufficiently good opinion of himself to make one among the admirers of Ellen Sparling. It is scarcely necessary to say that his suit was unsuccessful. Indeed the maiden was heard privately to declare her conviction that it was impossible there could be found anywhere a more ugly and disagreeable man, in every sense.

One fine frosty evening, the widow Moran's was more than usually crowded. The fire blazed cheerfully on the hearth, so as to render any other light unnecessary, although the night had already begun to close in. The mistress of the establishment was busily occupied in replenishing the wooden *noggins*, or drinking vessels, with which the board was covered; her glossy white hair turned up under a clean kerchief, and a general gala gladness spreading an unusual light over her shrivelled and attenuated features, as by various courtesies, addressed to the company around her, she endeavoured to make the gracious in her own house. Near the chimney-corner sat Dora Keys, a dark featured, bright eyed girl, who on account of her skill on the bagpipe, a rather unfeminine accomplishment, and a rare one in this district (where, however, as in most parts of Ireland, music of some kind or another was constantly in high request) filled a place of high consideration among the merry-makers. The remainder of the scene was filled up with fishermen, smugglers, and fish-jolters; the latter wrapt in their blue frieze coats, and occupying a more unobtrusive corner of the apartment, while Yamon, as noisy and imperious as usual, sat at the head of the rude table, giving the word to the whole assembly.

A knocking was heard at the slight hurdle-door. The good woman went to open it, and a young man entered. He was well formed, though rather thin and dark skinned, and a profusion of black curled hair clustered about his temples, corresponding finely with his glancing, dark, fiery eye. An air of sadness, or of pensiveness, too, hung about him, which gave an additional interest to his appearance and impressed the spectator with an involuntary respect. Mrs. Moran drew back with one of her lowest curtsies. "Don't you know me, mother?" he asked. The poor woman sprung to his neck with a cry of joy.

All was confusion in an instant. "Charles"—"Charlie"—"Mr. Moran"—was echoed from lip to lip in proportion to the scale of intimacy which was enjoyed by the several speakers. Many a rough hand grasped his, and many a good-humoured buffet and malediction he had to endure before the tumultuous joy of his old friends had subsided. At length after all questions had been answered, and all old friends, the dead, the living, and the absent, had been tenderly inquired for, young Moran took his place among the guests; the amusements of the evening were renewed, and Yamon, who had felt his importance considerably diminished by the entrance of the young traveller, began to resume his self-constituted sovereignty.

Gambling, the great curse of society in all climes, classes, ages, and states of civilization, was not unknown or unpractised in this wild region. Neither was it here unattended with its usual effects upon the mind, heart, and happiness of its votaries. The eager manifestation of assent which passed round the circle, when the proposition of just "a hand o' five-and-forty" was made, showed that it was by no means an unusual or unacceptable resource to any person present. The young exile, in particular, seemed to catch at it with peculiar readiness; and, in a few minutes, places and partners being arranged, the old woman deposited in the middle of the table a pack of cards, approaching in shape more to the oval than the oblong square, and in colour scarcely distinguishable from the black oaken board on which they lay. Custom, however, had rendered the players particularly expert at their use, and they were dealt round with as much flippancy as the newest pack in the hands of a demon of St. James's in our own time. One advantage, certainly, the fashionable gamesters possessed over these primitive gamblers: the latter were perfectly ignorant of the useful niceties of play, so much in request among the former. *Old gentlemen*, *stags*, *bridges*, etc., were matters totally unknown among our coast friends, and the only necessary consequences of play, in which they (perhaps) excelled, were the outrageous violence, good mouth-filling oaths, and the ferocious triumph which followed the winnings or the losses of the several parties.

After he had become so far acquainted with the dingy pieces of pasteboard in his hand, as to distinguish the almost obliterated impressions upon them, the superior skill of the sea-farer became apparent. Yamon, who played against him, soon began to show symptoms of turbulence, which the other treated with the most perfect coolness and indifference, still persevering in his good play, until his opponent, after lavishing abundance of abuse on every body around him, especially on his unfortunate partner in the game, acknowledged that he had no more to lose. The night had now grown late, and the guests dropping off one by one, Moran and his mother were left alone in the cottage.

"Mother", said the young man, as he threw the little window-shutter open, and admitted a gush of moonlight which illumined the whole room, "will you keep the fire stirring till I return: the night is fine, and I must go over the cliffs".

"The cliffs! to-night, child!" ejaculated the old woman. "You don't think of it, my heart?"

"I must go", was the reply; "I have given a pledge that I dare not be false to".

"The cliffs!" continued the old woman. "The way is uncertain even to the feet that know it best, and sure you wouldn't try it in the night, and after being away till you don't know, may be, a foot o' the way".

"When I left Ellen Sparling, mother", said the young man, "I pledged her my faith, that I would meet her on the night on which she should receive from me a token she gave me. She, in like manner, gave me hers. That token I sent to her before I entered your doors this evening, and I appointed her father's ould house, where he lived in his poor days, and where I first saw her, to meet me. I must keep my word on all hazards". And he flung the cottage-door open as he spoke.

"Then take care, take care", said the old woman, clasping her hands and extending them toward him, while she spoke in her native tongue. "The night, thank God! is a fine night, and the sea is still at the bottom of the cliffs, but it is an unsure path. I know the eyes that will be red, and the cheeks that will be white, and the young and fair ones too, if anything *contrary* should come to you this holy evening".

"I have given her my hand and word", was Moran's reply as he closed the door, and took the path over the sand hills.

The moon was shining brightly when he reached the cliffs, and entered on the path leading to the old rendezvous of the lovers, and from thence to the ruined building, where he expected to meet Ellen. He trudged along in the light-heartedness of feeling inspired by the conviction he felt, that the happiness of the times, which every object he beheld brought to his recollection, had not passed away with those days, and that a fair and pleasant future yet lay before him. He turned off the sand-hills while luxuriating in those visions of unchecked delight.

Passing the rocks of Duggara, he heard the plashing of oars, and the rushing of a canoe through the water. It seemed to make towards a landing-place further down, and lying almost on his path. He pursued his course, supposing, as in fact proved to be the case, that it was one of the fishermen drawing his canoe near to the caverns which were to be made the scene of a seal-hunt on the following day. As the little vessel glided through the water beneath him, a wild song, in the language of the country, rose to the broken crag on which he now rested, chaunted by a powerful masculine voice, with all the monotonous and melancholy intonation to which the construction of the music is peculiarly favourable. The following may be taken as a translation of the stanzas:—

I.

The Priest stood at the marriage board,
 The marriage cake was made:
With meat the marriage chest was stored,
 Decked was the marriage bed.
The old man sat beside the fire,
 The mother sat by him,
The white bride was in gay attire
 But her dark eye was dim,

Ululah! Ululah!

The night falls quick—the sun is set,
Her love is on the water yet.

II.

I saw the red cloud in the west,
    Against the morning light,
Heaven shield the youth that she loves best
    From evil chance to-night.
The door flings wide! Loud moans the gale
    Wild fear her bosom chills.
It is, it is the banthee's wail,
    Over the darkened hills,

Ululah! Ululah!

The day is past! the night is dark!
The waves are mounting round his bark.

III.

The guests sit round the bridal bed,
    And break the bridal cake,
But they sit by the dead man's head,
    And hold his wedding-wake.
The bride is praying in her room,
    The place is silent all!
A fearful call! a sudden doom!
    Bridal and funeral!

Ululah! Ululah!

A youth to Kilfiehera's ta'en.
That never will return again.

Before Moran had descended much further on his way, he perceived that the canoe had reached a point of the rock close upon his route. The fisherman jumped to land, made fast the painter, and turning up the path by which Moran was descending, soon encountered him. It was Yamon Macauntha.

"Ho! Mr. Moran! Out on the cliffs this hour o' the night, sir?"

"Yes, I have a good way to go. Good by to you".

"Easy a while, sir", said Yamon; "that is the same way I'm going myself, and I'll be with you".

Moran had no objection to this arrangement, although it was not altogether pleasing to him. He knew enough of the temper and habits of the smuggler to believe him capable of any design, and although he had been a stronger built man than he was, yet the odds, in case of any hostile attempt, would be fearfully in Yamon's favour. He remembered, too, certain rumours which had reached him of the latter being occasionally subject to fits of gloom approaching in their strength and intensity to actual derangement, and began to hesitate as to the more advisable course to be pursued. However, not to mention the pusillanimity of anything having the appearance of retreat, such a step would in all probability have been attempted in vain, for Yamon stood directly behind him, and the path was too narrow to admit the possibility of a successful struggle. He had only to obey the motion of the fisherman and move on.

"You don't know", said the latter, "or may be you never heard of what I'm going to tell you now; but easy, and you'll know all in a minute. Do you see that sloping rock down by the sea, where the horse-gull is standing at this minute, the same we passed a while ago. When my mother was little *better* than seven months married, being living hard by on the sand-hills, she went many's the time down to that rock, to fetch home some of the salt-water for pickle and things, and never made any work of going down there late or early, and at all hours. Well, it was as it might be this way, on a fine bright night, that she took her can in her hand, and down with her to the rock. The tide was full in, and when she turned off o' the path, what should see see fronting her, out, and sitting quite erect intirely upon the rock, only a woman, and she having the tail of her gown turned up over her head, and she sitting quite still, and never spaking a word, and her back towards my mother. '*Dieu uth*', says my mother, careless and civil, thinking of nothing, and wanting her to move; but she took no notice. 'Would it be troubling you if I'd just step down to get a drop o' the salt-water?' says my mother. Still no answer. So thinking it might be one of the neighbours that was funning, or else that it might be asleep she was, she asked her very plain and loud to move out o' the way. When there wasn't ere a word come after this, my mother stooped forward a little, and lifted the *gownd* from the woman's forehead, and peeped under—and what do you think she seen in the dark within? Two eyes as red as fire, and a shrively old face without any lips hardly, and they drawn back, and teeth longer than lobster's claws, and as white as the bleached bones. Her heart was down in her brogue* when *it* started up from her, and with a screech that made two halves of my mother's brains, *it* flew out over the wide sea.

"My mother went home and took to her bed, from which she never stirred till 'twas to be taken to Kilfiehera churchyard. It was in that week I was born. I never pass that place at night alone if I can help it—and that is partly the reason why I made so free to ask you to bear me company".

Moran had his confidence fully reëstablished by these words. He thought he saw in Yamon a wretch so preyed upon by remorse and superstition, as to be incapable of contemplating any deep crime, to which he had not a very great temptation. As Yamon still looked toward the rock beneath, the enormous horse-gull by which he had first indicated its position to Moran, took flight, and winged its way slowly to the elevation on which they stood. The bird rose above, wheeled round them, and with a shrill cry, that was repeated by a hundred echoes, dived again into the darkness underneath. Moran, at this instant, had his thoughts turned in another direction altogether, by the sight of the little recess in which Ellen and he had held their last conversation. He entered, followed by Yamon, who threw himself on the rude stone seat, observing that was a place "for the phuka to make her bed in".

The young traveller folded his arms, and gazed around for a few minutes in silence, his heart striving beneath the load of recollections which came upon him at every glance and motion. On a sudden, a murmured sound of voices was heard underneath, and Moran stooped down, and overlooked the brink of

*Shoe.

the tremendous precipice. There was a flashing of lights on the calm waters beneath, and in a few minutes a canoe emerged from the great cavern, bearing three or four men, with lighted torches, which, however, they extinguished as soon as they came into the clear moonlight. He continued to mark them until they were lost behind a projecting crag. He then turned, and in removing his hand detached a pebble, which, falling after a long pause into the sea, formed what is called by the peasant children, who practise it in sport, "a dead man's skull". It is formed when a stone is cast into the water, so as to emit no spray, but cutting rapidly and keenly through, in its descent, produces a gurgling evolution, bearing a momentary resemblance to the tables of a human skull. The sound ceased, and all again was still and silent, with the exception of the sound which the stirring of the waters made in the mighty cavern beneath.

"I remember the time when that would have won a button* for me", said Moran, turning round. He at the same instant felt his shoulder grasped with a tremendous force. He looked quickly up, and beheld Yamon, his eyes staring and wild with some frantic purpose, bending over him. A half uttered exclamation of terror escaped him, and he endeavoured to spring towards the path which led from the place. The giant arm of Yamon, however, intercepted him.

"Give me, cheat and plunderer that you are", cried the fisherman, while his limbs trembled with emotion, "give me the money you robbed me of this night, or by the great light that's looking down on us, I'll shake you to pieces".

"There, Yamon, there: you have my life in your power—there is your money, and now—" He felt the grasp of the fisherman tightening on his throat. He struggled, as a wretch might be expected to do, to whom life was new and dear; but he was as a child in the gripe of his enemy. There was a smothering shriek of entreaty—a wild attempt to twine himself in the limbs and frame of the murderer—and in the next instant he was hurled over the brow of the cliff.

---

*The practice of playing for *buttons* is very common among the peasant children.

"Another! another life!" said Yamon Dhu, as with hand stretched out, and fingers spread, as though yet in act to grasp, he looked out over the precipice. "The water is still again—Ha! who calls me?—From the caverns?—No.—Above?—Another life!—A deal of Christian's blood upon one man's soul!" and he rushed from the place.

About eleven o'clock on the following morning (as fine a day as could be), a young lad named Terry Mick (Terry, the son of Mick, a species of patronymic very usual in Ireland), entered, with considerable haste, the kitchen of Mr. Morty Shannon, a gentleman farmer, besides being coroner of the county, and as jolly a man as any in the neighbourhood. Terry addressed a brief tale in the ear of Aby Galaghar, Mr. Shannon's steward and fac-totum, which induced the said Sandy to stretch his long, well-seasoned neck, from the chimney corner, and directing his voice towards the door of an inner room, which was complimented with the appellation of a parlour, exclaimed: "Mr. Morty! you're *calling*, sir".

"Who am I *calling*?" asked a rich, waggish voice, from within.

"Mr. Sparling, the Palatine's boy, sir", replied Aby, quite unconscious of the *quid pro quo*.

"Indeed! More than I knew myself. Walk in, Terry".

"Go in to him, Terry dear", said Aby, resuming his comfortable position in the chimney-corner, and fixing a musing, contented eye upon a great cauldron of potatoes that hung over the turf-fire, and on which the first simmering froth, or *white horse* (as it is called in Irish cottages), had begun to appear.

"The master sent me to you, sir", said Terry, opening the door, and protruding an eye, and half a face into the sanctum sanctorum, "to know with his compliments—"

But first, I should let you have the glimpses that Terry got of the company within. The person to whom he immediately addressed himself sat at one end of a small deal table, on which were placed a jug of cold water, a broken bowl, half filled with coarse brown sugar, and a little jar which, by the frequent changes of position it underwent, seemed to contain the favourite article of the three. Imagine to yourself a middle sized man, with stout, well-set limbs, a short and thick head of hair, an indented forehead, eyes of a piercing gray, bright and sparkling, with an expression between leer and satire, and a nose running in a curvilineal direction toward the mouth. Nature had, in the first instance, given it a *sinister inclination*, and chance, wishing to rectify the *morals* of the feature, had by the agency of a blackthorn stick in the hands of a rebellious tenant, sent it again to the right. 'Twas kindly meant, as Mr. Morty himself used to say, though not dexterously executed.

"*The* master's compliments, sir", continued Terry, "to know if your honour would just step over to Kilkee, where there has been a bad business this morning—Charlie Moran being lying dead, on the broad side of his back, at the house, over".

When I say that an expression of involuntary satisfaction, which he in vain endeavoured to conceal, diffused itself over the tortuous countenance of the listener at this intelligence, it is necessary I should save his character by reminding the reader that he was a county coroner, and in addition to the four pounds which he was to receive for the inquest, there was the chance of an invitation to stay and dine with the Sparlings, people whose mode of living Mr. Morty had before now tried and approved.

"Come here, Terry, and take your morning", said he, filling a glass with ardent spirits, which the youth immediately disposed of with a speed that showed a sufficient familiarity with its use, although some affection of mincing decency induced him to colour the delicious relish with a grimace and shrug of comical dislike, as he replaced the glass on the table.

"E'then, that's good stuff, please your honour. Sure I'd know the master's anywhere over the world. This is some of the two year old, sir. 'Twas made the time Mr. Grady, the gauger, was stationed below there, at the white house—and faix, many a drop he tasted of it himself, in the master's barn".

"And is the still so long at work, Terry?"

"Oh, long life to you, sir,—aye is it and longer too. The master has *sech* a 'cute way with him in managing the still-hunters. 'Tis in vain for people to inform: to be sure, two or three tried it, but got nothing by it, barring a good lacing at the next fair-day. Mr. Grady used regularly to send notice when he got an information, to have him on his guard against he'd come with *the army*—and they never found anything there, I'll be your bail for it, more than what served to send 'em home as drunk as pipers, every mother's son. To be sure, that Mr. Grady was a pleasant man, and well liked whenever he came, among high and low, rich and poor, although being a gauger and a Protestant. I remember making him laugh hearty enough once. He asked me, says he, as it might be funning: 'Terry', says she, 'I'm very bad inwardly. How would you like to be walking after a gauger's funeral this morning?' 'Why thin, Mr. Grady', says I, 'I'd rather see a thousand of your *religion* dead than yourself, and meaning no love for *you*, neither'. And poor man, he did laugh hearty, to be sure. He had no pride in him—no pride, more than a child, had'nt Mr. Grady. God's peace be with him wherever he is this day".

In a few minutes Mr. Shannon's blind mare was saddled, and the head of the animal being directed toward Kilkee, away went Terry, trotting by the coroner's side, and shortening the road with his quaint talk. On arriving at the Palatine's house, they found it crowded with the inhabitants of the village. The fairy doctor of the district sat near the door; his brown and weather-beaten face wrapped in an extraordinary degree of mystery, and his eyes fixed with the assumption of deep thought on his twirling thumbs: in another part of the outer room was the schoolmaster of the parish, discussing the "crowner's quest law" to a circle of admiring listeners. In the chimney-corner, on stools which were ranged for the purpose, were congregated the 'knowledgable' women of the district. Two soldiers, detached from the nearest guard, were stationed at the door, and at a little distance from them, seated at a table, and basking in the morning sunshine, might be seen a number of fishermen and others, all deeply engaged in converse upon the occurrence which had summoned them together. One of them was in the act of speaking when the coroner arrived:—

"We had been drawing the little canoe up hard by the cavern, seeing would we be the first to be in upon the seals when the hunt would begin, when I see a black thing lying on the shore among the sea-weed, about forty yards or upwards from the rock where I stood; and 'tisnt itself I see first, either, only two sea-gulls, and one of 'em perched upon it, while the other *kep* wheeling round above it, and screaming as nait'rel as a christen; and so I ran down to Phil, here, and says I: 'There's murder down upon the rocks, let us have it in from the fishes'. So we brought it ashore. 'Twas pale and stiff, but there was no great harm done to it, strange to say, in regard of the great rocks, and the place. We knew poor Moran's face, and we said nothing to one another, only wrapt the spritsail about it, and had it up here to Mr. Sparling's (being handier to us than his own mother's), where we told our story".

Passing into the house, Mr. Morty Shannon was received with all the respect due to his exalted station. The women curtsied low, and the men raised their hands to their foreheads with that courteous action which is familiar to all, even the most unenlightened of the peasantry of the south of Ireland. The master of the mansion, a comfortable-looking farmer-like sort of person, rose from his seat near the hearth, and greeted the man of office with an air of greater familiarity, yet with a reserve becoming the occasion. As the door of an inner apartment stood open, Mr. Shannon could see the corpse of the murdered man laid out on a table near the window. Close to the head stood the mother of the dead, hanging over the corpse in silent grief, swaying herself backward and forward with a gentle motion, and wringing her hands; yet with so noiseless an action, that the profound silence of the room was never broken. On the opposite side, her fine head resting against the bier— her white, wan fingers wreathed together in earnest prayer above the body, while a half-stifled sob occasionally shook her delicate frame—and her long and curling tresses fell in flaxen masses over the bosom of the murdered, knelt Moran's betrothed love, Ellen Sparling. As she prayed, a sudden thought seemed to rush upon her, she raised her head, took from her bosom a light green ribbon, and kissing it fervently and repeatedly, she folded and placed it in that of the murdered youth, after which she resumed her kneeling posture. There are few, I believe, who have lived among scenes of human suffering to so little purpose as not to be aware, that it is not the heaviness of a particular calamity, nor the violence of the sorrow which it produces, that it is at any time the most powerful in awakening the commiseration of an uninterested spectator. The capability of deep feeling may be more or less a property of all hearts, but the power of communicating it is a gift possessed by few. The murmur of a bruised heart, the faint sigh of a broken spirit, will often stir and thrill all the strings of sympathy, while the frantic ravings of a wilder, though not less real woe, shall fail to excite any other sensation than that of pain and uneasiness. Perhaps it may be, that the selfishness of our nature is such, that we are alarmed and put on our guard, in proportion to the violence of the appeal which is made to us, and must be taken by surprise, before our benevolent emotions can be awakened. However all this might be, being no philosopher, I can only state the fact, that Mr. Morty Shannon, who had witnessed many a scene of frantic agony without experiencing any other feeling than that of impatience, was moved, even to a forget-fulness of his office, by the quiet, unobtrusive grief which he witnessed on entering this apartment.

It was the custom in those days, and is still the custom in most parts of Ireland, where any person is supposed to have "come by his end" unfairly, that all the inhabitants of his parish, or dis-trict, particularly those who, from any previous circumstances, may be rendered at all liable to suspicion, shall meet together and undergo a kind of ordeal, by touching the corpse, each in his turn. Among a superstitious people, such a regulation as this, simple though it was, had been frequently successful in betraying the guilty conscience; and it was a current belief among the peasantry, that in many instances where the perpe-trator of the horrid deed possessed strength of mind or callous-ness of heart to subdue all appearance of emotion in the moment of trial, some miraculous change in the corpse itself had been known to indicate the evil doer. At all events, there was a degree of solemnity and importance attached to the test, which invested it with a strong interest in the minds of the multitude.

Suspicion was not idle on this occasion. The occurrences of the previous evening at the widow's house, and the loss there sustained by Yamon, contributed in no slight degree to fix the attention of the majority upon him. It did not pass without

remark, neither, that he had not yet made his appearance at
Mr. Sparling's house. Many wild tales, moreover, were afloat
respecting Ellen Sparling, who had on that morning, before
sunrise, been seen by a fish jolter, who was driving his mule
loaded with fish along the road towards Kilrush, returning
across the hill towards her father's house, more like a mad
woman than a sober Christian. Before we proceed further in
our tale, it is necessary we should say something of the circumstances which led to this appearance.

When Ellen received the token on the previous evening from
young Moran's messenger, she tied her light chequered straw
bonnet under her chin, and stole out by a back entrance, with
a beating and anxious heart, to the appointed rendezvous. The
old ruined house which had been named to her, was situated at
the distance of a mile from her father's, and was at present
tenanted only by an aged herdsman in his employment. Not
finding Moran yet arrived, although the sun was already in the
west, she sent the old man away on some pretext, and took his
place in the little rush-bottomed chair by the fire-side. Two
hours of a calm and silent evening had already passed away,
and yet he came not. Wearied with the long expectation, and
by the tumult of thoughts and feelings which agitated her, she
arose, walked to a short distance from the cottage, and sitting
on a little knoll in the vicinity, which commanded a wide prospect of the sea, she continued to await his arrival, now and
then gazing in the direction of the cliffs by which the messenger told her he was to pass. No object, however, met her eye on
that path, and no sound came to her ear but the loud, full-
toned, and plaintive whistle of the ploughman, as he guided
his horses over a solitary piece of stubble-ground, lightening
his own and their labour by wild modulations of the *Keen-the-
cawn*, or death-wail; the effect of which, though it had often
delighted her under other circumstances, fell now with an oppressive influence upon her spirits.

Night fell at length, and she returned to the old house. As she
reached the neglected *haggart* on the approach, a light breeze
sprang up inland, and rustling in the thatch of the ruined out-
houses, startled her by its suddenness, almost as much as if it

had been a living voice. She looked up an instant, drew her handkerchief closer around her neck, and hurried on toward the door. It might be he had arrived by another path during her absence! High as her heart bounded at the suggestion, it sunk in proportion as she had lifted the latch, and entered the deserted room. The turf-embers were almost expiring on the hearth, and all was dark, cold, saddening, and comfortless. She felt vexed at the absence of the old servant, and regretted the caution which induced her to get rid of him. Amid all the intensity of her fondness, too, she could not check a feeling of displeasure at the apparent want of ardour on the part of her lover. It had an almost slighting look; she determined she would make it evident in her manner on his arrival. In the next moment the fancied sound of a footstep made her spring from her seat, and extend her arms in perfect oblivion of all her stern resolutions. Quite beaten down in heart by constant disappointments, and made nervous and feverish by anxiety, the most fearful suggestions began now to take place of her pettishness and ill-humour. She was alarmed for his safety. It was a long time since he had trod the path over the cliffs. The possibility that here rushed upon her, made her cover her face with her hands, and bend forward in her chair in an agony of terror.

Midnight now came on. A short and heavy breathing at the door, as she supposed, started her as she bent over the flame which she kept alive by placing fresh *sods* on the embers. She rose and went to the door. A large Newfoundland dog of her father's bounded by her as she opened it, and testified by the wildest gambols about the kitchen, the delight he felt in meeting her so unexpectedly, at such an hour, and so far from her home. She patted the faithful animal on the head, and felt restored in spirits by the presence even of this uncommunicative acquaintance. The sagacious servant had evidently traced her to the ruin by the fineness of its sense, and seemed overjoyed at the verification of his diagnostic. At length, after having sufficiently indulged the excitement of the moment, he took post before the fire, and after divers indecisive evolutions, he coiled himself up at her feet and slept. The maiden herself in a short time imitated his example.

The startling suggestions that had been crowding on her in her waking moments, now began to shape themselves in vivid and fearful visions to her sleeping fancy. As she lay back in her chair, her eyes not so entirely closed as to exclude the "lengthening rays" of the decaying fire before them, she became unaccountably oppressed by the sense of a person sitting close to her side. There was a hissing, as if of water falling on the embers just before the figure, and after a great effort she fancied that she could turn so far round as to recognise the face of her lover, pale, cold, with the long dark hair hanging drearily at each side, and as she supposed, dripping with moisture. She strove to move, but was perfectly unable to do so, and the figure continued to approach her, until at length, placing his chilling face so close to her cheek, that she thought she felt the damp upon her neck, he said gently: "Ellen, I have kept my hand and word: living, I would have done it; dead, I am permitted." At this moment a low grumbling bark from the dog Minos awoke her, and she started from her seat, in a state of nervousness which for a short time prevented a full conviction of the non-existence of the vision that had oppressed her slumber. The dog was sitting erect, and gazing with crouched head, fixed eyes, and lips upturned in the expression of canine fear, toward the door. Ellen listened attentively for a few minutes, and a gentle knocking was heard. She recognised too, or thought she recognised, a voice precisely similar to that of the figure in her dream, which pronounced her name with the gentlest tone in the world. What surprised her most, was that Minos, instead of starting fiercely up as was his wont on hearing an unusual sound at night, cowed, whimpered, and slunk back into the chimney-corner. Not in the least doubting that it was her lover, she rose and opened the door. The vividness of her dream, being yet fresh upon her, and perhaps the certainty she felt of seeing him, made her imagine for the instant that she beheld the same figure standing before her. It was but for an instant, however; on looking a second time, there was no person to be seen. An overwhelming sensation of terror now rushed upon her, and she fled from the place with the rapidity of madness. In a state half-frantic, half-fainting, she reached her father's house, and flung herself on her bed, where the news of Moran's death reached her the next morning.

To return, however, to the present position of our tale. A certain number of the guests were now summoned into the room where the body lay, and all things were prepared for the ordeal. At a table near the window, with writing materials before him, was placed the worthy coroner, together with the lieutenant of the guard at the lighthouse, who had arrived a few minutes before. Mr. Sparling stood close by them, his face made up into an expression of wise abstraction, his hands thrust into his breeches pockets, and jingling some half-pence which they contained. The betrothed lover of the murdered man had arisen from her knees, and put on a completely altered manner. She now stood in silence, and with tearless eyes, at the head of the bier, gazing with an earnestness of purpose, which might have troubled the carriage even of diffident innocence itself, into the face of every one who approached to touch the body. Having been aware of the suspicions afloat against Yamon, and the grounds for these suspicions, she expected with impatience the arrival of that person.

He entered at length. All eyes were instantly turned on him. There was nothing unusual in the manner or appearance of the man. He glanced round the room, nodded to a few, touched his forehead to the coroner and the lieutenant, and then walking firmly and coolly to the centre of the apartment, awaited his turn for the trial. A very close observer might have detected a quivering and wincing of the eyelid, as he looked toward Ellen Sparling, but it was only momentary, and he did not glance in that direction a second time.

"Isn't that droll,* Shawn?" whispered Terry in the ear of the fairy doctor, who stood near him. The latter did not deem it convenient to answer in words, but he compressed his lips, contracted his brow, and threw an additional portion of empty wisdom into his physiognomy.

"E'then," continued Terry, "only mark Tim Fouloo going to

---

*"Droll", in Ireland, means simply, *extraordinary*, and does not necessarily excite a comic association.

touch the dead corpse all a' one any body would sispect *him* to be taking the life body of a chicken, the *lahu-muthawn*" (half-natural), as a foolish looking, open-mouthed, open-eyed young booby advanced in his turn in a slow waddling gait to the corpse, and passing his hand over the face, retired with a stare of comic stupidity, which, notwithstanding the awful occasion, provoked a smile from many of the spectators.

Yamon was the last person who approached the corpse. From the moment he entered, the eye of Ellen Sparling had never been withdrawn from him for an instant, and its expression now became vivid and intense. He walked to the place, however, with much indifference, and passed his hand slowly and repeatedly over the cheek and brow of the dead man. Many a head was thrust forward as if in expectation that the inanimate lump of clay might stir beneath the feeler's touch. But no miracle took place, and they gazed on one another in silence as he slowly turned away, and folding his arms, resumed his place in the centre of the apartment.

"Well, Mr. Sparling", said his worship the coroner, "here is so much time lost: had we begun to take evidence at once, the business would be nearly at an end by this time".

The old Palatine was about to reply, when their conversation was interrupted by an exclamation of surprise from Ellen Sparling. Turning quickly round, they beheld her with one of the clenched hands of the corpse between hers, gazing at it in stirless amazement. Between the dead-stiff fingers appeared something of a bluish colour slightly protruded. Using the utmost strength of which she was mistress, Ellen forced open the hand, and took from it a small part of the lapel of a coat, with a button attached. And letting the hand fall, she rushed through the crowd, putting all aside without looking at one, until she stood before Yamon. A glance was sufficient. In the death-struggle, the unhappy Moran had torn away this portion of the murderer's dress, and the rent was visible at the moment.

"The murderer! blood for blood!" shrieked the frantic girl, grasping his garment, and looking almost delirious with passion. All was confusion and uproar. Yamon darted one glance around, and sprung toward the open door, but Ellen Sparling still clung as with a drowning grasp to her hold. He put forth the utmost of his giant strength to detach himself from her, but in vain. All his efforts seemed only to increase her strength, while they diminished his own. At last he bethought him of his fishing-knife; he plucked it from his belt and buried it in her bosom. The unfortunate girl relaxed her hold, reeled, and fell on the corpse of her lover, while Yamon bounded towards the door. Poor Terry crossed his way, but one blow laid him sprawling senseless on the earth, and no one cared to tempt a second. The rifles of the guard were discharged after him, as he darted over the sandhills; but just before the triggers were pulled, his foot tripped against a loose stone, he fell, and the circumstance perhaps saved his life (at least the marksmen said so). He was again in rapid flight before the smoke cleared away.

"*Shuil! Shuil!*"* The sand hills! the cliffs!" was now the general shout, and the chase immediately commenced. Many minutes elapsed ere they arrived at the cliffs, and half a dozen only of the most nimble-footed just reached the spot in time to witness the last desperate resource of the murderer. He stood and looked over his shoulder for an instant, then rushing to the verge of the cliff, where it walled in the land to a height of forty feet, he waved his hand to the pursuers, and cast himself into the sea.

The general opinion was that he had perished, but there was no trace ever seen that could make such a consummation certain. The body was never found, and it was suspected by a few, that, incredible as the story might appear, he had survived the leap, and gained the little rocky island opposite.

The few who returned at dusk to Mr. Sparling's house, found it the abode of sorrow, of silence, and of death. Even the voice of the hired keener was not called in on this occasion to mock the real grief that sat on every brow and in every heart. The lovers were waked together, and buried in the same grave at Kilfiehera.

*Come! Come!

THOMAS WATERS

(PSEUDONYM OF WILLIAM RUSSELL)

(1806–1876)

Despite the English dread of secret policing *à la française*, which festered throughout and after the bloody Revolution across the Channel, by the middle of the nineteenth century Brits were less opposed to the notion of non-military police. The Metropolitan Police had been launched in 1829 by Home Secretary Robert Peel—inspiring the term *bobbies* in England and *peelers* in Ireland—and a detective bureau opened in 1842, following a damaging public scandal that helped publicize the need for it. Immediately the term *plainclothes* was applied to the "disguise" of a policeman not required to wear a uniform.

In 1851, Charles Dickens—somehow dismissing his usual cynicism about authority—wrote a bouquet of love letters to police detectives in a series of articles that appeared in his own periodical, *Household Words*:

> We are not by any means devout believers in the old Bow Street Police. . . . On the other hand, the Detective Force organized since the establishment of the existing Police, is so well chosen and trained, proceeds so systematically and quietly, does its business in such a workmanlike manner, and is always so calmly and steadily engaged in the service of the public, that the public really do not know enough of it, to know a tithe of its usefulness.

A Dickens colleague, the flamboyant journalist George Augustus Sala, later complained in his autobiography: "Dickens had a curious and almost morbid partiality for communing with and entertaining police officers." Dickens loved to peacock around in the preferential treatment that fame bestowed upon him, and he may have been deliberately currying police favor; the next year he bragged to the novelist Edward Bulwer-Lytton, "Any of the Detective men will do anything for me."

Unquestionably Dickens helped raise the public profile of police detectives. In the title of his first article in the series, the profession was so little known that he placed the word *detective*—which dated only to the late 1830s in this usage—in quotation marks. The next decade, however, saw an explosion of interest in police and detectives in both journalism and fiction. At times the distinction between factual and fictional blurred. The familiar newspaper preoccupation with crime and scandal began to focus on those public employees who faced criminals and on those who deciphered crimes. "Just now books of narratives of detectives and ex-detectives are all the fashion," proclaimed the *Dublin Review* in 1861. Newspaper commentary from the 1860s demonstrates that, this early in the evolution of the detective story, the popular press was thinking of the genre as synonymous with police memoirs.

True, a few books were at least moderately factual and based upon the experiences of an actual policeman or detective (sometimes foreign), such as *Autobiography of a French Detective, from 1818 to 1858: Comprising the Most Curious Revelations of the French Detective Police System*, by former officer Louis Canler. Such glimpses behind the scenes helped inform the public but also provided fiction writers with details for verisimilitude. Thus many readers did not realize that most such accounts, whatever their claims of authenticity, were written not by police officers or detectives but by imaginative fiction writers. This trend of police-case "memoirs"—the so-called casebook school—is often mentioned in passing as a curious eddy in the growing current of detective stories, but it was actually a significant tributary.

One popular early exemplar of this field was "Richmond," in his 1827 series *Scenes in the Life of a Bow Street Runner*, which is considered the first volume of detective stories in English. The imposing group of buildings called Bow Street Magistrate's Court, in the old City bordering Covent Garden, was the headquarters of a group of proto-policemen founded in 1749 by magistrate Henry Fielding, who was also author of the comic novel *The History of Tom Jones*. The Runners operated out of Fielding's office at Number 4 Bow Street, joining the dusty network of watchmen, parish constables, and thief-takers.

But Richmond's cases are a bit windy and deal infrequently with homicide—not ideal for this anthology. In 1849 a more interesting writer began a series entitled *The Recollections of a Policeman* in *Chambers's Edinburgh Journal*, presented as factual accounts. The title page of the bound collection attributed the book to "Thomas Waters, an Inspector of the London Detective Corps." Curiously, it was published first in the United States, in 1852—with no international copyright law to channel royalties to the author—and not until seven years later in England.

The name seems to have been recognized early on as a pseudonym; the two-volume 1863 London edition attributes the book simply to "Waters," in quotation marks. It turns out to have been employed by a busy English writer named William Russell. He used a similar ploy in his nautical fiction, such as the 1856 *Tales of the Coast Guard*, attributed to "Lieutenant Warneford, R.N." (Royal Navy). So little is known about Russell that it is impossible to dispute the regalia with which he garbed his own name when he wrote under it, including at various times *Dr.* or *Esq.* or *LL.D.* He also wrote for *The London Journal* and other periodicals.

The Waters cases are vivid, convincing, and varied. Often they begin with Waters being dispatched by superiors to crime scenes far from his London headquarters—Liverpool, Guernsey. He employs disguise and other subterfuge that would become the stock-in-trade of everyone from Sherlock Holmes to Loveday Brooke. (For more on Brooke, see the introduction to "The Murder at Troyte's Hill" in this anthology.)

Russell's weakness for unfounded claims of authority makes it likely that he himself penned the grandiose preface trumpeting the patriotic and artistic virtues of one early edition:

The tales included in this volume possess a remarkable degree of literary merit, which renders no apology necessary for their appearance before the public at this time. The Detective Policeman is in some respects peculiar to England—one of the developments of the last twenty-five years. He differs as much from the informer and spy of the continent of Europe as the modern Protective Policeman does from the old-fashioned Watchman. His occupation is of the most exciting and dangerous character, calling into requisition patient endurance and skilful diplomacy. In ferreting out the legitimate objects of justice, his record is full of "hair-breadth 'scapes," which lend a strong odor of the romantic to his life. We think that the reader, after having perused the following pages, will unite with us in the remark, that the *true* stories contained therein have never been equalled for thrilling interest by any productions of modern fiction.

Russell revealed from page one of the first adventure, "A Detective in the Bud," that he was not going to traffic in pieties about law or government, and that he saw very clearly the kind of men (it would be only men for a half century to come) the police hired:

It may sound strangely, but is not the less true, that I joined the Metropolitan Detective Police Force—only the name of which is modern, the vocation itself being as old as corrupt, civilized and uncivilized humanity—before I had quite attained the ripe age of sixteen. My stepfather, at that time a well-known Bow-street officer—Bow-street Runner was the more common appellation—a stern, iron-willed, but just man, believed implicitly in the wisdom of Solomon, especially in the part thereof which teaches that to spare the rod is to spoil the child. He exemplified the sincerity of his faith by vigorous practice, and never more strikingly so than shortly before my sixteenth birthday, when it became necessary to peremptorily decide upon the groove into which, as we would now say, I should be shunted to make the journey of life. I myself had a strong predilection for the sea, and advanced reasons eminently satisfactory to myself why I should be at once bound 'prentice to Andrew Giles, skipper of a Newcastle collier trading between that port and the Thames, and a distant relative of my mother, long before that departed. My stepfather's views entirely differed from mine; I was more fitted to be a sweep than a sailor; but having noticed certain peculiarities of mine—indications of a character which in itself was not worthy of commendation, but might be turned to useful account in the business of life he had determined upon training me in the way I should go, whether I liked it or not, which way was the career of a Bow-street Detective Officer, his own profession. The proposal disgusted me. I told him so. Whereupon he at once had recourse to his favourite argument—the cane. Less than one week's daily drill in that exercise more than sufficed to convince me that he was right, I wrong; and with the consent of Sir Richard Bumie, I was given what may be called a cadet's commission in the celebrated corps of Bow-street "Runners," the pay to commence with twenty pounds per annum.

The year was 1819—that of the Peterloo Manchester Massacre, as the charge of the valiant yeomanry upon Orator Hunt's unarmed half-starved ragamuffins was termed by irreverent scribblers and spouters in Parliament and the press. . . .

Unlike in a collection of stand-alone stories, the adventures in *Recollections of a Policeman* connect and follow each other like chapters. The opening reference is to Chapter 1, the first story or case; "Guilty or Not Guilty" is the second.

GUILTY OR NOT GUILTY?

A few weeks after the lucky termination of the Sandford affair I was engaged in the investigation of a remarkable case of burglary, accompanied by homicide, which had just occurred at the residence of Mr. Bagshawe, a gentleman of competent fortune, situated within a few miles of Kendal in Westmoreland. The particulars forwarded to the London police authorities by the local magistracy were chiefly these:—

Mr. Bagshawe, who had been some time absent at Leamington, Warwickshire, with his entire establishment, wrote to Sarah King—a young woman left in charge of the house and property—to announce his own speedy return, and at the same time directing her to have a particular bedroom aired, and other household matters arranged for the reception of his nephew, Mr. Robert Bristowe, who, having just arrived from abroad, would, he expected, leave London immediately for Five Oaks' House. The positive arrival of this nephew had been declared to several tradesmen of Kendal by King early in the day preceding the night of the murder and robbery; and by her directions butcher-meat, poultry, fish, and so on, had been sent by them to Five Oaks for his table. The lad who carried the fish home stated that he had seen a strange young gentleman in one of the sitting-rooms on the ground-floor through the half-opened door of the apartment. On the following morning it was discovered that Five Oaks' House had been, not indeed broken *into*, but broken *out of.* This was evident from the state of the door fastenings and the servant-woman barbarously murdered. The neighbors found her lying quite dead and cold at the foot of the principal staircase, clothed only in her night-gown and stockings, and with a flat chamber candlestick tightly grasped in her right hand. It was conjectured that she had been roused from sleep by some noise below, and having descended to ascertain the cause, had been mercilessly slain by the disturbed burglars. Mr. Bagshawe arrived on the following day, and it was then found that not only a large amount of plate, but between three and four thousand pounds in gold and notes—the produce of government stock sold out about two months previously—had been carried off. The only person, except his niece, who lived with him, that knew there was this sum in the house, was his nephew Robert Bristowe, to whom he had written, directing his letter to the Hummums Hotel, London, stating that the sum for the long-contemplated purchase of Ryland's had been some time lying idle at Five Oaks, as he had wished to consult him upon his bargain before finally concluding it. This Mr. Robert Bristowe was now nowhere to be seen or heard of; and what seemed to confirm beyond a doubt the—to Mr. Bagshawe and his niece—torturing, horrifying suspicion that this nephew was the burglar and assassin, a portion of the identical letter written to him by his uncle was found in one of the offices! As he was nowhere to be met with or heard of in the neighborhood of Kendal, it was surmised that he must have returned to London with his booty; and a full description of his person, and the dress he wore, as given by the fishmonger's boy, was sent to London by the authorities. They also forwarded for our use and assistance one Josiah Barnes, a sly, sharp, vagabond-sort of fellow, who had been apprehended on suspicion, chiefly, or rather wholly, because of his former intimacy with the unfortunate Sarah King, who had discarded him, it seemed, on account of his incorrigibly idle, and in other respects disreputable habits. The *alibi* he set up was, however, so clear and decisive, that he was but a few hours in custody; and he now exhibited great zeal for the discovery of the murderer of the woman to whom he had, to the extent of his perverted instincts, been sincerely attached. He fiddled at the festivals of the humbler Kendalese; sang, tumbled, ventriloquized at their tavern orgies; and had he not been so very highly-gifted, might, there was little doubt, have earned a decent living as a carpenter, to which profession his father, by dint of much exertion, had about half-bred him. His principal use to us was, that he was acquainted with the features of Mr. Robert Bristowe; and accordingly, as soon as I had received my commission and instructions, I started off with him to the

Hummums Hotel, Covent Garden. In answer to my inquiries, it was stated that Mr. Robert Bristowe had left the hotel a week previously without settling his bill—which was, however, of very small amount, as he usually paid every evening—and had not since been heard of; neither had he taken his luggage with him. This was odd, though the period stated would have given him ample time to reach Westmoreland on the day it was stated he *had* arrived there.

"What dress did he wear when he left?"

"That which he usually wore: a foraging-cap with a gold band, a blue military surtout coat, light trousers, and Wellington boots."

The precise dress described by the fishmonger's errand-boy! We next proceeded to the Bank of England, to ascertain if any of the stolen notes had been presented for payment. I handed in a list of the numbers furnished by Mr. Bagshawe, and was politely informed that they had all been cashed early the day before by a gentleman in a sort of undress uniform, and wearing a foraging cap. Lieutenant James was the name indorsed upon them; and the address Harley Street, Cavendish Square, was of course a fictitious one. The cashier doubted if he should be able to swear to the person of the gentleman who changed the notes, but he had particularly noticed his dress. I returned to Scotland Yard to report *no* progress; and it was then determined to issue bills descriptive of Bristowe's person, and offering a considerable reward for his apprehension, or such information as might lead to it; but the order had scarcely been issued, when who should we see walking deliberately down the yard towards the police-office but Mr. Robert Bristowe himself, dressed precisely as before described! I had just time to caution the inspector not to betray any suspicion, but to hear his story, and let him quietly depart, and to slip with Josiah Barnes out of sight, when he entered, and made a formal but most confused complaint of having been robbed something more than a week previously—where or by whom he knew not—and afterwards deceived, bamboozled, and led astray in his pursuit of the robbers, by a person whom he now suspected to be a confederate with them. Even of this latter personage he could afford no tangible information; and the inspector, having quietly listened to his statement—intended, doubtless, as a mystification—told him the police should make inquiries, and wished him good-morning. As soon as he had turned out of Scotland Yard by the street leading to the Strand, I was upon his track. He walked slowly on, but without pausing, till he reached the Saracen's Head, Snow-Hill, where, to my great astonishment, he booked himself for Westmoreland by the night-coach. He then walked into the inn, and seating himself in the coffee-room, called for a pint of sherry wine and some biscuits. He was now safe for a short period at any rate; and I was about to take a turn in the street, just to meditate upon the most advisable course of action, when I espied three buckishly-attired, bold-faced looking fellows—one of whom I thought I recognised, spite of his fine dress—enter the booking-office. Naturally anxious in my vocation, I approached as closely to the door as I could without being observed, and heard one of them—my acquaintance sure enough; I could not be deceived in that voice—ask the clerk if there were any vacant places in the night-coach to Westmoreland. To Westmoreland! Why, what in the name of Mercury could a detachment of the swell-mob be wanting in that country of furze and frieze-coats? The next sentence uttered by my friend, as he placed the money for booking three insides to Kendal on the counter was equally, or perhaps more puzzling: "Is the gentleman who entered the office just now—him with a foraging cap I mean—to be our fellow-passenger?"

"Yes, he has booked himself; and has, I think, since gone into the house."

"Thank you: good-morning."

I had barely time to slip aside into one of the passages, when the three gentlemen came out of the office, passed me, and swaggered out of the yard. Vague, undefined suspicions at once beset me relative to the connection of these worthies with the "foraging-cap" and the doings at Kendal. There was evidently something in all this more than natural, if police philosophy could but find it out. I resolved at all events to try; and in order to have a chance of doing so, I determined to be of the party, nothing doubting that I should be able, in some way or other, to make one in whatever game they intended playing. I in my turn entered the booking-office, and finding there were still two places vacant, secured them both for James Jenkins and Josiah Barnes, countrymen and friends of mine returning to the "north countrie."

I returned to the coffee-room, where Mr. Bristowe was still seated, apparently in deep and anxious meditation, and wrote a note, with which I despatched the inn porter. I had now ample leisure for observing the suspected burglar and assassin. He was a pale, intellectual-looking, and withal handsome young man, of about six-and-twenty years of age, of slight but well-knit frame, and with the decided air—travel-stained and jaded as he appeared—of a gentleman. His look was troubled and careworn, but I sought in vain for any indication of the starting, nervous tremor always in my experience exhibited by even old practitioners in crime when suddenly accosted. Several persons had entered the room hastily, without causing him even to look up. I determined to try an experiment on his nerves, which I was quite satisfied no man who had recently committed a murder, and but the day before changed part of the produce of that crime into gold at the Bank of England, could endure without wincing. My object was, not to procure evidence producible in a court of law by such means, but to satisfy my own mind. I felt a growing conviction that, spite of appearances, the young man was guiltless of the deed imputed to him, and might be the victim, I could not help thinking, either of some strange combination of circumstances, or, more likely, of a diabolical plot for his destruction, essential, possibly, to the safety of the real perpetrators of the crime; very probably—so ran my suspicions—friends and acquaintances of the three gentlemen who were to be our fellow-travelers. My duty, I knew, was quite as much the vindication of innocence as the detection of guilt; and if I could satisfy myself that he was not the guilty party, no effort of mine should be wanting, I determined, to extricate him from the perilous position in which he stood. I went out of the room, and remained absent for some time; then suddenly entered with a sort of bounce, walked swiftly, and with a determined air, straight up to the box where he was seated, grasped him tightly by the arm, and exclaimed roughly, "So I have found you at last!"

There was no start, no indication of fear whatever—not the slightest; the expression of his countenance, as he peevishly replied, "What the devil do you mean?" was simply one of surprise and annoyance.

"I beg your pardon," I replied; "the waiter told me a friend of mine, one *Bagshawe*, who has given me the slip, was here, and I mistook you for him."

He courteously accepted my apology, quietly remarking at the same time that though his own name was Bristowe, he had, oddly enough, an uncle in the country of the same name as the person I had mistaken him for. Surely, thought I, this man is guiltless of the crime imputed to him; and yet— At this moment the porter entered to announce the arrival of the gentleman I had sent for. I went out; and after giving the new-comer instructions not to lose sight of Mr. Bristowe, hastened home to make arrangements for the journey.

Transformed, by the aid of a flaxen wig, broad-brimmed hat, green spectacles, and a multiplicity of waistcoats and shawls, into a heavy and elderly, well-to-do personage, I took my way with Josiah Barnes—whom I had previously thoroughly drilled as to speech and behavior towards our companions—to the Saracen's Head a few minutes previous to the time for starting. We found Mr. Bristowe already seated; but the "three friends," I observed, were curiously looking on, desirous no doubt of ascertaining *who* were to be their fellow-travelers before venturing to coop themselves up in a space so narrow, and, under certain circumstances, so difficult of egress. My appearance and that of Barnes—who, sooth to say, looked much more of a simpleton than he really was—quite reassured them, and in they jumped with confident alacrity. A few minutes afterwards the "all right" of the attending ostlers gave the signal for departure, and away we started.

A more silent, less social party I never assisted at. Whatever amount of "feast of reason" each or either of us might have silently enjoyed, not a drop of "flow of soul" welled up from one

of the six insides. Every passenger seemed to have his own peculiar reasons for declining to display himself in either mental
or physical prominence. Only one or two incidents—apparently
unimportant, but which I carefully noted down in the tablet of
my memory—occurred during the long, wearisome journey,
till we stopped to dine at about thirty miles from Kendal; when
I ascertained, from an over-heard conversation of one of the
three with the coachman, that they intended to get down at a
roadside tavern more than six miles on this side of that place.

"Do you know this house they intend to stop at?" I inquired
of my assistant as soon as I got him out of sight and hearing at
the back of the premises.

"Quite well: it is within about two miles of Five Oaks'
House."

"Indeed! Then you must stop there too. It is necessary I
should go on to Kendal with Mr. Bristowe; but you can remain
and watch their proceedings."

"With all my heart."

"But what excuse can you make for remaining there, when
they know you are booked for Kendal? Fellows of that stamp
are keenly suspicious; and in order to be useful, you must be
entirely unsuspected."

"Oh, leave that to me. I'll throw dust enough in their eyes to
blind a hundred such as they, I warrant ye."

"Well, we shall see. And now to dinner."

Soon after, the coach had once more started. Mr. Josiah
Barnes began drinking from a stone bottle which he drew from
his pocket; and so potent must have been the spirit it contained, that he became rapidly intoxicated. Not only speech,
but eyes, body, arms, legs, the entire animal, by the time we
reached the inn where we had agreed he should stop, was thoroughly, hopelessly drunk; and so savagely quarrelsome, too,
did he become, that I expected every instant to hear my real
vocation pointed out for the edification of the company. Strange
to say, utterly stupid and savage as he seemed, all dangerous
topics were carefully avoided. When the coach stopped, he got
out—how, I know not—and reeled and tumbled into the tap-
room, from which he declared he would not budge an inch till

next day. Vainly did the coachman remonstrate with him upon his foolish obstinacy; he might as well have argued with a bear; and he at length determined to leave him to his drunken humor. I was out of patience with the fellow; and snatching an opportunity when the room was clear, began to upbraid him for his vexatious folly. He looked sharply round, and then, his body as evenly balanced, his eye as clear, his speech as free as my own, crowed out in a low exulting voice, "Didn't I tell you I'd manage it nicely?"

The door opened, and, in a twinkling, extremity of drunkenness, of both brain and limb, was again assumed with a perfection of acting I have never seen equalled. He had studied from nature, that was perfectly clear. I was quite satisfied, and with renewed confidence obeyed the coachman's call to take my seat. Mr. Bristowe and I were now the only inside passengers; and as farther disguise was useless, I began stripping myself of my superabundant clothing, wig, spectacles, &c., and in a few minutes, with the help of a bundle I had with me, presented to the astonished gaze of my fellow-traveler the identical person that had so rudely accosted him in the coffee-room of the Saracen's Head inn.

"Why, what, in the name of all that's comical, is the meaning of this?" demanded Mr. Bristowe, laughing immoderately at my changed appearance.

I briefly and coolly informed him; and he was for some minutes overwhelmed with consternation and astonishment. He had not, he said, even heard of the catastrophe at his uncle's.

Still, amazed and bewildered as he was, no sign which I could interpret into an indication of guilt escaped him.

"I do not wish to obtrude upon your confidence, Mr. Bristowe," I remarked, after a long pause; "but you must perceive that unless the circumstances I have related to you are in some way explained, you stand in a perilous predicament."

"You are right," he replied, after some hesitation. "*It is* a tangled web; still, I doubt not that some mode of vindicating my perfect innocence will present itself."

He then relapsed into silence; and neither of us spoke again till the coach stopped, in accordance with a previous intimation I had given the coachman, opposite the gate of the Kendal prison. Mr. Bristowe started, and changed color, but instantly mastering his emotion, he calmly said, "You of course but perform your duty; mine is not to distrust a just and all-seeing Providence."

We entered the jail, and the necessary search of his clothes and luggage was effected as forbearingly as possible. To my great dismay we found amongst the money in his purse a Spanish gold piece of a peculiar coinage, and in the lining of his portmanteau, very dexterously hidden, a cross set with brilliants, both of which I knew, by the list forwarded to the London police, formed part of the plunder carried off from Five Oaks' House. The prisoner's vehement protestations that he could not conceive how such articles came into his possession, excited a derisive smile on the face of the veteran turnkey; whilst I was thoroughly dumb-founded by the seemingly complete demolition of the theory of innocence I had woven out of his candid open manner and unshakeable hardihood of nerve.

"I dare say the articles came to you in your sleep!" sneered the turnkey as we turned to leave the cell.

"Oh," I mechanically exclaimed, "in his sleep! I had not thought of that!" The man stared; but I had passed out of the prison before he could express his surprise or contempt in words.

The next morning the justice-room was densely crowded, to hear the examination of the prisoner. There was also a very numerous attendance of magistrates; the case, from the position in life of the prisoner, and the strange and mysterious circumstances of the affair altogether, having excited an extraordinary and extremely painful interest amongst all classes in the town and neighborhood. The demeanor of the accused gentleman was anxious certainly, but withal calm and collected; and there was, I thought, a light of fortitude and conscious probity in his clear, bold eyes, which guilt never yet successfully stimulated.

After the hearing of some minor evidence, the fishmonger's boy was called, and asked if he could point out the person he had seen at Five Oaks on the day preceding the burglary? The lad looked fixedly at the prisoner for something more than a minute without speaking, and then said, "The gentleman was standing before the fire when I saw him, with his cap on; I should like to see this person with his cap on before I say anything."

Mr. Bristowe dashed on his foraging-cap, and the boy immediately exclaimed, "That is the man!"

Mr. Cowan, a solicitor, retained by Mr. Bagshawe for his nephew, objected that this was, after all, only swearing to a cap, or at best to the *ensemble* of a dress, and ought not to be received. The chairman, however, decided that it must be taken *quantum valeat*, and in corroboration of other evidence. It was next deposed by several persons that the deceased Sarah King had told them that her master's nephew had positively arrived at Five Oaks. An objection to the reception of this evidence, as partaking of the nature of "hearsay," was also made, and similarly overruled. Mr. Bristowe begged to observe "that Sarah King was not one of his uncle's old servants, and was entirely unknown to him: it was quite possible, therefore, that he was personally unknown to her." The bench observed that all these observations might be fitly urged before a jury, but, in the present stage of the proceedings, were uselessly addressed to them, whose sole duty it was to ascertain if a sufficiently strong case of suspicion had been made out against the prisoner to justify his committal for trial. A constable next proved finding a portion of a letter, which he produced, in one of the offices of Five Oaks; and then Mr. Bagshawe was directed to be called in. The prisoner, upon hearing this order given, exhibited great emotion, and earnestly intreated that his uncle and himself might be spared the necessity of meeting each other for the first time after a separation of several years under such circumstances.

"We can receive no evidence against you, Mr. Bristowe, in your absence," replied the chairman in a compassionate tone of voice; "but your uncle's deposition will occupy but a few minutes. It is, however, indispensable."

"At least, then, Mr. Cowan," said the agitated young man, "prevent my sister from accompanying her uncle: I could not bear *that*."

He was assured she would not be present; in fact she had become seriously ill through anxiety and terror; and the crowded assemblage awaited in painful silence the approach of the reluctant prosecutor. He presently appeared—a venerable, white-haired man; seventy years old at least he seemed, his form bowed by age and grief, his eyes fixed upon the ground, and his whole manner indicative of sorrow and dejection. "Uncle!" cried the prisoner, springing towards him.

The aged man looked up, seemed to read in the clear countenance of his nephew a full refutation of the suspicions entertained against him, tottered forwards with out-spread arms, and, in the words of the Sacred text, "fell upon his neck, and wept," exclaiming in choking accents, "Forgive me—forgive me, Robert, that I ever for a moment doubted you. Mary never did—never, Robert; not for an instant."

A profound silence prevailed during this outburst of feeling, and a considerable pause ensued before the usher of the court, at a gesture from the chairman, touched Mr. Bagshawe's arm, and begged his attention to the bench. "Certainly, certainly," said he, hastily wiping his eyes, and turning towards the court. "My sister's child, gentlemen," he added appealingly, "who has lived with me from childhood: you will excuse me, I am sure."

"There needs no excuse, Mr. Bagshawe," said the chairman kindly; "but it is necessary this unhappy business should be proceeded with. Hand the witness the portion of the letter found at Five Oaks. Now, is that your handwriting; and is it a portion of the letter you sent to your nephew, informing him of the large sum of money kept for a particular purpose at Five Oaks?"

"It is."

"Now," said the clerk to the magistrates, addressing me, "please to produce the articles in your possession."

I laid the Spanish coin and the cross upon the table.

"Please to look at those two articles, Mr. Bagshawe," said the chairman. "Now, sir, on your oath, are they a portion of the property of which you have been robbed?"

The aged gentleman stooped forward and examined them earnestly; then turned and looked with quivering eyes, if I may be allowed the expression, in his nephew's face; but returned no answer to the question.

"It is necessary you should reply, Yes or No, Mr. Bagshawe," said the clerk.

"Answer, uncle," said the prisoner soothingly: "fear not for me. God and my innocence to aid, I shall yet break through the web of villany in which I at present seem hopelessly involved."

"Bless you, Robert—bless you! I am sure you will. Yes, gentlemen, the cross and coin on the table are part of the property carried off."

A smothered groan, indicative of the sorrowing sympathy felt for the venerable gentleman, arose from the crowded court on hearing this declaration. I then deposed to finding them as previously stated. As soon as I concluded, the magistrates consulted together for a few minutes; and then the chairman, addressing the prisoner, said, "I have to inform you that the bench are agreed that sufficient evidence has been adduced against you to warrant them in fully committing you for trial. We are of course bound to hear anything you have to say; but such being our intention, your professional adviser will perhaps recommend you to reserve whatever defence you have to make for another tribunal: here it could not avail you."

Mr. Cowan expressed his concurrence in the intimation of the magistrate; but the prisoner vehemently protested against sanctioning by his silence the accusation preferred against him.

"I have nothing to reserve," he exclaimed with passionate energy; "nothing to conceal. I will not owe my acquittal of this foul charge to any trick of lawyer-craft. If I may not come out of this investigation with an untainted name, I desire not to escape at all. The defence, or rather the suggestive facts I have to offer for the consideration of the bench are these:—On the evening of the day I received my uncle's letter I went to Drury Lane theatre, remaining out very late. On my return to the hotel, I found I had been robbed of my pocket-book, which contained not only that letter, and a considerable sum in bank-notes, but papers of great professional importance to me. It was too late to adopt any measures for its recovery that night; and the next morning, as I was dressing myself to go out, in order to apprise the police authorities of my loss, I was informed that a gentleman desired to see me instantly on important business. He was shown up, and announced himself to be a detective police-officer: the robbery I had sustained had been revealed by an accomplice, and it was necessary I should immediately accompany him. We left the hotel together; and after consuming the entire day in perambulating all sorts of by-streets, and calling at several suspicious-looking places, my officious friend all at once discovered that the thieves had left town for the west of England, hoping, doubtless, to reach a large town and get gold for the notes before the news of their having been stopped should have reached it. He insisted upon immediate pursuit. I wished to return to the hotel for a change of clothes, as I was but lightly clad, and night-traveling required warmer apparel. This he would not hear of, as the night-coach was on the point of starting. He, however, contrived to supply me from his own resources with a greatcoat—a sort of policeman's cape—and a rough traveling-cap, which tied under the chin. In due time we arrived at Bristol, where I was kept for several days loitering about; till, finally, my guide decamped, and I returned to London. An hour after arriving there, I gave information at Scotland Yard of what had happened, and afterwards booked myself by the night-coach for Kendal. This is all I have to say."

This strange story did not produce the slightest effect upon the bench, and very little upon the auditory, and yet I felt satisfied it was strictly true. It was not half ingenious enough for a made-up story. Mr. Bagshawe, I should have stated, had been led out of the justice-hall immediately after he had finished his deposition.

"Then, Mr. Bristowe," said the magistrate's clerk, "assuming this curious narrative to be correct, you will be easily able to prove an *alibi*?"

"I have thought over that, Mr. Clerk," returned the prisoner mildly, "and must confess that, remembering how I was dressed and wrapped up—that I saw but few persons, and those casually and briefly, I have strong misgivings of my power to do so."

"That is perhaps the less to be lamented," replied the county clerk in a sneering tone, "inasmuch as the possession of those articles," pointing to the cross and coin on the table, "would necessitate another equally probable, though quite different story."

"That is a circumstance," replied the prisoner in the same calm tone as before, "which I cannot in the slightest manner account for."

No more was said, and the order for his committal to the county jail at Appleby on the charge of "wilful murder" was given to the clerk. At this moment a hastily-scrawled note from Barnes was placed in my hands. I had no sooner glanced over it, than I applied to the magistrates for an adjournment till the morrow, on the ground that I could then produce an important witness, whose evidence at the trial it was necessary to assure. The application was, as a matter of course, complied with; the prisoner was remanded till the next day, and the court adjourned.

As I accompanied Mr. Bristowe to the vehicle in waiting to convey him to jail, I could not forbear whispering, "Be of good heart, sir, we shall unravel this mystery yet, depend upon it." He looked keenly at me; and then, without other reply than a warm pressure of the hand, jumped into the carriage.

"Well, Barnes," I exclaimed as soon as we were in a room by ourselves, and the door closed, "what is it you have discovered?"

"That the murderers of Sarah King are yonder at the Talbot where you left me."

"Yes: so I gather from your note. But what evidence have you to support your assertion?"

"This! Trusting to my apparent drunken imbecility, they occasionally dropped words in my presence which convinced me not only that they were the guilty parties, but that they had come down here to carry off the plate, somewhere concealed in the neighborhood. This they mean to do to-night."

"Anything more?"

"Yes. You know I am a ventriloquist in a small way, as well as a bit of a mimic: well, I took occasion when that youngest of the rascals—the one that sat beside Mr. Bristowe, and got out on the top of the coach the second evening, because, freezing cold as it was, he said the inside was too hot and close"——

"Oh, I remember. Dolt that I was, not to recall it before. But go on."

"Well, he and I were alone together in the parlor about three hours ago—I dead tipsy as ever—when he suddenly heard the voice of Sarah King at his elbow exclaiming, 'Who is that in the plate closet?' If you had seen the start of horror which he gave, the terror which shook his failing limbs as he glanced round the apartment, you would no longer have entertained a doubt on the matter."

"This is scarcely judicial proof, Barnes; but I dare say we shall be able to make something of it. You return immediately; about nightfall I will rejoin you in my former disguise."

It was early in the evening when I entered the Talbot, and seated myself in the parlor. Our three friends were present, and so was Barnes.

"Is not that fellow sober yet?" I demanded of one of them.

"No; he has been lying about drinking and snoring ever since. He went to bed, I hear, this afternoon; but he appears to be little the better for it."

I had an opportunity soon afterwards of speaking to Barnes privately, and found that one of the fellows had brought a chaise-cart and horse from Kendal, and that all three were to depart in about an hour, under pretence of reaching a town about fourteen miles distant, where they intended to sleep. My plan was immediately taken: I returned to the parlor, and watching my opportunity, whispered into the ear of the young gentleman whose nerves had been so shaken by Barnes' ventriloquism, and who, by the way, was *my* old acquaintance— "Dick Staples, I want a word with you in the next room." I spoke in my natural voice, and lifted, for his especial study and edification, the wig from my forehead. He was thunder-struck; and his teeth chattered with terror. His two companions were absorbed over a low game at cards, and did not observe us. "Come," I continued in the same whisper, "there is not a moment to lose; *if you would save yourself*, follow me!" He did so, and I led him into an adjoining apartment, closed the door, and drawing a pistol from my coat-pocket, said—"You perceive, Staples, that the game is up: you personated Mr. Bristowe at his uncle's house at Five Oaks, dressed in a precisely similar suit of clothes to that which he wears. You murdered the servant"——

"No—no—no, not I," gasped the wretch; "not I: I did not strike her"——

"At all events you were present, and that, as far as the gallows is concerned, is the same thing. You also picked that gentleman's pocket during our journey from London, and placed one of the stolen Spanish pieces in his purse; you then went on the roof of the coach, and by some ingenious means or other contrived to secrete a cross set with brilliants in his portmanteau."

"What shall I do—what shall I do?" screamed the fellow, half dead with fear, and slipping down on a chair; "what shall I do to save my life—my life?"

"First get up and listen. If you are not the actual murderer"——

"I am not—upon my soul I am not!"

"If you are not, you will probably be admitted king's evidence; though, mind, I make no promises. Now, what is the plan of operations for carrying off the booty?"

"They are going in the chaise-cart almost immediately to take it up: it is hidden in the copse yonder. I am to remain here, in order to give an alarm should any suspicion be excited, by showing two candles at our bedroom window; and if all keeps right, I am to join them at the cross-roads, about a quarter of a mile from hence."

"All right. Now return to the parlor: I will follow you; and remember that on the slightest hint of treachery I will shoot you as I would a dog."

About a quarter of an hour afterwards his two confederates set off in the chaise-cart: I, Barnes, and Staples, cautiously followed, the latter handcuffed, and superintended by the ostler of the inn, whom I for the nonce pressed into the king's service. The night was pitch dark, fortunately, and the noise of the cart-wheels effectually drowned the sound of our footsteps. At length the cart stopped; the men got out, and were soon busily engaged in transferring the buried plate to the cart. We cautiously approached, and were soon within a yard or two of them, still unperceived.

"Get into the cart," said one of them to the other, "and I will hand the things up to you." His companion obeyed.

"Hollo!" cried the fellow, "I thought I told you"——

"That you are nabbed at last!" I exclaimed, tripping him suddenly up. "Barnes, hold the horse's head. Now, sir, attempt to budge an inch out of that cart, and I'll send a bullet through your brains." The surprise was complete; and so terror-stricken were they, that neither resistance nor escape was attempted. They were soon handcuffed and otherwise secured; the remainder of the plate was placed in the cart; and we made the best of our way to Kendal jail, where I had the honor of lodging them at about nine o'clock in the evening. The news, late as it was, spread like wild-fire, and innumerable were the congratulations which awaited me when I reached the inn where I lodged. But that which recompensed me a thousandfold for what I had done, was the fervent embrace in which the white-haired uncle, risen from his bed to assure himself of the truth of the news, locked me, as he called down blessings from Heaven upon my head! There are blessed moments even in the life of a police-officer.

Mr. Bristowe was of course liberated on the following morning; Staples was admitted king's evidence; and one of his accomplices—the actual murderer—was hanged, the other transported. A considerable portion of the property was also recovered. The gentleman who—to give time and opportunity for the perpetration of the burglary, suggested by the perusal of Mr. Bagshawe's letter—induced Mr. Bristowe to accompany him to Bristol, was soon afterwards transported for another offence.

CHARLES MARTEL

(PSEUDONYM OF THOMAS DELF)

(1810–1865)

In 1862, when the New York firm of Carleton published the novel *Out of His Head*, the only author listed on the title page was Thomas Bailey Aldrich, who was known for two previous novels and for his magazine writings. Later he would edit various magazines, including almost a decade heading *The Atlantic Monthly*. In that role, Aldrich has the distinction of publishing the pioneer Black fiction writer Charles W. Chesnutt, one of whose fiercely candid stories—"The Sheriff's Children"—appears herein.

However, a second author ought to have been listed beside Aldrich, who had stolen chapters 11–14, which he presented as a stand-alone episode entitled "The Danseuse," from an earlier writer, Charles Martel, the pseudonym of Thomas Delf. A scholar, bookseller, and translator, Delf had a variety of works to his name, from *Appleton's Library Manual* to *Principles of Colouring in Painting* to the two story collections for which mystery fans remember him: *The Diary of an Ex-Detective* and *The Detective's Note-Book*, both published in 1860 as police "memoirs."

The stories in *The Detective's Note-Book*, which feature a detective identified only as F——, vary from headlong tales of pursuit to what we now think of as tales of detection, some with a Sherlockian scientific bent. Martel even appends a nonfictional note about bloodstains. However, one enigma not unraveled by F—— is why a dusty London bookseller would choose as his pseudonym the name of an eighth-century Frankish military hero, Charles, dubbed *Martel* from the Old French word for *hammer*, and grandfather of Charlemagne. However, there seems to be no mystery about why the historical Charles the Hammer, who led Frankish opposition to the Islamic Umayyad Caliphate's failed invasions of Gaul, has been chosen as totem and saint for a US-based white supremacist organization named after him. The Charles Martel Society, headquartered in Atlanta, publishes *The Occidental Quarterly*, a racist platform poorly disguised as an academic journal. Fortunately none of these issues concern the excellent story that follows.

The chapters copied by Aldrich and presented as his own had been published two years earlier in *The Detective's Note-Book*, as "Hanged by the Neck: A Confession." Except for changing the title, suturing a brief opening that fits the story to the rest of his novel, and inexplicably pasting on an ill-fitting new ending, Aldrich shamelessly copied Martel's story. Somehow this plagiarism remains little noticed in the field. Since the turn of the millennium, at least one anthologist has included Aldrich's version without mentioning Martel, even though in the 1970s the scholar and anthologist E. F. Bleiler resurrected the story under its original title and attribution. Perhaps few fans or anthologists read Martel nowadays, which is a shame, because he was an inventive writer. His detective seems to have been supplied by his creator with genuine research into investigative techniques. Martel also simply tells a lively story, even if it is marbled with laughable sexism.

HANGED BY THE NECK

A Confession

I.

I am about to lift the veil of mystery which for ten years has shrouded the murder of Maria G——; and, though I lay bare my own weakness, or folly, or what you will, I do not shrink from the unveiling. No hand but mine can perform the task. There was, indeed, a man who might have done this better than I; but he wrapped himself in silence and went his way.

I like a man who can hold his tongue.

On the corner of Dudley and Broad Streets stands a dingy-brown house, which, judging from its obsolete style of architecture, must have been built a century ago. It has a very cocked-hat air about it—an antique, unhappy look. It is now tenanted by an incalculable number of Irish families; but at the time of which I write it was a second-rate lodging-house of the more respectable sort, and rather largely patronised by poor but honest literary men, tragic actors, and pretty ballet-girls.

My apartments in Dudley Street were opposite this building, to which my attention was directed, soon after taking possession of the rooms, by the discovery of the following facts:— First, that a very charming *blonde* lodged on the second floor front of "over the way," and sang like a canary-bird every morning; second, that her name was Maria G——; third, that she had two lovers—short allowance for a *danseuse*. If ever poetry and pathos took human shape it was christened Maria G——. She was one of Beauty's best thoughts. I cannot tell if her eyes were black or hazel; but her hair was bronze-brown, silken, and wavy, and her mouth the perfection of tenderness. Her form was rich in those perfect curves which delighted the old Greek masters. I write this with no impure thought. But when she lay in her little room, stark, and lifeless, and horrible, the glory faded from her face, then I stooped down and kissed her, but not till then. How ghastly she looked! Eyes with no light in them, lips with no breath on them—white, cold, dead!

Maria G—— was a finer study to me than her lovers. One of them was commonplace enough—well dressed, well made, handsome, shallow. Nature manufactures such men by the gross. He was a lieutenant, in the navy I think, and ought to have been on the sea, or in it, instead of working ruin ashore. The other was a man of different mould. His character, like his person, had rough lines to it. Only for the drooping of his eyelids, and a certain coarseness about the mouth, he would have been handsome, in spite of those dark, deep-sunken eyes. His frame would have set an anatomist wild—tall, deep-chested, knitted with muscles of steel. "Some day," said I, as I saw him stalk by the house one evening, "he will throw the little lieutenant out of that second-floor window." It would have been a wise arrangement.

From the time I left off short jackets women have perplexed me. I have discovered what woman is not; but I have never found out what she is. I cannot tell to this day which of those two men Maria G—— loved, or if she loved either. The flirtation, however, was scandal enough for the entire neighbourhood; but little did the gossips dream of the tragedy which was being acted under their noses.

This affair had continued for several months, when it was reported that Maria and Julius Kenneth were affianced. The lieutenant was less frequently seen in Broad Street; and Julius waited upon Maria's footsteps with a humility and tenderness strangely out of keeping with his rough nature. Mrs. Grundy was somewhat appeased. Yet, though Maria went to the Sunday concerts with Julius Kenneth, she still wore the lieutenant's roses in her bosom!

If I could only meet with an unenigmatical woman!

II.

I was awakened one morning by several quick, nervous raps on my room door. The noise startled me from a most appalling dream.

"Oh, sir!" cried a voice on the landing, "there's been a dreadful murder done across the street! They've murdered Maria G——!"

"I will get up." That was all I said. I looked at my watch. It was nine o'clock. I had overslept myself; but then I sat up late the night before.

I dressed myself hastily, and, without waiting for breakfast, pushed my way through the crowd that had collected in front of the house, and passed upstairs unquestioned to the scene of the tragedy. When I entered the room there were six people present—a tall, slim gentleman, with a professional air, evidently a physician; two policemen; Adelaide Woods, an actress; Mrs. Marston, the landlady; and Julius Kenneth. In the centre of the chamber, on the bed, lay the body of Maria G——. The face of the corpse haunted me for years afterwards with its bloodless lips, the dark streaks under the eyes, and the long silken hair streaming over the pillow. I stooped over her for a moment, and turned down the counterpane, which was drawn up closely to her chin.

> "There was that across her throat
> Which you had hardly cared to see!"

At the head of the bed sat Julius Kenneth, bending over the icy hand which he held in his own. He seemed to be kissing it. The gentleman in black was conversing in undertones with Mrs. Marston, who wrung her hands every other moment and glanced towards the body. The two policemen were examining the doors, closets, and windows of the premises. There was no fire in the grate, but the room was suffocatingly close. I opened a window and leaned against the casement to catch the fresh air. The physician approached me. I muttered something to him.

"Yes," he began, "the affair looks very mysterious, as you

remark. Never saw so little evidence of anything. Thought at first 'twas a case of suicide: door locked, key on the inside, room in perfect order; but then we find no instrument with which the subject could have inflicted that wound on the neck. Party must have escaped by the window. But how? The windows are at least thirty feet from the ground. It would be impossible for a person to jump that distance without fracturing a limb, even if he could clear the iron railing below. Unpleasant things to jump on, those spikes. . . . Must have been done with a sharp knife. The party meant to make sure work of it. The carotid cleanly severed. Death in about a hundred seconds."

The medical man went on in this hideous style for ten minutes, during which time Kenneth did not raise his lips from Maria's hand. I spoke to him; but he only shook his head in reply. I understood his grief; and on returning to my room I wrote him a note, the purport of which will be shown hereafter.

The *Evening Herald* of that day contained the following article:—

"MURDER IN BROAD STREET.—This morning, at eight o'clock, Maria G——, the well-known *danseuse,* was found murdered in her bed, at her late residence on the corner of Broad and Endell Streets. There was but one wound on the body—a fearful gash on the neck, just below the left ear. The deceased was dressed in a ballet costume, and was evidently murdered immediately after her return from the theatre, by some person or persons concealed in the room. On a chair near the bed lay several fresh bouquets, and a long cloak which the deceased was in the habit of wearing over her dancing dress on coming home from the theatre at night. The perfect order of the apartment, and the fact that the door was locked on the inside, have induced many to believe that the poor girl killed herself. But we cannot think so. That the door was fastened on the inner side proves nothing, excepting that the murderer was hidden in the chamber. That the room gave no evidence of a struggle is also an insignificant fact. Two men, or even one strong man, grappling suddenly with the deceased, who was a very slight woman, would have prevented any great struggle. No weapon whatever was discovered on the premises. We give below all the material testimony elicited by the coroner's inquest. It explains nothing.

"*Harriet Marston* deposes: I keep a lodging-house at 131, Broad Street. The deceased has lodged with me for the past two years. Has always borne a good character. I do not think she had many visitors: certainly no male visitors, except a Lieutenant King and Mr. Kenneth, to whom she was engaged. I do not know when Lieutenant King was last at the house; not within three days I am confident. Deceased told me that he had gone away for ever. I did not see her last night when she returned from the theatre. The street door is never locked; each of the lodgers has a latch-key. The last time I saw the deceased was just before she went to the theatre, when she requested me to call her at eight o'clock, as she had promised to walk out with 'Jules,' meaning Mr. Kenneth. I knocked at the door eight or ten times, and received no answer. I then grew frightened, and called one of the lodgers, Adelaide Woods, who helped me to force the lock. The key fell out on the inside as we pressed against the door. Maria G—— was lying on the bed with her throat cut. The quilt and the strip of carpet beside the bed were covered with blood. She was not undressed. The room presented the same appearance it does now.

"*Adelaide Woods* deposes: I am an actress. I occupy a room next to that of the deceased. It was about eleven o'clock when she came home; she stopped ten or fifteen minutes in my chamber. The call-boy of the Olympic usually accompanied her home from the theatre. I let her in. Deceased had misplaced her night-key. I did not hear any noise in the night. The partition between our rooms is quite thick; but I do not sleep heavily, and should have heard any unusual noise. Two weeks ago deceased told me that she was to be married to Mr. Kenneth in June. She and Mr. Kenneth were in the habit of taking walks before breakfast. The last time I saw them together was yesterday morning. I assisted Mrs. Marston in breaking open the door. [Describes position of the body, &c., &c.]

"Here the call-boy was summoned, and testified to accompanying the deceased home on the night of the murder. He came as

far as the steps with her. The door was opened by a woman.
Could not swear it was Miss Woods, though he knows her by
sight. The night was very dark, and there was no lamp burning
in the entry.

"*Julius Kenneth* deposes: I am a machinist. I reside at No. —,
F—— Street. I have been acquainted with the deceased for eighteen months. We were engaged to be married. [Here the witness's
voice failed him.] The last time I saw her was yesterday morning,
on which occasion we walked out together. I did not leave my
room last evening. I was confined to the house by a cold all day.
A Lieutenant King used to visit the deceased frequently. It created considerable talk in the neighbourhood. I did not like it,
and requested her to break off the acquaintance. Deceased told
me yesterday morning that Lieutenant King had been ordered to
some foreign station, and would trouble me no more. Deceased
had engaged to walk with me this morning at eight o'clock.
When I reached Broad Street I first learned that she had been
murdered. [Here the witness, overcome by his emotions, was
permitted to retire.]

"*Dr. Underhill* deposes: [this witness was very voluble and
learned, and had to be checked several times by the coroner. We
give his testimony in brief.] I was called in to view the body of
the deceased. A deep wound on the throat, two inches below the
left ear, severing the left common carotid and the internal jugu-
lar vein, had been inflicted by some sharp instrument. Such a
wound would produce death almost immediately. The body bore
no other marks of violence. The deceased must have been dead
several hours, the *rigor mortis* having already supervened. On a
second examination with Dr. Rose the deceased was found to be
enceinte.

"*Dr. Rose* corroborated the above testimony.

"The policeman and several other people were examined, but
their statements threw no light on the case. The situation of Julius Kenneth, the lover of the unfortunate girl, excites the deepest commiseration. The deceased was nineteen years of age.
Who the criminal is, and what could have led to the perpetration
of the cruel act, are mysteries which, at present, threaten to baf-
fle the sagacity of the police."

I could but smile on reading all this solemn nonsense. After breakfast the next morning I made my toilet with extreme care, and presented myself at the police office. Two gentlemen, who were sitting with the magistrate at a table, started to their feet as I announced myself. I bowed to the magistrate very calmly and said,—

"*I am the person who murdered Maria G——!*"

Of course I was instantly arrested. The *Globe* of that evening favoured me with the following complimentary notice:—

"THE BROAD-STREET HOMICIDE: FURTHER DEVELOPMENTS: MORE MYSTERY.—The person who murdered the ballet-girl in Clarke Street on the night of the 3rd instant surrendered himself to the magistrate this morning. He gave his name as Paul Larkins, and resides opposite the scene of the tragedy. He is of medium height, and well made; has dark, restless eyes, and chestnut hair; his face is unnaturally pale, and by no means improved by the Mephistophilean smile which constantly plays upon his lips. Notwithstanding his gentlemanly address, there is that about him which stamps him villain. His voluntary surrender is not the least mysterious feature of this mysterious *affaire;* for, had he preserved silence, he would have escaped detection beyond a doubt. He planned and executed the murder with such skill that there is little or no evidence against him, save his own confession, which is inexplicable enough. He acknowledges the crime, but stubbornly refuses to enter into details. He expresses a desire to be hanged immediately! How he entered the room, and by what means he left it after committing the heinous deed, and why he brutally murdered a woman with whom, as it is proved, he had had no previous acquaintance, are enigmas which still perplex the public mind, and will not let curiosity sleep. These facts, however, will probably be brought to light during the trial. In the mean time the greatest excitement reigns throughout the city."

At four o'clock that afternoon the door of my cell turned on its hinges, and Julius Kenneth stood face to face with me. I ought to have cowered in the presence of that injured man, but I did not. I was cool, Satanic; he feverish and terrible.

"You got my note?" I said.

"Yes; and I have come here as you requested."

"You know, of course, that I have refused to reveal the circumstances connected with the murder? I wished to make the confession to you alone."

He turned his eyes on mine for a moment, and said, "Well?"

"But even to you I will assign no reason for having committed this crime. It was necessary that Maria G—— should die. I decided that she should die in her chamber, and to that end I purloined her night-key."

Julius Kenneth fixed his eyes on me.

"On Wednesday night, after Maria G—— had gone to the theatre, I entered the street door by means of the key, and stole unobserved into her chamber, and secreted myself under the bed, or in that small clothes press near the window—I forget which. Some time between eleven and twelve o'clock she returned; and as she lighted the candle I caught her by the waist, pressed a handkerchief saturated with chloroform over her mouth, and threw her on the bed. When she had ceased to struggle, and I could use my hand, I made a deep incision in her throat. Then I smoothed the bedclothes, and threw my gloves and the handkerchief into the grate. I am afraid there was not fire enough to burn them!"

Kenneth walked up and down the cell in great agitation; then he suddenly stopped and sat down on the bed.

"Are you listening? I then extinguished the light and proceeded to make my escape from the room, which I did in so simple a manner that the police, through their very desire to discover wonderful things, will never find it out, unless indeed *you* betray me. The night, you will remember, was remarkably foggy; it was so thick, indeed, that it was impossible to see a person at four yards' distance. I raised the window-sash cautiously, and let myself out, holding on by the sill until my feet touched on the left-hand shutter of the window beneath, which swung back against the house, and was made stationary by the catch. By standing on this—my arms are almost as long as yours—I was able to reach the iron water-spout of the adjacent building, and by that I descended to the pavement."

Kenneth glared at me like some ferocious animal.

"On gaining the street," I continued, "I found that I had thoughtlessly brought the knife with me—a long, slim-bladed knife. I should have left it in the room. It would have given the whole thing the appearance of suicide. I threw the knife——"

"Into the river!" exclaimed Kenneth, involuntarily.

And then I smiled.

"How did you know it was I?" he shrieked.

"It was as plain as day," I returned coolly. "Hush, they will hear you in the corridor. I knew it the moment I saw you sitting by the bed. First, because you shrunk instinctively from the corpse, though you seemed to caress it. Your grief throughout was clumsily done, sir; it was too melodramatic. Secondly, when I looked into the grate I saw a handkerchief partly consumed, and then I instantly remembered the faint, peculiar smell which I had observed in the room before the windows were opened. Thirdly, when I went to the window I noticed that the paint was scraped off the iron brackets which held the spout to the adjoining house. The spout had been painted three days previously; the paint on the brackets was thicker than anywhere else, and had not dried. On looking at your feet, which I did when I spoke to you, I remarked that the leather on the inner side of both your boots was slightly chafed."

"If you intend to betray me——" and Kenneth thrust his hand in his bosom. He had a pistol there.

"That I am *here* proves that I intend nothing of the kind. If you will listen patiently you shall learn why *I* acknowledge the crime, why *I* would bear the penalty. I believe there are vast, intense sensations, from which we are shut out by the fear of a certain kind of death. This pleasure, this ecstasy, this something which I have striven for all my life, is known only to the privileged few—innocent men, who, through some oversight of the law, are *hanged by the neck*. Some men are born to be hanged, some have hanging thrust upon them, and some (as I hope to do) achieve hanging. For years and years I have watched for such a chance as this. Worlds could not tempt me to divulge your guilt any more than worlds could have tempted me to commit your crime. A man's mind and heart should be at ease to enjoy, to the utmost, this delicious death. Now you may go."

And I turned my back on him. Kenneth came to my side and placed his heavy hand on my shoulder—that red right hand which all the tears of the angels could not wash white. It made me shudder.

"I shall go far from here," he said, hurriedly. "I cannot, I *will not,* die now. They dishonoured me. Maria was to have been my wife: so she would have hidden her shame! She is dead. When I meet *him* then I shall have done with life. I shall not die till then. And you—they will not harm you—you are a maniac!"

The cell door closed on Julius Kenneth.

I bite the blood into my lips with vexation when I think what a miserable failure I made of it. Three stupid friends who had played cards with me at my room on the night of the murder proved an *alibi.* I was literally turned out of prison, for I insisted on being executed. Then it was maddening to have all the papers call me "a monomaniac." I a monomaniac! I like that! What was Pythagoras, and Newton, and Fulton, and Brunel?

But I kept my peace; and impenetrable mystery shrouded the murder of Maria G——.

III.

Three years ago, in broad daylight, a man was shot dead in the park. A hundred eyes saw the deed. I went to the man's funeral. They buried him with military honours. So much for Lieutenant King!

The first grey light of dawn straggled through the narrow window of the cell, and drove the shadows into the farther corner, where Julius Kenneth lay sleeping. A summer morning was breaking on the city.

In cool green woods millions of birds stirred in their nests, waiting for the miracle of morning; the night trains dashed through quiet country towns; innumerable shop-boys took down innumerable shutters; the milkmen shrieked; the clocks struck; doors opened and closed; the glamour of sleep was broken, and all the vast machinery of life was put in motion.

But to the man in jail it was as if these things were not.

As he lay there, slumbering in the increasing light, the carpenters in the prison-yard were raising a wooden platform, with two hideous black uprights supporting a horizontal beam, in the centre of which was a small iron pulley. The quick sound of the hammers broke in on his dreams, if he had any. He turned restlessly once or twice, and pushed the hot pillow from him. Then he opened his eyes and saw the splendid blue sky through the window.

He listened to the hammers. He knew what the sound meant. It was his last day on earth. *Vive la bagatelle!* He would have more sleep; so he closed his eyes again.

At six o'clock the jailer brought him his breakfast, and he devoured it like an animal. An hour afterwards two attendants dressed him in a melancholy suit of black, and arranged his tangled hair. At seven the chaplain of the prison entered the cell.

"Would his poor friend," he said, approaching the wretch, "turn, in this last sad hour, to Him whose mercy, like the heavens, spanned all things? Would he listen for a while to the teachings of One whose life and death were two pure prayers for mankind? Would he have, at this awful moment, such consolation as he, a humble worker in God's vineyard, could give him?"

"No; but he would have some brandy."

The unscientific beast! I could pity him—not that he was to be hanged, but because he was not in the state of mind to enjoy the ecstatic sensations which I am convinced result from strangulation. The chaplain remained with the man, and the man yawned.

The ponderous bell of St. Paul's modestly struck eight as the High Sheriff paused at the foot of the scaffold, while the prisoner, followed by the indefatigable chaplain, complacently mounted the rough deal steps which lead to—can anybody tell me where? To the top of the scaffold. Quite right!

I shall not forget that insensible, stony face, as I saw it for a moment before the black cap screened it from the crowd. Why did they hide his face? I should like to have studied the convulsive workings of those features.

In the stillness of that June night they took the body away in a deal coffin, and buried it somewhere. I don't know where. I have not the slightest idea where they bury that sort of man.

JAMES McLEVY

(1796–1873)

In what is probably the best, and certainly the best-written, history of nineteenth century crime fiction, *The Invention of Murder*, historian Judith Flanders says of the "police-memoir" subgenre of detective stories that flourished in the mid–nineteenth century, "The main way of telling fictional memoirs from real ones is to look at the crimes."

Melodrama, byzantine plots, ciphers, vengeful machinations, dying messages, seemingly impossible crimes—all of these tropes already haunted the gleefully fictional detective stories of two centuries ago. Real-life policing, however, was largely a matter of stolen jewelry, unsolvable vandalism, misdemeanor fraud, and domestic violence with no mystery hiding the perpetrator and little likelihood of prosecution.

To Flanders's point, the following story, "The Dead Child's Leg," is not a typical case for Edinburgh police officer and detective James McLevy. He was an actual policeman and that was his real name. Most of the cases described in the stories attributed to him involve relatively minor property crimes—purloining ducks, picking pockets, stealing the last few pence off an old woman in a poorhouse. But naturally McLevy's unraveling of the grisly case of the child's leg seemed the best choice for an anthology about bloody murder.

Whatever real-life experiences may have inspired these stories, they read like fiction—lively and memorable fiction. Filled with dialogue beyond any that an officer's notebook might have recorded, the cases were presented as occurring long before they were written up during McLevy's retirement. He opened the first story by invoking Chance, whom he calls his "patroness." Not surprisingly, it turns out that often the culprit is unveiled by coincidence, in what feels like inattention to plot details perhaps resulting from McLevy's greater interest in portraying character. He also loved semicolons and em dashes.

He joined the newly established police force in 1830 as a night watchman. Three years later he became Scotland's first "criminal officer detective," assigned the number CO (Criminal Officer) 1. The introduction to the original 1861 volume claims that McLevy investigated twenty-two hundred cases and this number is often bandied about without documentation. In contrast to many accounts of early police and detectives, McLevy comes across as level-headed and humane, although he doesn't hesitate to show errors and short tempers within the force. He writes with compassion about "those scenes of which the quiet normal people of the world have no more idea than they have of what is going on in the molten regions of the middle of the earth, on the surface of which they are plucking roses."

In Scotland, the McLevy stories have remained much better known than most other nineteenth century crime writing. From 1999 to 2016, a popular BBC Radio 4 series brought the local hero a new audience, making the cases seem more than ever a collection of literary stories to be freely adapted. However, historical records corroborate details in some of McLevy's accounts. In one story set in 1845, for example, court records confirm details of interrogation and witnesses as described by McLevy; in another, the names of a marrying couple show up in the official marriage records of the correct year (1855), differing from McLevy's account only in forename. What makes McLevy so appealing nowadays, however, is not his accuracy as much as his compassion. He is a man of his time, but he cares about his fellow human beings.

Many of the stories cite the year of their occurrence, mostly in the 1840s. "The Dead Child's Leg" does not mention a date, but, typical of McLevy's offhand realism, it compassionately follows through the tragedy to the miscreant's trial and imprisonment. Two collections of McLevy stories, *Curiosities of Crime in Edinburgh* and *The Sliding Scale of Life*, were published in Edinburgh in 1861.

THE DEAD CHILD'S LEG

Some years ago, the scavenger whose district lies about the Royal Exchange, came to the office in a state of great excitement. He had a parcel in his hand, and laying it on the table, said, "I've found something this morning that you won't guess."

"A bag of gold, perhaps?" said I.

"I wish it had been," said the man, looking at the parcel, a dirty rolled-up napkin, with increased fear; "it's a bairn's leg."

"A bairn's leg!" said I, taking up the parcel, and undoing it with something like a tremor in my own hand, which had never shaken when holding by the throat such men as Adam M'Donald.

And there, to be sure, was a child's leg, severed about the middle of the thigh. On examining it, it was not difficult to see that it was a part of a new-born infant, and a natural curiosity suggested a special look to the severed end, to know what means had been taken to cut it from the body. The result was peculiar. It appeared as if a hatchet had been applied to cut the bone, and the operator had finished the work by dragging the member from the body,—a part of the muscle and integuments looking lacerated and torn. The leg was bleached, as if it had lain in water for a time, and it was altogether a ghastly spectacle.

"Where did you find it?" I asked.

"Why," replied the man, "I was sweeping about in Writers' Court at gray dawn, and, with a turn of my broom, I threw out of a sewer something white; then it was so dark I was obliged to stoop down to get a better look, and the five little toes appeared so strange that I staggered back, knowing very well now what it was. But I have always been afraid of dead bodies. Then I tied it up in my handkerchief, more to conceal it from my own sight than for any other reason."

"And you can't tell where it came from?" said I.

"Not certainly," answered he; "but I have a guess."

And the man, an Irishman, looked very wise, as if his guess

was a very dark ascertained reality, something terribly mysterious.

"Out with your guess, man," said I; "it looks like a case of murder, and we must get at the root of it."

"And I will be brought into trouble," answered he; "faith, I'll say no more. I've given you the leg, and that's pretty well, anyhow. It's not every day you get the like o' that brought to ye, all for nothing; and ye'er not content."

"You know more than you have told us," said I; "and how are we to be sure that you did not put the leg there yourself?"

"Put the leg there myself, and then bring it to you!" said he; "first kill the bairn, and then come to be hanged! Not just what an Irishman would do. We're not so fond of trouble as all that."

"Trouble or no trouble, you must tell us where you think it came from, otherwise we will detain you as a suspected murderer."

"Mercy save us! me a suspected murderer!" cried he, getting alarmed; "well now, to be plain, you see, the leg was lying just at the bottom of the main soil-pipe that comes from the whole of the houses on the east side of the court, and it must be somebody in some family in some flat in some house in some part of the row that's the mother,—that's pretty certain; and I think I have told you enough to get at the thief of a mother."

The man, no doubt, pointed at the proper source, however vaguely; so taking him along with me I walked over to Writers' Court, and, after examining the place where the leg was found, I was in some degree satisfied that the man was right. It was exceedingly unlikely that the member would be thrown down there by any one entering the court, or by any one from a window, for this would just have been to exhibit a piece of evidence that a murder, or at least a concealed birth had taken place somewhere in the neighbourhood, and to send the officers of the law upon inquiry. Besides, the leg was found in the gutter leading down from the main pipe of the tenements, and though there was no water flowing at the time there had been a sufficiency either on the previous night or early morning to wash it to where it had lain.

But after coming to this conclusion, the difficulty took another shape, not less unpromising. The pipe, as the man truly said, was a main pipe, into which all the pipes of the different houses led. One of these houses was Mr W——te's inn, which contained several females, of a higher grade from throughout the lands, and I shrunk from an investigation so general, and carrying an imputation so terrible. My inquiry was not among people of degraded character, where a search or a charge was only a thing of course,—doing no harm where they could not be more suspected than they deserved,—but among respectable families, some with females of tender feelings, regardful of a reputation which, to be suspected, was to be lost for ever; and I required to be on my guard against precipitation and imprudence.

Yet my course so far was clear enough. I could commit no imprudence, while I might expect help, in confining my first inquiries to the heads of the families; and this I had resolved upon while yet standing in the court in the hazy morning. The man and I were silent—he sleeping, and I meditating—when, in the stillness which yet prevailed, I saw a window drawn up in that stealthy way I am accustomed to hear when crime is on the outlook. It was clear that the greatest care had been taken to avoid noise; but ten times the care, and a bottle of oil to boot, would not have enabled this morning watcher to escape my ear. On the instant I slipt into an entry, the scavenger still sleeping away, and, notwithstanding of his shrewdness, not alive to an important part of the play. I could see without being seen; and looking up, I saw a white cap with a young and pale face under it, peering down upon the court. I had so good a look at the object, that I could have picked out that face, so peculiar was it, from among a thousand. I could even notice the eye, nervous and snatchy, and the secret-like movement of withdrawing the head as she saw the man, and then protruding it a little again as she observed him busy. Then there was a careful survey, not to ascertain the kind of morning, or to converse with a neighbouring protruding head, but to watch, and see, and hear what was going on below, where probably she had heard the voices of me and the man. Nay, I could have sworn that she directed her eye to the conduit—a suspicion on my part which afterwards appeared to me as absurd, as in the event of her being the criminal, and knowing the direction of the pipes, she never would have trusted her life to such an *open* mode of concealment as sending the mutilated body down through the inside pipes, to be there exposed.

After looking anxiously and timidly for some time, and affording me, as I have said, sufficient opportunity to scan and treasure up her features, she quietly drew in her pale, and, as I thought, beautiful face, let down the sash, almost with a long whisper of the wood, and all was still. I now came out of my hiding-place, and telling the man not to say a word to any one of what had been seen or done, I went round to the Exchange, and satisfied myself of the house thus signalised by the head of the pale watcher of the morning.

I need not say I had my own thoughts of this transaction but still I saw that to have gone and directly impeached this poor, timid looker-out upon the dawn for scarcely any other reason than she did then and there look out, and that she had a delicate appearance, would have been unauthorised, and perhaps fraught with painful consequences. What if I had failed in bringing home to her a tittle of evidence, and left her with a ruined reputation for life? The thought alarmed me, and I behoved to be careful, however strict, in the execution of my duty; so I betook myself during the forenoon to my first resolution of having conferences with the heads of the houses.

I took the affair systematically, beginning at one end and going through the families. No master or mistress could I find who could say they had observed any *signs* in any of their female domestics. The last house was a reservation—that house from which my watcher of the morning had been intent upon the doings of the court. It was the inn occupied, as I have said, by Mr W——te. Strangely enough, the door was opened by that same pale-faced creature. I threw my eye over her,—the same countenance, delicate and interesting,—the same nervous eye, and look of shrinking fear,—but now a smart cap on her head, which was like a mockery of her sadness and melancholy. She eyed me curiously and fearfully as I asked for

Mr W——te, and ran with an irregular and irresolute motion to show me in. I made no inquiry of her further, nor did I look at her intently to rouse her suspicion, for I had got all I wanted, even that which a glance carried to me. But if she showed me quickly in, I could see that she had no disposition to run away when the door of the room opened. No doubt she was about the outside of it. I took care she could learn nothing there, but few will ever know what she had suffered there.

I questioned Mr W——te confidentially; told him all the circumstances; and ended by inquiring whether any of his female domestics had shown any *signs* for a time bypast.

"No," said he; "such a thing could hardly have escaped me; and if I had suspected, I would have made instant inquiry, for the credit of my house."

"What is the name of the young girl who opened the door to me?"

"Mary B——n, but I cannot allow myself to suspect her; she is a simple-hearted, innocent creature, and totally incapable of such a thing."

"But is she not pale and sickly-looking as if some such event as that I allude to might have taken place in her case?"

"Why, yes, I admit," said he, "that she is paler than she used to be, but she has been so often with me; and then her conduct is so circumspect, I cannot listen to the suspicion."

"Might I see the others?" said I.

"Certainly;" replied he, "I can bring them here upon pretences."

"You may, except Mary B——n," said I; "I have seen enough of her."

And Mr W——te brought up several females on various pretences, all of whom I surveyed with an eye not more versed in these indications than what a very general knowledge of human nature might have enabled one to be. Each of them bore my scrutiny well and successfully—all healthy, blithe queens, with neither blush nor paleness to show anything wrong about the heart of conscience.

"All these are free," said I, "but I must take the liberty to ask you to show me the openings to the soil-pipe belonging to the tenement, but in such a way as not to produce suspicion; for I think you will find Mary about the door of the room."

And so it turned out, for no sooner had we come forth than we could see the poor girl escaping by the turn of the lobby.

"*That is my lass,*" said I to myself.

The investigation of the pipes showed me nothing. There was not in any of the closets a drop of blood, nor sign of any kind of violence to a child, nor in any bed-room a trace of birth, and far less a murder; but I could not be driven from my theory. My watcher of the morning of day was she who had taken the light of the morning of life from the new-born babe.

I consulted with the police doctor, and he saw at once difficulties of the case. The few facts, curious and adventitious as they were, which had come under my own eye, were almost for myself alone; no other would have been moved by them because they might have been supposed to be coloured by my own fancy. Yet I felt I had a case to make out in some way, however much the reputation of a poor young girl should be implicated, and not less my own character and feelings. As yet, proof there was none. To have taken up a girl merely because she had a pale face—the only indication I could point to that others could judge of—was not according to my usual tactics; but I could serve my purpose without injuring the character of the girl were she innocent, and yet convict her if guilty. So I thought: and my plan, which was my own, was a mere tentative one, free from the objection of hardship or cruelty to the young woman.

About twelve o'clock I rolled up the leg of the child in a neat paper parcel, and writing an address upon it to Mary B——n, at Mr W——te's, I repaired to the inn. Mary, who was not exclusively "the maid of the inn," did not this time open the door; it was done by one whose ruddy cheeks would have freed her from the glance of the keenest detective.

"Is Mary B——n in?" asked I.

"Yes," she replied somewhat carelessly; for I need not say there was not a suspicion in the house, except in the breast of Mr W——te, who was too discreet and prudent to have said a word.

"Tell her I have a parcel from the country for her," said I, walking in, and finding my way into a room.

The girl went for Mary, and I waited a considerable time; but then, probably, she might have been busy making the beds, perhaps her own, in a careful way, though she scarcely needed, after my eye had surveyed the sheets and blankets, as well as everything else. At length I heard some one at the door,—the hand not yet on the catch—a shuffling, a sighing, a flustering— the hand then applied and withdrawn—a sighing again—at length a firmer touch,—the door opened, and Mary stood before me. She was not pale now; a sickly flush overspread the lily—the lip quivered—the body swerved; she would have fallen had she not called up a little resolution not to betray herself.

"What—what—you have a parcel for me, sir?" she stuttered out.

"Yes, Mary," said I, as I still watched her looks, now changed again to pure pallor.

"Where is it from?" said she again, with still increased emotion.

"I do not know," said I, "but here it is," handing it to her.

The moment her hand touched it, she shrunk from the soft feel as one would do from that of a cold snake, or why should I not say the dead body of a child? It fell at her feet, and she stood motionless, as one transfixed, and unable to move even a muscle of the face.

"This is not the way to treat a gift," said I. "I insist upon you taking it up."

"O, God, I cannot!" she cried.

"Well, I must do so for you," said I, taking up the parcel. "Is that the way you treat the presents of your friends; come," laying it on the table, "come, open it; I wish to see what is in it."

"I cannot,—oh, sir, have mercy on me,—I cannot."

"Then do you wish *me* to do it for you?"

"Oh, no, no,—I would rather you took it away," she said with a spasm.

"But why so? what do you think is in it?" said I, getting more certain every moment of my woman.

"Oh, I do not know," she cried again; "but I cannot open that dreadful thing."

And as she uttered the words, she burst into tears, with a suppressed scream, which I was afraid would reach the lobby. I then went to the door, and snibbed it. The movement was still more terrifying to her, for she followed me, and grasped me convulsively by the arm. On returning to the table, I again pointed to the parcel.

"You must open that," said I, "or I will call in your master to do it for you."

"Oh,—for God's sake, no," she ejaculated; "I will,—oh yes, sir, be patient,—I will, I will."

But she didn't—she couldn't. Her whole frame shook, so that her hands seemed palsied, and I am sure she could not have held the end of the string.

"Well," said I, drawing in a chair, and seating myself, "I shall wait till you are able."

The sight of the poor creature was now painful to me, but I had my duty to do, and I knew how much depended on her applying her own hand to this strange work. I sat peaceably and silently, my eye still fixed upon her. She got into meditation—looked piteously at me, then fearfully at the parcel—approached it—touched it—recoiled from it—touched it again and again—recoiled;—but I would wait.

"Why, what is all this about?" said I calmly, and I suspect even with a smile on my face, for I wanted to impart to her at least so much confidence as might enable her to do this one act, which I deemed necessary to my object. "What is all this about? I only bear this parcel to you, and for aught I know, there may be nothing in it to authorise all this terror. If you are innocent of crime, Mary, nothing should move you. Come, undo the string."

And now, having watched my face, and seen the good-humour on it, she began to draw up a little, and then picked irresolutely at the string.

"See," said I, taking out a knife, "this will help you."

But whether it was that she had been busy with a knife that morning for another purpose than cutting the bread for her breakfast, I know not; she shrunk from the instrument, and, rather than touch it, took to undoing the string with a little more resolution. And here I could not help noticing a change that came over her almost of a sudden. I have noticed the same thing in cases where necessity seemed to be the mother of energy. She began to gather resolution from some thought; and, as it appeared, the firmness was something like new-born energy to overcome the slight lacing of the parcel. That it was an effort bordering on despair, I doubt not, but it was not the less an effort. Nay, she became almost calm, drew the ends, laid the string upon the table, unfolded the paper, laid the object bare, and—the effort was gone—fell senseless at my feet.

I was not exactly prepared for this. I rose, and seeing some spirits in a press, poured out a little, wet her lips, dropped some upon her brow, and waited for her to return to consciousness; and I waited longer than I expected,—indeed, I was beginning to fear I had carried my experiment too far. I thought the poor creature was dead, and for a time I took on her own excitement and fear, though from a cause so very different. I bent over her, watching her breath, and holding her wrist; at last a long sigh,—oh, how deep!—then a staring of the eyes, and a rolling of the pupils, then a looking to the table, then a rugging at me as if she thought I had her fate in my hands.

"Oh, where is it?" she cried. "Take it away; but you will hang me, will you? Say you will not, and I will tell you all."

I got her lifted up, and put upon a chair. She could now sit, but such was the horror she felt at the grim leg, torn as it was at the one end, and blue and hideous, that she turned her eyes to the wall, and I believe her smart cap actually moved by the rising of the black hair beneath it.

"Mary B——n," said I, calmly, and in a subdued voice, "you have seen what is in the parcel?"

"Oh, yes sir; oh, yes," she muttered.

"Do you know what it is?"

"Oh, too well, sire; too well."

"Then tell me," said I.

"Oh, sir," she cried, as she threw herself upon the floor on her knees, and grasped and clutched me around the legs and held up her face,—her eyes now streaming with tears, her cap off, her hair let loose,—"if I do, will you take pity on me, and not hang me?"

"I can say, at least, Mary," I replied, "that it will be better for you if you make a clean breast, and tell the truth. I can offer no promises. I am merely an officer of the law; but, as I have said, I know it will be better for you to speak the truth."

"Well, then, sir," she cried, while the sobbing interrupted every other word; "well, then, before God, whom I have offended, but who may yet have mercy upon a poor sinner left to herself,—and, of, sir, seduced by a wicked man,—I confess that I bore that child—but, sir, it was dead when it came into the world; and, stung by shame, and wild with pain, I cut it into pieces, and put it down into the soil pipe; and may the Lord Jesus look down upon me in pity!"

"Well, Mary," said I, as I lifted her up,—feeling the weight of a body almost dead,—and placed her again upon the chair; "you must calm yourself, and then go and get your shawl and bonnet, for you must—"

"Go with you to prison," she cried, "and be hanged. Oh, did you not lead me to believe you would save me?"

"No," said I; "but I can safely tell you, if what you have told me is true, that the child was still-born, you will not be hanged, you will only be confined for a little. Come," I continued, letting my voice down, "come, rise, and get your shawl and bonnet. Say nothing to any one, but come back to me."

But I had not an easy task here. She got wild again at the thought of prison, crying—

"I am ruined. Oh, my poor mother! I can never look her in the face again; no, nor hold up my head among decent people."

"Softly, softly," said I. "You must be calm, and obey; or see," holding up a pair of handcuffs, "I will put these upon your wrists."

Again necessity came to my help. She rose deliberately—stood for a moment firm—looked into my face wistfully, yet mildly—then turned up her eyes, ejaculating, "Thy will, O Lord, be done,"—and went out.

I was afraid, notwithstanding, she might try to escape, for

she seemed changeful; and a turn might come of frantic fear, which would carry her off, not knowing herself whither she went. I therefore, watched in the lobby, to intercept her in use of such an emergency; but the poor girl was true to her purpose. I tied up the fatal parcel which had so well served my object, put it under my arm, and quietly led her over to the office.

Her confession was subsequently taken down by the Crown officers, and she never swerved from it. I believe if I had not fallen upon this mode of extorting an admission, the proof would have failed, for every vestige of mark had been carefully removed; while the deception she had practised on the people of the inn had been so adroit, that no one had the slightest suspicion of her. The other parts of the child were not, I think, got; indeed it was scarcely necessary to search for them, confined as they were, probably, in the pipes. She was tried before the High Court; and, in the absence of any evidence to show that the child had ever breathed,—which could only have been ascertained by examining some parts of the chest,—she was condemned upon the charge of concealment, and sentenced to nine months' imprisonment.

ANDREW FORRESTER, JR.

(PSEUDONYM OF JAMES REDDING WARE)

c. 1832–1909

Now we come to the holder of a cherished title discussed in this book's introduction—"first female detective."

"Who am I?" begins the introduction to a collection published in London in early 1864 by the firm of Ward and Lock, who would later publish Arthur Conan Doyle's first novel about Sherlock Holmes. One early mention of this title gives the date 1861, but no other record of such an edition exists, so the date seems to be a misprint.

"It can matter little who I am," the narrator answers herself. "It may be that I took to the trade, sufficiently comprehended in the title of this work without a word of it being read, because I had no other means of making a living; or it may be that for the work of detection I had a longing which I could not overcome."

How unusual was this book? Consider the title: *The Female Detective*. It is satisfying to report that the first known collection of stories about such a character comprises not merely historical footnotes—the genre's incunabula, of note only to scholars—but lively and vivid fiction that stands the test of time.

The seven tales in this historic volume vary widely. One is a suspenseful novella about inheritance fraud that is too long for this anthology; another analyzes why a certain murder investigation failed to discover the culprit. "The Unknown Weapon" is the most straightforward account of crime and pursuit, but it has been reprinted occasionally. Written in short paragraphs as if for a newspaper supplement, it features a narrator aware of writing in the tradition of Poe's handful of detective stories.

In another story, in imitation of Poe's "Mystery of Marie Rogêt," the narrator applies his investigative imagination to a crime reported in newspapers. Two tales do not involve murder and thus are ineligible for inclusion in the present volume. But "The Judgement of Conscience" is ideal for *The Penguin Book of Murder Mysteries*—vivid, lively, homicidal, and unfamiliar.

The most curious story in *The Female Detective* is not actually narrated by Mrs. G. but instead presented as her retelling of an investigation by a police colleague. It turns out to be based upon the mystery of Road Hill House—the horrific 1860 murder of a young boy named Francis Kent, whose older sister Constance later confessed (rather unconvincingly) and served twenty years of a life sentence. She lived to the age of one hundred. Kate Summerscale resurrected this fascinating case in her suspenseful 2008 narrative *The Suspicions of Mr. Whicher*.

The title page of *The Female Detective* gave the author's name as Andrew Forrester, Jr. Despite the cleverly misleading adjective, the byline was long thought to be a pseudonym—but the man behind the mask remained unknown. It was his account of the Kent case, included in the collection as "A Child Found Dead: Murder or No Murder?" that revealed the author's identity long after his death. He turns out to have been James Redding Ware, a London-born novelist and playwright. The same story had appeared two years earlier in the periodical *Grave and Gay*. A revised edition appeared in 1865 as a pamphlet, *The Road Murder: Analysis of This Persistent Mystery*, by "J. Redding Ware." Fans of Victorian culture fondly recall Ware for his lively and amusing compendium *Passing English of the Victorian Era: A Dictionary of Heterodox English Slang and Phrase*, published in 1909, the year he died. Under the name Forrester, he wrote at least two other mystery collections— *The Revelations of a Private Detective* in 1863, and *Secret Service* the following year.

"I am called G. by the force," the narrator of the first Mrs. G. story explains. She identifies herself by the initial her colleagues use—"Mrs. G." When a surname is required during undercover work, she uses *Gladden*. "That is the name I assume most frequently," she remarks, which suggests that, although it shares her initial, it is not her actual name. However, you may see her referenced in crime scholarship under this name.

It's not surprising that, decades ahead of women joining the ranks of police officers, a writer would perceive the narrative opportunities in a female protagonist.

> It is the peculiar advantage of women detectives, and one which in many cases gives them an immeasurable value beyond that of their male friends, [says Mrs. G.] that they can get into houses outside which the ordinary men-detectives could barely stand without being suspected. . . . If there is a demand for men detectives there must also be one for female detective police spies. Criminals are both masculine and feminine—indeed, my experience tells me that when a woman becomes a criminal she is far worse than the average of her male companions, and therefore it follows that the necessary detectives should be of both sexes.

In this era of distinct gradations of class, Mrs. G. boasts a trained ear for the subtleties of spoken language, as does her creator, as the lively dialogue demonstrates. In listing methods of identification, she ends with "above all, by the unnumbered modes of speaking, the form of speaking, the subjects spoken of, and above all the impediments or peculiarities of speech. . . . He may change dress, voice, look, appearance, but never his mode of speaking—never his pronunciation." The stories move along quickly but provide vivid glimpses of the era. Like Sherlock Holmes, Mrs. G. depends upon her yellow-backed Bradshaw— *Bradshaw's Monthly Railway Guide*, an essential index in an age when England had as many as 150 competing railways issuing their own schedules.

Forrester has Mrs. G. introduce herself in the first story:

> For what reason do I write this book?
> I have a chief reason, and as I can have no desire to hide it from the reader, for if I were secretively inclined I should not be compiling these memoirs, I may as well at once say I write in order to show, in a small way, that the profession to which I be-

long is so useful that it should not be despised. . . . The reader will comprehend that the woman detective has far greater opportunities than a man of intimate watching, and of keeping her eyes upon matters near which a man could not conveniently play the eavesdropper. I am aware that the idea of family spies must be an unpleasant subject for contemplation; that to reflect that a female detective may be in one's own family is a disagreeable operation. But, on the other hand, it may be urged that only the man who has secrets to hide need fear a watcher, the inference standing that he who fears may justifiably be watched.

THE JUDGEMENT OF CONSCIENCE

He was in great poverty—yet a good citizen.

I came to know John Kamp over a very trifling affair—as you shall hear.

He was then about thirty years of age, and unmarried. I learnt very soon that he had a great desire to marry. Not any particular person. The desire appeared to be the result not of any individual passion, but the effect of reason.

I do not think I have said he was a shoemaker.

I am about to tell a romantic tale of this shoemaker, but I will not surround the narrative with any of the ordinary plaster-of-Paris conditions of romance. He was a plain, ungainly, and not remarkably tidy London shoemaker, earning a poor living, having meat but once a week—on Sunday to wit, and mealing on herrings, sprats, winkles, and such poor man's blessed food, all the week. Why do I call winkles, and herrings, and sprats blessed food? Simply because they are cheap and plentiful, and uphold the poor when otherwise they would sink under their low diet—sink not under the weight of it, but under its meagreness.

I never saw him drunk during the many months I knew him, I never heard a violent word pass his lips, and he was always following out some new train of thought.

He was one of the lower classes. Perhaps there are many such men as he amongst the lower classes. I hope there are; for though many live and die without making their mark in the world's history, they have honoured their lives—and seeing what we see daily amongst all classes, why, the memory of a well-spent, if lost, life must be a very great comfort on a death-bed.

He was not a happy man, though his unhappiness it appeared to me did not arise from the injustice the world did him, but from the consciousness that he was debarred from doing good in his generation.

Pray do not misunderstand me—or him.

He did not go about like a man who has a grievance with the world because it has failed to comprehend him. He had nothing in his constitution of the cynic, either lachrymose or scoffing. But I am quite sure he was generally sorry that he could do the world no good, beyond that of living the life of a good citizen (a condition which he did not sufficiently value), and that the world had so treated him he could not benefit society.

I do not say he was right in feeling that the world had not treated him well. I am quite aware that society cannot go about finding youthful genius or guessing at it. I am not destitute of the knowledge that the world is willing to pay for certain genius, and handsomely; but that it is not disposed to foster it before it is known. But, nevertheless, I do not condemn John Kamp for feeling more bitterly towards the world than he spoke generally of it, and clinging to the belief that it had injured in neglecting him.

It is true men make themselves or are helped by their friends; but it does not follow that a poor, ignorant man, who suffers in after life because the powers of the land did not foster him when neglectful parents let him run wild—it does not follow such an one shall reason in this fashion.

Take his argument.

"I know I have that in me which would benefit the world, but my hands are tied with the ignorance of my youth, and I am powerless; and I must live powerless; and I must die powerless."

What do you say to that argument? A wrong one to hold, but a very natural one.

It may be urged, however, that many men have raised themselves to eminence who held no higher social position than this John Kamp. But in their cases their early youth had as a rule been cared for—and a foundation to build upon had been made. Take Bloomfield, for instance—a genius who rose out of the menial trade to which Kamp belonged.

Again—the shape of his genius was one which called for help to demonstrate it. A man who has a genius for writing is set up with a quill, a quire of paper, an ink-bottle, and a penknife. A painter has to go farther in the way of an expensive nest of colours and a canvas; but when your genius takes the Eseulapian shape—when your thirst is to be a doctor, you cannot at once launch into the exercise of your genius—you must work through patient, expensive years, and then begin lowly and humbly to climb, not daring at first to use your knowledge, lest its novelty shall appear like ignorance, fighting for years and years, perhaps for a lifetime, before the world can look towards you, and cry out, "Behold him! he has benefited all men."

To benefit the world—this it was for which John Kamp, shoemaker, and indeed cobbler, aged thirty, thirsted.

And as I write I remember the occasion upon which we first met. A crowd in the street is always an attraction to a detective, for it may happen, indeed generally does, that he is wanted to complete the performance.

I saw a crowd one night in the classic regions of Whitechapel, and making one of it directly, I found a woman in a fit, with a weakly-looking but clear-brained man superintending the unfortunate.

Neither born to command, nor used to that luxury, I felt certain directly I saw him, here he appeared to be in his element—to be doing what he knew it was within his province, and without that of those about him, to effect.

"Stand aside, mates!" I heard him say, as I approached; "if there's one thing more than another she wants, it's fresh air. Do stand aside, mates!"

This the "mates" proceeded to do by falling back about two feet, and then immediately advancing over one and a half.

"Look here, mates—don't hold her back like that." These remarks were addressed to the men who were holding the wretched woman with an energy which would have arrested the vigour of a grenadier. "Hold her well up," he continued, "and a little on one side, so that her head hangs a little on one side; if she gets anything in her throat she will choke if you hold her back, mates. P'r'aps it's one of them fits which comes on through want. Will one o' you, mates, go and get three-penn'orth of brandy?"

One of the mates did; a raffish-looking young man, whose true vocation very much I fear was that of the general thief; but, to the credit of humanity, even amongst thieves, I am bound to say he returned with the spirit (and some water) in a public-house basin.

The case was one of those ordinary fits which are in truth the result of want acting upon a frame which tends to epilepsy. Poor creature—dank, thin, ragged, haggard, we police people see such miseries daily, and until we get so used to it that the less amiable amongst us look upon them as nuisances.

I waited till the poor woman "come to," as the expression goes, till once more she looked about her, as though she had been born into a strange world—till once more she recovered her poor wretched senses, and putting herself together, uttered some few shamefaced sentences, which sounded like excuses, and prepared to slink away.

"Come, mates," said the impromptu doctor, "let's give her some coppers—let's make a collection."

I grieve to say that doubt was rife in a moment, and that calumny, looking the good Samaritan in the face, said it was "all a do."

And as every grain of calumny tells, the collection, I remember, amounted only to twopence-halfpenny, which he who had spoken handed (with some scorn flashing from his eyes at the crowd), to the poor old woman, who appeared more shame-facedly apologetic than ever upon receiving this douceur.

As for me, I followed the Samaritan, whom I saw by his clothing was a mechanic of a very ordinary character.

I followed him with no bad intent to the neighbourhood of the Tower, when he entered a house which was so poor and so temptationless that the door swung idly and without a lock.

That same evening I made some inquiries at the parlour-shop of a widow, who exhibited so little a desire to sell, and so great a desire to talk, that I looked upon the hundred and one articles she had for sale as mere commercial excuses—a kind of business-like umbrella for harbouring scandal.

I was not wrong. When I came to know the vicinity better, I ascertained that the Widow Green's was the street club, and one which emulated any social gathering of the sort at the west end, as far as dealing with reputations went. I calculated that a character was ruined per sixty minutes during business hours.

I learnt a good deal from the Widow Green, who by the way also played upon that piano of the poor, the mangle.

It appeared he was John Kamp, a nice young man, but objectionable on this score—that he was "a little orf 'is 'ed."

This statement inquired into, it appeared that he was a respectable young man, looking after his sister, never getting too much (this was a delicate east-end mode of reference to strong drink), always paying his rent, though rather despising credit (this was a reference to his want of patronage of the parlour-shop, I saw); but what "were agin him were this—that he were crotchetty," though nevertheless mending a shoe with punctuality to time and the best of thread and leather.

I need not say it was no difficulty for me to make acquaintance with the Kamps. I was engaged at that time (though it may appear to my reader an odd case to call for the operations of a woman detective) upon what has since taken the name of the great sugar-baking case, and therefore I was living in the neighbourhood of Aldgate and Whitechapel. And inasmuch as my professional abilities could only be exercised at certain hours, I had a good deal of time at my disposal.

The meeting with Kamp took place on the second day of my sojourn in that quarter of London, and it was on the third that I made his acquaintance, with the help of a pair of mendable shoes, which I bought of my landlady to her eminent suspicion, for my act was unusual.

I knocked as well as I could the two knocks which I had learnt was the dose for the Kamps; and, after some time, for the knocker was loose and askew, to say nothing of its having no anvil, the sister, as I afterwards learnt, came down to the door.

She was not pleasant to look upon, her jaw being so under-hung as to give her at first sight that malevolent expression which is too suggestive of the bull-dog—but accustomed to search rather than glance at faces, I perceived very quickly that she was a pleasant, and (her mouth and jaw apart) an attractive young person.

I need not here dilate upon my first interviews with John Kamp, because I have more important matter to write about. Let me, therefore, but just say that I found he was an earnest-looking man as he sat at his hard work, and the faint, fog-drenched light fell upon his forehead, which was wide and massive, though coarse-grained, and framed with rather dull-looking and not too well kept soft, black hair.

It is a part of my profession to bring people out, and I soon effected that object with Kamp.

After a few days we got on very pleasantly together. He accepted perfectly my position as a visitor, and not a customer. He would look up from his work when I went in, and give a pleasant but rather worn smile, and then he would drop over his lapstone, and tap away at his work.

He was assuredly very unfortunate in many ways. Certainly superior to his trade, and not inclined to rest content in that place in which chance and his own will had placed him: he was forced even to yield an outward respect to his poor trade which he could not feel. He never attempted to take a high place in his trade, because, though a good workman, he had not regularly served his time to shoemaking. Forced early in life from a bad home, he had become errand-boy at a shoe-shop, and here he watched the trade and ultimately practised it.

And as there are always men who avail themselves of all advantages, many of those master-makers who employed Kamp, had given him the worst pay for the best work, simply because he could not show an ordinary indenture.

I am afraid this system tended to make him more discontented with his lot than he would even otherwise have been.

On my third visit I found him operating on a thick-headed loading labourer, and pulling a back tooth from his heavy jaw with the ordinary pair of pincers with which he stretched his leather.

For you see, exactly as at an evening party, the gentleman most rallied and patronized is he who does more than anybody for the general amusement, so with John Kamp. The general neighbourhood pitied him in a small-beer kind of way as an oddity, and availed themselves of all those oddities which they could turn to their own advantage.

"Thank ye, mate," said the heavy-headed labourer; and without a word to the sister he left the room.

"He did not pay you!" said I.

"No; I never take any payment for medical advice," he replied.

I admit the answer was a little bumptious, but he was a poorly-informed man, and it is not always the unlearned who alone are vain. And I would have you remark that when a poor man who makes but from fifteen to eighteen shillings a week refuses a payment which is justly *his*, there must be more in the abnegation than at first we see.

"But he would have had to pay a shilling," said I, "had he gone to a dentist; you ought to have charged him sixpence."

"Oh, he could have got an order from the relieving officer to the parish doctor, and had his tooth extracted for nothing."

"But then he would have lost his time."

"Yes, he would," said Kamp.

By the way, it was the dinner hour, and Kamp had left his meal gratuitously to take out the labourer's tooth.

The sister and I did not get on very well together. It appeared to me that she resented my intrusion, though I am sure I in no way impeded them. The curse of poverty was evident in her, whereas the brother had gained a victory over it by his wisdom. For he was wise though he had little knowledge. I am aware that wisdom presupposes knowledge, but my experience tells me that much wisdom may exist accompanied by very little knowledge. Furthermore, my experience tells me that it too frequently happens that an immensity of knowledge is accompanied by no wisdom whatever.

Somehow I grew to like this John Kamp.

But his vanity was by no means flattered.

And by this sentence perhaps the reader apprehends a personal secret which may not already have been very difficult to learn.

He knew much of medicine, and more of its philosophy. His

favourite work was "Johnston's Chemistry of Common Life." He knew the book almost by heart, and he would dilate upon it in a manner which was almost touching, when was taken into consideration his hopeless passion for a profession in which in all probability he could never practise.

In politics he was of course a thorough liberal, but he was not governed by those extreme views which it must be confessed are generally held by the self-educated. Self-educated this man wholly was. In after times I received letters from him, and I am bound to say they showed a height of education which was most praiseworthy. It could be seen he had been his own master perhaps. There were too many capital letters, and much faint obscurity in the composition, but it could be seen that the man was earnest and straight-forward. Every sentence had bone in it, and every line had something in it, and every letter was a something perfect in its way, and in itself.

No, he was not in the ordinary sense of the word a chartist.

He has said to me—

"I once went to a chartist meeting, but I never attended a second. If chartism means anything it means that those who suffer shall suffer no longer. Well, I went, and found the men there were hearty hale mechanics, they were those especially who are luckiest amongst us workers—such as engineers and smiths—the men who get the best pay amongst us. *They* had little cause of complaint, whereas now those mechanics who are really down-trod—I mean all those that use the needle, such as shoemakers and tailors—they that can hardly get a bit o' bread, much less cheese, *they* weren't at the meeting at all. They had not got time to go. I was shouldered out of the way, and my voice could not have been heard amongst all those big men, shouting and yelling. It struck me I had never imagined so tyrannical a meeting as that. So I did not go to another of them, for they are a lie, and no better."

During these talkings, while he worked, and I also, the sister said nothing, but bent over her hard, hard work, which was military tailoring.

I have seen her fingers quite blue and rough through the action of the harsh serge used for artillery uniforms, and at other times I have seen her looking wonderfully faded and worn in the midst of red linesmen's tunics.

I think I have said she was very pleasant-faced, apart from the under-hung jaw; but the mass of people had not looked beyond her deformity, which was very apparent when she ate her poor meals, and they had been prejudiced against her. She had accepted this life-long condemnation in a quiet way, without resentment, but not without knowledge, and had fallen into a kind of meekly-repelling apathy which must have tended, in a general way, to increase that want of prepossession with which people I am afraid regarded her.

It was about two weeks after I came to know this far from ordinary man that, as I was talking with Kamp on one of the chapters of Johnston's Chemistry, a copy of which I admit I purchased and read up, and as Johanna Kamp was working under new conditions, as far as my experience went, for she was surrounded by the white flannel devoted to the summer wear of the marines—I say it was as we were thus occupied, it being at three o'clock in the afternoon and a pleasant April day, with the one window open and the light wind waving over a quivering penny pot of primroses, that a heavy, solid step was heard on the stairs.

Upon this Kamp looks up at his sister, and she at the door. And it may be it was only that her pale countenance was heightened in colour by being contrasted with the unordinary white materials about her, but it seemed to me a something like warm-hearted blood rose to the poor woman's face.

Without any preliminary tap, the door was rattled open, and a well-built but intolerably plain soldier of the line entered the room.

It may be that my presence made a difference in their meeting, but whether this was the case or not I am bound to say that the working woman met the soldier's "how do ye do?" with no enthusiasm, but with much pleasant, calm cordiality.

He was a very honest sort of man, this soldier, who, I gathered, had (like most of the soldiery) gone a little astray in youth, and been brought back again by the discipline of the army.

"My company's back at the Tower, Johanna," he said cheerily

to the woman; adding, to Kamp, "So you'll see plenty of me, Jack."

"Perhaps I am intruding," I said, at this point.

"Oh no, ma'am," replied the soldier, evidently with the air of having some proprietorship in the room himself—"it ull hold four on us"—looking about the premises with a soldierly air.

Then he slipped off his coat, unhitched his braces, and taking a seat at Johanna's table, he began to thread a needle.

For the poor have no time to waste, and I saw at a glance he was at an old office—he helped to gain bread in that poor place.

As he took up the pieces of cloth Johanna laid before him ready basted together, he said, "And where's the table and them other things?"

She pointed to a covered pile in the room, which had often given me cause to wonder of what it was composed.

"One half look," said the soldier (he was a corporal, I saw). "One half look"—already apologizing for wasting time—and he went in three strides to the pile, took off the dingy cover, gave a glance at a table, two or three chairs, and other matters, covered the whole again, and then returned with three more strides to his seat. I think these three strides were taller and handsomer than those which had preceded them.

As he sat down, he tapped himself with one hand upon the other arm.

"I shall get 'em soon now, Johnny, and then!"

Here a bright look came on his face, which made it momentarily prepossessing.

Of course, it did not require any profound detection to comprehend what was going on.

The soldier and seamstress were engaged to be married, some of the furniture had been bought, and they were only waiting till he got his serjeant's stripes upon his coat.

Well, well, it was very pleasant to see them hard at work. He was no bad needle-man, as indeed few soldiers are. Indeed, I believe the army contractor got better work out of him than any one. He did certainly appear to take every stitch with a will.

This was the only occasion on which I saw the soldier.

One day in the same week, and when Johanna was away taking home a huge bundle of completed clothing to her employer, a sub-army clothing contractor, whom I had once seen (he was a kind of Hebrew Adonis)—on that day Kamp told me the history of the engagement.

Exactly as she had met with nothing but inattention from men during her life, so he had been made the butt of women. When they by chance met (in that little East London paradise, the Victoria Park), it was clear they had both felt grateful for the frankness with which each met the other, and the conversation had begun by his picking up her umbrella. They had experienced a good deal of pain at the way in which the world had treated them, and as it is the knack of mental pain to purify people, why they soon found out that they were fitted to each other.

When they walked out of a Sunday (this I learnt from Kamp) they were frequently laughed at. And I must confess at first sight they were an ugly pair, and their ugliness was all the more remarkable from the contrast between them, for his chin and jaw shelved away in a very remarkable manner. But I believe the public ridicule gave them the benefit of feeling a kind of mutual pity for the public unkindness, which after a time was a kind of satisfaction to them, as showing how much they ought to be to one another.

For my part I think, in a quiet, sad, earnest way, Johanna Kamp and Tom Hapsy were happy, and loved each other very truly in a poor, plain way.

I have said that I did not see the corporal again. This loss—I felt it one, for I had taken a liking to the ugly fellow—arose from the fact that I was recalled from the neighbourhood and set upon other business.

I heard nothing more of the Kamps. I may add that they had never learnt my true occupation, but supposed me a small annuitant, a little eccentric, but very kindly disposed upon the whole.

Six months passed away—six months to me in my profession of very great importance.

I had been out of London, and it was the second night after

my return, that, going down to the office, I found my fellow-workwomen very earnestly discussing a piece of news which had arrived. This was made up of the particulars of a murder in the east of London.

Two hours before, and at about eight o'clock in the evening, and when, therefore, the night had fairly set in, a tradesman in a large way of business had been shot dead. He had received the charge full in the breast, and therefore his enemy must have faced him; but though the alarm was immediately taken and the murdered man was alive when several people reached his side, he was unable to utter a word, and he died speechless as when found.

This affair had occurred at a place called New Ford, and very near to a running stream.

The spot upon which the unfortunate man fell was not many hundred yards from his own house, and he had been seen walking up and down a field as though waiting for some one. I may add at once that this was so—he expecting a young person who it appeared was notoriously in the habit of meeting him in the field where he was found dying.

The usual government reward in cases of evident murder was in this case very rapidly advertised.

Now, I need not tell the reader that detectives are as much excited by one of these rich government rewards as—as a ladies' school by the appearance of a new and an elegant master.

Every man or woman amongst us has an equal chance in the first place of gaining the prize, and as one hundred pound bank notes are not going begging every day in the week, we of the force look upon them with a considerable amount of respect.

I went down to New Ford and obtained a view of the dead man.

I knew the face, for I never forget features I have once seen, but I could not identify it, owing to that marvellous new expression which death lays on the human countenance.

For a full hour I tried to recall where I had seen the face, and what were the associations connected with it.

I confess I failed, and I turned once more into the station at which the chief particulars of the case were known—the station within the district of which the crime had been committed—and sat down more fatigued than though I had been walking half a score miles.

I was known well at the office, and therefore no impediment was thrown in my way in relation to this matter.

"Have you got any clue?" I asked in, I am quite sure, a worn and tired voice.

"Only a bit of a one," said to me a sergeant, who at horse and turf cases is supposed to be quite unapproachable.

The clue to which he referred is one which in cases of ordinary shooting has on many occasions brought home his guilt to the actual murderer. I refer to the wadding, or rather stopping, used to fix the charge in the barrel of the firearm. If this stopping is not a disc of pasteboard, or a material sold for charging purposes, it frequently happens that it is a piece of paper torn from a supply in the possession of the person using the firearm.

It has in many instances happened where this stopping has not taken fire and burnt itself out, that enough of the paper, either written or printed on, has been found to bring home the shot to certain parties; and indeed there are cases on record where the rough line of the edge of the bit of half-burnt paper has agreed so certainly with another morsel found in the pocket of a suspected man, that upon such circumstantial evidence as this to begin upon, murder has been brought home to the guilty man.

In the case under consideration a crumpled stopping, which had in all probability been in the barrel of a firearm, in company with the bullet that had been found in the body of Mr. Higham, was picked up near the spot at which the murdered man had fallen, and within an hour of the catastrophe.

It was the scorched blackened remains of the upper half of a printed page of what the printers would call a demy-octavo book.

It bore the title of the work in the running-head line—"Johnston's Chemistry of Common Life."

I knew now where I had seen the dead man when in life. Once accompanying Johanna Kamp, with a large bundle of work to her employer's (it was in the evening, and she feared she might have the work snatched away if she went alone), I recalled that we saw the dead man, and I further recalled that in taking her work he had paid her a kind of marked attention which was half mirthful and half real.

I recalled also that she said to me, it was hard how much poor folk had to put up with in order to get a crust.

I declare that the idea shot into my brain in the moment of seeing the scrap of printed paper—had it been torn from John Kamp's copy.

This was a matter which, as far as I was concerned, could easily be found out. I had but to pay the shoemaker a visit to bring the conversation round to Johnston, and then ask to see the book.

Perhaps it was cruel to spy upon the man who had met me daily as a something more than an acquaintance; but if such a consideration were always to arrest the course of justice the ordinary affairs of the world could not go on.

A man is your friend, but if he transgresses that law which it is your duty to see observed you have no right to spare him because he is so; for in doing this you admit, by implication, that you did not spare other men because they were no friends.

I went down to Kamp's house next morning.

I did not knock at the swinging door of the house. The knocker was still hanging to the door all askew, and still wanting the anvil.

I went direct upstairs—something beating at my heart and saying, "cruel, cruel!" as I did so. I tapped at the door.

I remember how earnest and emphatic those sounds appeared to me. The last time I stood in that room I was there as the man's friend; now I was entering it as his enemy—as one suspecting him of murder, for that was my errand.

Yes, I was about to use that past friendship as the means of prosecuting my profession. I know I was but doing my duty—I feel certain at this moment I was but doing my duty; but something, which I suppose was conscience, told me that this was not well.

"Come in," said a weak voice.

Hearing a quick, beating sound—and which, indeed, was the rushing of my blood through my heart, I opened the door and entered.

My heart failed me as I did so, for hope sank within me.

He was sitting desolately upon his work-stool.

He had not been working.

As I came in he recognised me, but he did not rise or hold out his hand.

"How are you?" he said, abstractedly, and then in a distressingly absent manner he took up one of his most ordinary tools—one he used a thousand times a day—and looked at it with an odd, distant expression, as though he had never seen it before.

Then he laid this down and took up a piece of the wax used in his trade and began abstractedly pressing it into different forms.

The room looked very desolate, and though it had not been distinguishable for cleanliness when I had been in the habit of seeing it, the place now looked indescribably more dirty than it did, while there was a forlorn expression upon it which was totally absent when I had seen it daily.

There was no evidence of the sister—no threads, no shreds of cloth, no waiting chair, or draggled work-basket. The table at which she used to work was put away against the wall, and upon the spot where the covered furniture used to stand.

The linnet's cage still hung in the window.—Ah! I did not mention the tailless linnet the sister fed and called "Tweet." But the bird was dead surely; at all events the cage was empty, and dry, and dusty.

Kamp looked very worn and broken down; and, for we detectives have to look at everything, I saw that the silky, black hair, which had never had those proper pains taken with it which its natural beauty deserved, was all bestreaked with grey.

I think I need hardly tell the reader that not for two moments had I been in the room before I felt that the old life of that chamber had passed away never to return.

Between him and me, as I entered the room, there was the space of the dusty unswept floor. He was seated on his stool, listless and broken down.

There was an ugly stoop in his shoulders, which had not been there when I was a visitor. His hands, so adroit and earnest as I had seen them, lay inert and drooping one over each knee, and there was a substantial shadow on his face beyond the darkness of his room, for though the day was bright the glass was thick with old, old dirt.

"The sister has not been here for weeks," I thought, "and perhaps not for months."

The first volume of "Johnston's Chemistry of Common Life," lay open and face downwards, on a pile of work-a-day tools and scraps of leather at his feet.

I saw that the heap of dirt and rubbish round about him (and which seems to be a condition of correct shoemaking), was far larger and higher than when I used to come almost every morning for several weeks together, and, I hope, make the time pass pleasantly to him, while I listened to his half-learned and wiser talk.

He looked very desolate—poor fellow.

It seemed to me that his heart was bleeding.

All the brightness had passed from his face; and all the patience, and all the blunted hope. All his countenance sat with despair, all its desire seemed to be annihilation.

For my part I hardly knew what to say.

I looked about for some moments, and then I said—

"I hope you have been well since I saw you last?"

"Yes, well," he said, looking mournfully round the room.

A pause.

I found that my sense of justice could flag.

At last I said—

"Have you perfected your machine yet?"

For the poor fellow, amongst other ideas, had given his attention to the shaping of a machine at which shoemakers could do their work without bending and curving themselves over it in the ordinary way, to which is attributable so much of the lung and liver disease to which the men of his trade are subject.

"No," he said, with a dead wild look out beyond him—far past the walls of that narrow dirty room—"I've not thought of it lately."

And now I fell to my duty.

"But I see you still study your book," I said, pointing to the volume lying face down upon the ground.

"I've been trying to read," he said, "but I can't."

He was speaking like a sick, patient child. I know I might have struck him, say upon the cheek, and he would not have resented it.

I knelt down to take the book—feeling, I am afraid, much like Judas when he held out the red hand for the thirty pieces of silver.

These words stopped my action:

"Those were very happy days when you came here and talked about old Johnston with me—wasn't they?"

I could not take up the book.

"But where is your sister?" I asked. I was going to add in a gayer tone—"married?" But a something, 'twas sympathy I suppose with the place and man, stopped the word.

He did not move, he did not look at me, as he answered, his eyes once more looking forward with that seeing blindness, if I dare use such an expression, to which I have already referred.

"Dead."

"Dead!" I replied, something like an echo.

"Oh yes; Johanna has been dead a month or more, only I don't quite exactly know how time goes."

I hardly knew what to say, indeed I had a very great mind to confess to him what my errand was, and to ask him to forgive me for having wronged him.

As the history will show, I did well to keep my confession to myself.

"Indeed," I said. "It must have been a sad blow to Tom Hapsy."

A fierce look came over his face for a moment and then died again.

"It was partly his fault," said he, "since he would not trust her."

"Not trust her?" I said, and I confess that heartily as I was pitying the poor fellow I saw before me, it struck me as wonderful that Johanna Kamp should have excited jealousy in her lover.

"No," said Kamp, "he would not trust her. He couldn't understand that she had to be civil at the warehouse, and that it only was civility."

"Surely they didn't quarrel, John?"

"Yes, they quarrelled."

"And did they part?"

"Yes, they parted."

He uttered these sentences with a patience of despair which almost made me love the man.

"And—and what happened then?"

"What happened—why what happens to most women when they are disrespected? Don't they disrespect themselves? She was a good woman," he continued, with a smile which was sweet though it was so ghastly; "a good woman," he repeated, with a sound something like a dry hard sob, "and Tom Hapsy should not have been so hard upon her, for she would have lost her work, and I'd give my life on it there was nothing to complain of till he left her."

"Did he leave her?" I asked.

"Yes; he set to watching for her one night outside the warehouse, and when she came out, laughing, though it was all in the way of business, poor thing, he caught her by the arm. I saw the marks black and blue the next day, and then he flung her away from him as he called her an under-hung—," here he stopped and a something like a blush overcame his countenance, and he continued, "I beg your pardon, I was going to use a word you would not care to hear."

"But what happened?"

"What happened?" he asked, with a soft kind of fierceness; "what happens to any woman, whether she is under-hung or not, when she does not care what comes of her? She had lived patient enough, never thinking any man would honourably notice her, living here in my poor home, till Tom Hapsy took up with her—and then when he went off she did not care what became of her."

He stopped for a moment, and then he went on:

"I was ill at the time, and we were poorer than usual, or I would not have let her go still to the cursed warehouse. How did it end? There—I remember reading amongst the ancients that there was a woman who asked her husband to kill her, and she flung herself upon the sword. That was just the way with poor Johanna. He had not much trouble with her, and he flung her off as you'd fling away a down-at-heel shoe."

"Who was he?" I asked, with my breath coming and going nervously. I was beginning to be afraid that I saw the whole tragedy, and in which I was to play a terrible part that I had brought upon myself.

His answer was as I suspected; *he* was the man who lay dead, shot through the left lung; *he* was the sub-army tailoring contractor who had employed Johanna Kamp, and who, to my own knowledge, had distinguished her in a marked manner (whatever the cause) from the other workwomen.

Whatever the cause!

Can it be guessed at?

I think it can. The dead man had been a sensualist in the strictest sense of that term. Now, what is the career of the sensualist? It will be found that as satiety approaches the appetite requires a stronger and stronger stimulation. If it were possible I could here give some awful examples of what depths of depravity the professed sensualist can fall to, but their narration is not admissible. Yet I can illustrate the sin by referring to the opening chapter of a tale of Eugène Sue's, in which the career of a sensualist is depicted. As he sinks and darkens in iniquity beauty palls upon him, innocence is contemptible, and his passions are aroused in exact proportion to the brutality and coarseness of the objects who surround him.

A purer and better-fitted comparison may be found in one's frequent experience of a very handsome man, or beautiful woman, mating with an extremely ordinary companion for life.

I assume that this wretched man—poverty having been the handmaiden of his sin—had luxuriated in so many instances in the youth and good looks of those who sought his employ, as a large army sub-contractor, that by a natural moral decay, or immoral progress, he became enamoured of poor, ugly, unprepossessing Johanna Kamp.

After a pause, a very long pause, the desolate man said—

"I see her there now when they brought her in wet and dead out of the dock. I didn't know her at first, for it's black mud in the docks. I can't get away from poor Joan—there she is, *there*, with her poor hands that worked so hard, down on each side of her, and the black water coming from her closed eyes just like tears. They laid her down just here," he said plaintively, as he stooped upon one knee, and pointed to a spot with his hard right hand, the fingers of which were flattened with many hard, hard years' work; "and she seemed to be smiling almost. And when I stooped forward to kiss her they pulled me back, and asked me if I was mad. Joan and I were all alone in the world; our mother died when she was an hour old, and father never cared for us. There she was," he continued, pointing to the spot again, "and she and I was here four days together," and he pointed to the cupboard-room which she had used as a bedroom. "When they took Joan away, they took my heart and buried it with you, Joan—buried it with you."

He dropped forward on the ground, and over the spot where the ill-featured sister had been laid. But no tears wetted his face—his grief was too hard for that.

And now, what should I do?

There lay the book; there, farther off, perhaps lay a murderer.

What if he who had been shot had been a heartless wretch—what if he was better out of the world than in it? In the face of the law all men are equal, and their lives are sacred.

Thou shalt not kill.

This rule stands whether it be godly man or fallen, true or false. Thou shalt do no murder.

The book was nearer to me than to him.

And he lay in a kind of stupor, with his eyes gazing in another direction than mine. Had he been looking on me I could not have stooped and turned the pages of the book.

The folios of the half-burnt fragment lying as witness at the station-house were 75, 76. I turned the pages of the book without noise and with the least movement.

Page 74—no pages 75, 76. Then followed page 77.

The leaf comprising the pages 75, 76, had been roughly torn

from the book, leaving some jagged fragments about the thread used in the sewing of the sheets.

Certain now that he was a murderer, I looked upon him with dread.

And yet I pitied him.

What was I to do?

What could I do—except my duty.

I do not know how long a time passed from the moment of my discovery until that in which he spoke to me. But by rough calculation, really I think minutes must have elapsed before the silence was broken.

"Good-bye," he said, "we shan't see each other again."

"Why not?" I asked, a little shamefacedly.

"I'm going to give myself up to the police."

Of course there could be no doubt in my mind as to who was the murderer of the Hebrew army contractor.

"Why give yourself up to the police?" I returned, awkwardly.

"Because I have done murder."

He uttered these words in the simplest and most immoveable manner, with no fear, no pain, no shame. It has since appeared to me that he was in that condition of which most men have had some experience, when a great shock has so stupified the mind that there appears to be no ability to exercise reason; when the acts we commit ourselves, or those of others, affect us so little, that under such circumstances we may be declared in a sort of half-trance.

He was so despairingly callous that he did not notice the absence of all alarm on my part. As for me I could play no double game with this man. He was so candid with me that to lie to him would have been indeed the depth of meanness.

"I am a detective," I said.

He looked up, but did not by his face betray any astonishment or distrust at my words.

"Do you understand?" I continued, my eyes upon the ground; "I am a female detective."

"Are you?" he said, with piteous simplicity.

"What made you kill him?"

Suddenly he looked wild, as he replied—

"Why should bad men live?"

I shook my head. I replied—

"Why should better men kill the bad?"

"They ought not to live—they are no good on the earth."

You see the poor creature had been so "hardly entreated" by the world, that he had turned against it when a common crime which the world does not punish very rigorously had crushed *his* home.

It is very well, perhaps, to preach, but there are times and places for sermons, and I felt that before his despair there was no need for me to give out a text. If despair outrages the law, well and good. The law must be satisfied. But let us leave despair alone, if we can only preach to it. For my part, whatever the man, I think I feel inclined to take his hand if he is despairing.

So I turned to facts.

"How did you do it?" I asked.

He got up from the floor where they had laid down the ill-favoured sister—the boards were still marked with the black dock mud in which the body was enveloped when brought to the poorhouse (for I may add the dead face was recognised while yet the water was streaming from it by a fellow-workwoman of the deceased), he got up from the ground quite mechanically, if that expression is allowable, and going to the pile of dirt and leather cuttings which lay heaped near his working stool, he put his hand in a wandering, awkward manner into the rubbish, and after feeling for a few moments, produced a common rusty pistol.

It was charged.

The natural thought to occur to a detective was this—"Why is the pistol loaded?"

So I said to him—

"Why, it's charged."

"Yes," he replied, with some appearance of stupid confusion.

"Surely," I said, "you were not going to—to let anything happen to yourself?"

He looked up. And this was the only moment throughout

our interview when anything like an expression which was not abject dejection appeared upon his face. And as he raised his face he said—

"Do you think I could kill myself? No! I know myself too well for that."

I will leave the reader to ponder on the apparent contradiction in his declaration of murder on the one hand, and his evident abhorrence of suicide on the other.

"Then, why is the pistol loaded?" I asked.

"I—I don't know," said he.

So I continued—

"But how came you to do this?"

"How?" he replied, relapsing into his apathy, "I thought he ought to be killed, like so much carrion, and I bought the pistol, and paid the shopboy to show me how to load it; and then I went to the field where I knew he was to meet another of 'em. I learnt that from one of the women at the warehouse, who knew all about it. I came up with him, that is near him, and then—"

Here he stopped, and appeared to fall into an abstruse chain of thought.

"Well?" I asked.

"Why—why, then he fell, shot!" he replied, in a quick, half-astonished manner.

His words even then appeared to me extraordinary, from the peculiar mode in which they were put together.

But the great question stood—Why was the pistol loaded?

I will pass over the actual giving of the poor fellow into custody, for there can be no need to launch into detail upon so painful a subject. Suffice it to say, that he exhibited no emotion whatever upon being charged with wilful murder, and went with many sighs, but no repugnance, to the dark cell.

For my part, I felt there was something, beyond what he had said, wanted in order to elucidate the matter.

Now, when we detectives doubt we question.

This was my plan in the case of which I am now writing.

The first person I questioned was the girl who was to have met Higham on the night when he was killed.

She only had benefited by that crime—she benefited but for a short time. She was a pert, saucy, bold-eyed, young person, who replied to my questions in a tone which clearly argued that she should much prefer slapping my face to answering me.

Had she seen a stooping man about the spot, with long black hair hanging quite to his shoulders? No, she had *not*. How should she? *She* had not been looking for persons with long black hair, *she* had been looking for poor Mr. Higham. What? Had she seen anybody about? No; of course not. She did not go there to be seen by *any*body but poor Mr. Higham. What? Had she seen anybody about? Yes, if she must answer. She had seen a soldier. What? Could she describe him? No, she could not describe him. She saw him once under the gas-lamp at the corner of the field near the road, and that was quite enough for *her*. Why was it quite enough for her? Why, because when *she* looked at a man a second time it was because he was worth looking at. Yes.

This was all the information I got from this extremely pert young person, who, I may remark, in quitting her at this place, came under my especial attention about two years after the termination of the case, "A Judgment of Conscience."

Now to the detective all people who by any chance may be guilty, are not considered innocent till they have been proved guiltless.

Therefore, the confession of the shoemaker apart, the unknown soldier who had been seen by the girl I had questioned was quite likely to be the guilty person.

The inquest was to take place that evening—the evening following the giving in custody of John Kamp. Of course I attended.

The case created some commotion, by the fact that the murderer had given himself up to justice; but I need not tell you that the inquest proceeded, as far as evidence went, precisely as though Kamp had been still at liberty.

I need here only refer to the evidence of the medical man, for his depositions alone affect the course of this tale.

He produced the bullet he had extracted from the body of

the dead man, and then proceeded to describe the course the ball had taken.

Judge my surprise when upon asking for and fitting the bullet to the pistol Kamp had given me, I found that it would not run down the barrel.

Therefore it was evident that if Kamp had shot the man, he had used some other weapon than the one he had given me. But if so, why had he deceived me in reference to the pistol? Not seeking to hide the crime, why should he seek to mystify me in reference to the weapon?

Nay, upon further consideration, I saw that he could not, of course, know that the evidence of the bullet would be in his favour.

I gave my testimony, which exhibited very fully the discrepancy between Kamp's statement and the evidence given by the doctor in relation to the bullet.

It was quite impossible to reconcile the contradictions, and, after much bald and unequal suggestion, the inquest was adjourned.

The night, however, was not to pass without the mystery being cleared up.

I was at the district station, and it was about eleven p.m., when the ears of all the officers at the station were pricked up at hearing a crowd of approaching footsteps.

We went to the door, the jailer, I remember, clashing his keys loudly, and there coming towards us was a stretcher carried by a couple of policemen and surrounded by a number of people—for the greater part, of the lowest class—the hum of whose voices on our practised ears told us that it was no drunken case which was being carried in.

A policeman leading the *cortége*, and who had an air of startled dignity upon him, stopped as he approached the office-door.

"It's sooicide for a pot!" said the jailer, who stood behind me.

"Sooicide!" said the sergeant, as he stopped, and as the official part of the procession followed his example—not followed however by the rabble, who flocked round and gorged intelligence with all their eyes, their mouths meanwhile being wide open with excitement.

"I know'd it," said the jailer. "*I* should have won."

"What is it, Brogley?" asked the inspector of the sergeant.

"Military case, sir," said the sergeant; "soldier shot hisself in a room in Hare's-street, in the room where the prisoner Kamp, the shoemaker, lived."

It was no good guess on my part, after hearing these words, to feel certain that the soldier was Tom Hapsy.

I raised the poor quilt that had been thrown over the body—a quilt that had been taken from "the prisoner Kamp's" room—and there sure enough I saw, as the eager crowd herded about me, glad of this chance to see a horror—there I saw what remained of the features of Tom Hapsy.

So in six months, I thought, as after some official directions the body was borne on towards the dead house, Johanna Kamp had destroyed herself, so also had the cheerful soldier Tom Hapsy, and the third of that humble trio, John Kamp, lay in prison self-accused of murder.

Nor let the reader suppose this case untrue because it may appear overdrawn. The poor and the wretched too often find death sweeter than life. And indeed in this particular case, the man and woman, by reason of their physical drawbacks, had been so desolate before they met, that it is no wonder they fell into despair when the love they felt for each other was broken down by a selfish, heartless man.

The searcher at the dead-house found that letter on the poor dead body which exculpated John Kamp, though I could have saved him had the letter fallen from the body in its passage to the dead-house.

For the bullet extracted from Higham's body exactly fitted the pistol found in Hapsy's right hand, and what is more, the bullet taken from Tom's temple, where it had lodged, had been cast in the same mould (as the mark of a fracture proved) as the lead which the doctor produced at the inquest upon the sub-army contractor.

Thereupon I went by permission to John Kamp's cell.

By the way I will not reproduce Tom Hapsy's letter found on

his dead body, for it was badly spelt, and written in a high-flown, sentimental style, which might appear ridiculous to the more unthinking of my readers. It is sufficient to say that he declared he had taken the law into his own hands, first in destroying "Johanna's seducer," and then himself.

I went, I say, to John Kamp's cell.

"John Kamp," said I, "you did not kill Mr. Higham."

He looked up amazedly.

And then I told him all the news.

He did not weep. He was too thoroughly broken-down for that. He did not betray any surprise when I told him about the cartridge-paper being a leaf from the work of which he was so fond. He took little notice of my explanation to the effect that the soldier must have torn the leaf from the book when contemplating the murder.

All he said was—"Poor Tom."

Some time afterwards I comprehended how it happened that both men were at the same time in the field where the catastrophe occurred.

The young person who was to meet Higham, viciously proud of the interview, had confided the news to a companion (who of course knew all about the talk concerning Johanna's death), and she it was who informed the brother and soldier the of the coming meeting. With what intention I have never learnt. But I have surmised that she did so with some idea of that rough, terrible justice called vengeance, and which more or less lurks in every human heart.

Yes, all he said was, "Poor Tom!"

At last I said to him—"But, John, why did you say you killed the man?"

He looked up to me with most weary simplicity, and he said—

"I went out to kill him, and should have done so if Tom had not. I did not know who shot him at the time. I was a murderer in intention, and I gave myself up."

So, there you have my tale of "The Judgement of Conscience."

John Kamp is in Australia now, and doing well. Nor am I sorry that I helped him to do well. He has long since paid me back; and he tells me if ever I want a pound or two I am to let him know.

I think he is happy for being in Australia, where they are not so socially particular as in England, even in the matter of doctors. He has long since managed to become a kind of under-assistant at a dispensary; and I am sure that I for one would not at all hesitate to swallow a prescription made up by him, even though he had put the dose together in the dark.

MARY FORTUNE

(1833?—1911?)

Bradbury and Evans, a British firm of printers-turned-publishers, are remembered now primarily for publishing Charles Dickens—some of the novels he wrote and one of the periodicals he edited. Even without Boz, however, they were a diverse and influential company. In 1850 they began producing a monthly magazine entitled *The Ladies' Companion: An Illustrated Monthly Magazine of the Fashions, Interesting Facts, and Select Fiction*. One of the many literarily significant decisions the editors made in the next few years was to invite a promising young writer in Canada, Mary Helena Fortune, to immigrate to Australia and write about the gold rush there. Each issue of the *Companion* sold for a shilling, twelve times the cost of the penny sheets. Handsomely produced and well-illustrated, the magazine could afford to invest in such a popular story as the fairy-tale wealth to be dug like buried treasure from the gold-filled hills of the British colony.

Born in Belfast around the year 1833, Mary Helena Wilson had moved to Canada with her father following the tragic early death of her mother. In Canada, probably still in her late teens, she married a surveyor named Joseph Fortune and gave birth to a son. When her father moved far away again, this time to Australia, young Mary followed him, accompanied by her son but not her husband. She arrived in Melbourne in 1855 with little except the invitation from *The Ladies' Companion*.

Gifted with intelligence and imagination and energy, and faced with few well-paying jobs available to women lacking social capital, Fortune was soon writing for numerous Australian newspapers. Like many female writers of the time, she published under masculine pseudonyms, strange aliases, gender-neutral initials, and sometimes completely anonymously. The gold rush economy was launching many periodicals, and like those in both her native Ireland and her adopted nation of Canada, they published a great deal of fiction. An editor at one, the *Mount Alexander Mail* in Victoria, soon admired Fortune's skill and wrote to offer a position as subeditor. When she revealed to him that the author behind the pseudonym was a woman, however, he withdrew the job offer. She kept scribbling, both fiction and nonfiction. At times she wrote under a sad nickname she had for herself—Waif Wander. In 1858 she married a policeman, Percy Brett, whose work experience would provide much of Fortune's impressive details of detective work.

In 1865 she submitted a story to a recently launched Melbourne-based magazine entitled *The Australian Journal*. Modeled after successful British periodicals such as *Family Herald* and *Cassell's Illustrated Family Paper*, it was intended by its editor to capture the burgeoning audience of literate women and teenagers. For this periodical Fortune wrote romances, scattered journalism, and a Gothic novel, *Clyzia the Dwarf*, described by crime fiction scholar Lucy Sussex as "exquisitely excessive."

The magazine's editor, formerly with the Victoria Mounted Police, liked crime stories and featured them from the beginning. The *Journal* ran a series entitled "Memoirs of an Australian Police Officer," launched by James Skipp Borlase, a Cornish immigrant who also wrote the penny dreadful *Ned Kelly, the Ironclad Australian Bushranger*, which was later described as "as disgraceful and disgusting a production as has ever been printed." Soon Borlase was fired for plagiarism and other sins, and 1866 saw publication of Fortune's first contribution to the series, "The Dead Witness," now considered the first detective-series short story written by a woman. Later Borlase republished some of his stories, and, with his usual disregard of law and decency, included among them a story that Fortune had contributed anonymously to his series.

On November 7, 1868, Fortune launched her own series in the paper, *The Detective's Album*, with the story "The Red Room." It was the first of what would prove to be a long line of serial detective stories, centered around and narrated by the investigator, a policeman named Mark Sinclair. For the next *four decades*, Fortune wrote one story about the likable and not painfully upright Sinclair for each monthly issue, although the editor at this point shrank her pseudonym to a genderless "W.W." The only collection of her stories that appeared during Fortune's lifetime was from this series—*The Detective's Album: Tales of the Australian Police*—published in 1871. It begins with an elaboration of Fortune's conceit that Sinclair is recounting memories inspired by the mug shots and crime scene photos he has filed away over the years in his official album—which is why, in the following story, she invites the reader to examine a photo that does not actually appear in the text.

Not until the 1950s did a Melbourne bibliophile, John Kinmont Moir, unearth the real identity of W.W. In the 1980s the mystery scholar Lucy Sussex edited the first modern volume of Fortune's work, and the first ever about her, with her real name featured in the title—*The Fortunes of Mary Fortune*. During Moir's inquiries about Fortune's life, the current editor of the *Australian Journal* wrote to him in 1952 about Fortune's drinking, "for which, God knows, she probably had every reason, as she wrote more, and doubtless got less for it, than any other Australian writer of the time." Sussex's research found that in 1874 a police report, seeking Fortune as "a reluctant witness in a case of rape," said she was "much given to drink and she has been locked up several times for drunkenness."

Later in her career, Fortune wrote autobiographical sketches such as "Twenty-Six Years Ago; or, the Diggings from '55," which appeared in 1882 and 1883, using her own experience to highlight the previously unrecorded experiences of white immigrant women to the Australian bush. Scholars applaud her ongoing critique of colonialization, her documentation of the bustling city of Melbourne and of the goldfields, as well as her determination to spotlight the travails and contributions of women. She also told a lively and vivid story.

THE RED ROOM

In the pursuit and arrest of criminals in every corner of the world, what a powerful assistance has the art of photography been to policemen of every grade. Before its perfection and dissemination to every quarter of the globe, the detective had little to guide him save the imperfect and stereotyped description in the *Police Gazette*, of the verbally given impression of some not over-observant victim, perhaps. Now it is different. In almost three cases out of every five the first mail puts us in possession of a *facsimile* on paper of the object of our search, and we are in a position to pounce upon him at once, with a certainty as to his identity of which nothing can deprive us.

When I promised to give to the public the police histories of some of the pictured forms and faces in my detective album, I had not duly considered the task I was about to undertake. It will be a harrowing one. There is not one of those portraits that does not bring vivid remembrances to me; and some of them most terrible ones, that are calculated, even at this distance of time, to make me shudder, and the blood run colder in my veins.

The album generally lies in the drawer of my office desk at my headquarters; and it is not kept for the amusement of visitors, or, indeed, for anyone's inspection save my own. It has a horrible fascination for me, and one which is very strange in a person so used to such scenes as those in which the originals of my portraits have played the principal part. And so deeply interesting, at least to my recollection, are every one of the episodes connected with those pictured faces that I have turned the leaves over and over again for many minutes without being able to decide which of its pages I should first unfold. But selection would be only invidious, and I shall take the simplest way, relating my acquaintance with the history of each leaf as it comes, commencing with the first page.

I could not have done better, I think; for the tale of crime connected with this one will take me back to the early days of the Victorian diggings, and to the scenes which are already becoming a recollection of the past, and which are not likely to be renewed. There are many who will read these pages to whom the localities into which my reminiscences will lead me will be familiar, but they will recognize no topographical correctness in the names I shall apply to the places I shall have to describe. There remain still, in many of the scenes I shall find it necessary to portray, persons to whom my stories must bring terrible memories, and with whom the real names must inevitably connect the tragedies. Under these circumstances, it will be more charitable to select colonial names at random, and without attempting to locate them at proper distances from each other.

It is, let me see, twelve years ago now, since I was riding, one lovely spring day, through one of the prettiest bits of wild country in Victoria. A most beautiful and perfect specimen of the "bush track" led over plain and through gorge, and by winding creek; now but lightly marking its rarely-travelled path through an old box forest, and anon emerging upon a broad and rolling plain, where the scattered trees flourished restingly, like the old oaks in an English demesne. Sometimes it climbed tortuously up a steep and rooky range; sometimes it vanished entirely on the arid side of a sloping sun-browned eminence. Sometimes it carried me on through a perfect richness of soft, green wattles, or stopped lazily at a deep, still water pool; but always beautiful, and always enjoyable in the soft genial brightness of an Australian September day.

I had just reached such a spot—a still, dark-bosomed waterhole, that lay but a little distance from the faint track. That wayfarers had made it a resting-place was evident from the marks of hoof and foot that trampled one place at its edge, and from the bits of half-burnt wood and white ashes that lay at the foot of a near tree. But there had not been enough of this to destroy the natural beauty of the spot; and the soft bushes around were green and fresh-looking, and the lordly trees as grand, and the dark water as restful, as if the eye of man had never looked upon the scene.

My horse seemed to have an inclination to drink, so I turned him, or rather let him take his own course, towards the pool; and then I dismounted, and while he satisfied his thirst by long draughts of the cool water, I stood by his side holding the bridle in my hand, and admired the surroundings of the quiet bush waterhole.

Every one at all familiar with Australian country scenery knows the value of these deep pools in a country so ill-watered as ours is. They are generally to be met with on the beds of dry creeks, where their steep edges, worn away by many a winter torrent, are fringed by the spring-blossomed wattle, or guarded by the old gnarled gum-tree, that stands like a silent sentinel over the secrets of the pool. Of what value they are in the hot and droughty summer of our eastern land, let the foot-sore swagsman tell, who, faint and weary, at last reaches one to refresh and to cool.

I was not faint and weary, yet the dark water pool had an attraction for me that I did not attempt to resist. "What a dark hiding-place for the victim dead," I thought; "and if it were even so, not less placidly would its surface reflect those feathery wattle boughs laden with their clusters of golden down, and not less sweetly would that joyous magpie warble his notes as he plumes himself, with the water for a mirror."

At this moment my horse lifted his head from the water with a long sigh of content, but as he did so he pricked up his ears and started. Looking behind me to see what had alarmed him, I saw something that startled myself, being, as I was, unaware of the presence of a living being.

It was a man seated upon a dead log by the water's side, with his elbows on his knees, and his face buried in his hands. The usual swag lay beside him, and he was dusty and way-worn looking; but he did not seem like a digger, but, to my accustomed eyes, like a new chum, viz., one who had not been long in the colony.

His whole attitude was one of the deepest dejection. If he had heard my approach, he must have paid no attention to it, for his bowed head remained upon his hands even as the horse's feet began to shift in the water preparatory to his dipping his lips in a fresh part of the pool. I don't know how it was, but my heart was drawn towards this lonely man, sitting there so desolate by the bush waterhole, and I did what I would not perhaps have done in a less lonely place—I addressed him.

"Hallo, mate! What's the matter with you? Not sick, eh?"

The stranger lifted his head slowly, and as if with an effort, and when he did so I perceived that the face was that of a young man of evident gentle breeding.

"You are not ill, or in want any way, I hope?" I asked again, as he did not immediately answer.

"No, I am only thoroughly tired out, and—and low-spirited," he added, hesitatingly. "Can you tell me how far the Bridge Hotel is from this?"

"Well, I have never been here before," I replied, "but I think I can make a tolerably good guess. The Bridge Hotel is about a mile and a half from Carrick police-station, and Carrick police-station is about two miles from where you sit. You are some three and a half miles from the Bridge Hotel."

"It's a good walk yet," he said, with a sigh of weariness.

"I'll tell you what you can do to shorten the road," I observed, impulsively. "Come with me to the camp—company will lighten the way, and you can have a rest there and start fresh."

"Are you going to the police camp?" he asked, with interest, looking me all over quickly as he spoke.

I was in plain clothes, having only recently been removed into the detective force.

"Yes—I am going straight there."

"You are not a policeman? You have nothing to do with the force?" he inquired eagerly.

"I have quite enough to do with it to insure you a welcome at any rate," was my evasive reply, "if you are coming with me; and if you are not, why I must be going, for the sun dips fast in Australia when he gets as low as he is at present."

At this moment occurred one of those apparently simple incidents, the life and death consequences of which it is too hard for materialism to account for. Upon such simple things hang the whole issue of a person's future life. The delay of a moment—the breaking of a strap—the falling of a few raindrops—the stumbling of a foot against a stone—upon these, and such things as these, have rested the issue of life in how many re-corded and unrecorded instances.

The animal I had ridden, being satisfied with his long draught of the refreshing element, at this moment withdrew his forefoot from the clayey brink of the pool. As he did so, I turned to re-cover a firmer foothold, a something caught in his foot, or rather around it, and tripped him. It was apparently a black string, one end of which was embedded in the mud; but the horse's foot detached it, and he climbed to the sward by my side with it hanging, limp and dirty, yet dripping with water, around his ankle.

I stooped down and removed it, lifting it at the same time to examine it more closely. It was a black silk necktie, with an em-broidery in what had once been richly-colored floss in the cor-ners; but the action of the water had left only faint hues where had once been a brilliant imitation of natural flowers. Satisfied with my inspection, I threw it from me—was it chance that made it alight upon the foot of my new acquaintance? His eye followed it from my hand—I saw that as I cast it away—and when it rested on his boot I was looking into his face, and saw a lividness spread over it too decided not to be noticed. Follow-ing my example, he stooped and raised the dripping rag from the ground, and examined it closely, with a head so bent down that the brim of his hat shaded his face from my eyes. But I could see the hands that held the bit of silk, and the long delicate-looking fingers trembled like leaves in a breeze.

Apparently the sight of this rag, dragged from the muddy edge of an Australian bush waterhole, recalled memories or feelings which the traveler could not bear; his legs trembled under him, his very lips grew ashen hued, and he fell back upon the log from which he had arisen at his last question to myself. He clasped the necktie firmly in his fingers, and once more bent his head over them, and groaned as one in agony of mind that could not be given utterance to.

My curiosity as well as my pity was deeply aroused. What could this stranger have possibly found in this dirty, soiled string to arouse such evident distress? "What on earth is the matter, my good friend?" I asked, laying my hand kindly on his shoulder. "That dripping thing that my horse has unconsciously pulled out of the mud has affected you strangely. Won't you tell me what it is?"

"It is murder," he replied, hoarsely, "and a murder that I have come half around the globe to find. Oh God," he added, rising to his feet and excitedly lifting the hand that held the bit of black silk, in an attitude of invocation, "help me to discover and avenge! But why should I doubt? Hast Thou not led me here, all unconsciously, to the very spot—to the very spot? I thank thee, Oh my God!" and he sat down once more and burst into a passion of tears.

I was glad to see the tears—painful as it is at all times to see them flow from a man's eyes—for I knew they would act as a safety-valve to the intensity of his feelings, of whatever nature they might be. And so I did not attempt to interrupt him until the first burst was over, and his grief had subsided into deep sobs that seemed to tear him. Then I spoke to him kindly.

"My dear fellow, I do not know the cause of your trouble, of course, and I do not ask to know it, if you do not wish to tell me; but I do not like to leave you here alone in this state. You have spoken of murder. Can I not help you? I am an officer of detectives, and I am on my way to Carrick Police Station. Here, put your swag on my horse, and I will walk with you. We may help you. Come, now."

"A detective! Oh, yes, I will go with you! Surely heaven is ready to help me, since you are sent to throw at my feet the first clue to the lost. I am ready;" and looking a long look first at the cold deep water we were about to leave, he lifted his swag to be able to throw it over my saddle.

I daresay we walked half a mile before the silence was broken between us, the stranger walking on one side of the horse, with his hand resting on the swag to steady it, and I on the other, carelessly holding the bridle of my well-trained animal. The man seemed almost completely absorbed in thought, and I don't believe that he was conscious in any degree of the nature of the country we were journeying over. He still held the necktie in his hand, and every now and then he looked at it sadly; but at length he folded it up, placed it in his breast, and then spoke to me.

"Shall we go near the Bridge Hotel at all on our way to the camp?"

"No—it is a mile and a half from the station. Are you anxious to get there? Do you expect to meet anyone?" I asked, wishing to get him into conversation.

"I expect to meet a murderer," he answered, hurriedly; "but, see, I'm going to tell you my story now. Mine is a retiring disposition at any time, and by-and-bye I may not be inclined to speak in the presence of your companions. Pray, listen to every word, for I do not speak from any motive but one, which requires your help as a detective."

And, as he concluded, he arranged the swag more securely, and letting the horse move on until he passed him, placed himself by my side.

I had already noticed what a handsome young fellow he was. His features were aquiline, and his hair and beard a dark brown. He had large, dark, melancholy-looking eyes, and his face was deathly pale; and his years might have numbered twenty-five, but not more.

"It is three years ago now," he began, "since the news of the great gold finds of Australia reached the quiet country town where our widowed mother shared the home and the affections of her two only children. We were both boys. Edward was two years younger than I; and when he heard of the suddenly-acquired fortunes of the land of gold, ropes would not have held him at home.

" 'Why should I not go and make money?' he asked. 'We may plod on here in poverty for ever. No, mother, do not say me nay. I shall soon return to fill your lap with a golden shower, and then George need not grow any paler at that weary desk.'

"And so he went, and I was left alone with our mother, keeping on still my situation to support us both. Edward was even more fortunate than he had dreamed, for the first letter we received from him brought home a handsome sum, the produce of his first gold-mining speculation in the colony.

"I will not tire you with a description of my mother's delight when, at the end of the first year of his absence, we received a letter from Edward stating his intention of returning home at once. He had been so fortunate that a handsome fortune was to be shared with us; and the boy's letter was like a burst of sunshine, it was so full of delight and joy, and it made my poor mother's heart young again. Edward was her favourite too, and he was worthy of her love.

"Well, months passed away wearily, and we heard no more of my brother, and my mother began to droop and pine, and to fancy all sorts of evil had befallen the lad. He had told us in his letter that he was on his way to Melbourne when he wrote it, and that he carried his gold with him. A 'heavy swag' he called it; determined to entrust it to no one, so fearful was he of losing it. At last, yielding to my poor mother's entreaties, I wrote a note to the postmaster at Reid's Creek—the place where my brother had been working—acquainting him with the particulars of our anxiety, and requesting that he would try to gain any particulars that he could for us.

"By the very next mail came a reply from a mate of poor Edward's, who had fortunately happened to be at Reid's Creek when the postmaster got mine. His tidings fell like a thunderbolt upon us, and from the very hour of its receipt my mother sank rapidly.

"It stated that the writer had accompanied Edward on his way to town until they reached the Bridge Hotel, at Coghill Creek. There he had heard such news as induced him to say farewell to Edward, and turn his steps in the direction of the new rush at McIvors.

"Things at McIvors not proving as he had anticipated, he had retraced his steps without loss of time, but only to find that Edward had left the Bridge Hotel.

"He went on to say that he had followed the Sydney-road to town, step by step, and inquired in every direction for his late mate, and all to no purpose. He was certain that he had not sailed in any vessel that had left the port, and from the large quantity of gold he carried on his person, and the great temptation it would have proved to the cupidity of anyone of the many bad characters to whom his simplicity might expose his gold after he had parted with his more prudent mate, that mate dreaded the worst.

"I have told you," continued the speaker, forgetting weariness and pace in the trouble of his own words, and walking on rapidly—"I have already told you that this letter grievously affected my mother—it killed her. From the moment of its receipt she conjured up continual pictures of her boy lying in a bloody and hidden grave—a martyr to the gold he had gone to procure for her sake, and she died gladly, in the full certainty of meeting him all the sooner.

"I am afraid, stranger," continued the young man, pausing, and looking sadly into my face, "that I could not in a year make you understand the deep love I bore for this young brother. People said that our faces were so similar that strangers might well mistake the one for the other; but there was no similarity in our dispositions. I was always quiet, and, it may be, moody, and he was full of life and life's sunshine; but my heart was not moody towards my brother Edward, and I loved him with a 'love passing the love of woman.'

"Yes," cried the traveler, passionately, and stopping in his walk to hold my arm excitedly, "I loved him more as a father would love an affectionate son, than as one brother feels for another; and I have come sixteen thousand miles to find the necktie his dead mother's fond fingers wrought for him lying at my feet! Tell me, what does it mean? You who live in an atmosphere of such things and read them, tell me, does this mean murder, or only madness?" and he dragged the wet silk rag again from his breast, and held it at arm's length before my eyes.

He asked me if it meant murder or madness, and, sooth to say, I did not know what to answer him. The wild light in his eyes made me dread that his mind was unsettled, but that he had told me a true story, and had good reason to dread the murder of a brother, I had my own reasons for believing.

"Listen to me, my dear fellow," I said gently, looking kindly into his craving, anxious eyes meanwhile. "You have come a long distance to find out a cruel secret and to discover the guilty, and will you now render further efforts hopeless by encouraging an excitement which will be pernicious to your objects as well as to your own health? I am able, believe me, to sympathize with your feelings and affection for your lost brother, but I shall be obliged to cease doing so if you give way to weakness in the matter. There, give me your hand, and accept mine, as that of one in every way willing to help you to discover the truth so long as you will try to be calm and to trust him. Will you?"

He laid his hand frankly in my own, looked searchingly into my eyes once more, and then pressed my hand in a firm grasp.

"I will—I *will* try," he said, walking; onward again, and so permitting me to do the same; "but it is very hard to be quiet with a burning heart, and every footstep following the track of a murdered brother."

"Now listen to me again," I continued, "while I tell you something that will deeply interest you. By a strange coincidence, my business at Carrick Police Station is so nearly connected with the object that drew you from your English home, that I might just as well have been dispatched up here for the very purpose of elucidating *your* mystery. About a month ago, a man of property was lost track of in the vicinity of this very Bridge Hotel, and as he had a large sum of money in his possession, his friends have naturally become very anxious about him. I have been sent up to try for any trace that might be discovered of him in this neighborhood, and I meet with you, come so very far to tell me, as it were, of a lost brother at this same Bridge Hotel. You are *sure* your brother has been here, since you find his necktie lying at your foot, and *I* am sure that the woman who keeps this hotel is an intriguing, unprincipled creature, whose inordinate love of dress and display might urge her to any crime of which cupidity is capable. Now, what do you think of all this, my friend?"

"I think that the hand of God is in it," he replied, solemnly. "And see," I added, opening my pocket-book and producing from it a *carte*, which I handed him, "here is a likeness of this landlady of the Bridge Hotel. Look at it and see if it seem like the portrait of a woman base enough to assist in murder for the sake of gold."

"Must it of necessity be this woman?" he said, with a shudder. "It is the portrait of a bold yet handsome woman, of a low intellectual type, and a fierce untamable temper; but I hate to believe it possible that one of the same sex as my dead mother—the gentle and the good—should be even suspected of so horrible a deed."

"And yet such deeds they do," I replied, "and do with a coldness and a cruelty at times that men cannot do more than equal. I have come up with a strong suspicion against this Mrs. Henry, as she calls herself. She has been living at this house now five years, passing as a widow, and in such a style that she must have some other source of wealth than the hotel, which to the certain knowledge of the police, does not pay her license. She drives a buggy and pair, and rides a blood horse fit for a queen. There is not a lady in Victoria can outshine her in dress, and she exhibits it far and near on every opportunity. She has been known to spend eighty pounds with a travelling jeweler on a single ornament, and we must find out where the gay lady gets her money."

"It is your province to be suspicious," said the young traveler, as he handed me back the portrait of Mrs. Henry; "but a woman who enjoys the frivolities of life would be the last I would suspect of blood-spilling, and yet somebody murdered our boy."

"Bah!" I answered, looking with a sneering lip at the picture, ere I replaced it in my pocket. "I *am* suspicious, and that is a bad, bold, vicious countenance."

Will you have a look at it, reader? It is the portrait that I have chosen from my detective album to illustrate this story with. Would you ever suppose that the original of that regal figure, with the beautiful face full of consciousness of its own beauty, could have lured men to death with as little pity as a ghoul? Or those soft-looking rounded fingers, loaded with rings, could have been remorselessly dabbled in the warm blood of a dozen victims? There is a tragic air in the attitude in which the artist has depicted her in her heavy silken robes. She stands with half averted face, one hand grasping the back of a rich arm-chair, the other hanging carelessly by her side, and contrasting its whiteness with the dark hue of the dress. Her hair is a wealth of gloss and waves, but it is pushed carelessly back from a broad, smooth brow, and the face seems half turned toward the watcher with an expression of haughty astonishment at your presumption in daring to scan it.

Such was the portrait of one of the most remorseless criminals Victoria has ever produced.

My companion and I walked on with but few words more until we came within sight of Carrick Station. It was one of those up-country stations that seems to have been planted in the most out-of-the-way spots, in total defiance of common sense. There were not three houses within as many miles of it; and the constables who were unfortunate enough to be stationed there passed a most wretched and lonely time of it.

The sun was just dipping behind the tops of the trees as we approached the camp, and the low beams tinged with a last flush the salient points of the landscape. Grey rooks were ruddy with his warm tints; long, pendant branches of box swayed in the evening breeze, catching ever and anon the red flush as they momentarily escaped the shadow of their own foliage. Long shadows lay on the soft grass, and made but the greener every bit of herbage by the dark contrast. Carrick was a pretty spot under such influences.

And so my companion seemed to think; he stood still for a moment when the beauty of the scene appeared first to strike him, and then he strode on again silently. Suddenly, however, he started again, and, turning a white face toward me, asked abruptly, "Who is that?"

Following with my eye the direction of his pointing finger, I saw my old friend, Sergeant Thomson, leading a horse toward the stable, and in earnest conversation with a man who was walking by his side. The two figures were only about thirty yards from us, and I could see that the stranger was of a slight, delicate-seeming figure, and walked as one who was either weakly or much fatigued.

"The policeman is Sergeant Thomson," I answered, "a very clever fellow, and one who will be of great assistance to us in managing Mrs. Henry. The man who is with him I do not know; he is evidently a stranger who is going to stop at the camp all night."

As I spoke, the constable went on alone, and his companion turned on his track and came directly toward us. His eyes were bent upon the ground as in deep thought, and he was entirely unaware of our approach. He was, as a nearer view further convinced me, very delicate, but there was another fact that struck me still more vividly when he had come within a distance of twenty yards, and that was his astonishing likeness to my new friend. At the same moment that this likeness attracted my attention the approaching young man lifted his eyes and perceived us, and as he did so, he uttered an exclamation of astonishment, and darted forward hastily.

My companion stopped short and lifted his hand as if to ward off the contact of the stranger. But as he stared wildly into his face, the hand dropped, and the arms of the young man were around my new friend. There was a muttered, smothered, half-choked cry of "Edward! My brother!" that told its own tale, and I passed on, leaving the brothers to exhibit their feelings in solitude. What those feelings were I could well guess, for to one, at least, it was the recovery of the dead.

I daresay you will either feel, or affect to feel, very much shocked when I tell you that I felt most heartily disappointed at this disappointment to the tragedy I had already interwoven with my visit to the bush water-hole.

Before I recalled the memory of my companion's deep affection for this young brother, I would have much preferred that he should have been waiting in the bottom of the hole for me to pull him up, so that he might have been, dead although he was, a witness against Mrs. Henry. Better feelings, however, soon got the mastery over the hard heart of the detective, and I was prepared to reciprocate the kindly expressions of my new friend when he shortly after introduced his brother to me, with a deep joy in his eyes, and in the very tones of his voice that one must have been of adamant not to have sympathized with.

Talking of being introduced, I think it is almost time that I introduced you to the name of these young men. They were called Mansfield, and that knowledge, shared between you and me, will facilitate the course of my story considerably.

The night had closed round the station when the "quartette," composed of the two brothers, myself, and Sergeant Thomson, were gathered in one of the little barrack rooms, interestedly listening to the strange story by which Edward Mansfield at once accounted for his suspicious disappearance and his unexpected arrival in the vicinity of the Bridge Hotel. The brothers had spent some time in intercourse, which the sergeant and I took care not to interrupt, after supper; but when at length the darkness had fallen densely down upon forest and plain, they came in together, and I could see in the sad eyes of the lad that his mother's memory had not been tearless.

"Let us sit close," said the elder, drawing chairs forward, "Edward has a wild story to tell you. If," he added, vehemently, as he turned to me with the same wild light in his eyes that I had seen at the waterhole—"if God permits to go unpunished the inhuman woman who murders for gold, and brought the widow's grey hairs with sorrow to the grave, then is He not a God of justice!"

With strongly excited curiosity we seated ourselves, and prepared to listen to the young man's tale. It was a tale that deeply affected even me at the time, and one which urged me on the track of the murderess, as the smell of blood might the sleuth hound; and if it does not thrill your hearts to listen to it now, I don't know what hearts are made of.

"I can't take time to tell you day and date, my friends," commenced the youth with the pale, sad face, as he sat with his hand on his brother's shoulder, and his eyes fixed on that older, yet similar face, as if he feared he might again lose it, "but it is unnecessary. You all know when I left the Ovens diggings, and how I came here to the Bridge Hotel, carrying gold that was to make my poor mother rich and happy. It seems but yesterday that I shook Bob's hand as he started for McIvors, and yet a twelvemonth of such heaviness has passed since as might well build up a barrier of forgetfulness between me and it.

"It had been well for me had I gone with him and left the Bridge Hotel and its siren mistress far behind me, but I couldn't—I couldn't do it, George. You know how susceptible I was always to female influence; and the happiness induced by my great success, and my near prospect of returning to the comfort of home, and the society of its beloved inmates, rendered me even more liable to be imposed upon by the allurements of this woman.

"You have seen her likeness, George, but it can give you no idea of her diabolical fascination of manner. I was as helpless as a child in her hands—nay, more than helpless, for I was a willing slave. Oh, may heaven curse her!" ejaculated the youth, clenching his hand while a red flush mounted angrily into his white face, and a fierce light glowed in his dark eyes, "and the fascination that allures men to death.

"By why do I so speak? Is she not already accursed? The demon with the fair face and the devil's heart, bought with blood dabbed hands full of gold? It kills me to feel," he added vehemently, "that, by this indulgence of a criminal weakness, I lost the light of my mother's old age, that I had so long worked for; and that to punish *me* God saw fit to take her away without her boy's hand to press in death. But I was only a lad, George," he added, pleading, as if begging for his brother's forgiveness—"was only a lad, and like putty in the hands of this inhuman woman."

"My poor Edward, you were in nothing to blame," said the elder, soothingly, as he pressed his brother's hand in a warm grip. "You were sinned against, my poor boy, but in nothing have you sinned. Be calm, Edward, retribution is coming . . ."

With an effort the young man continued, "In but a very short time I had confided to this creature every hope and aspiration of my heart—my love for you, George, my devotion to my widowed mother. I had told her of the delight I anticipated in pouring my gold into my mother's lap, and telling her that we should feel trouble or want no more. And she, the vile thing, feigned to sympathize in feelings which she understood no more than the animals in her stable. Good God! How she

must have laughed at the fool who spoke of his deep consciousness of a mother's holy affection, and yet permitted himself to
be molded by a word from such a woman as she!

"I don't know how many days had passed, but they were not
many, when the end came. They were days full of the delight of
young and foolish passion—days spent in the woods around
the Bridge Hotel, or in the luxurious private rooms of her own
cottage. I longed to go toward the home of my affections, but
an invincible chain appeared to bind me to the siren's side.

"Every morning I rose with the determination of proceed-
ing, only to meet with wooings and smiles that bound me to
her side like iron. She had installed me in the best room of the
hotel and given me the key of a safe which it contained; and
there I placed my gold, and did not fail to often assure myself
of its safe keeping.

"And in this room I retired to rest on the last frightful night
of my stay at the hotel. They called it the red room, from, as I
supposed, the colour of its furniture and decorations. God
knows, it might well be called the room of that sanguinary
hue; for although every luxury that could gratify the senses
and minister to sleep was gathered there, it was the room of
blood.

"Oh, the recollection of that night is more than I can bear;
it seems to bring me face to face with a violent death once
more!"

The wine which I poured out and offered the young narrator
at this moment was not unneeded. The perspiration was gathering in heavy drops on his pale forehead, and every limb trembled as he ceased. His brother sat and listened with clenched
hands and corrugated brow, the picture of fierce determination; and even Sergeant Thomson, the phlegmatic, showed
unmistakable symptoms of deep interest.

As for myself, I was more than deeply interested; I was craving for a further confirmation of my suspicions respecting Mrs.
Henry, and beginning to see a strange ending to my young
friend's story. I already hated this woman's character, but if she
had done as my expectations led me to believe from the tendency of Edward Mansfield's tale, it was a satisfaction to me to

feel assured that no punishment the law could adjudge would be sufficient to expiate her crimes.

"You will think me childishly weak," continued young Mansfield, after he had recovered himself enough to proceed; "but you can have no conception of the sufferings of that terrible night. The terror and the pain I then endured have weakened me, mind and body, for life. But I must go on, or your patience will be exhausted.

"I don't know what had come over me that night, but I could not sleep. I had retired earlier than was my wont, because a traveler had arrived at the house, and taken up so much of Mrs. Henry's attention that there seemed little left for me. I was jealously disposed, and sought my room in a huff; and fully determined to leave for Melbourne in the morning of the following day.

"With the weakness of a spoony feeling, however, I was no sooner in bed than a thousand thorns seemed to be under me, and I regretted that I had left the society of the woman who had such influence over me, and half determined to re-seek it.

"Under these feelings I rose and assumed my clothes again; as I buttoned my vest, however, I felt the key of the safe that contained my gold. An invincible inclination to see it was aroused by the contact of the key, and I had soon lighted my candle and drawn from the closet the chamois bag containing the metal so precious to me. The very touch of the nuggets brought home, and the prospects the wealth had opened, so vividly before me, that a complete revulsion of feeling was the consequence. The wretched cause of my infatuation was as totally forgotten as if she had never existed.

"I threw myself once more on the bed, dressed as I was, and with the long bag of gold laid on my chest, and my hands laid on it, I abandoned myself to a delightful picture of home that my imagination conjured up before me. The very weight of the gold that lay on my breast, a precious incubus, was so far from being oppressive that, instead of being a discomfort, I positively enjoyed the sensation. There was over forty pounds in weight of the precious metal, all the result of my own digging. It would have been a heavy load to carry many tens of miles had it been iron or flour, or indeed anything but gold; but we never felt it, neither Bob nor I, save as a delightful certainty of our future independence.

"And so I lay there and caressed it, and built such fond castles in the future air, as boyhood and youth will build, though death is standing at the threshold. And I pictured my mother's sweet smile, and George's beloved face, without a care that my gold would not smooth, until the candle flickered and went out, and left me alone in the darkness.

"But I scarcely noted the change, so full of the absent was I; and I only gathered up the gold closer to my face with both hands, as if it held light as well as all other blessings; and in this instance it was more to me, for it was life itself. Had it not been for the gold laying as it did in so unlikely a spot, I should never have sat here to tell you how they murdered me, brother George.

"Unconsciously I fell asleep. The soothing influence of dear home thoughts had banished the unholy unrest that had kept me awake hitherto. I had no intention of sleeping when I lay down there dressed to think of you and mother, but I did sleep; and only wakened as one wakens from sleep to die.

"Oh, it was terrible, brother George, to wake up with the consciousness of a fearful and unavoidable death certainly at your heart, and a sense, though but a momentary one, that never—never again would your eyes rest upon the features of a loving face.

"It was what seemed to be a sharp tug that awoke me—a tug that appeared, at the same time, to wrench and to smother me; and—oh, God!—I felt as if my eyes were burst open to see for only one moment a sight that I shall recall with horror to my dying day.

"My first consciousness was, as I have said, suffocation; and simultaneously with the opening of my eyes, I involuntarily lifted my hand to my throat. A strong cord encircled it, but it also encircled the bag of gold that I had gathered up caressingly over the lower part of my face, and that fact was the saving of my life, since it partially nullified the effects of the strangling rope that was momentarily compressing my throat more and more.

"Just as I opened my eyes, life seemed leaving me, but the one frightful stare I was enabled to give, as my apparent last, showed me a scene that cannot be forgotten.

"The whole wall behind the red-curtained bed had disappeared, and in the illuminated opening were two figures that I knew only too well. One was that of Mrs. Henry, and the other Karl Schwitz, a German, surly and silent, who seemed to be *factotum* at the Bridge Hotel. The man held in his hand the end of the cord which was throttling me, and which, by some mechanical contrivance, was tightly stretched from side to side of the bed.

"The woman was anxiously watching my face, and I encountered her bloodthirsty eyes as mine opened in the last agony of consciousness.

" 'How hard he dies!' said the monstrous woman in a whisper, that I heard as if it had been shouted in my ears. 'Ah! Look at this—this is it! That will finish it, Schwitz!'

"And she dragged the bag of gold from under the cord.

"Immediately it tightened. I tried to scream—to beg, to implore, for a second, but my brain, for one horrid moment, seemed wrenching from my skull, and I felt the blood gush from my nose, and mouth, and ears, and a flood of blood seemed to rush between my eyes and the woman's face, and it was all over; I was unconscious.

"It could not have been for very long that I remained so, and it was with an almost unbearable sense of agony that I partially regained my senses. The cold night air was fanning my face, over which I felt the dabbling blood as it dripped slowly over my forehead. Over my forehead! Yes; for my head was hanging down, and I looked strangely at the apparently inverted heaven, with its dark expanse and bright, twinkling stars, that hung above me so silently. As consciousness slowly returned, I became aware that I was lying strangely over the back of a horse, and that some one was mounting behind me.

"At that moment I felt a hand, warm and life-like it seemed, against my pained frame, stealing up against my heart, where it rested for a moment, ere that woman's remorseless whisper was again heard.

"There is no fear, Schwitz; he is quite dead. But be sure and sink him well."

"My God, the agony of that moment! Like lightning it flashed over me that my only chance of life was to feign death—one groan, one sigh, nay, one breath, and I was lost! And I was going to be sank—where . . . ?

"How I ever lived during that fearful ride through the dark bush heaven only knows. I was in the most fearful pain, yet dared not move, when my very position was the most acute torture. I formed a hundred plans, but my sense of utter prostration rendered them all futile. Had I possessed but my ordinary strength, how easily I could have fallen from the horse, and grappled with my intended murderer, or fled into the hiding of the night; but I felt my entire helplessness, and that, should I fall, it would be but to lie on the grass, and be dispatched by the knife of him whose life mine would too certainly endanger.

"And yet, could I have known the fate before me, I think I would have tried even to grapple with a death in the dark to avoid it. After an apparently interminable ride, the animal was pulled up, and his living rider dismounted. As for me, I was a corpse only—a thing but to be hidden in the deep bush water-hole; and so I was tossed to the ground, and fell with the weight of death to the earth.

"With a celerity induced by fear, the German assassin commenced attaching to my body by means of a strong cord, some object which I could only guess to be a heavy one, for the purpose of sinking me to the bottom of the hole.

"Oh! good heavens, George, if I could only make you understand one tithe of what I felt in that agonized moment! The inertness of a half-death was pressing on my brain like an iron weight; and yet I was fully conscious of my own helplessness, and of the sounds of earth around me. I could hear the lonely soughing of the night air among the branches that waved in the darkness above me, and through the leafy branches of which I could see faintly the twinkle of far away stars. I could hear the sad ripple of the water far down below the steep brink where I lay, as some overhanging limb dip-dipped into it with the swaying motion of the wind; and more than all—louder than all, could I hear the quick, hard breathing of the murderer above me, as he bound my helpless form with his accursed rope.

"I couldn't think: I tried to pray, but ineffectually. Oh, it was dreadful. I knew that my moments were numbered, and already I seemed to feel the suffocating water pressing me down—down to eternity, while my weighted body was dragged helplessly to the slimy bottom of my last resting-place.

"There was no longer any necessity that I should feign death, for I was as helpless as any dead man could be, save only that my mind was alive to my position, and my brain maddened with a sense of my hopeless condition.

"All at once I remembered that I had a knife in my pocket, and it was as if a ray of heaven had entered my almost bloodless heart. George, do you remember us reading Dumas' tale of the prisoner's escape from the terrible Château D'If? He was sewn up in a sack and a weight attached to his feet, and he was thrown into the sea from the high rocks near the chateau. But he had purposely provided himself with a knife and managed to extricate himself from his shroud before he was stifled by the waves. What if I could manage to do the same? There was no terrible depth of air for my helpless body to cleave. Was there a shadow of a hope for me!

"As this thought surged painfully through my brain, Schwitz rose to his feet; the task was completed.

"There was no time for consideration now, and, with one last effort, I lifted my arm and plunged my hand into my pocket. I had gained the knife, opened it, and held it with a grip like death, ere the assassin had drawn a long breath, and once more stooped over me, and gathered me up roughly in his arms with a hideous strength. A moment more, and I was flung out into the darkness—was gasping for breath in the swiftly-divided air—met the water with a deathly rush, and was sinking down, down coldly, like a stone, to oblivion.

"I can hardly tell you how I cut the rope that bound the iron to my waist; it was all done with the instinct of desperation.

However, it could not have been many seconds ere I found my-self, weak and panting, and gasping for breath at the surface, and grasping for life the heavy branch that I had heard but a little before dipping desolately in the dark water.

"Weak and trembling as I was, and hard as I found it to re-tain my clutch of the yielding branch, I knew that the least noise would betray me. My limbs seemed freezing, and my helpless hands incapable of a moment's grasp, when my quick-ened sense of hearing caught the sound of a horse's feet quickly leaving the scene of my terror. The murderer was gone, and I managed to crawl along the branch; and at last finding grass beneath my feet, I fell forward on my face and wept, and prayed, and offered up such thanksgiving as my almost inani-mate frame could devise.

"And there I lay, without once thinking what I should do, or how punish the wretches who had treated me so vilely. I was conscious only that I had escaped, and was thankful, when a quick sound of wheels nearing the water fell upon my ear. It ceased almost close to me, and voices, in no low tone, greeted my gladdened senses.

"'It used to be here, at any rate; turn the lamp this way, Mac. Oh, I'm sure the water is here, I can feel the cold air of it. Damn it! What have we here?'

"The speaker had seen me lying at his feet, and a picture of wretchedness I must have appeared. Two men stooped over me, and ruddy, although with a softness of voice more in ac-cordance with my condition than their own natures, asked me what had brought me there and thus.

"'I have been strangled and thrown into the water for dead,' I managed to whisper. 'For God's sake, and if you have the hearts of human beings, take me out of this, or they will find me again.'

"I remember no more—I fainted; and it was many miles dis-tant that I once more became conscious. The rest of my story is soon told, my friends. It was into the care of two noted bush-rangers I had fallen, and they were on their hurried route to the border. They dared not, had they been ever so much inclined, stop to get any assistance for me; and in one of their rocky hiding-places I remained until but a week ago, entirely help-less, and a hoverer between life and death. My story won their commiseration, and when I was once more able to travel, they furnished me with a horse, and means, to return and punish the would-be murderers. I came for vengeance, and to recover my gold, and I have found my brother."

And the young man stretched out his hand and grasped that of the brother who had sought him so far and so hopelessly.

"You shall win both!" I exclaimed, starting to my feet; "if man's help can do it, you shall have both revenge and your gold! Come, Thomson, I want a yarn with you, and, if you take my advice, you two young men will turn in and get all the rest you can; you both need it."

The tale of this poor young fellow's sufferings made a deep impression on me, and intensified, if possible, my feelings of hatred against the vile woman I had come to entrap. There was no need of watch or trap now, it was true, since such a witness had arisen from the dead, as it were, to testify against her; but I couldn't be satisfied with simply going in my official capacity and arresting her and her accomplice for murder. I wanted to see more of her—to observe the wiles of the enchantress which she used as nets to entrap the unwary traveler. Besides, I had the death or loss of the man whose fate I had come especially to ascertain to lay at her door, and prove against her, if I could, and so I could not rest until my course of action was com-menced.

It was yet early in the evening, and it did not take too long to assume my disguise, which was simply the complete dress of a man of fashion with every evidence of wealth about it that custom would permit of my displaying; and in less than an hour the sergeant and I were on our way to the Bridge Hotel. Our plans were all laid, at least so far as we could lay any, where so much depended on chance, and no lover ever felt the road longer between him and his *inamorata* than I did that which separated me from Mrs. Henry.

"I hope there will be no travelers to take her attention off," I said. "I do hope that she will take a fancy to me, just such a fancy as she took to poor Edward Mansfield—the she devil!"

No wonder I spoke strongly, humanity could not help it after having listened to the lad's sad tale.

"There is little danger of company," answered Thomson; "but very rarely indeed is the Red Room called upon. By George, I want to overhaul that room, Sinclair! I have many a time admired the rich appearance of it when, on rare occasions, I have been admitted to the adjoining luxurious drawing-room; but *you* are sure to get it made over to your use; rich fellows like you are sure to be patronized."

And my mate's jolly laugh sounded strangely in the quiet bush. It was not long ere our quick pace brought us to the door of the Bridge Hotel, and we dismounted. Our horses were taken in charge by a man whose appearance the darkness did not permit me to examine, but a whisper from my companion assured me that it was Schwitz, the midnight murderer.

"Welcome, gentlemen! Welcome to the Bridge Hotel! Ah! It is you, Thomson; I'm delighted to see you! Pray, bring the gentleman in."

Those were the first words I heard Mrs. Henry utter, and in a voice as sweet and clear as the sound of a silver bell. She had one of those rare musical voices that linger long in the memory— one that once heard will repeat itself to the memory years after, with a freshness unaffected by time. And such a face and form! As she stood there under the full blaze of a brightly-burning lamp, with her lips wreathed in a winning smile, and face aglow with welcome and expectation, I thought I had never seen such a beautiful creature. Her portrait had scarcely prepared me for such a soft, lovable expression as seemed incorporated with every lovely feature; and yet—and yet she was a murderess!

"I have brought you a gentleman that would be lost at the camp, Mrs. Henry," observed the sergeant as we entered—"an old friend who has, although so fortunate, not forgotten the unlucky policeman. But we can't be all rich, Mrs. Henry, and the station is no place for a gent accustomed to such comforts as Mr. Murray, Mrs. Henry, Mr. Murray. He is going to stop a week or so, Mrs. Henry, and I know you can give him rooms fit for a prince."

"Faith, Thomson, you'll have to spend your time with me

then, instead of me passing it with you," I said, as I bowed gallantly to the hostess. "The attractions of the Bridge Hotel will be greater than those of old friendship, I foresee."

"I hope so," responded Mrs. Henry, frankly, presenting her hand to my clasp.

It was a soft, warm, and jeweled hand, but I shuddered as I forced myself to press it warmly; yet the pressure increased the rich colour of Mrs. Henry's cheeks. "How strange that such a creature should still know how to blush!" I thought, as her eyes fell beneath a gaze that I tried to make as ardent as possible.

"I shall have the pleasure of showing you to your rooms. You are not going to leave us, Mr. Thomson?"

"I am sorry to say I must not stay now, but I'll be down bright and early in the morning;" and bidding us good-night, the sergeant took himself away, and left me to form my own opinion of the fascinating criminal.

And I formed it; but no words can describe my varied feelings as I sat for hours in her society within the enchanted precincts or the richly-furnished sitting-room, from which opened the terrible Red Room. It was impossible—utterly impossible, to resist the influence of a manner in which every allurement of tone and gesture and apparent sweetness assisted to overcome. She was fascination—its very self-possessor of the terrible fatal power of the brilliant serpent, that forces to destruction the victims of its gleaming eyes. In spite of my knowledge of this woman's character—in spite of the bloody memories that enveloped her as a mantle—in spite of the shudder that occasionally awoke me as from a dream, only to sleep again but too willingly, I was overpowered by this woman's presence, won by her sweet, affectionate voice, and bewildered by the liquid eyes that looked deeply into mine.

It was with an effort that I at last dragged myself away, and entered the Red Room, escorted by my fair hostess.

"I hope you will be comfortable here," she said laughingly, as she placed a candlestick on the luxuriously-appointed and lace-draped toilet; "and indeed you must be, unless, indeed, a ruffled heart as well as the couch want making!"

"And how else?" I exclaimed, seizing both fair hands as she

was leaving the chamber—"how can it be else? Who *could* rest after spending an evening with you?"

"Flatterer!" she answered, bending towards me as I drew her with both hands, but trying to disengage herself at the same time, "Flatterer! There now—let me go!"

"Until to-morrow. Thank heaven, only for a few hours!" I said passionately, as I released her, and she closed the door behind her rustling silks.

Yes, it's true! On my word as a man, it's as true as that I tell it! And I was in earnest; my blood was at fever heat, and my brain on fire with the glamour this accursed woman had cast over me. But it was quickly over; no sooner had the door closed and the influence of her presence been withdrawn, than I became faint with very shame for my own weakness, and fell like a child for support against the door that separated me from her.

There I leaned, and the red hue of the chamber seemed to cry out murder against me; the crimson Turkish carpet, the deep-red satin paper, with its cornice of gold, that decorated the walls; the heavy satin damask curtains that clouded the windows and fell around the couch like palls; all seemed to cry out blood against me, who had so soon forgotten the murderer in the woman, and found delight in her smile! I tell you I was faint, and had it not been for death, I would have lain down upon that bed for the rest that my sinking body required.

That couch! My God! *who* could rest there? Where the dying victims had writhed in agony, and from whence had gone up to heaven such aspirations for mercy and for vengeance. Could any human being sleep in such a haunted room? I went over to the splendid mirror and looked at my white, damp face, and the disordered hair, and the diamonds that gleamed and glistened in my shirt and on my fingers, and an idiotic wonder possessed me if I was myself at all, and had not been transformed by the spell of a sorceress into something infinitely worse than herself.

"I'm mad!" I thought, "Or I'm a coward! But this must not be. Rouse up, man, and do your work! Remember poor Edward Mansfield!"

I passed a most miserable and wretched night, sitting in a deep arm-chair, where I longed for light and morning as I had never longed before. Let a man be ever so little of a coward, he must feel uncomfortable in such a position. When the candle had burned itself out the darkness was intense, and every sound startled. I knew that midnight had witnessed murder in that fated chamber, and that I was myself at the mercy of the assassins every moment, but I did not fear attack as yet, since I had exhibited nothing to tempt their cupidity sufficiently, yet a strange horror drove sleep far away for hours.

But at length I slept, and was awakened by a peculiar knock at the door. I knew the signal, and admitted young Edward Mansfield.

"Is it so late?" I asked. "And Thomson and your brother?"

"Are outside. All is prepared." The lad was pale as death, and he trembled violently as he looked on the bed of crimson hue, "My God, what I suffered there!" was his exclamation, as he fell into a seat.

Hurriedly, I freshened my toilet a little, and leaving Edward in the chamber, I went out.

How comfortable everything looked in the handsome sitting-room! A bright fire burned in the grate, and close to it was drawn a breakfast-table set for two, and glittering with white-ness of china and gleaming of plate and damask of linen. We were to breakfast together then—my enslaver and I. Ah!

I passed out towards the other building—for that in which I had slept was an attached cottage entirely shut out from the hotel save by one door of communication. In the bar I found Thomson and George Mansfield, who had his face as much concealed as possible, to hide his likeness to his brother. Schwitz was attending in the bar—a heavy-faced man, with a suspicious, silent manner, and a furtive look, that would have told against him anywhere.

"I leave Schwitz to you," I said to Thomson in a low tone; "and for God's sake, don't let him escape. Cheer up, Mansfield—we are near the end."

Hastily swallowing the drink which my friend had ordered—and of which, truth to say, I stood much in need—I returned to the breakfast-room to meet Mrs. Henry just entering the door. How fresh and lovely she looked! Attired in a floating muslin, with every addition in lace and ornament that could add to the attraction of her appearance, her beauty was almost irresistible, had I not been so fearfully changed from the fool of the previous night. Even as it was, it went hard with me to meet the winning, and apparently sincere smile with which I was greeted, and to know that my act was about to drive smiles from that face forever.

"Ah! You are then up, Mr. Murray. I have been quite longing for your appearance. I thought you squatter gentlemen were very early risers. Shall we have breakfast? But how pale you do look! I am afraid you have rested badly."

She said this with that dangerous conscious smile that had so fettered and bewildered me the previous evening. There was in her arch look an evident allusion to my complimentary words on parting at the bedroom door, but she met no answering look in my stony face. I was adamant once more. God knows what she saw in my face to arouse her conscience however, but she did see something, and her face grew pale as a corpse as she still gazed at me, with the light fading out of her eyes, and an unspeakable terror growing into them.

"You have not slept," she murmured, unconsciously as it were.

"No, I have not slept," I answered, bending down over her, and looking more closely into the trembling woman's face. "Could *you* sleep in there?"

And I pointed with my finger at the door of the Red Room.

She did not answer; she only raised her hand and clutched convulsively at her white throat, as if she were choking.

"Come with me," I continued, "and I will show you the thing that kept me from sleeping in your red chamber."

And I led her helplessly to the door of the bedroom, and almost lifted her inside.

Edward Mansfield was sitting in the scarlet arm-chair opposite the door as I pushed the murderess in before him; but at the first sight of the heartless fiend, he started to his feet, and held out both hands, as if to ward her off. As for Mrs. Henry, who doubtless saw in Edward's pale face, contrasted as it was by the deep red of the dimly lighted apartment, that of one risen from the dead, she threw up her arms in the very extremity of terror, and cried out a cry sufficient to curdle the blood in a fainthearted man's veins.

"Oh, God! The dead—the dead—the dead!"

"No, the living!" I interposed—"the living whom He has preserved by an almost miracle to work out His earthly vengeance against the murderer. There Edward, the criminal is secured."

And I clasped the handcuffs on the rounded wrists I had so lately admired.

She never spoke afterwards, at least during the day and night which followed. She was as one crushed under the weight of Almighty justice. I doubt if, from the moment of her arrest she was ever fully conscious of all the horrors of her position, but only as one who lived in a terrible dream, from which only a violent and fearful death awaited her.

Long ere this scene in the Red Room was enacted, Schwitz had been secured, and acted the part of the absolute coward, pleading for mercy, whining, sobbing, tearing his hair, and accusing his accomplice of inciting him to do it all. He confessed to everything, and revealed murders that had never been suspected. With his assistance, a goodly "plant" was discovered buried in a secure place, and with the rest, Edward's bag intact.

Sergeant Thomson had the satisfaction of overhauling the secret of the chamber of horrors, when a most complicated arrangement of machinery to assist the work of murder was brought to light. The back of the bed was indeed moveable, and the cord, that terminated the sleeping victim's life almost instantaneously, was worked by a small windlass, that the fair hand of Mrs. Henry had often turned. Altogether it was a frightful trap, and enough to make the greatest believer almost lose faith in the humanity which could practice such cruelty for gold.

The murderers were both hung. Schwitz was believed to have died of fear before the drop fell, and his partner in guilt suffered as one utterly unconscious of what is passing around her. Pray turn over the leaf, and hide that fear-recalling face in the "Detective's Album."

RICHARD DOWLING

(1846–1898)

Apparently "Negative Evidence," which was published in the magazine *East and West* in 1888, was the first detective story to employ photographic evidence. The invention of photography had been announced in France in 1839, though it was still not a common hobby but rather a craft that required expertise. At about the time this story was published, some of Arthur Conan Doyle's first published writing recounted his interest in photography.

Richard Dowling was born in Clonmel, in County Tipperary in southern Ireland, in 1846. He began his writing career as a journalist for the liberal periodical *The Nation*, and edited a humor magazine entitled *Zozimus*, named after a legendary street rhymer. (The fame of this "Last of the Gleemen" lingers in Dublin, where both a bar and an art gallery bear his name.) Dowling lived only fifty-two years but left behind more than two dozen books, mostly thrillers such as *The Mystery of Killard* and *A Dark Intruder*, many of them triple-deckers published by the London firm of Ward and Downey—the latter partner apparently his cousin. A mark of Dowling's fame at his height was that he was asked, along with Arthur Conan Doyle and Bram Stoker and twenty-one other authors, to contribute a chapter to the consecutive novel *The Fate of Fenella*, which appeared in weekly installments in *The Gentlewoman*. Male and female writers took turns adding a chapter. "The plot is ridiculous; the characters waver and change from chapter to chapter," complained one reviewer, and then conceded, "but there are occasionally strong situations, and scraps of fairly good dialogue."

Dowling could be a charming writer. His 1887 collection *Ignorant Essays* gathers informal rambles about bookish matters, including what is probably the only passionate celebration of Nuttall's *Standard Dictionary of the English Language*. Readers interested in Victorian culture ought to seek out Dowling's lively survey *London Town: Sketches of London Life and Character*, which features visits to such legendary sites as the Bow Street police court and the Billingsgate fish market, portraits of a hansom cabdriver and a street "flower girl," and even rambles to Madame Tussauds and the new underground railway. It lacks the admirable social-justice crusade of Henry Mayhew's *London Labour and the London Poor*, but in its appreciation of diverse humanity stands companionably beside Dickens's *Sketches by Boz*.

NEGATIVE EVIDENCE

John Hastings of Barford had, as a matter of course, promised to dine at Charcombe House that evening. The next morning he was to be married to Maud Bathurst, the only child of Mr Frank Bathurst, who owned Charcombe House. John had seen Maud the day before, and it had been arranged he was to come over in the afternoon of this day. He had some business to transact in Dunfield, the nearest town, and as soon as he had made an end of it, he told Maud he should walk over Charcombe Hill, so that they might have a few hours together before dinner. She was not to come to meet him, as he did not know how long his business would detain him in Dunfield. After dinner he would drive back to his own place, The Oaks. It would take less time to walk from Dunfield to Charcombe over the hill, than to drive round the hill from the town to the House. Hence he had decided upon walking. Maud might expect him at any time between four and six. Dinner would not be until half-past seven.

The marriage between John Hastings and Maud Bathurst had been arranged by mutual inclination, and with the cordial approval of her parents. Indeed, it seemed as though Nature and Fate had destined them for one another. He was tall and dark and sincere, she small and fair and light-hearted and affectionate. He was alone in the world, and in choosing a wife need consult no one but the girl upon whom he had set his heart, and her relations or guardians. The lands of Charcombe, which in time would be hers, adjoined the lands of Barford, which now were his. The families had been friendly neighbours for generations. Both in London and in the neighbourhood of their own homes Maud and he had met continually for years, and successive heads of the families had wished that the two races might be joined in one, the two properties go down to a common heir. But somehow this hope had never seemed likely to be realised until now. Formerly there had never been a marriageable heir when there happened to be a marriageable heiress, and Mr and Mrs Bathurst rejoiced that a traditional aspiration was about to be fulfilled at last.

As for the two young people themselves, they cared nothing for traditional aspirations. They were simply in love with one another, and they wanted to get married and live all their lives together, just as do thousands, millions of other people, who have neither ancestors nor acres.

It was bright July weather. As four o'clock struck in the tiny tower that stood over the gate of the coach-house, the sun appeared hardly lower in the heavens than at noon. It seemed tireless, and full of light that could never die. It was king absolute of the pale azure realms, and ruled in lonely despotism, its sway unchallenged by subtlest conspirator cloud.

The pendulum of the clock in the tower swung backward and forward with a dull, mechanical, despairing tick, tick. It had no more interest in its work than a felon at the oar. The sun noiselessly continued its imperceptible, invincible triumph towards the west. It did not move because of any law that bound it, but because of its slowness to remain.

In the sky the only events are clouds; in the tower the only events are hours. But it matters not whether clouds came into the sky or the hammer of the clock struck the hour, the sun and pendulum went on unheeding. The sun might be lost in the clouds, the ticking of the pendulum drowned in the booming of the bell, but the progress of the sun westward and the oscillation of the pendulum over the central point of earth suffered no mutation.

From her own window she could best get sight of John as he came over the brow of the hill. She knew the point of the hill from which his head would strike upwards against the pale sky. She was in her room, and on that point her blue eyes were fixed when the clock struck four.

As soon as she should see him, she would fly on tip-toe out of the room, along the corridor and down the stairs. Should she meet anyone, she would slacken her pace and go demurely— except that someone was her mother. If she met her mother she would kiss hands and flee past without abating her speed, for her mother would know and understand that she was speeding because he was coming over the hill. Once in the open air she would have to go quietly, for many windows looked on the lawn. But as soon as she was round the garden wall she might hasten again until she came to their favourite resting-place, the rustic bench under the great chestnut-tree. There no one could see them meet, and by the time she had reached the chestnut he would be near enough to speak to her—to speak to her! And then they should sit down and rest.

Maud waited minute after minute, and yet that figure did not start up against the sky. She knew he had many things to do in Dunfield that day, and, young and inexperienced as she was, she felt that when a man has many things to do, although he may happen to be a bridegroom-elect, he cannot always calculate to a nicety how long his business may take him, for though he may be a model of punctuality he may meet men who do not estimate that royal virtue at its proper worth.

John had said he would be with her between four and six, and it was not yet five. It would, of course, have been delightful if he had appeared on the top of the hill just as the clock struck four, but then one must not expect in this ordinary climate and time to have things fall out as they do in an Eastern fairy tale of long ago. Even to desire such a miracle would be childish and absurd.

She leaned against the window for support, and kept her wide-open blue eyes fixed on that heather-clad slanting ridge. Gradually, as minutes of expectancy unfulfilled went by, the brightness and animation faded from her face, until it became almost pensive, and the full rose-red of her cheeks paled to pink. She put one of her hands upon the sash of the window, and leaned her forehead against the glass. This pushed her hat back, and disclosed the rich waves of golden hair that lay over the mantling white forehead. She was physically tired of standing so long in almost the same position, but she was not conscious she was tired. She only thought—

"He will come presently. The moment his head rises above the hill I shall see him, and, oh, then!"

Suddenly she started. The clock struck five. She looked at

the sun. It was plainly lower in the heavens than when she looked at it last, as she began her vigil. She looked to the east. A low, slender smoke-coloured cloud lay along the horizon, visible between the house and the precipitous ends of the hills. Still the light was superb.

John had now got half way through the time he had allowed himself. But after all this was the better way; for, while before it struck five there was, let her say, one chance of his appearing each minute, now there were two chances. In the hour gone by luck might keep him away from her for a couple of hours. Now that was impossible. All the rich chances of his coming were packed and crowded into the little space of sixty minutes. Every second that went by brought him nearer to her. She was so easy about him, now that it was less than an hour from the time of his absence to the time of his presence, that she might as well make herself comfortable.

She sat down, leaning her elbow on the high window sill and keeping her eyes still fixed on the brow of the hill.

As minutes went by those between the present moment and six grew thicker and thicker with promises of him, until suppressed excitement took the place of languor, and she fancied she could feel him pressing forward towards the verge of that hill.

Still the hard, sharp line of the distant heather lay flat and unbroken against the darkening blue of the sky. The margin of smoke-colour cloud had advanced far westward, and down in the east lay a sombre shadow under a bank of dun vapour.

The sun passed slowly westward. The pendulum of the clock swung monotonously backward and forward with its slow, unwearying tick, tick.

Once more the girl started. She stood hastily up. The clock had begun to strike six.

Surely before it had finished striking he would appear. He had said six as the last moment which could delay him from her. It could not be that he would tarry beyond the last second of the hour.

The clock ceased striking. The girl sighed, and, sitting down, clasped her hands in her lap. Still no figure rose between her and the sky above the edge of that hill.

It was strange to her that on this, the last evening of her maiden life, he should for the first time be late in keeping his appointment. They had now been engaged six months, and during all that time he had never been one moment late. She had already told herself that one or several of many things might have delayed him beyond all reasonable calculation. But when the heart is anxious or hungry there is small consolation in the reason. She did not want to think he was blameless in being late. What she wanted was his presence, not a knowledge of what caused his absence. In a short time the ordinary common-place guests of the evening would begin to arrive, and she would have to go down and meet them, and talk dull, pointless nothings to them, while her heart and its attendant senses were in expectation on that hill-top.

Half an hour went by. The sun was now getting low in the west.

The clock went on impassively. Maud's spirits fell low. A feeling akin to fear had gradually begun to gather in her mind. She resolved upon one thing: Here she would wait till the last moment. Then, when duties to others called, she should go and try to smile as though she had suffered no disappointment.

What!—seven o'clock striking and yet he had not come! The sun was now far down in the west. It would set in about an hour. The last day of her girlhood would come to an end when the clock struck again. Surely, surely it was hard he had not come. There was now no further time for watching or waiting. She should dress and go down. She had put on her hat and gloves in vain. Well, it would not do to be gloomy. It would not do to show she was disappointed. She did not blame him for not coming. She was only sorry he had not come. She knew he had to go to a number of places in Dunfield—his lawyer's and his banker's, and several tradesmen's, and the post-office; but still it was a pity he had not come. There was so much she had to say to him in those two hours she had promised herself with him before dinner. Well, there was no use in fretting now, and perhaps, after all, when he did come, when a little while hence she turned round and unexpectedly saw him, the delight of that moment would recompense her for the disappointment of this.

Dinner came and went, and brought no lover—no message from him, no news of him. A hundred different harmless and blameless reasons were assigned by her father and mother and sympathetic friends for his absence. But they fell idly into her ears. If all was well, why was not he here? If anything were wrong, what was it? If anything had happened to him, then— She did not finish the thought. She did not weep.

What would happen tomorrow?

Next morning came, and brought no news of John Hastings. The hour for the marriage came, but no bridegroom with it. In the meantime inquiries had been made.

As far as could be discovered, the history of John Hastings's action the previous day was as follows:

At about noon he arrived in Dunfield, put up his horse and dog-cart at "The Oaks", and went first to his lawyer, with whom he had a long interview. Nothing of any unusual interest occurred at this meeting; it was merely for the purpose of arranging tedious and uninteresting details connected with the missing man's approaching and with the routine business of the six weeks which Mr Hastings intended passing abroad after the ceremony.

From his lawyer's Mr Hastings went to the bank, out of which he drew in Bank of England notes, a sum of £300. Mr Hastings did not stay more than ten minutes in the bank. After this he called on three tradesmen, who were concerned in certain alterations and repairs going on at his place, Barford.

When he had finished with the tradesmen, he went to "The Oaks", the principal inn of the town, and gave orders that his dog-cart should be sent for him to Charcombe House, so as to arrive about eleven o'clock. He said he was going to walk over the hill to Charcombe, which he expected to reach at four. He owed the landlord of "The Oaks" a baiting account, and paid it out of the bundle of notes he had that day got from the bank. He paid the money in the bar. Several people saw him pay the money, and, in honour of his marriage, he left some money with the landlord to be distributed among the servants and hangers-on at the inn. Then he set off in the direction of the House, taking the way that led over the hill. From that time to this he had not been seen by anyone.

What humour did he seem in?

The very best possible. He spoke in a friendly way to everyone, and received congratulations and good wishes with cheerful graciousness.

Was it known if he had any enemies, if there were any people who owed him a grudge?

As far as was known he had no enemy, and no one owed him a grudge. On the contrary, he was popular and universally respected in the neighbourhood. It was the general impression that no one in or near Dunfield would do him harm.

Then, if no one in the district was likely to injure him, and if he had been injured or made away with, in all likelihood a stranger had had something to do with it. Were there any strangers or suspicious-looking people in the town? Particularly was any stranger or suspicious-looking person in the bank when he got the money?

No. Mr Hastings was the only one in the bank, beyond the officials, when he drew the money.

Was any strange or suspicious-looking person in "The Oaks" when he so injudiciously pulled out that bundle of notes to pay the land lord?

Ah! that was a different matter. Wait a moment. Yes. Now it was recollected, while Mr Hastings was paying his account in the bar, a man named William Laycroft, a photographer he appeared to be, who had been staying at "The Oaks" a few days, came downstairs with his apparatus in his hand, and passed through. He left the bar before Mr Hastings, taking his apparatus with him, and went in the direction of Charcombe Hill, but not exactly by the same route as the missing man had taken.

Where was the photographer now? Had he left the town?

It was believed not. He had been seen that morning at "The Oaks", and the impression was that there he might still be staying.

The photographer was sought at "The Oaks", and found there.

He was a low, wiry, thin man, of swarthy complexion and nervous manner. He was clad in rusty black cloth coat, waistcoat, and trousers, and wore a black silk hat, much the worse for wear. His clothes fitted him ill, and his hat was too big for him, so that he had every now and then to thrust it back off his forehead, or it would have come down on his nose.

When first interrogated as to his movements the day before, he said that was no business of anyone but himself, and that he did not intend giving any answers; but upon having matters explained, and the gravity of the position pointed out to him, he said he would reply to any question. He offered in extenuation of his reluctance to speak when first asked, the statement that he was secretly getting together a certain class of photograph landscapes for a particular purpose, and if this purpose became known, someone else might forestall him, and so render all his labour up to this valueless. His account of his actions after leaving "The Oaks" the day before was:

He had made up his mind to take a photograph of a piece of broken ground on the Dunfield side of Charcombe Hill. He set off at a brisk pace and soon after gained the place he had selected for placing his camera. The point (which he minutely described, commanded the route by which the missing man would go) was in a little hollow well sheltered from sun and wind, and sight for that matter, because a large stone hung over the camera, and, save by standing directly in front of what he might describe as a cave, no one could see him or his instrument.

The day was most favourable to his purposes, the air being pure and the light full and strong. He had prepared almost everything for his work before setting out from "The Oaks". In a few minutes all was ready, and he slipped off the cap. As he had explained, he wanted this photograph for a particular purpose, and one of the essentials for this purpose was that the period of exposure should be long. He lit his pipe and looked around him, although the plate was ready for removal. When he had everything tidy once more he set off back to the inn, encountering no one on the way. He had not seen Mr Hastings or anyone else on the hill, or from the time he began to ascend the hill until he got to the bottom again. He now wished to apologise for his brusqueness of manner when first asked about his experience on the hill yesterday. His temper had been somewhat soured by the ill success of that plate; for, although the day had been everything his heart could wish, the plate turned out defective. There was an unaccountable smudge on the right-hand side of it at the horizon line.

The people who were listening had paid great attention to all his story, until he came to his apology and grievance towards the end. They felt that the apology ought to have come earlier, and that the grievance ought not to have been mentioned at all. It was little short of impertinence to intrude upon so grave and anxious an inquiry as the present, the success or want of success with a paltry photograph negative.

All felt, moreover, that though there was nothing like evidence against William Laycroft, the itinerant photographer, his position was far from being free from suspicion. The informal inquiry was being held by a few friends of both families in the little private parlour of "The Oaks".

As soon as Laycroft had finished his story he withdrew. It was desirable that everything should be kept as quiet as possible for the present, and so, as yet, the police had not been communicated with. A couple of men had gone over the road John Hastings had intended following, but they had come back with no tidings of the missing man. The friends were beginning to think of calling in the police at last. It was now past noon, and the wedding could not take place that day. Half a dozen different scouts, besides those who went over the hill, had been sent out, but each returned with no word or clue.

All at once, and without a word of warning, William Laycroft, the itinerant photographer, burst into the room in a state of great excitement. He held a thin film of paper in his hand.

"Quick!" he cried, looking round him and holding up the limp piece of paper. "Quick, I say! Some men come with me. I know the ground well. I've been over it all before, I think. Quick, I say! Who will follow me?"

The other men stared at one another. They thought him mad.

"I call you no men if you sit there and will not follow me. I'm going up the hill to find the body of the gentleman you are looking for, the gentleman whom, I could see by your looks, you thought a while ago I had murdered. Whoever wants to be at the finding of the body of Mr John Hastings will follow me."

There was something startling, and at the same time impressive, in the man's manner, and the men in the parlour rose and asked, "Where? where?"

"Follow me!" he cried, and they could get no other words from him.

He led the way up the hill, but kept more to the east than the way John Hastings had taken. The men told him this. "Follow me," was all the reply he would deign.

For some time he held on almost due east, and then made a sharp turn north. This brought him, on a lower level than the hill, to a kind of shelf here running along the whole side of the hill. Over this shelf an almost perpendicular wall of rock rose to the height of forty feet. The shelf or ledge, which was quite level, appeared like a road cut into the side of the hill.

The little party kept on at a quick pace for half an hour. All at once Laycroft stopped and looked eagerly around. Nothing unusual was to be seen. He then looked up the face of the rock. Here, also, was nothing unusual.

He seemed inexpressibly perplexed and confounded. The men who had accompanied him were about to turn and desert him, when all were startled by hearing a strange sound, a moan from some part of the cliff above them.

"He is there! He is there, and alive!" said Laycroft.

Search was instantly made, and at last John Hastings was found jammed between two rocks a few feet below the cliff.

When he was extricated, and had recovered somewhat, he said that everything had gone well with him until, upon reaching a point a little south of where they found him, and a couple of hundred yards further west, he received a tremendous blow on the back of the head, and he remembered nothing till he awoke in the middle of the night where he was found. Here he was helpless, and too weak to call out or give any sufficient sign.

Laycroft's account was that, after his interrogation in the parlour, he "printed an impression from the negative taken the evening before, and upon examining the horizon line at the right or left-hand corner he came to the conclusion that this defect was caused by something moving over the heather from west to east in the direction of the horizon. Upon scrutinising the blur carefully with a magnifying glass, he came to the further conclusion that there was a human figure for a brief moment between the lens and the sky. Still further examination showed him that this figure carried another in its arms. At this moment he felt convinced that this would prove to be the photograph of the last scene in a tragedy.

However, although John Hastings got a bad shaking and lost £300, he did not die. The man who robbed him and tried to kill him was never found. The marriage had to be postponed for a month. There is now no further relique of that afternoon's bad work save the negative of a certain photograph hanging in Maud's room, a negative which John says has been, excepting herself, the cause of the greatest mercy ever shown to man.

CHARLES W. CHESNUTT

(1858–1932)

"I think I must write a book," Charles W. Chesnutt confided to his journal when he was twenty-two years old in 1880. "I am almost afraid to undertake a book so early and with so little experience in composition." He undertook this dream with passionate energy, however, and soon acquired the experience he sought. When he died fifty-two years later, having lived from before the Civil War through the Harlem Renaissance, Chesnutt left behind a hugely influential legacy as a pioneer Black writer. He was celebrated as an author of works of fiction, who at the start of his career published regularly in New York literary magazines such as *The Atlantic Monthly*.

He began as many writers do, with short pieces for local periodicals, then trying those with an ever larger reach. Chesnutt's career added books to his magazine work by the end of the nineteenth century, with publication of two volumes of short stories. His early stories resulted in interest from Houghton Mifflin, the respected Boston publishing house that had evolved from the firm of Ticknor and Fields, the first white-owned company to publish a book promoting the abolition of slavery. After rejecting a couple of Chesnutt's novel manuscripts, Houghton Mifflin published *The Conjure Woman* in 1899, which blended the harsh daily reality of the postwar South with the magic and occult powers from African folklore. Later the same year Houghton Mifflin published Chesnutt's second collection, *The Wife of His Youth and Other Stories of the Color-Line*. This same annus mirabilis saw publication of his biography of Frederick Douglass.

Chesnutt's paternal grandmother had been enslaved, his grandfather her enslaver; his mother was from a similar racial mix but in what Chesnutt called a "free mulatto" family. He described himself as "seven-eighths white," but that was enough to make him legally Black—*octoroon*, by the terminology of his era's racism. According to contemporary descriptions and photographs, he could have "passed" as white. He chose not to. Marriage between Black and white people had been illegal since the 1600s, but many white people accepted that the hidden rape of Black women was always part of slavery and remained common throughout Reconstruction and beyond. Thus Chesnutt returned often to the theme of miscegenation, with a clarity that drew fierce criticism from white supremacy's eager deniers and defenders. But at the same time, the elegance and clarity of his writing drew serious literary attention. Not surprisingly, however, Chesnutt's books did not sell well. Supporting himself as a stenographer, he kept writing.

He insisted upon writing about the horrors of lynching and other forms of terrorism employed against people of color, and about the systematic disenfranchisement resulting from the inequalities of segregation. His commitment to honest realism included careful attention to spoken language, including how Black characters spoke differently after education and exposure to the larger world and how those who could "pass" for white learned to code-switch. As would Ralph Ellison and other writers later, Chesnutt also insisted upon historically accurate language as a reflection of racist characters, as in his use of the most objectionable word a white person can call a Black person.

In his 1900 novel *The House Behind the Cedars*, he wrote about "passing" three decades before Nella Larsen made it the title of her own brilliant novel. A courageous, insightful writer, Chesnutt seems now well ahead of his time, but some people of his own era recognized and celebrated his talent. The novelist and critic William Dean Howells praised Chesnutt's stories in *The Atlantic*. As early as 1901, the *Boston Evening Transcript* was profiling Chesnutt, talking with him about his background and his working methods.

"The Sheriff's Children" appeared in the November 7, 1889, issue of *The Independent*.

THE SHERIFF'S CHILDREN

Branson County, North Carolina, is in a sequestered district of one of the staidest and most conservative States of the Union. Society in Branson County is almost primitive in its simplicity. Most of the white people own their own farms, and even before the War there were no very wealthy families to force their neighbors, by comparison, into the category of "poor whites."

To Branson County, as to most rural communities in the South, the War is the one historical event that overshadows all others. It is the era from which all local chronicles are dated— births, deaths, marriages, storms, freshets. No description of the life of any Southern community would be perfect that failed to emphasize the all-pervading influence of the great conflict.

And yet the fierce tide of war that had rushed through the cities and along the great highways of the country, had, comparatively speaking, but slightly disturbed the sluggish current of life in this region remote from railroads and navigable streams. To the north in Virginia, to the west in Tennessee, and all along the seaboard the war had raged; but the thunder of its cannon had not disturbed the echoes of Branson County, where the loudest sounds heard were the crack of some hunter's rifle, the baying of some deep-mouthed hound, or the yodel of some tuneful Negro on his way through the pine forest. To the east, Sherman's army had passed on its march to the sea; but no straggling band of "bummers" had penetrated the confines of Branson County. The war, it is true, had robbed the county of the flower of its young manhood; but the burden of taxation, the doubt and uncertainty of the conflict, and the sting of ultimate defeat, had been borne by the people with an apathy that robbed misfortune of half its sharpness.

The nearest approach to town life afforded by Branson County is found in the little village of Troy, the county-seat, a hamlet with a population of four or five hundred.

Ten years makes little difference in the appearance of these remote Southern towns. If a railroad is built through one of them, it infuses some enterprise; the social corpse is galvanized by the fresh blood of civilization that pulses along the farthest ramifications of our great system of commercial highways. At the period of which I write, no railroad had come to Troy. If a traveler, accustomed to the bustling life of cities, could have ridden through Troy on a summer day, he might easily have fancied himself in a deserted village. Around him he would have seen weather-beaten houses, innocent of paint, the shingled roofs in many instances covered with a rich growth of moss. Here and there he would have met a razor-backed hog lazily rooting his way along the principal thoroughfare; and more than once be would probably have had to disturb the slumbers of some yellow dog, dozing away the hours in the ardent sunshine, and reluctantly yielding up his place in the middle of the dusty road.

On Saturdays the village presented a somewhat livelier appearance, and the shade-trees around the court-house square and along Front Street served as hitching-posts for a goodly number of horses and mules and stunted oxen, belonging to the farmer-folk who had come in to trade at the two or three local stores.

A murder was a rare event in Branson County. Every well-informed citizen could tell the number of homicides committed in the county for fifty years back, and whether the slayer, in any given instance, had escaped, either by flight or acquittal, or had suffered the penalty of the law. So, when it became known in Troy early one Friday morning in summer, about ten years after the war, that old Captain Walker, who had served in Mexico under Scott, and had left an arm on the field of Gettysburg, had been foully murdered during the night, there was intense excitement in the village. Business was practically suspended, and the citizens gathered in little groups to discuss the murder, and speculate upon the identity of the murderer. It transpired from testimony at the coroner's inquest, held during the morning, that a strange mulatto had been seen going in the direction of Captain Walker's house the night before, and had been met going away from Troy early Friday morning, by a farmer on his way to town. Other circumstances seemed to connect the stranger with the crime. The sheriff organized a *posse* to search for him, and early in the evening, when most of the citizens of Troy were at supper, the suspected man was brought in and lodged in the county jail.

By the following morning the news of the capture had spread to the farthest limits of the county. A much larger number of people than usual came to town that Saturday—bearded men in straw hats and blue homespun shirts, and butternut trousers of great amplitude of material and vagueness of outline; women in homespun frocks and slat-bonnets, with faces as expressionless as the dreary sandhills which gave them a meager sustenance.

The murder was almost the sole topic of conversation. A steady stream of curious observers visited the house of mourning, and gazed upon the rugged face of the old veteran, now stiff and cold in death; and more than one eye dropped a tear at the remembrance of the cheery smile, and the joke—sometimes superannuated, generally feeble, but always good-natured—with which the captain had been wont to greet his acquaintances. There was a growing sentiment of anger among these stern men, toward the murderer who had thus cut down their friend, and a strong feeling that ordinary justice was too slight a punishment for such a crime.

Toward noon there was an informal gathering of citizens in Dan Tyson's store.

"I hear it 'lowed that Square Kyahtah's too sick ter hole co'te this evenin'," said one, "an' that the purlim'nary hearin' 'll haf ter go over tel nex' week."

A look of disappointment went round the crowd.

"Hit's the durndes', meanes' murder ever committed in this caounty," said another, with moody emphasis.

"I s'pose the Nigger 'lowed the Cap'n had some greenbacks," observed a third speaker.

"The Cap'n," said another, with an air of superior information, "has left two bairls of Confedrit money, which he 'spected 'ud be good some day er nuther."

This statement gave rise to a discussion of the speculative

value of Confederate money; but in a little while the conversation returned to the murder.

"Hangin' air too good fer the murderer," said one; "he oughter be burnt, stidier bein' hung."

There was an impressive pause at this point, during which a jug of moonlight whisky went the round of the crowd.

"Well," said a round-shouldered farmer, who, in spite of his peaceable expression and faded gray eye, was known to have been one of the most daring followers of a rebel guerrilla chieftain, "what air yer gwine ter do about it? Ef you fellers air gwine ter sed down an' let a wuthless Nigger kill the bes' white man in Branson, an' not say nuthin' ner do nuthin', *I'll* move outen the caounty."

This speech gave tone and direction to the rest of the conversation. Whether the fear of losing the round-shouldered farmer operated to bring about the result or not is immaterial to this narrative; but, at all events, the crowd decided to lynch the Negro. They agreed that this was the least that could be done to avenge the death of their murdered friend, and that it was a becoming way in which to honor his memory. They had some vague notions of the majesty of the law and the rights of the citizen, but in the passion of the moment these sunk into oblivion; a white man had been killed by a Negro.

"The Cap'n was an ole sodger," said one of his friends, solemnly. "He'll sleep better when he knows that a co'te-martial has be'n hilt an' jestice done."

By agreement the lynchers were to meet at Tyson's store at five o'clock in the afternoon, and proceed thence to the jail, which was situated down the Lumberton Dirt Road (as the old turnpike antedating the plank-road was called), about half a mile south of the courthouse. When the preliminaries of the lynching had been arranged, and a committee appointed to manage the affair, the crowd dispersed, some to go to their dinners, and some to quietly secure recruits for the lynching party.

It was twenty minutes to five o'clock, when an excited Negro, panting and perspiring, rushed up to the back door of Sheriff Campbell's dwelling, which stood at a little distance from the jail and somewhat farther than the latter building from the court-house. A turbaned colored woman came to the door in response to the Negro's knock.

"Hoddy, Sis' Nance."

"Hoddy, Brer Sam."

"Is de shurff in," inquired the Negro.

"Yas, Brer Sam, he's eatin' his dinner," was the answer.

"Will yer ax 'im ter step ter de do' a minute, Sis' Nance?"

The woman went into the dining-room, and a moment later the sheriff came to the door. He was a tall, muscular man, of a ruddier complexion that is usual among Southerners. A pair of keen, deep-set gray eyes looked out from under bushy eyebrows, and about his mouth was a masterful expression, which a full beard, once sandy in color, but now profusely sprinkled with gray, could not entirely conceal. The day was hot; the sheriff had discarded his coat and vest, and had his white shirt open at the throat.

"What do you want, Sam?" he inquired of the Negro, who stood hat in hand, wiping the moisture from his face with a ragged shirt-sleeve.

"Shurff, dey gwine ter hang de pris'ner w'at's lock' up in de jail. Dey're comin' dis a-way now. I wuz layin' down on a sack er corn down at de sto', behine a pile er flour-bairls, w'en I hearn Doc' Cain en Kunnel Wright talkin' erbout it. I slip' outen de back do', en run here as fas' as I could. I hearn you say down ter de sto' once't dat you wouldn't let nobody take a pris'ner 'way fum you widout walkin' over yo' dead body, en I thought I'd let you know 'fo dey come, so yer could pertec' de pris'ner."

The sheriff listened calmly, but his face grew firmer, and a determined gleam lit up his gray eyes. His frame grew more erect, and he unconsciously assumed the attitude of a soldier who momentarily expects to meet the enemy face to face.

"Much obliged, Sam," he answered. "I'll protect the prisoner. Who 's coming?"

"I dunno who-all *is* comin'," replied the Negro. "Dere's Mistah McSwayne, en Doc' Cain, en Maje' McDonal', en Kunnel Wright, en a heap er yuthers. I wuz so skeered I done furgot mo'd'n half un em. I spec' dey mus' be mos' here by dis time, so I'll git outen de way; fer I doan want nobody fer ter think I wuz mix' up in dis business." The Negro glanced nervously down the road toward the town, and made a movement as if to go away.

"Won't you have some dinner first?" asked the sheriff.

The Negro looked longingly in at the open door, and sniffed the appetizing odor of boiled pork and collards.

"I ain't got no time fer ter tarry, Shurff," he said, "but Sis' Nance mought gin me sump'n I could kyar in my han' en eat on de way."

A moment later Nancy brought him a huge sandwich, consisting of split corn-pone, with a thick slice of fat bacon inserted between the halves, and a couple of baked yams. The Negro hastily replaced his ragged hat on his head, dropped the yams in the pocket of his capacious trousers, and taking the sandwich in his hand, hurried across the road and disappeared in the woods beyond.

The sheriff re-entered the house, and put on his coat and hat. He then took down a double-barreled shot-gun and loaded it with buckshot. Filling the chambers of a revolver with fresh cartridges, he slipped it into the pocket of the sack-coat which he wore.

A comely young woman in a calico dress watched these proceedings with anxious surprise.

"Where are you goin', Pa," she asked. She had not heard the conversation with the Negro.

"I am goin' over to the jail," responded the sheriff. "There's a mob comin' this way to lynch the Nigger we've got locked up. But they won't do it," he added, with emphasis.

"Oh, Pa! don't go!" pleaded the girl, clinging to his arm; "they'll shoot you if you don't give him up."

"You never mind me, Polly," said her father reassuringly, as he gently unclasped her hands from his arm. "I'll take care of myself and the prisoner, too. There ain't a man in Branson County that would shoot me. Besides, I have faced fire too often to be scared away from my duty. You keep close in the house," he continued, "and if any one disturbs you just use the old horse-pistol in the top bureau drawer. It's a little old-fashioned, but it did good work a few years ago."

The young girl shuddered at this sanguinary allusion, but made no further objection to her father's departure.

The sheriff of Branson was a man far above the average of the community in wealth, education and social position. His had been one of the few families in the county that before the war had owned large estates and numerous slaves. He had graduated at the State University at Chapel Hill, and had kept up some acquaintance with current literature and advanced thought. He had traveled some in his youth, and was looked up to in the county as an authority on all subjects connected with the outer world. At first an ardent supporter of the Union, he had opposed the secession movement in his native State as long as opposition availed to stem the tide of public opinion. Yielding at last to the force of circumstances, he had entered the Confederate service rather late in the war, and served with distinction through several campaigns, rising in time to the rank of colonel. After the war he had taken the oath of allegiance, and had been chosen by the people as the most available candidate for the office of sheriff, to which he had been elected without opposition. He had filled the office for several terms, and was universally popular with his constituents.

Colonel, or Sheriff Campbell, as he was indifferently called, as the military or the civil title happened to be most important in the opinion of the person addressing him, had a high sense of the responsibility attaching to his office. He had sworn to do his duty faithfully, and he knew what his duty was, as sheriff, perhaps more clearly than he had apprehended it in other passages of his life. It was, therefore, with no uncertainty in regard to his course that he prepared his weapons and went over to the jail. He had no fears for Polly's safety.

The sheriff had just locked the heavy front door of the jail behind him when a half-dozen horsemen, followed by a crowd of men on foot, came round a bend in the road and drew near the jail. They halted in front of the picket fence that surrounded the building, while several of the committee of arrangements rode on a few rods farther to the sheriff's house. One of them dismounted and rapped on the door with his riding-whip.

"Is the sheriff at home?" he inquired.

"No, he has just gone out," replied Polly, who had come to the door.

"We want the jail keys," he continued.

"They are not here," said Polly. "The sheriff has them himself." And then she added, with assumed indifference, "He is at the jail now."

The man turned away, and Polly went into the front room, from which she peered anxiously between the slats of the green blinds of a window that looked toward the jail. Meanwhile the messenger returned to his companions and announced his discovery. It looked as tho the sheriff had got wind of their design and was preparing to resist it.

One of them stepped forward and rapped on the jail door.

"Well, what is it?" said the sheriff, from within.

"We want to talk to you, Sheriff," replied the spokesman.

There was a little wicket in the door, this the sheriff opened, and answered through it.

"All right, boys, talk away. You are all strangers to me, and I don't know what business you can have." The sheriff did not think it necessary to recognize anybody in particular on such an occasion; the question of identity sometimes comes up in the investigation of these extra-judicial executions.

"We're a committee of citizens and we want to get into the jail."

"What for? It ain't much trouble to get into jail. Most people are anxious to keep out."

The mob was in no humor to appreciate a joke, and the sheriff's witticism fell dead upon an unresponsive audience.

"We want to have a talk with the Nigger that killed Cap'n Walker."

"You can talk to that Nigger in the court-house, when he's brought out for trial. Court will be in session here next week. I know what you fellows want; but you can't get my prisoner to-day. Do you want to take the bread out of a poor man's mouth? I get seventy-five cents a day for keeping this prisoner, and he's the only one in jail. I can't have my family suffer just to please you fellows."

One or two young men in the crowd laughed at the idea of Sheriff Campbell's suffering for want of seventy-five cents a day; but they were frowned into silence by those who stood near them.

"Ef yer don't let us in," cried a voice, "we'll bu's' the do' open."

"Bu'st away," answered the sheriff, raising his voice so that all could hear. "But I give you fair warning. The first man that tries it will be filled with buckshot. I'm sheriff of this county, and I know my duty, and I mean to do it."

"What's the use of kicking, Sheriff," argued one of the leaders of the mob. "The Nigger is sure to hang anyhow; he richly deserves it; and we've got to do something to teach the Niggers their places, or white people won't be able to live in the county."

"There's no use talking, boys," responded the sheriff. "I'm a white man outside, but in this jail I'm sheriff; and if this Nigger's to be hung in this county, I propose to do the hanging. So you fellows might as well right-about-face, and march back to Troy. You've had a pleasant trip, and the exercise will be good for you. You know *me*. I've got powder and ball, and I've faced fire before now, with nothing between me and the enemy, and I don't mean to surrender this jail while I'm able to shoot." Having thus announced his determination the sheriff closed and fastened the wicket, and looked around for the best position from which to defend the building.

The crowd drew off a little, and the leaders conversed together in low tones.

The Branson County jail was a small, two-story brick building, strongly constructed, with no attempt at architectural ornamentation. Each story was divided into two large cells by a passage running from front to rear. A grated iron door gave entrance from the passage to each of the four cells. The jail seldom had many prisoners in it, and the lower windows had been boarded up. When the sheriff had closed the wicket, he ascended the steep wooden stair to the upper floor. There was no window at the front of the upper passage, and the most available position from which to watch the movements of the crowd below was the front window of the cell occupied by the solitary prisoner.

The sheriff unlocked the door and entered the cell. The

prisoner was crouched in a corner, his yellow face, blanched with terror, looking ghastly in the semi-darkness of the room. A cold perspiration had gathered on his forehead, and his teeth were chattering with affright.

"For God's sake, Sheriff," he murmured hoarsely, "don't let 'em lynch me; I didn't kill the old man."

The sheriff glanced at the cowering wretch with a look of mingled contempt and loathing.

"Get up," he said sharply. "You will probably be hung sooner or later, but it will not be to-day, if I can help it. I will unlock your fetters, and if I can't hold the jail, you will have to make the best fight you can. If I am shot, I will consider my responsibility at an end."

There were iron fetters on the prisoner's ankles, and handcuffs on his wrist. These the sheriff unlocked, and they fell clanking to the floor.

"Keep back from the window," said the sheriff. "They might shoot if they saw you."

The sheriff drew toward the window a pine bench which formed a part of the scanty furniture of the cell, and laid his revolver upon it. Then he took his gun in hand, and took his stand at the side of the window where he could with least exposure of himself watch the movements of the crowd below.

The lynchers had not anticipated any determined resistance. Of course they had looked for a formal protest, and perhaps a sufficient show of opposition to excuse the sheriff in the eye of any stickler for legal formalities. But they had not come prepared to fight a battle, and no one of them seemed willing to lead an attack upon the jail. The leaders of the party conferred together with a good deal of animated gesticulation, which was visible to the sheriff from his outlook, tho the distance was too great for him to hear what was said. At length one of them broke away from the group, and rode back to the main body of the lynchers, who were restlessly awaiting orders.

"Well, boys," said the messenger, "we'll have to let it go for the present. The sheriff says he'll shoot, and he's got the drop on us this time. There ain't any of us that want to follow Cap'n Walker jest yet. Besides, the sheriff is a good fellow, and we don't want to hurt 'im. But," he added, as if to reassure the crowd, which began to show signs of disappointment, "the Nigger might as well say his prayers, for he ain't got long to live."

There was a murmur of dissent from the mob, and several voices insisted that an attack be made on the jail. But pacific counsels finally prevailed, and the mob sullenly withdrew.

The sheriff stood at the window until they had disappeared around the bend in the road. He did not relax his watchfulness when the last one was out of sight. Their withdrawal might be a mere feint, to be followed by a further attempt. So closely, indeed, was his attention drawn to the outside, that he neither saw nor heard the prisoner creep stealthily across the floor, reach out his hand and secure the revolver which lay on the bench behind the sheriff, and creep as noiselessly back to his place in the corner of the room.

A moment after the last of the lynching party had disappeared there was a shot fired from the woods across the road; a bullet whistled by the window and buried itself in the wooden casing a few inches from where the sheriff was standing. Quick as thought, with the instinct born of a semi-guerrilla army experience, he raised his gun and fired twice at the point from which a faint puff of smoke showed the hostile bullet to have been sent. He stood a moment watching, and then rested his gun against the window, and reached behind him mechanically for the other weapon. It was not on the bench. As the sheriff realized this fact, he turned his head and looked into the muzzle of the revolver.

"Stay where you are, Sheriff," said the prisoner, his eyes glistening, his face almost ruddy with excitement.

The sheriff mentally cursed his own carelessness for allowing him to be caught in such a predicament. He had not expected anything of the kind. He had relied on the Negro's cowardice and subordination in the presence of an armed white man as a matter of course. The sheriff was a brave man, but realized that the prisoner had him at an immense disadvantage. The two men stood thus for a moment, fighting a harmless duel with their eyes.

"Well, what do you mean to do?" asked the sheriff, with apparent calmness.

"To get away, of course," said the prisoner, in a tone which caused the sheriff to look at him more closely, and with an involuntary feeling of apprehension; if the man was not mad, he was in a state of mind akin to madness, and quite as dangerous. The sheriff felt that he must speak the prisoner fair, and watch for a chance to turn the tables on him. The keen-eyed, desperate man before him was a different being altogether from the groveling wretch who had begged so piteously for life a few minutes before.

At length the sheriff spoke:

"Is this your gratitude to me for saving your life at the risk of my own? If I had not done so, you would now be swinging from the limb of some neighboring tree."

"True," said the prisoner, "you saved my life, but for how long? When you came in, you said Court would sit next week. When the crowd went away they said I had not long to live. It is merely a choice of two ropes."

"While there's life there's hope," replied the sheriff. He uttered this commonplace mechanically, while his brain was busy in trying to think out some way of escape. "If you are innocent you can prove it."

The mulatto kept his eye upon the sheriff. "I didn't kill the old man," he replied; "but I shall never be able to clear myself. I was at his house at nine o'clock. I stole from it the coat that was on my back when I was taken. I would be convicted, even with a fair trial, unless the real murderer were discovered beforehand."

The sheriff knew this only too well. While he was thinking what argument next to use, the prisoner continued:

"Throw me the keys—no, unlock the door."

The sheriff stood a moment irresolute. The mulatto's eye glittered ominously. The sheriff crossed the room and unlocked the door leading into the passage.

"Now go down and unlock the outside door."

The heart of the sheriff leaped within him. Perhaps he might make a dash for liberty, and gain the outside. He descended the narrow stair, the prisoner keeping close behind him.

The sheriff inserted the huge iron key into the lock. The rusty bolt yielded slowly. It still remained for him to pull the door open.

"Stop!" thundered the mulatto, who seemed to divine the sheriff's purpose. "Move a muscle, and I'll blow your brains out."

The sheriff obeyed; he realized that his chance had not yet come.

"Now keep on that side of the passage, and go back upstairs."

Keeping the sheriff in front of him, the mulatto followed the other up the stairs. The sheriff expected the prisoner to lock him into the cell and make his own escape. He had about come to the conclusion that the best thing he could do under the circumstances was to submit quietly, and take his chances of recapturing the prisoner after the alarm had been given. The sheriff had faced death more than once upon the battle-field. A few minutes before, well armed, and with a brick wall between him and them he had dared a hundred men to fight; but he felt instinctively that the desperate man in front of him was not to be trifled with, and he was too prudent a man to risk his life against such heavy odds. He had Polly to look after, and there was a limit beyond which devotion to duty would be quixotic and even foolish.

"I want to get away," said the prisoner, "and I don't want to be captured; for if I am, I know I will be hung on the spot. I am afraid," he added, somewhat reflectively, "that in order to save myself I shall have to kill you."

"Good God!" exclaimed the sheriff, in involuntary terror; "you would not kill the man to whom you owe your own life."

"You speak more truly than you know," replied the mulatto. "I indeed owe my life to you."

The sheriff started. He was capable of surprise, even in that moment of extreme peril. "Who are you?" he asked, in amazement.

"Tom, Cicely's son," returned the other. He had closed the

door and stood talking to the sheriff through the grated opening. "Don't you remember Cicely—Cicely, whom you sold, with her child, to the speculator on his way to Alabama?"

The sheriff did remember. He had been sorry for it many a time since. It had been the old story of debts, mortgages and bad crops. He had quarreled with the mother. The price offered for her and her child had been unusually large, and he had yielded to the combination of anger and pecuniary stress.

"Good God!" he gasped, "you would not murder your own father?"

"My father?" replied the mulatto. "It were well enough for me to claim the relationship, but it comes with poor grace from you to ask anything by reason of it. What father's duty have you ever performed for me? Did you give me your name, or even your protection? Other white men gave their colored sons freedom and money, and sent them to the free States. *You* sold *me* to the rice swamps."

"I at least gave you the life you cling to," murmured the sheriff.

"Life?" said the prisoner, with a sarcastic laugh. "What kind of a life? You gave me your own blood, your own features—no man need look at us together twice to see that—and you gave me a black mother. Poor wretch! She died under the lash, because she had enough womanhood to call her soul her own. You gave me a white man's spirit, and you made me a slave, and crushed it out."

"But you are free now," said the sheriff. He had not doubted, could not doubt, the mulatto's word. He knew whose passions coursed beneath that swarthy skin and burned in the black eyes opposite his own. He saw in this mulatto what he himself might have become had not the safeguards of parental restraint and public opinion been thrown around him.

"Free to do what?" replied the mulatto. "Free in name, but despised and scorned and set aside by the people to whose race I belong far more than to that of my mother."

"There are schools," said the sheriff. "You have been to school." He had noticed that the mulatto spoke more eloquently and used better language than most Branson County people.

"I have been to school and dreamed when I went that it

would work some marvelous change in my condition. But what did I learn? I learned to feel that no degree of learning or wisdom will change the color of my skin and that I shall always wear what in my own country is a badge of degradation. When I think about it seriously I do not care particularly for such a life. It is the animal in me, not the man, that flees the gallows. I owe you nothing," he went on, "and expect nothing of you; and it would be no more than justice if I were to avenge upon you my mother's wrongs and my own. But still I hate to shoot you; I have never yet taken human life—for I did *not* kill the old captain. Will you promise to give no alarm and make no attempt to capture me until morning, if I do not shoot?"

So absorbed were the two men in their colloquy and their own tumultuous thoughts that neither of them had heard the door below move upon its hinges. Neither of them had heard a light step come stealthily up the stair, nor seen a slender form creep along the darkening passage toward the mulatto.

The sheriff hesitated. The struggle between his love of life and his sense of duty was a terrific one. It may seem strange that a man who could sell his own child into slavery should hesitate at such a moment when his life was trembling in the balance. But the baleful influence of human slavery poisoned the very fountains of life, and created new standards of right. The sheriff was conscientious; his conscience had merely been warped by his environment. Let no one ask what his answer would have been; he was spared the necessity of a decision.

"Stop," said the mulatto, "you need not promise. I could not trust you if you did. It is your life for mine; there is but one safe way for me; you must die."

He raised his arm to fire, when there was a flash—a report from the passage behind him.

His arm fell heavily at his side, and the pistol dropped at his feet.

The sheriff recovered first from his surprise, and throwing open the door secured the fallen weapon. Then seizing the prisoner he thrust him into the cell and locked the door upon him; after which he turned to Polly, who leaned half-fainting against the wall, her hands clasped over her heart.

"Oh, Pa, I was just in time!" she cried hysterically, and, wildly sobbing, threw herself into her father's arms.

"I watched until they all went away," she said. "I heard the shot from the woods and I saw you shoot. Then when you did not come out I feared something had happened, that perhaps you had been wounded. I got out the other pistol and ran over here. When I found the door open, I knew something was wrong, and when I heard voices I crept up-stairs, and reached the top just in time to hear him say he would kill you. Oh, it was a narrow escape!"

When she had grown somewhat calmer, the sheriff left her standing there and went back into the cell. The prisoner's arm was bleeding from a flesh wound. His bravado had given place to a stony apathy. There was no sign in his face of fear or disappointment or feeling of any kind. The sheriff sent Polly to the house for cloth, and bound up the prisoner's wound with a rude skill acquired during his army life.

"I will have a doctor come and dress the wound in the morning," he said to the prisoner. "It will do very well until then, if you will keep quiet. If the doctor asks you how the wound was caused, you can say that you were struck by the bullet fired from the woods. It would do you no good to have it known that you were shot while attempting to escape."

The prisoner uttered no word of thanks or apology, but sat in sullen silence. When the wounded arm had been bandaged, Polly and her father returned to the house.

The sheriff was in an unusually thoughtful mood that evening. He put salt in his coffee at supper, and poured vinegar over his pancakes. To many of Polly's questions he returned random answers. When he had gone to bed he lay awake for several hours.

In the silent watches of the night, when he was alone with God, there came into his mind a flood of unaccustomed thoughts. An hour or two before, standing face to face with death, he had experienced a sensation similar to that which drowning men are said to feel—a kind of clarifying of the moral faculty, in which the veil of the flesh, with its obscuring passions and prejudices, is pushed aside for a moment, and all the acts of one's life stand out, in the clear light of truth, in their correct proportions and relations—a state of mind in which one sees himself as God may be supposed to see him. In the reaction following his rescue, this feeling had given place for a time to far different emotions. But now, in the silence of midnight, something of this clearness of spirit returned to the sheriff. He saw that he had owed some duty to this son of his—that neither law nor custom could destroy a responsibility inherent in the nature of mankind. He could not thus, in the eyes of God at least, shake off the consequences of his sin. Had he never sinned, this wayward spirit would never have come back from the vanished past to haunt him.

And as he thought, his anger against the mulatto died away, and in its place there sprang up a great, an ineffable pity. The hand of parental authority might have restrained the passions he had seen burning in the prisoner's eyes when the desperate man spoke the words which had seemed to doom his father to death. The sheriff felt that he might have saved this fiery spirit from the slough of slavery; that he might have sent him to the free North, and given him there, or in some other land, an opportunity to turn to usefulness and honorable pursuits the talents that had run to crime, perhaps to madness; he might, still less, have given this son of his the poor simulacrum of liberty which men of his caste could possess in a slave-holding community; or least of all, but still something, he might have kept the boy on the plantation, where the burdens of slavery would have fallen lightly upon him.

The sheriff recalled his own youth. He had inherited an honored name to keep untarnished; he had had a future to make; the picture of a fair young bride had beckoned him on to happiness. The poor wretch now stretched upon a pallet of straw between the brick walls of the jail had had none of these things—no name, no father, no mother—in the true meaning of motherhood—and until the past few years no possible future, and then one vague and shadowy in its outline, and dependent for form and substance upon the slow solution of a problem in which there were many unknown quantities.

From what he might have done to what he might yet do was

an easy transition for the awakened conscience of the sheriff. It occurred to him, purely as a hypothesis, that he might permit his prisoner to escape; but his oath of office, his duty as sheriff, stood in the way of such a course, and the sheriff dismissed the idea from his mind. But he could investigate the circumstances of the murder, and move Heaven and earth to discover the real criminal, for he no longer doubted the prisoner's innocence; he could employ counsel for the accused, and perhaps influence public opinion in his favor. An acquittal once secured, some plan could be devised by which the sheriff might in some degree atone for his neglect of what he now clearly perceived to have been a duty.

When the sheriff had reached this conclusion he fell into an unquiet slumber, from which he awoke late the next morning.

He went over to the jail before breakfast and found the prisoner lying on his pallet; his face turned to the wall: he did not move when the sheriff rattled the door.

"Good-morning," said the latter, in a tone intended to waken the prisoner.

There was no response. The sheriff looked more keenly at the recumbent figure; there was an unnatural rigidity about its attitude.

He hastily unlocked the door and, entering the cell, bent over the prostrate form. There was no sound of breathing; he turned the body over, it was cold and stiff. The prisoner had torn the bandage from his wound and bled to death during the night. He had evidently been dead several hours.

C. L. PIRKIS

(1839–1910)

"She is the most sensible and practical woman I ever met," says private detective Ebenezer Dyer of his trusted operative Loveday Brooke. In the last decade of the nineteenth century, such adjectives were seldom part of compliments to women—and these words, in fact, were placed in a male character's mouth by his female creator. After setting up her detective's strengths by showing them admired by a man, C. L. Pirkis demonstrated them throughout her entire series of seven stories about Loveday Brooke. Pirkis disguised her suspect femininity behind initials, as in the next century would S. E. Hinton, P. D. James, and J. K. Rowling. Catherine Louisa Lyne was born in London. Her grandfather was author of a popular primer for students of Latin, and she grew up aware of books and the possibility of writing them. In 1872 she married Frederick Edward Pirkis, a fleet paymaster with the Royal Navy.

Five years later, she began her publishing career with a romantic potboiler of a sensation novel, *Disappeared from Her Home*, under the name "Mrs. Fred E. Pirkis." Growing out of Gothic Sturm und Drang, "sensation novels" brought together passionate romance and everyday realism, which had previously been treated like matter and antimatter—as if they would combust in each other's presence. Instead adventurous new authors demonstrated that, like a waltz in a pantry, antic plots could take place in ordinary settings and wake each to the other's dramatic potential. In scholarship about the genesis of this movement, the usual trinity invoked is *The Woman in White*, by Wilkie Collins, with its proto-detective and absolute mazurka of a plot; Ellen Wood's *East Lynne*, a byzantine rigmarole about double identities; and *Lady Audley's Secret*, in which Mary Elizabeth Braddon accompanies a homicidal bigamist along her merry way. Pirkis followed her own contribution with a dozen other novels and numerous short stories before the sole collection for which she is remembered in the twenty-first century, *The Experiences of Loveday Brooke, Lady Detective*, published by Hutchinson & Company in 1894.

Unlike many women detectives conjured by men—Hugh Weir's Madelyn Mack, for example, or M. McDonnell Bodkin's Dora Myrl—Brooke is not presented as hyperfeminine in beauty or instinct to make up for her allegedly unfeminine profession. "Neither handsome nor ugly," Pirkis describes her, and even "nondescript"—surely a useful attribute in an investigator. Nor is Brooke romantically noble, like George R. Sims's character Dorcas Dene, who becomes a detective because her artist husband goes blind after they inherit debt, or Anna Katharine Green's character Violet Strange, who recklessly chooses private inquiry as a way to earn money to support her disowned sister. Nor does Brooke coo at her husband (she is happily single) or name a dog Toddlekins—misdemeanors committed by Dorcas Dene.

Loveday Brooke is simply a professional private investigator who does her job and earns the respect of her employer, Ebenezer Dyer. Adept at disguise and mimicry, Brooke serves Pirkis as a navigator through the social conventions that she wants to critique. Often, through stratified English society, she moves almost invisibly, disguised as a servant. With more concern for a just community than many of the cheerfully escapist purveyors of crime stories, Pirkis employs Brooke to show the dehumanizing labor of immigrants, poor women working behind the scenes of wealth, the tragic poverty of the ordinary urban streets. She is quick to notice aberrations; like Sherlock Holmes, she is suspicious of overpaid labor in a culture that habitually underpays. Pirkis also resisted shaping the stories into a cycle that evolves toward an almost-novel, a device popular at the time—and one that has returned in twenty-first century TV series. Her adventures stand alone, like those of Sherlock Holmes.

The Brooke stories appeared in *The Ludgate Monthly*, one of a myriad of periodicals that fed the demand for brief entertainment before the invention of radio, motion pictures, and television. It launched in 1891 and survived under variations of this name for a decade. The huge success of *The Strand Magazine*, now famous for serializing the Holmes saga, was based in part upon its commitment to the innovative notion of featuring an illustration on every page. *The Ludgate Monthly* at first tried an old-fashioned approach, emphasizing text and a more traditional look, in contrast to *The Strand*. Then it surrendered to the zeitgeist, reinvented itself as *The Ludgate Illustrated Magazine*, and within a couple of years transformed into *The Ludgate*. By the mid-1890s photographs could be reproduced well enough to become a feature of periodicals and *The Ludgate* relied heavily upon them.

The scholar John Sutherland estimated that of the 800 weekly newspapers throughout Great Britain around this time, 240 published detective or crime stories. Many periodicals reviewed one another's offerings, just as now podcasts and newspapers review TV programs. During the early days of the magazine and of Pirkis's contributions to it, a reviewer wrote, "*The Ludgate Monthly* seems to improve in attractiveness each month, just as month by month Miss Loveday Brooke continues to outshine the detective Sherlock Holmes in preternatural prescience." Then the reviewer felt compelled to add, "We are just afraid that Miss Brooke is too clever in catching criminals ever to catch a husband." Advertisements for the eventual Brooke collection reproduced a phrase from a review in *The Glasgow Herald*: "A Female Sherlock Holmes."

"The Murder at Troyte's Hill" was second in the series, appearing in March 1893. Four more followed. A seventh story was published in the magazine after its name change and included when Hutchinson & Company published a collection, *The Experiences of Loveday Brooke, Lady Detective*, in 1894. Pirkis chose to label Brooke's cases as "experiences," not "adventures," which makes them sound more felt and personally significant than mere larks. In a masterpiece of book publicity, the publisher printed thousands of business cards for their imaginary detective and pasted one to the front of each red cloth cover. They identified the heroine without the label "Mrs."—

merely as *Loveday Brooke, Lady Detective, Lynch Court, Fleet Street.*

It was Pirkis's last book. She abandoned fiction for more hands-on work in the real world. Three years earlier, she and her husband had helped found the National Canine Defence League, since renamed the Dogs Trust and still the nation's foremost charity for dogs. Pirkis had dedicated her 1887 triple-decker *A Dateless Bargain* to a prominent anti-vivisectionist. She noticed animals and their fates throughout the Brooke series. One character is discovered to be cruelly abusing animals—even attacking a dog with a hammer—to confirm a crackpot theory. It's a sin to spoil a literary surprise, so we won't reveal which story includes this vile character.

Pirkis described her detective in this introductory scene from the first story in the series:

Loveday Brooke, at this period of her career, was a little over thirty years of age, and could be best described in a series of negations.

She was not tall, she was not short; she was not dark, she was not fair; she was neither handsome nor ugly. Her features were altogether nondescript; her one noticeable trait was a habit she had, when absorbed in thought, of dropping her eyelids over her eyes till only a line of eyeball showed, and she appeared to be looking out at the world through a slit, instead of through a window.

Her dress was invariably black, and was almost Quaker-like in its neat primness. Some five or six years previously, by a jerk of Fortune's wheel, Loveday had been thrown upon the world penniless and all but friendless. Marketable accomplishments she had found she had none, so she had forthwith defied convention, and had chosen for herself a career that had cut her off sharply from her former associates and her position in society. For five or six years she drudged away patiently in the lower walks of her profession; then chance, or, to speak more precisely, an intricate criminal case, threw her in the way of the experienced head of the flourishing detective agency in Lynch Court. He quickly enough found out the stuff she was made of, and threw her in the way of better-class work—work, indeed, that brought increase of pay and of reputation alike to him and to Loveday.

Ebenezer Dyer was not, as a rule, given to enthusiasm; but he would at times wax eloquent over Miss Brooke's qualifications for the profession she had chosen.

"Too much of a lady, do you say?" he would say to anyone who chanced to call in question those qualifications. "I don't care twopence-halfpenny whether she is or is not a lady. I only know she is the most sensible and practical woman I ever met. In the first place, she has the faculty—so rare among women—of carrying out orders to the very letter: in the second place, she has a clear, shrewd brain, unhampered by any hard-and-fast theories; thirdly, and most important item of all, she has so much common sense that it amounts to genius—positively to genius, sir."

THE MURDER AT
TROYTE'S HILL

"Griffiths, of the Newcastle Constabulary, has the case in hand," said Mr. Dyer; "those Newcastle men are keen-witted, shrewd fellows, and very jealous of outside interference. They only sent to me under protest, as it were, because they wanted your sharp wits at work inside the house."

"I suppose throughout I am to work with Griffiths, not with you?" said Miss Brooke.

"Yes; when I have given you in outline the facts of the case, I simply have nothing more to do with it, and you must depend on Griffiths for any assistance of any sort that you may require."

Here, with a swing, Mr. Dyer opened his big ledger and turned rapidly over its leaves till he came to the heading "Troyte's Hill" and the date "September 6th."

"I'm all attention," said Loveday, leaning back in her chair in the attitude of a listener.

"The murdered man," resumed Mr. Dyer, "is a certain Alexander Henderson—usually known as old Sandy—lodge-keeper to Mr. Craven, of Troyte's Hill, Cumberland. The lodge consists merely of two rooms on the ground floor, a bed-room and a sitting-room; these Sandy occupied alone, having neither kith nor kin of any degree. On the morning of September 6th, some children going up to the house with milk from the farm, noticed that Sandy's bed-room window stood wide open. Curiosity prompted them to peep in; and then, to their horror, they saw old Sandy, in his night-shirt, lying dead on the floor, as if he had fallen backwards from the window. They raised an alarm; and on examination, it was found that death had ensued from a heavy blow on the temple, given either by a strong fist or some blunt instrument. The room, on being entered, presented a curious appearance. It was as if a herd of monkeys had been turned into it and allowed to work their impish will. Not an article of furniture remained in its place: the bed-clothes had been rolled into a bundle and stuffed into the chimney; the bedstead—a small iron one—lay on its side; the one chair in the room stood on the top of the table; fender and fire-irons lay across the washstand, whose basin was to be found in a farther corner, holding bolster and pillow. The clock stood on its head in the middle of the mantelpiece; and the small vases and ornaments, which flanked it on either side, were walking, as it were, in a straight line towards the door. The old man's clothes had been rolled into a ball and thrown on the top of a high cupboard in which he kept his savings and whatever valuables he had. This cupboard, however, had not been meddled with, and its contents remained intact, so it was evident that robbery was not the motive for the crime. At the inquest, subsequently held, a verdict of 'willful murder' against some person or persons unknown was returned. The local police are diligently investigating the affair, but, as yet, no arrests have been made. The opinion that at present prevails in the neighbourhood is that the crime has been perpetrated by some lunatic, escaped or otherwise and enquiries are being made at the local asylums as to missing or lately released inmates. Griffiths, however, tells me that his suspicions set in another direction."

"Did anything of importance transpire at the inquest?"

"Nothing specially important. Mr. Craven broke down in giving his evidence when he alluded to the confidential relations that had always subsisted between Sandy and himself, and spoke of the last time that he had seen him alive. The evidence of the butler, and one or two of the female servants, seems clear enough, and they let fall something of a hint that Sandy was not altogether a favourite among them, on account of the overbearing manner in which he used his influence with his master. Young Mr. Craven, a youth of about nineteen, home from Oxford for the long vacation, was not present at the inquest; a doctor's certificate was put in stating that he was suffering from typhoid fever, and could not leave his bed without risk to his life. Now this young man is a thoroughly bad sort, and as much a gentleman-blackleg as it is possible for such a young fellow to be. It seems to Griffiths that there is something suspicious about this illness of his. He came back from Oxford on the verge of delirium tremens, pulled round from that, and then suddenly, on the day after the murder, Mrs. Craven rings the bell, announces that he has developed typhoid fever and orders a doctor to be sent for."

"What sort of man is Mr. Craven senior?"

"He seems to be a quiet old fellow, a scholar and learned philologist. Neither his neighbours nor his family see much of him; he almost lives in his study, writing a treatise, in seven or eight volumes, on comparative philology. He is not a rich man. Troyte's Hill, though it carries position in the county, is not a paying property, and Mr. Craven is unable to keep it up properly. I am told he has had to cut down expenses in all directions in order to send his son to college, and his daughter from first to last has been entirely educated by her mother. Mr. Craven was originally intended for the church, but for some reason or other, when his college career came to an end, he did not present himself for ordination—went out to Natal instead, where he obtained some civil appointment and where he remained for about fifteen years. Henderson was his servant during the latter portion of his Oxford career, and must have been greatly respected by him, for although the remuneration derived from his appointment at Natal was small, he paid Sandy a regular yearly allowance out of it. When, about ten years ago, he succeeded to Troyte's Hill, on the death of his elder brother, and returned home with his family, Sandy was immediately installed as lodge-keeper, and at so high a rate of pay that the butler's wages were cut down to meet it."

"Ah, that wouldn't improve the butler's feelings towards him," ejaculated Loveday.

Mr. Dyer went on: "But, in spite of his high wages, he doesn't appear to have troubled much about his duties as lodge-keeper, for they were performed, as a rule, by the gardener's boy, while he took his meals and passed his time at the house, and, speaking generally, put his finger into every pie. You know the old adage respecting the servant of twenty-one years' standing: 'Seven years my servant, seven years my equal, seven years my master.' Well, it appears to have held good in the case of Mr. Craven and Sandy. The old gentleman, absorbed in his philological studies, evidently let the reins slip through his fingers, and Sandy seems to have taken easy possession of them. The servants frequently had to go to him for orders, and he carried things, as a rule, with a high hand."

"Did Mrs. Craven never have a word to say on the matter?"

"I've not heard much about her. She seems to be a quiet sort of person. She is a Scotch missionary's daughter; perhaps she spends her time working for the Cape mission and that sort of thing."

"And young Mr. Craven: did he knock under to Sandy's rule?"

"Ah, now you're hitting the bull's eye and we come to Griffiths' theory. The young man and Sandy appear to have been at loggerheads ever since the Cravens took possession of Troyte's Hill. As a schoolboy Master Harry defied Sandy and threatened him with his hunting-crop; and subsequently, as a young man, has used strenuous endeavours to put the old servant in his place. On the day before the murder, Griffiths says, there was a terrible scene between the two, in which the young gentleman, in the presence of several witnesses, made use of strong language and threatened the old man's life. Now, Miss Brooke, I have told you all the circumstances of the case so far as I know them. For fuller particulars I must refer you to Griffiths. He, no doubt, will meet you at Grenfell—the nearest station to Troyte's Hill, and tell you in what capacity he has procured for you an entrance into the house. By-the-way, he has wired to me this morning that he hopes you will be able to save the Scotch express to-night."

Loveday expressed her readiness to comply with Mr. Griffiths' wishes.

"I shall be glad," said Mr. Dyer, as he shook hands with her at the office door, "to see you immediately on your return—that, however, I suppose, will not be yet awhile. This promises, I fancy, to be a longish affair?" This was said interrogatively.

"I haven't the least idea on the matter," answered Loveday. "I start on my work without theory of any sort—in fact, I may say, with my mind a perfect blank."

And anyone who had caught a glimpse of her blank, expressionless features, as she said this, would have taken her at her word.

Grenfell, the nearest post-town to Troyte's Hill, is a fairly busy, populous little town—looking south towards the black country, and northwards to low, barren hills. Pre-eminent among these stands Troyte's Hill, famed in the old days as a border keep, and possibly at a still earlier date as a Druid stronghold.

At a small inn at Grenfell, dignified by the title of "The Station Hotel," Mr. Griffiths, of the Newcastle constabulary, met Loveday and still further initiated her into the mysteries of the Troyte's Hill murder.

"A little of the first excitement has subsided," he said, after preliminary greetings had been exchanged; "but still the wildest rumours are flying about and repeated as solemnly as if they were Gospel truths. My chief here and my colleagues generally adhere to their first conviction, that the criminal is some suddenly crazed tramp or else an escaped lunatic, and they are confident that sooner or later we shall come upon his traces. Their theory is that Sandy, hearing some strange noise at the Park Gates, put his head out of the window to ascertain the cause and immediately had his death blow dealt him; then they suppose that the lunatic scrambled into the room through the window and exhausted his frenzy by turning things generally upside down. They refuse altogether to share my suspicions respecting young Mr. Craven."

Mr. Griffiths was a tall, thin-featured man, with iron-grey hair, but so close to his head that it refused to do anything but stand on end. This gave a somewhat comic expression to the upper portion of his face and clashed oddly with the melancholy look that his mouth habitually wore.

"I have made all smooth for you at Troyte's Hill," he presently went on. "Mr. Craven is not wealthy enough to allow himself the luxury of a family lawyer, so he occasionally employs the services of Messrs. Wells and Sugden, lawyers in this place, and who, as it happens, have, off and on, done a good deal of business for me. It was through them I heard that Mr. Craven was anxious to secure the assistance of an amanuensis.

I immediately offered your services, stating that you were a friend of mine, a lady of impoverished means, who would gladly undertake the duties for the munificent sum of a guinea a month, with board and lodging. The old gentleman at once jumped at the offer, and is anxious for you to be at Troyte's Hill at once."

Loveday expressed her satisfaction with the programme that Mr. Griffiths had sketched for her, then she had a few questions to ask.

"Tell me," she said, "what led you, in the first instance, to suspect young Mr. Craven of the crime?"

"The footing on which he and Sandy stood towards each other, and the terrible scene that occurred between them only the day before the murder," answered Griffiths, promptly. "Nothing of this, however, was elicited at the inquest, where a very fair face was put on Sandy's relations with the whole of the Craven family. I have subsequently unearthed a good deal respecting the private life of Mr. Harry Craven, and, among other things, I have found out that on the night of the murder he left the house shortly after ten o'clock, and no one, so far as I have been able to ascertain, knows at what hour he returned. Now I must draw your attention, Miss Brooke, to the fact that at the inquest the medical evidence went to prove that the murder had been committed between ten and eleven at night."

"Do you surmise, then, that the murder was a planned thing on the part of this young man?"

"I do. I believe that he wandered about the grounds until Sandy shut himself in for the night, then aroused him by some outside noise, and, when the old man looked out to ascertain the cause, dealt him a blow with a bludgeon or loaded stick, that caused his death."

"A cold-blooded crime that, for a boy of nineteen?"

"Yes. He's a good-looking, gentlemanly youngster, too, with manners as mild as milk, but from all accounts is as full of wickedness as an egg is full of meat. Now, to come to another point—if, in connection with these ugly facts, you take into consideration the suddenness of his illness, I think you'll admit that it bears a suspicious appearance and might reasonably give rise to the surmise that it was a plant on his part, in order to get out of the inquest."

"Who is the doctor attending him?"

"A man called Waters; not much of a practitioner, from all accounts, and no doubt he feels himself highly honoured in being summoned to Troyte's Hill. The Cravens, it seems, have no family doctor. Mrs. Craven, with her missionary experience, is half a doctor herself, and never calls in one except in a serious emergency."

"The certificate was in order, I suppose?"

"Undoubtedly. And, as if to give colour to the gravity of the case, Mrs. Craven sent a message down to the servants, that if any of them were afraid of the infection they could at once go to their homes. Several of the maids, I believe, took advantage of her permission, and packed their boxes. Miss Craven, who is a delicate girl, was sent away with her maid to stay with friends at Newcastle, and Mrs. Craven isolated herself with her patient in one of the disused wings of the house."

"Has anyone ascertained whether Miss Craven arrived at her destination at Newcastle?"

Griffiths drew his brows together in thought.

"I did not see any necessity for such a thing," he answered. "I don't quite follow you. What do you mean to imply?"

"Oh, nothing. I don't suppose it matters much: it might have been interesting as a side-issue." She broke off for a moment, then added:

"Now tell me a little about the butler, the man whose wages were cut down to increase Sandy's pay."

"Old John Hales? He's a thoroughly worthy, respectable man; he was butler for five or six years to Mr. Craven's brother, when he was master of Troyte's Hill, and then took duty under this Mr. Craven. There's no ground for suspicion in that quarter. Hales's exclamation when he heard of the murder is quite enough to stamp him as an innocent man: 'Serve the old idiot right,' he cried: 'I couldn't pump up a tear for him if I tried for a month of Sundays!' Now I take it, Miss Brooke, a guilty man wouldn't dare make such a speech as that!"

"You think not?"

Griffiths stared at her. "I'm a little disappointed in her," he thought. "I'm afraid her powers have been slightly exaggerated if she can't see such a straight-forward thing as that."

Aloud he said, a little sharply, "Well, I don't stand alone in my thinking. No one yet has breathed a word against Hales, and if they did, I've no doubt he could prove an *alibi* without any trouble, for he lives in the house, and everyone has a good word for him."

"I suppose Sandy's lodge has been put into order by this time?"

"Yes; after the inquest, and when all possible evidence had been taken, everything was put straight."

"At the inquest it was stated that no marks of footsteps could be traced in any direction?"

"The long drought we've had would render such a thing impossible, let alone the fact that Sandy's lodge stands right on the graveled drive, without flower-beds or grass borders of any sort around it. But look here, Miss Brooke, don't you be wasting your time over the lodge and its surroundings. Every iota of fact on that matter has been gone through over and over again by me and my chief. What we want you to do is to go straight into the house and concentrate attention on Master Harry's sick-room, and find out what's going on there. What he did outside the house on the night of the 6th, I've no doubt I shall be able to find out for myself. Now, Miss Brooke, you've asked me no end of questions, to which I have replied as fully as it was in my power to do; will you be good enough to answer one question that I wish to put, as straightforwardly as I have answered yours? You have had fullest particulars given you of the condition of Sandy's room when the police entered it on the morning after the murder. No doubt, at the present moment, you can see it all in your mind's eye—the bedstead on its side, the clock on its head, the bed-clothes half-way up the chimney, the little vases and ornaments walking in a straight line towards the door?"

Loveday bowed her head.

"Very well. Now will you be good enough to tell me what this scene of confusion recalls to your mind before anything else?"

"The room of an unpopular Oxford freshman after a raid upon it by undergrads," answered Loveday promptly.

Mr. Griffiths rubbed his hands.

"Quite so!" he ejaculated. "I see, after all, we are one at heart in this matter, in spite of a little surface disagreement of ideas. Depend upon it, by-and-bye, like the engineers tunneling from different quarters under the Alps, we shall meet at the same point and shake hands. By-the-way, I have arranged for daily communication between us through the post-boy who takes the letters to Troyte's Hill. He is trustworthy, and any letter you give him for me will find its way into my hands within the hour."

It was about three o'clock in the afternoon when Loveday drove in through the park gates of Troyte's Hill, past the lodge where old Sandy had met with his death. It was a pretty little cottage, covered with Virginia creeper and wild honeysuckle, and showing no outward sign of the tragedy that had been en-acted within.

The park and pleasure-grounds of Troyte's Hill were exten-sive, and the house itself was a somewhat imposing red brick structure, built, possibly, at the time when Dutch William's taste had grown popular in the country. Its frontage presented a somewhat forlorn appearance, its centre windows—a square of eight—alone seeming to show signs of occupation. With the exception of two windows at the extreme end of the bedroom floor of the north wing, where, possibly, the invalid and his mother were located, and two windows at the extreme end of the ground floor of the south wing, which Loveday ascertained subsequently were those of Mr. Craven's study, not a single window in either wing owned blind or curtain. The wings were extensive, and it was easy to understand that at the extreme end of the one the fever patient would be isolated from the rest of the household, and that at the extreme end of the other Mr. Craven could secure the quiet and freedom from interruption which, no doubt, were essential to the due prosecution of his philological studies.

Alike on the house and ill-kept grounds were present the stamp of the smallness of the income of the master and owner of the place. The terrace, which ran the length of the house in front, and on to which every window on the ground floor opened, was miserably out of repair: not a lintel or door-post, window-ledge or balcony but what seemed to cry aloud for the touch of the painter. "Pity me! I have seen better days," Loveday could fancy written as a legend across the red-brick porch that gave entrance to the old house.

The butler, John Hales, admitted Loveday, shouldered her portmanteau and told her he would show her to her room. He was a tall, powerfully-built man, with a ruddy face and dogged expression of countenance. It was easy to understand that, off and on, there must have been many a sharp encounter between him and old Sandy. He treated Loveday in an easy, familiar fashion, evidently considering that an amanuensis took much the same rank as a nursery governess—that is to say, a little below a lady's maid and a little above a house-maid.

"We're short of hands, just now," he said, in broad Cumberland dialect, as he led the way up the wide stair case. "Some of the lasses downstairs took fright at the fever and went home. Cook and I are single-handed, for Moggie, the only maid left, has been told off to wait on Madam and Master Harry. I hope you're not afeared of fever?"

Loveday explained that she was not, and asked if the room at the extreme end of the north wing was the one assigned to "Madam and Master Harry."

"Yes," said the man; "it's convenient for sick nursing; there's a flight of stairs runs straight down from it to the kitchen quarters. We put all Madam wants at the foot of those stairs and Moggie herself never enters the sick-room. I take it you'll not be seeing Madam for many a day, yet awhile."

"When shall I see Mr. Craven? At dinner to-night?"

"That's what naebody could say," answered Hales. "He may not come out of his study till past midnight; sometimes he sits there till two or three in the morning. Shouldn't advise you to wait till he wants his dinner—better have a cup of tea and a chop sent up to you. Madam never waits for him at any meal."

As he finished speaking he deposited the portmanteau outside one of the many doors opening into the gallery.

"This is Miss Craven's room," he went on; "cook and me thought you'd better have it, as it would want less getting ready than the other rooms, and work is work when there are so few hands to do it. Oh, my stars! I do declare there is cook putting it straight for you now." The last sentence was added as the opened door laid bare to view, the cook, with a duster in her hand, polishing a mirror; the bed had been made, it is true, but otherwise the room must have been much as Miss Craven left it, after a hurried packing up.

To the surprise of the two servants Loveday took the matter very lightly.

"I have a special talent for arranging rooms and would prefer getting this one straight for myself," she said. "Now, if you will go and get ready that chop and cup of tea we were talking about just now, I shall think it much kinder than if you stayed here doing what I can so easily do for myself."

When, however, the cook and butler had departed in company, Loveday showed no disposition to exercise the "special talent" of which she had boasted.

She first carefully turned the key in the lock and then proceeded to make a thorough and minute investigation of every corner of the room. Not an article of furniture, not an ornament or toilet accessory, but what was lifted from its place and carefully scrutinized. Even the ashes in the grate, the debris of the last fire made there, were raked over and well looked through.

This careful investigation of Miss Craven's late surroundings occupied in all about three quarters of an hour, and Loveday, with her hat in her hand, descended the stairs to see Hales crossing the hall to the dining-room with the promised cup of tea and chop.

In silence and solitude she partook of the simple repast in a dining-hall that could with ease have banqueted a hundred and fifty guests.

"Now for the grounds before it gets dark," she said to herself, as she noted that already the outside shadows were beginning to slant.

The dining-hall was at the back of the house; and here, as in the front, the windows, reaching to the ground, presented easy means of egress. The flower-garden was on this side of the house and sloped downhill to a pretty stretch of well-wooded country.

Loveday did not linger here even to admire, but passed at once round the south corner of the house to the windows which she had ascertained, by a careless question to the butler, were those of Mr. Craven's study.

Very cautiously she drew near them, for the blinds were up, the curtains drawn back. A side glance, however, relieved her apprehensions, for it showed her the occupant of the room, seated in an easy-chair, with his back to the windows. From the length of his outstretched limbs he was evidently a tall man. His hair was silvery and curly, the lower part of his face was hidden from her view by the chair, but she could see one hand was pressed tightly across his eyes and brows. The whole attitude was that of a man absorbed in deep thought. The room was comfortably furnished, but presented an appearance of disorder from the books and manuscripts scattered in all directions. A whole pile of torn fragments of foolscap sheets, overflowing from a waste-paper basket beside the writing-table, seemed to proclaim the fact that the scholar had of late grown weary of, or else dissatisfied with his work, and had condemned it freely.

Although Loveday stood looking in at this window for over five minutes, not the faintest sign of life did that tall, reclining figure give, and it would have been as easy to believe him locked in sleep as in thought.

From here she turned her steps in the direction of Sandy's lodge. As Griffiths had said, it was graveled up to its doorstep. The blinds were closely drawn, and it presented the ordinary appearance of a disused cottage.

A narrow path beneath over-arching boughs of cherry-laurel and arbutus, immediately facing the lodge, caught her eye, and down this she at once turned her footsteps.

This path led, with many a wind and turn, through a belt of shrubbery that skirted the frontage of Mr. Craven's grounds, and eventually, after much zig-zagging, ended in close proximity to the stables. As Loveday entered it, she seemed literally to leave daylight behind her.

"I feel as if I were following the course of a circuitous mind," she said to herself as the shadows closed around her. "I could not fancy Sir Isaac Newton or Bacon planning or delighting in such a wind-about-alley as this!"

The path showed greyly in front of her out of the dimness. On and on she followed it; here and there the roots of the old laurels, struggling out of the ground, threatened to trip her up.

Her eyes, however, had now grown accustomed to the half-gloom, and not a detail of her surroundings escaped her as she went along.

A bird flew from out the thicket on her right hand with a startled cry. A dainty little frog leaped out of her way into the shriveled leaves lying below the laurels. Following the movements of this frog, her eye was caught by something black and solid among those leaves. What was it? A bundle—a shiny black coat? Loveday knelt down, and using her hands to assist her eyes, found that they came into contact with the dead, stiffened body of a beautiful black retriever. She parted, as well as she was able, the lower boughs of the evergreens, and minutely examined the poor animal. Its eyes were still open, though glazed and bleared, and its death had, undoubtedly, been caused by the blow of some blunt, heavy instrument, for on one side its skull was almost battered in.

"Exactly the death that was dealt to Sandy," she thought, as she groped hither and thither beneath the trees in hopes of lighting upon the weapon of destruction.

She searched until increasing darkness warned her that search was useless. Then, still following the zig-zagging path, she made her way out by the stables and thence back to the house.

She went to bed that night without having spoken to a soul beyond the cook and butler. The next morning, however, Mr. Craven introduced himself to her across the breakfast-table. He was a man of really handsome personal appearance, with a fine carriage of the head and shoulders, and eyes that had a forlorn, appealing look in them. He entered the room with an air of great energy, apologized to Loveday for the absence of his wife, and for his own remissness in not being in the way to receive her on the previous day. Then he bade her make herself at home at the breakfast-table, and expressed his delight in having found a coadjutor in his work.

"I hope you understand what a great—a stupendous work it is?" he added, as he sank into a chair. "It is a work that will leave its impress upon thought in all the ages to come. Only a man who has studied comparative philology as I have for the past thirty years, could gauge the magnitude of the task I have set myself."

With the last remark, his energy seemed spent, and he sank back in his chair, covering his eyes with his hand in precisely the same attitude as that in which Loveday had seen him overnight, and utterly oblivious of the fact that breakfast was before him and a stranger-guest seated at table. The butler entered with another dish. "Better go on with your breakfast," he whispered to Loveday, "he may sit like that for another hour."

He placed his dish in front of his master.

"Captain hasn't come back yet, sir," he said, making an effort to arouse him from his reverie.

"Eh, what?" said Mr. Craven, for a moment lifting his hand from his eyes.

"Captain, sir—the black retriever," repeated the man.

The pathetic look in Mr. Craven's eyes deepened.

"Ah, poor Captain!" he murmured; "the best dog I ever had."

Then he again sank back in his chair, putting his hand to his forehead.

The butler made one more effort to arouse him.

"Madam sent you down a newspaper, sir, that she thought you would like to see," he shouted almost into his master's ear, and at the same time laid the morning's paper on the table beside his plate.

"Confound you! leave it there," said Mr. Craven irritably. "Fools! dolts that you all are! With your trivialities and interruptions you are sending me out of the world with my work undone!"

And again he sank back in his chair, closed his eyes and became lost to his surroundings.

Loveday went on with her breakfast. She changed her place at table to one on Mr. Craven's right hand, so that the newspaper sent down for his perusal lay between his plate and hers. It was folded into an oblong shape, as if it were wished to direct attention to a certain portion of a certain column.

A clock in a corner of the room struck the hour with a loud, resonant stroke. Mr. Craven gave a start and rubbed his eyes.

"Eh, what's this?" he said. "What meal are we at?" He looked around with a bewildered air. "Eh!—who are you?" he went on, staring hard at Loveday. "What are you doing here? Where's Nina?—Where's Harry?"

Loveday began to explain, and gradually recollection seemed to come back to him.

"Ah, yes, yes," he said. "I remember; you've come to assist me with my great work. You promised, you know, to help me out of the hole I've got into. Very enthusiastic, I remember they said you were, on certain abstruse points in comparative philology. Now, Miss—Miss—I've forgotten your name—tell me a little of what you know about the elemental sounds of speech that are common to all languages. Now, to how many would you reduce those elemental sounds—to six, eight, nine? No, we won't discuss the matter here, the cups and saucers distract me. Come into my den at the other end of the house; we'll have perfect quiet there."

And utterly ignoring the fact that he had not as yet broken his fast, he rose from the table, seized Loveday by the wrist, and led her out of the room and down the long corridor that led through the south wing to his study.

But seated in that study his energy once more speedily exhausted itself.

He placed Loveday in a comfortable chair at his writing-table, consulted her taste as to pens, and spread a sheet of foolscap before her. Then he settled himself in his easy-chair, with his back to the light, as if he were about to dictate folios to her.

In a loud, distinct voice he repeated the title of his learned work, then its sub-division, then the number and heading of the chapter that was at present engaging his attention. Then he put his hand to his head. "It's the elemental sounds that are my stumbling-block," he said. "Now, how on earth is it possible to get a notion of a sound of agony that is not in part a sound of terror? or a sound of surprise that is not in part a sound of either joy or sorrow?"

With this his energies were spent, and although Loveday remained seated in that study from early morning till daylight began to fade, she had not ten sentences to show for her day's work as amanuensis.

Loveday in all spent only two clear days at Troyte's Hill.

On the evening of the first of those days Detective Griffiths received, through the trustworthy post-boy, the following brief note from her:

"I have found out that Hales owed Sandy close upon a hundred pounds, which he had borrowed at various times. I don't know whether you will think this fact of any importance.—L. B."

Mr. Griffiths repeated the last sentence blankly. "If Harry Craven were put upon his defence, his counsel, I take it, would consider the fact of first importance," he muttered. And for the remainder of that day Mr. Griffiths went about his work in a perturbed state of mind, doubtful whether to hold or to let go his theory concerning Harry Craven's guilt.

The next morning there came another brief note from Loveday which ran thus:

"As a matter of collateral interest, find out if a person, calling himself Harold Cousins, sailed two days ago from London Docks for Natal in the *Bonnie Dundee*?"

To this missive Loveday received, in reply, the following somewhat lengthy dispatch:

"I do not quite see the drift of your last note, but have wired to our agents in London to carry out its suggestion. On my part, I have important news to communicate. I have found out what Harry Craven's business out of doors was on the night of the murder, and at my instance a warrant has been issued for his arrest. This warrant it will be my duty to serve on him in the course of to-day. Things are beginning to look very black against him, and I am convinced his illness is all a sham. I have seen Waters, the man who is supposed to be attending him, and have driven him into a corner and made him admit that he has only seen young Craven once—on the first day of his illness—and that he gave his certificate entirely on the strength of what Mrs. Craven told him of her son's condition. On the occasion of this, his first and only visit, the lady, it seems, also told him that it would not be necessary for him to continue his attendance, as she quite felt herself competent to treat the case, having had so much experience in fever cases among the blacks at Natal.

"As I left Waters's house, after eliciting this important information, I was accosted by a man who keeps a low-class inn in the place, McQueen by name. He said that he wished to speak to me on a matter of importance. To make a long story short, this McQueen stated that on the night of the sixth, shortly after eleven o'clock, Harry Craven came to his house, bringing with him a valuable piece of plate—a handsome epergne—and requested him to lend him a hundred pounds on it, as he hadn't a penny in his pocket. McQueen complied with his request to the extent of ten sovereigns, and now, in a fit of nervous terror, comes to me to confess himself a receiver of stolen goods and play the honest man! He says he noticed that the young gentleman was very much agitated as he made the request, and he also begged him to mention his visit to no one. Now, I am curious to learn how Master Harry will get over the fact that he passed the lodge at the hour at which the murder was most probably committed; or how he will get out of the dilemma of having repassed the lodge on his way back to the house, and not noticed the wide-open window with the full moon shining down on it?

"Another word! Keep out of the way when I arrive at the house, somewhere between two and three in the afternoon, to serve the warrant. I do not wish your professional capacity to get wind, for you will most likely yet be of some use to us in the house.

"S.G."

Loveday read this note, seated at Mr. Craven's writing-table, with the old gentleman himself reclining motionless beside her in his easy-chair. A little smile played about the corners of her mouth as she read over again the words—"for you will most likely yet be of some use to us in the house."

Loveday's second day in Mr. Craven's study promised to be as unfruitful as the first. For fully an hour after she had received Griffiths' note, she sat at the writing-table with her pen in her hand, ready to transcribe Mr. Craven's inspirations. Beyond, however, the phrase, muttered with closed eyes—"It's all here, in my brain, but I can't put it into words"—not a half-syllable escaped his lips.

At the end of that hour the sound of footsteps on the outside gravel made her turn her head towards the window. It was Griffiths approaching with two constables. She heard the hall door opened to admit them, but, beyond that, not a sound reached her ear, and she realized how fully she was cut off from communication with the rest of the household at the farther end of this unoccupied wing.

Mr. Craven, still reclining in his semi-trance, evidently had not the faintest suspicion that so important an event as the arrest of his only son on a charge of murder was about to be enacted in the house.

Meantime, Griffiths and his constables had mounted the stairs leading to the north wing, and were being guided through the corridors to the sick-room by the flying figure of Moggie, the maid.

"Hoot, mistress!" cried the girl, "here are three men coming up the stairs—policemen, every one of them—will ye come and ask them what they be wanting?"

Outside the door of the sick-room stood Mrs. Craven—a tall, sharp-featured woman with sandy hair going rapidly grey.

"What is the meaning of this? What is your business here?" she said haughtily, addressing Griffiths, who headed the party.

Griffiths respectfully explained what his business was, and requested her to stand on one side that he might enter her son's room.

"This is my daughter's room; satisfy yourself of the fact," said the lady, throwing back the door as she spoke.

And Griffiths and his confrères entered, to find pretty Miss

Craven, looking very white and scared, seated beside a fire in a long flowing robe de chambre.

Griffiths departed in haste and confusion, without the chance of a professional talk with Loveday. That afternoon saw him telegraphing wildly in all directions, and dispatching messengers in all quarters. Finally he spent over an hour drawing up an elaborate report to his chief at Newcastle, assuring him of the identity of one, Harold Cousins, who had sailed in the *Bonnie Dundee* for Natal, with Harry Craven, of Troyte's Hill, and advising that the police authorities in that far-away district should be immediately communicated with.

The ink had not dried on the pen with which this report was written before a note, in Loveday's writing, was put into his hand.

Loveday evidently had had some difficulty in finding a messenger for this note, for it was brought by a gardener's boy, who informed Griffiths that the lady had said he would receive a gold sovereign if he delivered the letter all right.

Griffiths paid the boy and dismissed him, and then proceeded to read Loveday's communication.

It was written hurriedly in pencil, and ran as follows:

"Things are getting critical here. Directly you receive this, come up to the house with two of your men, and post yourselves anywhere in the grounds where you can see and not be seen. There will be no difficulty in this, for it will be dark by the time you are able to get there. I am not sure whether I shall want your aid to-night, but you had better keep in the grounds until morning, in case of need; and above all, never once lose sight of the study windows." (This was underscored.) "If I put a lamp with a green shade in one of those windows, do not lose a moment in entering by that window, which I will contrive to keep unlocked."

Detective Griffiths rubbed his forehead—rubbed his eyes, as he finished reading this.

"Well, I daresay it's all right," he said, "but I'm bothered, that's all, and for the life of me I can't see one step of the way she is going."

He looked at his watch: the hands pointed to a quarter past

six. The short September day was drawing rapidly to a close. A good five miles lay between him and Troyte's Hill—there was evidently not a moment to lose.

At the very moment that Griffiths, with his two constables, were once more starting along the Grenfell High Road behind the best horse they could procure, Mr. Craven was rousing himself from his long slumber, and beginning to look around him. That slumber, however, though long, had not been a peaceful one, and it was sundry of the old gentleman's muttered exclamations, as he had started uneasily in his sleep, that had caused Loveday to open, and then to creep out of the room to dispatch, her hurried note.

What effect the occurrence of the morning had had upon the household generally, Loveday, in her isolated corner of the house, had no means of ascertaining. She only noted that when Hales brought in her tea, as he did precisely at five o'clock, he wore a particularly ill-tempered expression of countenance, and she heard him mutter, as he set down the tea-tray with a clatter, something about being a respectable man, and not used to such "goings on."

It was not until nearly an hour and a half after this that Mr. Craven had awakened with a sudden start, and, looking wildly around him, had questioned Loveday who had entered the room.

Loveday explained that the butler had brought in lunch at one, and tea at five, but that since then no one had come in.

"Now that's false," said Mr. Craven, in a sharp, unnatural sort of voice; "I saw him sneaking round the room, the whining, canting hypocrite, and you must have seen him, too! Didn't you hear him say, in his squeaky old voice: 'Master, I knows your secret—'" He broke off abruptly, looking wildly round. "Eh, what's this?" he cried. "No, no, I'm all wrong—Sandy is dead and buried—they held an inquest on him, and we all praised him up as if he were a saint."

"He must have been a bad man, that old Sandy," said Loveday sympathetically.

"You're right! you're right!" cried Mr. Craven, springing up excitedly from his chair and seizing her by the hand. "If ever a man deserved his death, he did. For thirty years he held that rod over my head, and then—ah where was I?"

He put his hand to his head and again sank, as if exhausted, into his chair.

"I suppose it was some early indiscretion of yours at college that he knew of?" said Loveday, eager to get at as much of the truth as possible while the mood for confidence held sway in the feeble brain.

"That was it! I was fool enough to marry a disreputable girl—a barmaid in the town—and Sandy was present at the wedding, and then—" Here his eyes closed again and his mutterings became incoherent.

For ten minutes he lay back in his chair, muttering thus; "A yelp—a groan," were the only words Loveday could distinguish among those mutterings, then suddenly, slowly and distinctly, he said, as if answering some plainly-put question: "A good blow with the hammer and the thing was done."

"I should like amazingly to see that hammer," said Loveday; "do you keep it anywhere at hand?"

His eyes opened with a wild, cunning look in them.

"Who's talking about a hammer? I did not say I had one. If anyone says I did it with a hammer, they're telling a lie."

"Oh, you've spoken to me about the hammer two or three times," said Loveday calmly; "the one that killed your dog, Captain, and I should like to see it, that's all."

The look of cunning died out of the old man's eye—"Ah, poor Captain! splendid dog that! Well, now, where were we? Where did we leave off? Ah, I remember, it was the elemental sounds of speech that bothered me so that night. Were you here then? Ah, no! I remember. I had been trying all day to assimilate a dog's yelp of pain to a human groan, and I couldn't do it. The idea haunted me—followed me about wherever I went. If they were both elemental sounds, they must have something in common, but the link between them I could not find; then it occurred to me, would a well-bred, well-trained dog like my Captain in the stables, there, at the moment of death give an unmitigated currish yelp; would there not be something of a human note in his death-cry? The thing was worth putting to the test. If I could hand down in my treatise a fragment of fact on the matter, it would be worth a dozen dogs' lives. So I went out into the moonlight—ah, but you know all about it—now, don't you?"

"Yes. Poor Captain! did he yelp or groan?"

"Why, he gave one loud, long, hideous yelp, just as if he had been a common cur. I might just as well have let him alone; it only set that other brute opening his window and spying out on me, and saying in his cracked old voice: 'Master, what are you doing out here at this time of night?'"

Again he sank back in his chair, muttering incoherently with half-closed eyes.

Loveday let him alone for a minute or so; then she had another question to ask.

"And that other brute—did he yelp or groan when you dealt him his blow?"

"What, old Sandy—the brute? he fell back—Ah, I remember, you said you would like to see the hammer that stopped his babbling old tongue—now didn't you?"

He rose a little unsteadily from his chair, and seemed to drag his long limbs with an effort across the room to a cabinet at the farther end. Opening a drawer in this cabinet, he produced, from amidst some specimens of strata and fossils, a large-sized geological hammer.

He brandished it for a moment over his head, then paused with his finger on his lip.

"Hush!" he said, "we shall have the fools creeping in to peep at us if we don't take care." And to Loveday's horror he suddenly made for the door, turned the key in the lock, withdrew it and put it into his pocket.

She looked at the clock; the hands pointed to half-past seven. Had Griffiths received her note at the proper time, and were the men now in the grounds? She could only pray that they were.

"The light is too strong for my eyes," she said, and rising from her chair, she lifted the green-shaded lamp and placed it on a table that stood at the window.

"No, no, that won't do," said Mr. Craven; "that would show

everyone outside what we're doing in here." He crossed to the window as he spoke and removed the lamp thence to the mantelpiece.

Loveday could only hope that in the few seconds it had remained in the window it had caught the eye of the outside watchers.

The old man beckoned to Loveday to come near and examine his deadly weapon. "Give it a good swing round," he said, suiting the action to the word, "and down it comes with a splendid crash." He brought the hammer round within an inch of Loveday's forehead.

She started back.

"Ha, ha," he laughed harshly and unnaturally, with the light of madness dancing in his eyes now; "did I frighten you? I wonder what sort of sound you would make if I were to give you a little tap just there." Here he lightly touched her forehead with the hammer. "Elemental, of course, it would be, and—"

Loveday steadied her nerves with difficulty. Locked in with this lunatic, her only chance lay in gaining time for the detectives to reach the house and enter through the window.

"Wait a minute," she said, striving to divert his attention; "you have not yet told me what sort of an elemental sound old Sandy made when he fell. If you'll give me pen and ink, I'll write down a full account of it all, and you can incorporate it afterwards in your treatise."

For a moment a look of real pleasure flitted across the old man's face, then it faded. "The brute fell back dead without a sound," he answered; "it was all for nothing, that night's work; yet not altogether for nothing. No, I don't mind owning I would do it all over again to get the wild thrill of joy at my heart that I had when I looked down into that old man's dead face and felt myself free at last! Free at last!" his voice rang out excitedly— once more he brought his hammer round with an ugly swing.

"For a moment I was a young man again; I leaped into his room—the moon was shining full in through the window—I thought of my old college days, and the fun we used to have at Pembroke—topsy turvey I turned everything—" He broke off abruptly, and drew a step nearer to Loveday. "The pity of it all was," he said, suddenly dropping from his high, excited tone to a low, pathetic one, "that he fell without a sound of any sort." Here he drew another step nearer. "I wonder—" he said, then broke off again, and came close to Loveday's side. "It has only this moment occurred to me," he said, now with his lips close to Loveday's ear, "that a woman, in her death agony, would be much more likely to give utterance to an elemental sound than a man."

He raised his hammer, and Loveday fled to the window, and was lifted from the outside by three pairs of strong arms.

"I thought I was conducting my very last case—I never had such a narrow escape before!" said Loveday, as she stood talking with Mr. Griffiths on the Grenfell platform, awaiting the train to carry her back to London. "It seems strange that no one before suspected the old gentleman's sanity—I suppose, however, people were so used to his eccentricities that they did not notice how they had deepened into positive lunacy. His cunning evidently stood him in good stead at the inquest."

"It is possible," said Griffiths thoughtfully, "that he did not absolutely cross the very slender line that divided eccentricity from madness until after the murder. The excitement consequent upon the discovery of the crime may just have pushed him over the border. Now, Miss Brooke, we have exactly ten minutes before your train comes in. I should feel greatly obliged to you if you would explain one or two things that have a professional interest for me."

"With pleasure," said Loveday. "Put your questions in categorical order and I will answer them."

"Well, then, in the first place, what suggested to your mind the old man's guilt?"

"The relations that subsisted between him and Sandy seemed to me to savour too much of fear on the one side and power on the other. Also the income paid to Sandy during Mr. Craven's absence in Natal bore, to my mind, an unpleasant resemblance to hush-money."

"Poor wretched being! And I hear that, after all, the woman he married in his wild young days died soon afterwards of

drink. I have no doubt, however, that Sandy sedulously kept up
the fiction of her existence, even after his master's second marriage. Now for another question: how was it you knew that Miss
Craven had taken her brother's place in the sick-room?"

"On the evening of my arrival I discovered a rather long lock
of fair hair in the unswept fireplace of my room, which, as it
happened, was usually occupied by Miss Craven. It at once occurred to me that the young lady had been cutting off her hair
and that there must be some powerful motive to induce such a
sacrifice. The suspicious circumstances attending her brother's
illness soon supplied me with such a motive."

"Ah! that typhoid fever business was very cleverly done. Not
a servant in the house, I verily believe, but who thought Master
Harry was upstairs, ill in bed, and Miss Craven away at her
friends' in Newcastle. The young fellow must have got a clear
start off within an hour of the murder. His sister, sent away the
next day to Newcastle, dismissed her maid there, I hear, on the
plea of no accommodation at her friends' house—sent the girl
to her own home for a holiday and herself returned to Troyte's
Hill in the middle of the night, having walked the five miles
from Grenfell. No doubt her mother admitted her through one
of those easily-opened front windows, cut her hair and put her
to bed to personate her brother without delay. With Miss Craven's strong likeness to Master Harry, and in a darkened room,
it is easy to understand that the eyes of a doctor, personally
unacquainted with the family, might easily be deceived. Now,
Miss Brooke, you must admit that with all this elaborate chi-
canery and double dealing going on, it was only natural that
my suspicions should set in strongly in that quarter."

"I read it all in another light, you see," said Loveday. "It
seemed to me that the mother, knowing her son's evil proclivi-
ties, believed in his guilt, in spite, possibly, of his assertions of
innocence. The son, most likely, on his way back to the house
after pledging the family plate, had met old Mr. Craven with the
hammer in his hand. Seeing, no doubt, how impossible it would
be for him to clear himself without incriminating his father, he
preferred flight to Natal to giving evidence at the inquest."

"Now about his alias?" said Mr. Griffiths briskly, for the

train was at that moment steaming into the station. "How did you know that Harold Cousins was identical with Harry Craven, and had sailed in the *Bonnie Dundee*?"

"Oh, that was easy enough," said Loveday, as she stepped into the train; "a newspaper sent down to Mr. Craven by his wife, was folded so as to direct his attention to the shipping list. In it I saw that the *Bonnie Dundee* had sailed two days previously for Natal. Now it was only natural to connect Natal with Mrs. Craven, who had passed the greater part of her life there; and it was easy to understand her wish to get her scape-grace son among her early friends. The alias under which he sailed came readily enough to light. I found it scribbled all over one of Mr. Craven's writing pads in his study; evidently it had been drummed into his ears by his wife as his son's alias, and the old gentleman had taken this method of fixing it in his memory. We'll hope that the young fellow, under his new name, will make a new reputation for himself—at any rate, he'll have a better chance of doing so with the ocean between him and his evil companions. Now it's good-bye, I think."

"No," said Mr. Griffiths; "it's au revoir, for you'll have to come back again for the assizes, and give the evidence that will shut old Mr. Craven in an asylum for the rest of his life."

GERALDINE BONNER

(1870–1930)

Popular a century ago but now forgotten, Geraldine Bonner began by writing short stories for various US and British periodicals—*Harper's*, *Vogue*, *Pall Mall*. The periodical press was hungry for short fiction in a time after widespread education had become the norm but before radio and movies encroached upon the entertainment market. The first decade of the new century found Bonner coauthoring plays.

Childhood experiences in the mining camps of Colorado inspired her first novel. *Hard-Pan: A Story of Bonanza Fortunes* was published in 1900. The term seems to have derived from prospectors and referred to a hard layer of compressed soil, usually clay, not far beneath the ground's surface; by the time of Bonner's writing, it also meant a bedrock or foundation and a reliable money-making venture. Later Bonner used "Hard Pan" as an occasional pseudonym.

She wrote several successful murder mysteries. Her style was lively and informal, often a confiding sort of first-person, as in *The Girl at Central*, which is narrated by switchboard operator and amateur sleuth Molly Morgenthau. Most of Bonner's books did not feature series characters, but this untrained "detective"—no less improbable than Miss Marple, come to think of it, and a lot livelier—went on to feature in other cases. She narrates half of *The Black Eagle Mystery* and a smaller part of *Miss Maitland, Private Secretary*.

In 1895 a new magazine appeared that published only short stories—*The Black Cat*. The editor, Herman Umbstaetter, sought new writers and often lured them with contests. In this transitional era, he published everyone from Jack London to Henry Miller, from O. Henry to early work by Rex Stout, later the creator of genius detective Nero Wolfe. Geraldine Bonner's

"The Statement of Jared Johnson" appeared in the June 1899 issue. It is one of her non-series stories, narrated by a participant in the mystery, not a professional observer. The narrator's slang includes a rude term for speakers of Spanish, Portuguese, and Italian, nowadays thought of as archaic racism for all things Italian.

THE STATEMENT OF
JARED JOHNSON

I am going to write my side of the famous "Johnson Case."

It's a pretty hard thing to go over in cold blood, but I want the public to hear my version of the story. They know the case against me has been dismissed and they've read in the papers what I said, but it's been so mixed up and so misrepresented that I've decided to make my own statement to write down as simply and as honestly as I can just how it was I came to be suspected.

My name is Jared Johnson and until I was arrested on the 23d of last December, I was the janitor of the Fremont Building, and had been so for two years past.

The Fremont, as people know now, since the trial made it famous, is an old building off Washington Square. It was one of those houses that still exist in that quarter of the city, which used to be the homes of the gentry and gradually got down in the world till they were first sliced off into flats, and then split up into offices.

The Fremont had been a fine, well built house in the beginning, and even when I came into it was in good repair. But it was old-fashioned, without elevators or electric lights, and the offices rented for low prices.

The top story had been used as a photograph gallery, and had long glass skylights in the ceiling. But that was before my time. Ever since I'd been janitor it had been leased by a society of ladies for a studio. One batch painted there all the morning and another all the afternoon. They had models who used to pose for them and who were forever clattering up and down stairs—mostly Italians and generally a pretty tough-looking lot.

This room was a good deal of a charge on me, for I had to keep it heated up to a tremendous temperature, because the models stood up to be painted in their skins as God made them. And, if they were dagoes, I couldn't let them take their deaths. One end of the room, under the corner skylight, was curtained off for them to use as a dressing room.

Below this were four floors of offices and lodgings, and in the basement I and my wife, Rosy, had our rooms. I have to be particular about describing all this, because I want those who read my statement to have everything clear in their minds.

Just about the middle of December there was a great frost, the worst cold snap I remember, and I came to New York from Ohio when I was twelve. On the morning of December 17th Rosy told me that the thermometer outside Miss Maitland, the type-writer's, window, had dropped to 3 above zero. It was mortal cold. I was kept busy building fires and seeing that the steam heat was on full pressure.

I was proud of the old Fremont for not a pipe in her burst or froze. And next door in the Octagon Building, a brand new skyscraper, twelve stories, and with all the modern improvements, the pipes on our side burst and froze so that the ice was clogged down the sides of them in a huge mass with icicles as long as your arm.

I noticed this on the morning of December 17th when I was rubbing off the skylights in the studio. I was standing on a step-ladder when I looked up at the wall of the Octagon rising like a cliff, and just on the angle, a little above our roof, were the pipes with the ice wrapped round them like a winding sheet. I couldn't help laughing for they'd blown so about the Octagon and her "modern improvements."

Two days later the black frost broke and there was the biggest thaw that ever was seen. It got soft and warm like Spring, the streets began to swim with water, and all day long the boys were coming down from the offices complaining of the steam heat. I was on the rush all day, for to add to everything else it was Saturday, and Rosy and I have most of the building to ourselves that day and we do the cleaning.

But we didn't do as much as usual that Saturday, for, as I had to tell on the trial, and so must repeat it now, Rosy and I had fallen out. We'd been bickering for quite a while past and Saturday it seemed as if we couldn't meet on the stairs or hand each other a broom or a pail without snapping and nagging. I'm not blaming her, for I was as ugly as she, only my temper is not of that kind. It's the still, sulky sort, and it rises slowly but takes a long time to cool.

The trouble between us was this—Heaven forgive me for raking it all up after Rosy proved herself to be the truest wife a man ever had, but it's part of my statement, and has to go in—Rosy was jealous. She'd always been inclined that way, and when we were first married and everything she did seemed just about right, I tried never to bother or annoy her.

But after five years of marriage I wasn't quite so considerate, and though I swear before Heaven I never did aught that any man mightn't do without shame or blame, I wasn't so mindful of what Rosy liked or disliked. I know now that, without meaning it, I must have provoked her often. I suspect I did it to tease her a little, and I suspect I did it to prove to her that I was my own master and wasn't going to have any woman dictating to me.

It was one of the models up in the ladies' studio that Rosy was jealous about. Most of them being dagoes, as black as mulattoes, and only speaking their own talk, I had no words with them. But there was one of them, Alice Merrion, that was of Irish parentage but American born, and with her I struck up an acquaintance, and we used to stop and pass the time of day when we met on the stairs or in the hall.

Rosy took a dislike to Alice Merrion right from the start. She said she couldn't bear her because she was a model. Nothing that you could say would make Rosy believe that a girl could be honest and earn her living that way.

As for Alice Merrion's looks—she couldn't understand why any one wanted to paint her picture. To tell the truth, I often thought this too, for Alice wasn't what I'd call a pretty girl. She had freckles, yellowish-green eyes and a big bush of red hair that stood out like flames round her head.

I liked the girl and I was sorry for her. She was one of the best I ever knew, honest as a die and straight as a string for all her being a model. She supported her mother, and if ever I was sure of anything in my life, I was sure of Alice Merrion's character.

But I wasn't any more taken with her than a married man might be honestly taken with any decent girl.

On Saturday afternoon, the ladies going home early, I made it my business to clean up the studio and lock it till Monday morning. On Saturday, December 19th, the ladies left even earlier than usual, the day settling down dark and threatening rain, and about four I went up with my broom and pail.

I was mightily surprised when I opened the door to see Alice sitting huddled up, cowering over the stove. She was right under the middle skylight and the gray, wintery light fell in on her red hair that was loosely knotted up and looked like a fiery crown. From under her skirt her bare feet were thrust out on the stove ledge, and she had a shawl folded round her shoulders, with her bare arms, white as marble, coming out.

"Why, Alice," said I, "what's up? It's past four and here you are, not even dressed yet."

She looked up at me and I saw that her cheeks were pale and her eyes looked dull and heavy.

"I feel sick," she said, drawing her hand over her forehead, and pushing back her hair. "I've got something sure. A little while ago I was as hot as this stove, and now I'm freezing."

She crouched over it spreading out her hands. I touched one of them; it was like ice. As I stood looking at her I heard the first drops of rain—big, heavy, slow drops—fall on the skylight.

"You've caught a bad cold," I said to her. "You want something to warm you up. Don't you think a cup of tea would do you good?"

Her face brightened directly.

"Oh, Mr. Johnson," she said, "do you think you could get me one? I didn't have a bite of lunch to-day. I felt so bad. And then I stood here for two hours and that's hard work, even when you're well. I think if I could get something hot I'd feel better."

She looked up at me with her big, yellowish eyes shining through the gray light, and if ever I was sorry for a woman it was for her. I wished that Rosy wasn't so down on her and I'd have taken her to our rooms and given her a good meal.

"Rest here easy," I said to her, "and I'll get you a bite that will brace you up. I won't be long," and I went out and down the stalls feeling angrier than ever with Rosy for her senseless prejudice.

I hoped and prayed that there might be no one in the kitchen and things went my way for once. Rosy was not there. So I made a little brew of tea, cut some bread and butter, put it on a tray and set off up the stairs.

And it was here that my luck deserted me. For, on the second landing, I met Miss Maitland going out.

"What's the matter?" says she, looking at the tray. "Any one sick?"

It didn't cross my mind not to tell the truth and I answered:

"The model, ma'am, on the top floor, has caught a chill and feels bad."

Miss Maitland laughed and went down the stairs and her testimony in court, if you remember, was pretty damaging for me.

On the fourth floor I ran into Mr. Raymond on the landing. Mr. Raymond is my favorite in the whole Fremont. He is a stenographer and rents all the back rooms on that floor, some of them for offices and the rest for his own lodgings.

"Hullo, Johnson," he says to me in his jolly way, "taking that up to me? Made a mistake this time. That's not my particular tipple."

I laughed, for we all knew that Mr. Raymond's tipple was a pretty strong one.

"No, sir," I said. "It's for Alice Merrion in the studio. She's taken with a chill. She's had nothing to eat since morning and I thought this would warm her up a little."

"Ah, poor girl!" he says, going on down the passage to his own rooms. Then over his shoulder he called, "If you want anything stronger—if she feels faint, or anything—just drop in on me and I'll give it to you."

And he went down the passage. Those two meetings were about as bad for me as they could be, as it turned out afterward.

I went into the studio and found Alice just as I had left her. She drank the tea and ate the bread with a relish and I began to get things ready for my cleaning. Now and then we spoke to each other, and between whiles we could hear the rain drumming on the skylight. It grew dark and leaden, and, as I moved, I could see through the skylights the big wall of the Octagon, with the windows springing out in yellow squares as the gases were lit.

When Alice had finished, I knew she'd want to dress and go home, so I made an excuse to go. She watched me as I set the tea things back on the tray and then said suddenly:

"You're very good to me; let's shake hands."

I was surprised, but took her hand and shook it.

"You're a good girl," I said to her, "mind you remember that I'm always your friend."

"Thanks, Jared Johnson," said she quite solemnly, "I know that. Good-by."

I turned round and went, some way or other feeling sort of strange and awed. I shut the door behind me and as I was on the stairs I heard her lock it.

In the kitchen I found Rosy. The moment she saw the tray her face darkened, and she pulled up short in her work and eyed me with a sharp look. I was irritable myself, angry with her for her treatment of Alice Merrion, and when she looked at me that way, it made me blaze up. Without waiting for her to ask me, I told her who the tray was for and where I had been.

I don't think it's necessary for me to tell just what we said to each other, but we had a quarrel—a bitter one. Now that both of us have felt what real misery is, we realize with shame what a pair of crazy fools we were.

But we thought of nothing then but our own anger. I don't remember all I said. I felt that black rage a man sometimes feels when a woman he loves and honors flings in his teeth low meannesses he never thought of doing. In the middle of it I got up and ran out of the room, banging the door. I went down to the cellar, and stayed there all night sleeping on a pile of gunny sacks in front of the furnace.

The next day Rosy and I were about as stiff to each other as we could be. We hardly spoke at all and ate our meals in a heavy silence. Monday morning broke with a blue sky and sunlight outside, but between us there was still cloudy weather.

I got up early, for I had to build fires in some of the offices, especially in the studio, which, by eight o'clock, was supposed to be warmed and ready for the first class. As I went up the third flight of stairs, Mr. Raymond came out on the landing.

"Hullo! Johnson," says he, "what the devil's the matter with this building? Is she settling?"

"The Fremont's as good as she ever was, sir," I answered. "What's the matter?"

"The ceiling's come down in my bathroom," says he. "Early this morning—whang! bang!—down she came. Come and see the scene of carnage."

I followed him into the bathroom, which opened off the end of the passage, and there, sure enough, the ceiling was down. I picked up a piece of the plaster and felt that it was wet.

"A leak," I said, "the rain's come in above."

"Oh, then," he says, suddenly, "that explains the crash of glass I heard Saturday evening. There was a tremendous smashing of glass from somewhere up there."

This startled me. I suppose I looked sort of alarmed, for Mr. Raymond said,

"I'll go up with you. Probably the skylight's broken."

We ran up the last flight and tried the studio door. It was locked, and when I tried my key I found that there was one already in the keyhole.

I don't know then just what I thought, but I know a deadly feeling of fear took hold of my heart. Mr. Raymond must have seen it in my face.

"Break in the door," says he in a low voice, and, as he spoke, he put his shoulder to the panel and pressed. In a moment we had ripped off the old socket that held the lock and the door burst in.

There was a sudden sharp current of air, cold and wet, and the brown curtain over the models' dressing corner swelled out on the draught. A window was open somewhere and part of the floor was dark with rain stains.

We shut the door with the key still in the lock and ran to where the curtain fell back into its straight folds. Behind it we saw a sight that neither of us will ever forget.

Alice Merrion lay on her face on the floor, the skylight above her broken, and the fragments of glass scattered in every direction.

She was fully dressed, except for her shoes, one of which she held in her hand. Through the broken skylight the rain had beaten upon her till her clothes, the floor, her hair, were oozing moisture. The latter was wet with something else which dyed it a deeper red. The back of her skull was fractured and partly driven in. She was rigid in death, her eyes open, and an expression of strange, terrified surprise stamped upon her features.

That first glimpse impressed every detail of the room upon my mind. Her hat and jacket were hanging from a peg in the wall. On the shelf under the square of looking-glass lay some hair-pins and her purse. All about—on her dress, in her hair, on the floor—shone bits of the shivered skylight. The panes of glass were of a good size and were fitted into light, thin supports of iron. Just in the middle two of these were bowed downward.

We bent over her to see if there were any signs of life, but she was cold and stiff as a marble statue. The physicians afterward said that when we found her she had been dead about thirty-six hours. She had evidently been putting on her shoes when struck down by the terrific blow that killed her.

That is as truthful a description as I can write of the finding of Alice Merrion's body. I ought to know how to do it by this time. I've not only told it so often, but I've dreamed it night after night till I wonder if I'm going to go on dreaming it forever.

The next day I was arrested on suspicion as the murderer and a week later was indicted by the Grand Jury. My trial followed in two months.

I never knew until I was in danger of losing my life on circumstantial evidence how important the most insignificant things can become when people are looking for incriminating actions and words. Foolish things I had said came up against me as black as night. The cup of tea I took the girl was as bad for me as if it had been a cup of poison. But worst of all was the quarrel I had with Rosy. It all had to come out, and the newspapers that were not on my side said it was as bad for me as if I'd been caught red-handed.

I could see as plain as anybody that the case against me was a strong one. It started on the theory that I was in love with Alice Merrion. Both Rosy and I acknowledged that we'd more than once quarrelled about her. On the afternoon of December 19th I had had a final interview with her. There were different opinions as to what this had been about. Some had it that she'd threatened to expose me to my wife, who was jealous already; others that she'd given me to understand she wouldn't have anything to do with me. Whatever she'd said, she'd scared or angered me till I'd crept up on her from the back and struck her dead with one—or some thought two—savage blows.

To turn aside suspicion I had then locked the door and left the key in it, had broken the skylight—the noise of which Mr. Raymond had heard at a few minutes after five—and, under cover of the dark, had dropped from the roof to the fire-escapes. When I got to the kitchen my nerves were naturally unstrung and I had quarrelled with my wife, left the room, and had not been seen again until the morning.

The one link in the chain which did not fit was how I had brought the tea tray down with me. The only way I could have done this was to have put it outside the door, and then, after escaping by the fire-ladders, crept back for it and come down again. This, people said, was a proof of my fiendish coolness and cunning.

The fact that the evidence pointed to no one else made it all the worse for me. There did not seem to be a human creature but myself who could be suspected. The girl had no enemies and no follower that anybody knew of. She had led a quiet and perfectly respectable life. That the object was not theft was proved by the fact that her purse, containing twenty dollars, was untouched. There was no doubt that somebody had murdered her, and the murder could be fastened on no one but me.

One of the questions over which there was great argument was what instrument or weapon had been used to deliver the blow. On the upper part of the occiput, just below the crown, the skin and flesh had been cleanly cut as though struck with something sharp-edged or pointed.

There were expert surgeons called up to examine the wounds and they each had their own ideas as to what the murderer had used. One thought a bayonet, or something shaped like a bayonet, such as a pickaxe or an ice-pick. Another said a hatchet or axe. And one—he was the most celebrated of the lot—said he thought that not one but two implements had been employed, a sharp one which cut the scalp, and a heavy one which fractured the skull.

It was this man who said that the murderer had evidently been in a state of frenzy, as the blow or blows must have been of terrific force to so crush the skull. His evidence started the theory that the girl had been killed by a maniac who had entered and come out by the skylight.

The first days of the trial were so terrible I hate to think of them. The whole world seemed against me. The reporters used to come and talk with me and then write me up as "a man with the face of an assassin" or describe me as "the human bloodhound."

Some of them were friendly fellows too—used to clap me on the back and say, "Brace up, old boy, they've not got enough evidence to convict you"; but when it came to believing in me, that was quite another story. I was Jared Johnson The Suspect, as they called me, a good case to make copy out of, and that was all.

There was one of them that I didn't take much notice of or stock in at first. He was the youngest looking chap for his age I ever saw. When I first saw him I thought he was about eighteen. He was a little, thin, smooth-faced, light-haired boy, and new to the business, as you could see by the quiet bashful sort of way he hung round when the others were there.

One day he got at me alone and began to talk to me, easy and natural, as man to man. He told me he was from Ohio, as I was, and that broke the ice right off. Then he said his name was John Paul Hayne, and he was twenty-six years old. He sat quite a while talking of places in the old state we both knew, and I got to feel as if I was a civilized Christian once more, not an Apache Indian that all the world was chasing. When he got up to go, he stood round for a minute in an uneasy sort of way, and then he suddenly says to me, looking me straight in the eye:

"Jared Johnson, you're not guilty of that murder."

He didn't say it as if he was asking a question, or as if he was trying to persuade himself—he just stated a fact. I looked back at him and I said as quietly as he:

"You're right. But what makes you think so?"

"Oh," says he, speaking in a queer sort of way he had with him, "I can see a church by daylight. I've seen a lot while I've been loafing round here."

The next time he came we had a long talk. He told me he'd viewed the premises and the body the morning the murder was discovered. He was sent by his paper. *The Scoop.* And since then he'd been there several times on his own account.

"And you know," says he, "I've come to a conclusion. The thing that killed Alice Merrion didn't *go* through the skylight, it *came* through it."

"What makes you think that?" I asked.

"The way the iron stanchions were bent. They say the weight of the man hanging to them and pulling himself up bowed them down. Now, I say that's a mistake. To bend those rods that way a man would have to be a giant—a second Sandow. It was the weight of something that struck them from above—a tremendous weight—that bent and almost broke them."

"What could strike down from there?" I asked. "There's nothing between the roof of the Fremont and Heaven."

"That's the trick," said he. "You tell me what could, and I'll tell you what killed Alice Merrion."

It seemed to me all idle talk, but I couldn't help saying:

"I don't see how you make that out. Alice was struck on the back of the head. If a thing fell on her it would have caught her on the top of her head. She must have been standing right under the skylight."

He leaned forward and put his fingers on my arm, his eyes shining like jewels.

"Johnson," says he, "you're an honest man. I've no doubt, but you've not got much sense. Don't you remember that she was putting on her shoes? Did you ever see a woman put on her shoes? She leans over so that her head's bent forward this way—" and he bent his head far down till the back of his neck was stretched out beyond his collar.

"I guess you and the doctor have got the same idea," said I. "There is nothing that could come down on her from above and strike her dead with one blow but a madman who had been creeping about on the roofs."

"I worked over that theory for some time," says he, "but I've come to the conclusion that there's nothing in it. Between the breaking of the glass and the falling of the blow she could have got to the door. No—she was surprised as she was putting on her shoes—surprised and killed in the same instant."

I thought of the expression of her face that morning when we found her dead and stiff, and I looked at John Paul Hayne and nodded without speaking.

After this I saw him every few days. He asked me lots of questions and I got to answering him pretty freely, for I saw that he didn't publish what I said, and I got a great liking for him. He was forever starting theories, but I didn't see that they came to anything.

It was just about this time that the second cold snap struck the city. It was precious cold in my cell and I thought of the old Fremont and Rosy's sitting room with a fire shining through the bars of the grate. Lord! but those times seemed a long way off!

Rosy came to see me with her ears tied up in a worsted scarf. She said it was not as cold as the first snap, but, none the less, the Octagon pipes had frozen and burst again. Some of the Octagon people had come over to the Fremont to ask for rooms. They said the Octagon was a sham, run up by contract and badly built from the curbstone to the chimneys.

Because of these applications the owners of the Fremont were thinking of tearing out the inside of the studio and fitting it up for offices. But, so far, it stood just as it did the morning Alice Merrion's body was found there. The detectives working on the case wouldn't have it touched.

The cold spell was a short one. The back of the winter was

broken and it gave way in three days with a big thaw. The sun beat down like Spring and everything ran water.

My trial was going on daily. The evidence for the defence was nearly all in. I was in a strange state of mind—sometimes I felt wild as if I was being smothered; then again I'd be dull and dead-like, not caring what happened.

People kept on saying "They can't convict you on the evidence they've got." But I didn't care much for that. Even if the jury disagreed I was ruined. I'd have to go back to the world and for the rest of my life be pointed out as the man who had brutally murdered a poor, sick, defenceless girl. I'd rather have died, only for Rosy.

It was the afternoon of the third warm day. I'll never forget that day if I live to be two hundred. The window of the cell was open and every now and then a little breath of soft air came in—air full of Spring.

I was alone, sick at heart and dead beat. I'd been in the court room since morning. They'd had Rosy on the stand, and the poor girl had got mixed up and made things between us look as bad as could be. Then, seeing what she had done, and being weak and frightened, she'd gone off into hysterics, and they could not get her into any sort of condition to go on. So the case had been called off until Monday and I'd seen Rosy taken out sobbing and half dead, and been brought back to my cell.

I was sitting on the edge of the bed when I heard the rattling of bolts and voices at the door, and in came Hayne. The light from the window fell full on his face and it shone as if there was a lamp lit inside it. The look of him brought me on to my feet as if I'd been yanked up by a derrick. I said something, I don't know what. Maybe I didn't speak at all, but I know I tried to.

Without saying a word he took off his hat and held it out to me. I looked at it stupidly. It was a brown derby, the top broken and split.

"Look at that, Johnson," he said, shaking it under my eyes— "look at it well. It's saved you. Do you understand me? It's saved your life."

I stared at him and tried to say something but my tongue wouldn't work.

He pushed me back on the bed and, holding the hat in front of me, began to talk quick with his breath catching in between like a man who's been running.

"My hat's been ruined in that studio of yours—the studio of the Fremont. Fortunately, Raymond and his assistant stenographer were there and saw the catastrophe. See," he said, thrusting his hand through the hole in the crown. "What a blow!"

"A blow!" I said. "Who struck it?"

"The same person who struck Alice Merrion."

We were silent for a second, staring at each other. I could hear my heart beating like a hammer. Then he began:

"I've been in the studio a good deal lately, studying the place. To-day I stopped there at about mid-day, to have another look at those bent rods we've so often spoken of. On the landing I met Raymond and his assistant, and they went in with me, as I wanted to explain to them my idea about the rods. I got on a chair under the broken skylight and they stood below, listening to my explanation. As I stood that way the sun beat down on my head almost as hot as summer and I could hear the dripping of the water from the icicles on the Octagon pipes.

"All of a sudden, without warning, I heard a sharp, snapping sound, there was a crushing noise, and something struck me on the head a stultifying blow. I shouted and struck up, and Raymond and the stenographer caught me as I fell, for I was stunned for a moment. When I pulled myself together I saw that the floor was covered with icicles and chunks of solid ice. Looking up we could see that the great bunch which had been hanging to the pipes had broken off, snapped by its own weight in the thaw."

I fell back on the bed, holding his hand, and stammering something—Heaven knows what.

"Brace up, old man," says he. "You can see daylight now all right. Raymond says that the icicles on the pipes in the last frost were triple that size and weight. *They* bent the iron rods and tore the skylight out. *They* murdered Alice Merrion. All you can say is that they killed her quickly. They must have fallen in two detachments, the vibration of the first break dislodging the second mass, which came almost in the same instant. The glass was broken and the huge, jagged iceberg with its pointed dag-gers, must have plunged through the opening and in one breath struck the girl senseless and lifeless. Why, pull yourself together old man—you're as white as chalk."

Well, that's all.

The rest of the story is too well known through the papers for me to tell it. The case of the State against Jared Johnson was dismissed. There was a great day when I said good-by to them all and came out into the daylight again—an innocent man.

But I'm not going to stay here. No. Too many people know me by sight and stare at me, and I can't bear to pass the old Fremont. Rosy and I are going back to Ohio; my brother has a farm there and I'm to help work it with him.

As for John Paul Hayne, I'm glad to say they've raised his salary on *The Scoop*. One of those sensational papers offered him a hundred dollars a week, but he wouldn't take it. He's a fine boy. He's promised to write to me every two weeks.

ELLEN GLASGOW

(1873–1945)

The shipboard discussion in "A Point in Morals" at first seems to be heading in the direction followed by Alfred Hitchcock's 1948 experimental film *Rope*, in which an onstage murder results in a hidden corpse around which the rest of the action pivots. Ellen Glasgow does not go that far, but she builds suspense while cleverly exploring the very definition of "murder," within the kind of conversation story popular at the time and later resurrected by such writers as Agatha Christie in her Tuesday Night Club series and Isaac Asimov in his Black Widowers series, both of which comprise stories of various characters telling stories about crimes they have encountered.

Unlike most of the other writers in *The Penguin Book of Murder Mysteries*, Glasgow was a mainstream literary novelist, not a crime writer. During her thirty-five-year career, she explored class differences and their barriers to love and friendship, the rise of industrial capitalism, opposition to women's freedom, and eventually racial inequality. Descended mostly from moneyed and influential Southern white people who supported the Civil War, Glasgow could not write about race with the kind of blistering authenticity demonstrated by her contemporary Charles W. Chesnutt, whose own murder story "The Sheriff's Children" appears herein. Indeed, Glasgow's early writings show her working away from the default racism of her upbringing. She joined the suffrage movement and gradually wrote from a more feminist point of view, mining the raw ore of her own romantic disappointments and struggles with social barriers to write a succession of realistic explorations of the American South. She was awarded a Pulitzer Prize for her novel *In This Our Life*, which featured both Black and white characters. It was made into a 1942 movie starring Bette Davis—

the trailer for which carefully omits mention of race or any glimpse of dark skin. Inevitably, in Jim Crow America, the movie toned down the Black characters and the systemic racism they faced. Both the author of the novel and the star of the movie were publicly critical of the script's failure to measure up to the novel.

Alongside her nineteen novels, Glasgow published one collection each of her stories, essays, and poems. Unlike many of the other writers in this anthology, Glasgow had little regular presence in periodicals. She did not agree to serial publication of any of her novels, and wrote no more short stories after her 1923 collection *The Shadowy Third and Other Stories*. This volume reprinted one new tale and six previously published— four of them ghost stories—including her murder story "A Point in Morals," which first appeared in *Harper's New Monthly Magazine* in May 1899.

A POINT IN MORALS

"The question seems to be—" began the Englishman. He looked up and bowed to a girl in a yachting-cap who had just come in from deck and was taking the seat beside him. "The question seems to be—" The girl was having some difficulty in removing her coat, and he turned to assist her.

"In my opinion," broke in a well-known alienist on his way to a convention in Vienna, "the question is simply whether or not civilization, in placing an exorbitant value upon human life, is defeating its own aims." He leaned forward authoritatively, and spoke with a half-foreign precision of accent.

"You mean that the survival of the fittest is checkmated," remarked a young journalist travelling in the interest of a New York daily, "that civilization should practise artificial selection, as it were?"

The alienist shrugged his shoulders deprecatingly. "My dear sir," he protested, "I don't mean anything. It is the question that means something."

"Well, as I was saying," began the Englishman again, reaching for the salt and upsetting a spoonful, "the question seems to be whether or not, under any circumstances, the saving of a human life may become positively immoral."

"Upon that point—" began the alienist: but a young lady in a pink blouse who was seated on the Captain's right interrupted him.

"How could it?" she asked. "At least I don't see how it could; do you, Captain?"

"There is no doubt," remarked the journalist, looking up from a conversation he had drifted into with a lawyer from one of the Western States, "that the more humane spirit pervading modern civilization has not worked wholly for good in the development of the species. Probably, for instance, if we had followed the Spartan practice of exposing unhealthy infants, we should have retained something of the Spartan hardihood. Certainly if we had been content to remain barbarians both our digestions and our nerves would have been the better for it, and melancholia would perhaps have been unknown. But, at the same time, the loss of a number of the more heroic virtues is overbalanced by an increase of the softer ones. Notably, human life has never before been regarded so sacredly."

"On the other side," observed the lawyer, lifting his hand to adjust his eye-glasses, and pausing to brush a crumb from his coat, "though it may all be very well to be philanthropic to the point of pauperizing half a community and of growing squeamish about capital punishment, the whole thing sometimes takes a disgustingly morbid turn. Why, it seems as if criminals were the real American heroes! Only last week I visited a man sentenced to death for the murder of his two wives, and, by Jove, the jailer was literally besieged by women sympathizers. I counted six bunches of heliotrope in his cell, and at least fifty notes."

"Oh, but that is a form of nervous hysteria!" said the girl in the yachting-cap, "and must be considered separately. Every sentiment has its fanatics—philanthropy as well as religion. But we don't judge a movement by a few overwrought disciples."

"That is true," said the Englishman, quietly. He was a middle-aged man, with an insistently optimistic countenance, and a build suggestive of general solidity. "But to return to the original proposition. I suppose we will all accept as a fundamental postulate the statement that the highest civilization is the one in which the highest value is placed upon individual life—"

"And happiness," added the girl in the yachting-cap.

"And happiness," assented the Englishman.

"And yet," commented the lawyer, "I think that most of us will admit that such a society, where life is regarded as sacred because it is valuable to the individual, and not because it is valuable to the state, tends to the non-production of heroes—"

"That the average will be higher and the exception lower," observed the journalist. "In other words, that there will be a general elevation of the mass, accompanied by a corresponding lowering of the few."

"On the whole, I think our system does very well," said the Englishman, carefully measuring the horseradish he was placing upon his oysters. "A mean between two extremes is apt to be satisfactory in results. If we don't produce a Marcus Aurelius or a Seneca, neither do we produce a Nero or a Phocas. We may have lost patriotism, but we have gained cosmopolitanism, which is better. If we have lost chivalry, we have acquired decency; and if we have ceased to be picturesque, we have become cleanly, which is considerably more to be desired."

"I have never felt the romanticism of the Middle Ages," remarked the girl in the yachting-cap. "When I read of the glories of the Crusaders, I can't help remembering that a knight wore a single garment for a lifetime, and hacked his horse to pieces for a whim. Just as I never think of that chivalrous brute, Richard the Lion-Hearted, that I don't see him chopping off the heads of his three thousand prisoners."

"Oh, I don't think that any of us are sighing for a revival of the Middle Ages," returned the journalist. "The worship of the past has usually for its devotees people who have only known the present—"

"Which is as it should be," commented the lawyer. "If man was confined to the worship of the knowable, all the world would lapse into atheism."

"Just as the great lovers of humanity were generally hermits," added the girl in the yachting-cap. "I had an uncle who used to say that he never really loved mankind until he went to live in the wilderness."

"I think we are drifting from the point," said the alienist, helping himself to potatoes. "Was it not—can the saving of a human life ever prove to be an immoral act? I once held that it could."

"Did you act upon it?" asked the lawyer, with rising interest. "I maintain that no proposition can be said to exist until it is acted upon. Otherwise it is in merely an embryonic state—"

The alienist laid down his fork and leaned forward. He was a notable-looking man of some thirty-odd years, who had made a sudden leap into popularity through several successful cases.

He had a nervous, muscular face, with singularly penetrating eyes, and hair of a light sandy color. His hands were white and well shaped.

"It was some years ago," he said, bending a scintillant glance around the table. "If you will listen—"

There followed a stir of assent, accompanied by a nod from the young lady upon the Captain's right. "I feel as if it would be a ghost story," she declared.

"It is not a story at all," returned the alienist, lifting his wineglass and holding it against the light. "It is merely a fact."

Then he glanced swiftly around the table as if challenging attention.

"As I said," he began, slowly, "it was some few years ago. Just what year does not matter, but at that time I had completed a course at Heidelberg, and expected shortly to set out with an exploring party for South Africa. It turned out afterwards that I did not go, but for the purpose of the present story it is sufficient that I intended to do so, and had made my preparations accordingly. At Heidelberg I had lived among a set of German students who were permeated with the metaphysics of Schopenhauer, von Hartmann, and the rest, and I was pretty well saturated myself. At that age I was an ardent disciple of pessimism. I am still a disciple, but my ardor has abated—which is not the fault of pessimism, but the virtue of middle age—"

"A man is usually called conservative when he has passed the twenties," interrupted the journalist, "yet it is not that he grows more conservative, but that he grows less radical—"

"Rather that he grows less in every direction," added the Englishman, "except in physical bulk."

The alienist accepted the suggestions with an inclination, and continued. "One of my most cherished convictions," he said, "was to the effect that every man is the sole arbiter of his fate. As Schopenhauer has it, '*that there is nothing to which a man has a more unassailable title than to his own life and person.*' Indeed, that particular sentence had become a kind of motto with our set, and some of my companions even went so far as to preach the proper ending of life with the ending of the power of individual usefulness."

He paused to help himself to salad.

"I was in Scotland at the time, where I had spent a fortnight with my parents, in a small village on the Kyles of Bute. While there I had been treating an invalid cousin who had acquired the morphine habit, and who, under my care, had determined to uproot it. Before leaving I had secured from her the amount of the drug which she had in her possession—some thirty grains— done up in a sealed package, and labelled by a London chemist. As I was in haste, I put it in my bag, thinking that I would add it to my case of medicines when I reached Leicester, where I was to spend the night with an old schoolmate. I took the boat at Tighnabruaich, the small village, found a local train at Gourock to reach Glasgow with one minute in which to catch the first express to London. I made the change and secured a first-class smoking-compartment, which I at first thought to be vacant, but when the train had started a man came from the dressing-room and took the seat across from me. At first I paid no heed to him, but upon looking up once or twice and finding his eyes upon me, I became unpleasantly conscious of his presence. He was thin almost to emaciation, and yet there was a muscular suggestion of physical force about him which it was difficult to account for, since he was both short and slight. His clothes were shabby, but well made, and his cravat had the appearance of having been tied in haste or by nervous fingers. There was a trace of sensuality about the mouth, over which he wore a drooping yellow mustache tinged with gray, and he was somewhat bald upon the crown of his head, which lent a deceptive hint of intellectuality to his uncovered forehead. As he crossed his legs I saw that his boots were carefully blacked, and that they were long and slender, tapering to a decided point."

"I have always held," interpolated the lawyer, "that to judge a man's character you must read his feet."

The alienist sipped his claret and took up his words:

"After passing the first stop I remembered a book at the bottom of my bag, and, unfastening the strap, in my search for the book I laid a number of small articles upon the seat beside me, among them the sealed package bearing the morphine label and the name of the London chemist. Having found the book, I turned to replace the articles, when I noticed that the man across from me was gazing attentively at the labelled package. For a moment his expression startled me, and I stared back at him from across my open bag, into which I had dropped the articles. There was in his eyes a curious mixture of passion and repulsion, and, beyond it all, the look of a hungry hound when he sees food. Thinking that I had chanced upon a victim of the opium craving, I closed the bag, placed it in the net above my head, and opened my book.

"For a while we rode in silence. Nothing was heard except the noise of the train and the clicking of our bags as they jostled each other in the receptacle above. I remember these details very vividly, because since then I have recalled the slightest fact in connection with the incident. I knew that the man across from me drew a cigar from his case, felt in his pocket for an instant, and then turned to me for a match. At the same time I experienced the feeling that the request veiled a larger purpose, and that there were matches in the pocket into which he thrust his fingers.

"But, as I complied with his request, he glanced indifferently out of the window, and following his gaze, I saw that we were passing a group of low-lying hills flecked with stray patches of heather, and that across the hills a flock of sheep were filing, followed by a peasant girl in a short skirt. It was the last faint suggestion of the Highlands.

"The man across from me leaned out, looking back upon the neutral sky, the sparse patches of heather, and the flock of sheep.

" 'What a tone the heather gives to a landscape!' he remarked, and his voice sounded forced and affected.

"I bowed without replying, and as he turned from the window, and I sat upon the back seat in the draught of cinders, I bent forward to lower the sash. In a moment he spoke again:

" 'Do you go to London?'

" 'To Leicester,' I answered, laying the book aside, impelled by a sudden interest. 'Why do you ask?'

"He flushed nervously.

" 'I—oh, nothing,' he answered, and drew from me.

"Then, as if with swift determination, he reached forward

and lifted the book I had laid upon the seat. It was a treatise of von Hartmann's in German.

" 'I had judged that you were a physician,' he said—'a student, perhaps, from a German university?'

" 'I am.'

"He paused for an instant, and then spoke in absent-minded reiteration, 'So you don't go on to London?'

" 'No,' I returned, impatiently; 'but can I do anything for you?'

"He handed me the book, regarding me resolutely as he did so.

" 'Are you a sensible man?'

"I bowed.

" 'And a philosopher?'

" 'In amateur fashion.'

"With fevered energy he went on more quickly, 'You have in your possession,' he said, 'something for which I would give my whole fortune.' He laid two half-sovereigns and some odd silver in the palm of his hand. 'This is all I possess,' he continued, 'but I would give it gladly.'

"I looked at him curiously.

" 'You mean the morphia?' I demanded.

"He nodded. 'I don't ask you to give it to me,' he said; 'I only ask—'

"I interrupted him. 'Are you in pain?'

"He laughed softly, and I really believe he felt a tinge of amusement. 'It is a question of expediency,' he explained. 'If you happen to be a moralist—'

"He broke off. 'What of it?' I inquired.

"He settled himself in his corner, resting his head against the cushions.

" 'You get out at Leicester,' he said, recklessly. 'I go on to London, where Providence, represented by Scotland Yard, is awaiting me.'

"I started. 'For what?'

" 'They call it murder, I believe,' he returned; 'but what they call it matters very little. I call it justifiable homicide—that also matters very little. The point is—I will arrive, they will be there before me. That is settled. Every station along the road is watched.'

"I glanced out of the window.

" 'But you came from Glasgow,' I suggested.

" 'Worse luck! I waited in the dressing-room until the train started. I hoped to have the compartment alone, but—' He leaned forward and lowered the window-shade. 'If you don't object,' he said, apologetically; 'I find the glare trying. It is a question for a moralist,' he repeated. 'Indeed, I may call myself a question for a moralist,' and he smiled again with that ugly humor. 'To begin with the beginning, the question is bred in the bone and it's out in the blood.' He nodded at my look of surprise. 'You are an American,' he continued, 'and so am I. I was born in Washington some thirty years ago. My father was a politician of note, whose honor was held to be unimpeachable— which was a mistake. His name doesn't matter, but he became very wealthy through judicious speculations—in votes and other things. My mother has always suffered from an incipient hysteria, which developed shortly before my birth.' He wiped his forehead with his pocket-handkerchief, and knocked the ashes from his cigar with a flick of his finger. 'The motive for this is not far to seek,' he said, with a glance at my travelling-bag. He had the coolest bravado I have ever met. 'As a child,' he went on, 'I gave great promise. Indeed, we moved to England that I might be educated at Oxford. My father considered the atmospheric ecclesiasticism to be beneficial. But while at college I got into trouble with a woman, and I left. My father died, his fortune burst like a bubble, and my mother moved to the country. I was put into a banking office, but I got into more trouble with women—this time two of them. One was a low variety actress, and I married her. I didn't want to do it. I tried not to, but I couldn't help it, and I did it. A month later I left her. I changed my name and went to Belfast, where I resolved to become an honest man. It was a tough job, but I labored and I succeeded— for a time. The variety actress began looking for me, but I escaped her, and have escaped her so far. That was eight years ago. And several years after reaching Belfast I met another woman. She was different. I fell ill of fever in Ireland, and she nursed me. She was a good woman, with a broad Irish face, strong hands, and motherly shoulders. I was weak and she was strong, and I fell in love with her. I tried to tell her about the variety actress, but somehow I couldn't, and I married her.' He shot the stump of his cigar through the opposite window and lighted another, this time drawing the match from his pocket. 'She is an honest woman,' he said—'as honest as the day. She believes in me. It would kill her to know about the variety actress—and all the others. There is one child, a girl—a freckle-faced mite just like her mother—and another is coming.'

" 'She knows nothing of this affair?'

" 'Not a blamed thing. She is the kind of woman who is good because she can't help herself. She enjoys it. I never did. My mother is different, too. She would die if other people knew of this; my wife would die if she knew of it herself. Well, I got tired, and I wanted money, so I left her and went to Dublin. I changed my name and got a clerkship in a shipping office. My wife thinks I went to America to get work, and if she never hears of me she'll probably think no worse. I did intend going to America, but somehow I didn't. I got in with a man who signed somebody's name to a check and got me to present it. Then we quarrelled about the money, and the man threw the job on me and the affair came out. But before they arrested me I ran him down and shot him. I was ridding the world of a damned traitor.'

"He raised the shade with a nervous hand, but the sun flashed into his eyes, and he lowered it.

" 'I suppose I'd hang for it,' he said; 'there isn't much doubt of that. If I waited I'd hang for it, but I am not going to wait. I am going to die. It is the only thing left, and I am going to do it.'

" 'And how?'

" 'Before this train reaches London,' he replied, 'I am a dead man. There are two ways. I might say three, except that a pitch from the carriage might mean only a broken leg. But there is this—' He drew a vial from his pocket and held it to the light. It contained an ounce or so of carbolic acid.

" 'One of the most corrosive of irritants,' I observed.

" 'And there is—your package.'

"My first impulse promised me to force the vial from him. He was a slight man, and I could have overcome him with but little exertion. But the exertion I did not make. I should as soon have thought, when my rational humor reasserted itself, of knocking a man down on Broadway and robbing him of his watch. The acid was as exclusively his property as the clothes he wore, and equally his life was his own. Had he declared his intention to hurl himself from the window I might not have made way for him, but I should certainly not have obstructed his passage.

"But the morphia was mine, and that I should assist him was another matter, so I said,

" 'The package belongs to me.'

" 'And you will not exchange?'

" 'Certainly not.'

"He answered, almost angrily:

" 'Why not be reasonable? You admit that I am in a mess of it?'

" 'Readily.'

" 'You also admit that my life is morally my own?'

" 'Equally.'

" 'That its continuance could in no wise prove to be of benefit to society?'

" 'I do.'

" 'That for all connected with me it would be better that I should die unknown and under an assumed name than that I should end upon the scaffold, my wife and mother wrecked for life, my children discovered to be illegitimate?'

" 'Yes.'

" 'Then you admit also that the best I can do is to kill myself before reaching London?'

" 'Perhaps.'

" 'So you will leave me the morphine when you get off at Leicester?'

" 'No.'

"He struck the window-sill impatiently with the palm of his hand.

" 'And why not?'

"I hesitated an instant.

" 'Because, upon the whole, I do not care to be the instrument of your self-destruction.'

" 'Don't be a fool!' he retorted. 'Speak honestly, and say that because of a little moral shrinkage on your part you prefer to leave a human being to a death of agony. I don't like physical pain. I am like a woman about it, but it is better than hanging, or life-imprisonment, or any jury finding.'

"I became exhortatory.

" 'Why not face it like a man and take your chances? Who knows—"

" 'I have had my chances,' he returned. 'I have squandered more chances than most men ever lay eyes on—and I don't care. If I had the opportunity, I'd squander them again. It is the only thing chances are made for.'

" 'What a scoundrel you are!' I exclaimed.

" 'Well, I don't know,' he answered; 'there have been worse men. I never said a harsh word to a woman, and I never hit a man when he was down—"

"I blushed. 'Oh, I didn't mean to hit you,' I responded.

"He took no notice.

" 'I like my wife,' he said. 'She is a good woman, and I'd do a good deal to keep her and the children from knowing the truth. Perhaps I'd kill myself even if I didn't want to. I don't know, but I am tired—damned tired.'

" 'And yet you deserted her.'

" 'I did. I tried not to, but I couldn't help it. If I was free to go back to her to-morrow, unless I was ill and wanted nursing, I'd see that she had grown shapeless, and that her hands were coarse.' He stretched out his own, which were singularly white and delicate. 'I believe I'd leave her in a week,' he said.

"Then with an eager movement he pointed to my bag.

" 'That is the ending of the difficulty,' he added, 'otherwise I swear that before the train gets to London I will swallow this stuff, and die like a rat.'

" 'I admit your right to die in any manner you choose, but I don't see that it is my place to assist you. It is an ugly job.'

" 'So am I,' he retorted, grimly. 'At any rate, if you leave the train with that package in your bag it will be cowardice—

sheer cowardice. And for the sake of your cowardice you will damn me to this—' He touched the vial.

" 'It won't be pleasant,' I said, and we were silent.

"I knew that the man had spoken the truth. I was accustomed to lies, and had learned to detect them. I knew, also, that the world would be well rid of him and his kind. Why I should preserve him for death upon the gallows I did not see. The majesty of the law would be in no way ruffled by his premature departure; and if I could trust that part of his story, the lives of innocent women and children would, in the other case, suffer considerably. And even if I and my unopened bag alighted at Leicester, I was sure that he would never reach London alive. He was a desperate man, this I read in his set face, his dazed eyes, his nervous hands. He was a poor devil, and I was sorry for him as it was. Why, then, should I contribute, by my refusal to comply with his request, an additional hour of agony to his existence? Could I, with my pretence of philosophic latitudinarianism, alight at my station, leaving him to swallow the acid and die like a rat in a cage before the journey was over? I remembered that I had once seen a guinea-pig die from the effects of carbolic acid, and the remembrance sickened me suddenly.

"As I sat there listening to the noise of the slackening train, which was nearing Leicester, I thought of a hundred things. I thought of Schopenhauer and von Hartmann. I thought of the dying guinea-pig. I thought of the broad-faced Irish wife and the two children.

"Then 'Leicester' flashed before me, and the train stopped. I rose, gathered my coat and rug, and lifted the volume of von Hartmann from the seat. The man remained motionless in the corner of the compartment, but his eyes followed me.

"I stooped, opened by bag, and laid the chemist's package upon the seat. Then I stepped out, closing the door after me." As the speaker finished, he reached forward, selected an almond from the stand of nuts, fitted it carefully between the crackers, and cracked it slowly.

The young lady upon the Captain's right shook herself with a shudder.

"What a horrible story!" she exclaimed; "for it is a story, after all, and not a fact."

"A point, rather," suggested the Englishman; "but is that all?"

"All of the point," returned the alienist. "The next day I saw in the *Times* that a man, supposed to be James Morganson, who was wanted for murder, was found dead in a first-class smoking-compartment of the Midland Railway, Coroner's verdict, 'Death resulting from an overdose of morphia, taken with suicidal intent.'"

The journalist dropped a lump of sugar in his cup and watched it attentively.

"I don't think I could have done it," he said. "I might have left him with his carbolic. But I couldn't have deliberately given him his death-potion."

"But as long as he was going to die," responded the girl in the yachting-cap, "it was better to let him die painlessly."

The Englishman smiled. "Can a woman ever consider the ethical side of a question when the sympathetic one is visible?" he asked.

The alienist cracked another almond. "I was sincere," he said. "Of that there is no doubt. I thought I did right. The question is—did I do right?"

"It would have been wiser," began the lawyer, argumentatively, "since you were stronger than he, to take the vial from him, and to leave him to the care of the law."

"But the wife and children," replied the girl in the yachting-cap. "And hanging is so horrible!"

"So is murder," responded the lawyer, dryly.

The young lady on the Captain's right laid her napkin upon the table and rose. "I don't know what was right," she said, "but I do know that in your place I should have felt like a murderer."

The alienist smiled half cynically. "So I did," he answered; "but there is such a thing, my dear young lady, as a conscientious murderer."

AUGUSTE GRONER

(1850–1929)

In the last decade of the nineteenth century, Auguste Groner, an Austrian novelist who began her career writing historical fiction and children's books, saw publication of her initial story about Josef Müller, the hero of the first series of police detective stories in the German language. (In English commentary, her name is often misspelled as *Augusta*.) Critics now compare Müller to Constable Studer, a hardworking Swiss policeman created by Friedrich Glauser, who died in 1938 but whose Studer novels have only recently been translated into English. Probably Müller will remind more readers of George Simenon's quietly dogged Jules Maigret, and perhaps at times of TV's Lieutenant Columbo. Please note that in the following story Groner has a character employ a then-common derogatory term for the Romany people.

Born Auguste Kopallik in Vienna in 1850—to a staid accountant who found himself father of a theologian, an artist, and a writer—she taught school before trying her hand at writing. In her late twenties she married Richard Groner, whose steadily updated encyclopedia of Vienna would still bear his name a half century after his death in 1931. His wife is still remembered there, better known than ever.

Her first collection about Josef Müller in English appeared in 1910 under the title *Joe Muller, Detective: Being the Account of Some Adventures in the Professional Experience of a Member of the Imperial Austrian Police*. Curiously, the first edition shows on its red cloth cover the name of the translator, Grace Isabel Colbron, rather than the author. Under his anglicized name, Muller quickly gained popularity in the United States—until the international interest in German-speaking writers plummeted after World War I.

For many years, Groner was more popular in English than in German. Colbron's translation of the first collection began with an introduction to the character, some of which follows:

Joseph Muller, Secret Service detective of the Imperial Austrian police . . . is a small, slight, plain-looking man, of indefinite age, and of much humbleness of mien. A naturally retiring, modest disposition, and two external causes are the reasons for Muller's humbleness of manner, which is his chief characteristic. One cause is the fact that in early youth a miscarriage of justice gave him several years in prison, an experience which cast a stigma on his name and which made it impossible for him, for many years after, to obtain honest employment. But the world is richer, and safer, by Muller's early misfortune. For it was this experience which threw him back on his own peculiar talents for a livelihood, and drove him into the police force. Had he been able to enter any other profession, his genius might have been stunted to a mere pastime, instead of being, as now, utilised for the public good. . . . Muller's official rank is scarcely much higher than that of a policeman, although kings and councillors consult him and the Police Department realises to the full what a treasure it has in him. But official red tape, and his early misfortune, prevent the giving of any higher official standing to even such a genius. . . . The kindest-hearted man in the world, he is a human bloodhound when once the lure of the trail has caught him. . . . The high chiefs and commissioners grant a condescending permission when Muller asks, "May I do this? . . . or may I handle this case this way?" both parties knowing all the while that it is a farce, and that the department waits helpless until this humble little man saves its honour by solving some problem before which its intricate machinery has stood dazed and puzzled. . . . Sometimes his unerring instinct discovers secrets in high places, secrets which the Police Department is bidden to hush up and leave untouched. Muller is then taken off the case, and left idle for a while if he persists in his opinion as to the true facts. And at other times, Muller's own warm heart gets him into trouble.

THE CASE OF THE
POOL OF BLOOD IN
THE PASTOR'S STUDY

Translated by Grace Isabel Colbron

The sun rose slowly over the great bulk of the Carpathian mountains lying along the horizon, weird giant shapes in the early morning mist. It was still very quiet in the village. A cock crowed here and there, and swallows flew chirping close to the ground, darting swiftly about preparing for their higher flight. Janci the shepherd, apparently the only human being already up, stood beside the brook at the point where the old bridge spans the streamlet, still turbulent from the mountain floods. Janci was cutting willows to make his Margit a new basket.

Once the shepherd raised his head from his work, for he thought he heard a loud laugh somewhere in the near distance. But all seemed silent and he turned back to his willows. The beauty of the landscape about him was much too familiar a thing that he should have felt or seen its charm. The violet hue of the distant woods, the red gleaming of the heather-strewn moor, with its patches of swamp from which the slow mist arose, the pretty little village with its handsome old church and attractive rectory—Janci had known it so long that he never stopped to realise how very charming, in its gentle melancholy, it all was.

Also, Janci did not know that this little village of his home had once been a flourishing city, and that an invasion of the Turks had razed it to the ground leaving, as by a miracle, only the church to tell of former glories.

The sun rose higher and higher. And now the village awoke to its daily life. Voices of cattle and noises of poultry were heard about the houses, and men and women began their accustomed round of tasks. Janci found that he had gathered enough willow twigs by this time. He tied them in a loose bundle and started on his homeward way.

His path led through wide-stretching fields and vineyards past a little hill, some distance from the village, on which stood a large house. It was not a pleasant house to look at, not a house one would care to live in, even if one did not know its use, for it looked bare and repellant, covered with its ugly yellow paint, and with all the windows secured with heavy iron bars. The trees that surrounded it were tall and thick-foliaged, casting an added gloom over the forbidding appearance of the house. At the foot of the hill was a high iron fence, cutting off what lay behind it from all the rest of the world. For this ugly yellow house enclosed in its walls a goodly sum of hopeless human misery and misfortune. It was an insane asylum.

For twenty years now, the asylum had stood on its hill, a source of superstitious terror to the villagers, but at the same time a source of added income. It meant money for them, for it afforded a constant and ever-open market for their farm products and the output of their home industry. But every now and then a scream or a harsh laugh would ring out from behind those barred windows, and those in the village who could hear, would shiver and cross themselves. Shepherd Janci had little fear of the big house. His little hut cowered close by the high iron gates, and he had a personal acquaintance with most of the patients, with all of the attendants, and most of all, with the kind elderly physician who was the head of the establishment. Janci knew them all, and had a kind word equally for all. But otherwise he was a silent man, living much within himself.

When the shepherd reached his little home, his wife came to meet him with a call to breakfast. As they sat down at the table a shadow moved past the little window. Janci looked up. "Who was that?" asked Margit, looking up from her folded hands. She had just finished her murmured prayer.

"Pastor's Liska," replied Janci indifferently, beginning his meal. (Liska was the local abbreviation for Elizabeth.)

"In such a hurry?" thought the shepherd's wife. Her curiosity would not let her rest. "I hope His Reverence isn't ill again," she remarked after a while. Janci did not hear her, for he was very busy picking a fly out of his milk cup.

"Do you think Liska was going for the old man?" began Margit again after a few minutes.

The "old man" was the name given by the people of the village, more as a term of endearment than anything else, to the generally loved and respected physician who was the head of the insane asylum. He had become general mentor and oracle of all the village and was known and loved by man, woman and child.

"It's possible," answered Janci.

"His Reverence didn't look very well yesterday, or maybe the old housekeeper has the gout again."

Janci gave a grunt which might have meant anything. The shepherd was a silent man. Being alone so much had taught him to find his own thoughts sufficient company. Ten minutes passed in silence since Margit's last question, then some one went past the window. There were two people this time, Liska and the old doctor. They were walking very fast, running almost. Margit sprang up and hurried to the door to look after them.

Janci sat still in his place, but he had laid aside his spoon and with wide eyes was staring ahead of him, murmuring, "It's the pastor this time; I saw him—just as I did the others."

"Shepherd, the inn-keeper wants to see you, there's something the matter with his cow." Count ——, a young man, came from the other direction and pushed in at the door past Margit, who stood there staring up the road.

Janci was so deep in his own thoughts that he apparently did not hear the boy's words. At all events he did not answer them, but himself asked an unexpected question—a question that was not addressed to the others in the room, but to something out and beyond them. It was a strange question and it came from the lips of a man whose mind was not with his body at that moment—whose mind saw what others did not see.

"Who will be the next to go? And who will be our pastor now?" These were Janci's words.

"What are you talking about, shepherd? Is it another one of

your visions?" exclaimed the young fellow who stood there before him. Janci rubbed his hands over his eyes and seemed to come down to earth with a start.

"Oh, is that you, Ferenz? What do you want of me?"

The boy gave his message again, and Janci nodded good-humouredly and followed him out of the house. But both he and his young companion were very thoughtful as they plodded along the way. The boy did not dare to ask any questions, for he knew that the shepherd was not likely to answer. There was a silent understanding among the villagers that no one should annoy Janci in any way, for they stood in a strange awe of him, although he was the most good-natured mortal under the sun.

While the shepherd and the boy walked toward the inn, the old doctor and Liska had hurried onward to the rectory. They were met at the door by the aged housekeeper, who staggered down the path wringing her hands, unable to give voice to anything but inarticulate expressions of grief and terror. The rest of the household and the farm hands were gathered in a frightened group in the great courtyard of the stately rectory which had once been a convent building. The physician hurried up the stairs into the pastor's apartments. These were high sunny and airy rooms with arched ceilings, deep window seats, great heavy doors and handsomely ornamented stoves. The simple modern furniture appeared still more plain and common-place by contrast with the huge spaces of the building.

In one of the rooms a gendarme was standing beside the window. The man saluted the physician, then shrugged his shoulders with an expression of hopelessness. The doctor returned a silent greeting and passed through into the next apartment. The old man was paler than usual and his face bore an expression of pain and surprise, the same expression that showed in the faces of those gathered downstairs. The room he now entered was large like the others, the walls handsomely decorated, and every corner of it was flooded with sunshine. There were two men in this room, the village magistrate and the notary. Their expression, as they held out their hands to the doctor, showed that his coming brought great relief.

And there was something else in the room, something that drew the eyes of all three of the men immediately after their silent greeting.

This was a great pool of blood which lay as a hideous stain on the otherwise clean yellow-painted floor. The blood must have flowed from a dreadful wound, from a severed artery even, the doctor thought, there was such a quantity of it. It had already dried and darkened, making its terrifying ugliness the more apparent.

"This is the third murder in two years," said the magistrate in a low voice.

"And the most mysterious of all of them," added the clerk.

"Yes, it is," said the doctor. "And there is not a trace of the body, you say?—or a clue as to where they might have taken the dead—or dying man?"

With these words he looked carefully around the room, but there was no more blood to be seen anywhere. Any spot would have been clearly visible on the light-coloured floor. There was nothing else to tell of the horrible crime that had been committed here, nothing but the great, hideous, brown-red spot in the middle of the room.

"Have you made a thorough search for the body?" asked the doctor.

The magistrate shook his head. "No, I have done nothing to speak of yet. We have been waiting for you. There is a gendarme at the gate; no one can go in or out without being seen."

"Very well, then, let us begin our search now."

The magistrate and his companion turned towards the door of the room but the doctor motioned them to come back. "I see you do not know the house as well as I do," he said, and led the way towards a niche in the side of the wall, which was partially filled by a high bookcase.

"Ah—that is the entrance of the passage to the church?" asked the magistrate in surprise.

"Yes, this is it. The door is not locked."

"You mean you believe—"

"That the murderers came in from the church? Why not? It is quite possible."

"To think of such a thing!" exclaimed the notary with a shake of his head.

The doctor laughed bitterly. "To those who are planning a murder, a church is no more than any other place. There is a bolt here as you see. I will close this bolt now. Then we can leave the room knowing that no one can enter it without being seen."

The simple furniture of the study, a desk, a sofa, a couple of chairs and several bookcases, gave no chance of any hiding place either for the body of the victim or for the murderers. When the men left the room the magistrate locked the door and put the key in his own pocket. The gendarme in the neighbouring apartment was sent down to stand in the courtyard at the entrance to the house. The sexton, a little hunchback, was ordered to remain in the vestry at the other end of the passage from the church to the house.

Then the thorough search of the house began. Every room in both stories, every corner of the attic and the cellar, was looked over thoroughly. The stable, the barns, the garden and even the well underwent a close examination. There was no trace of a body anywhere, not even a trail of blood, nothing which would give the slightest clue as to how the murderers had entered, how they had fled, or what they had done with their victim.

The great gate of the courtyard was closed. The men, reinforced by the farm hands, entered the church, while Liska and the dairy-maids huddled in the servants' dining-room in a trembling group around the old housekeeper. The search in the church as well as in the vestry was equally in vain. There was no trace to be found there any more than in the house.

Meanwhile, during these hours of anxious seeking, the rumour of another terrible crime had spread through the village, and a crowd that grew from minute to minute gathered in front of the closed gates to the rectory, in front of the church, the closed doors of which did not open although it was a high feast day. The utter silence from the steeple, where the bells hung mute, added to the spreading terror. Finally the doctor came out from the rectory, accompanied by the magistrate, and announced to the waiting villagers that their venerable pastor had disappeared under circumstances which left no doubt that he had met his death at the hand of a murderer. The peasants listened in shuddering silence, the men pale-faced, the women sobbing aloud with frightened children hanging to their skirts. Then at the magistrate's order, the crowd dispersed slowly, going to their homes, while a messenger set off to the near-by county seat.

It was a weird, sad Easter Monday. Even nature seemed to feel the pressure of the brooding horror, for heavy clouds piled up towards noon and a chill wind blew fitfully from the north, bending the young corn and the creaking tree-tops, and moaning about the straw-covered roofs. Then an icy cold rain descended on the village, sending the children, the only humans still unconscious of the fear that had come on them all, into the houses to play quietly in the corner by the hearth.

There was nothing else spoken of wherever two or three met together throughout the village except this dreadful, unexplainable thing that had happened in the rectory. The little village inn was full to overflowing and the hum of voices within was like the noise of an excited beehive. Everyone had some new explanation, some new guess, and it was not until the notary arrived, looking even more important than usual, that silence fell upon the excited throng. But the expectations aroused by his coming were not fulfilled. The notary knew no more than the others although he had been one of the searchers in the rectory. But he was in no haste to disclose his ignorance, and sat wrapped in a dignified silence until some one found courage to question him.

"Was there nothing stolen?" he was asked.

"No, nothing as far as we can tell yet. But if it was the gypsies—as may be likely—they are content with so little that it would not be noticed."

"Gypsies?" exclaimed one man scornfully. "It doesn't have to be gypsies, we've got enough tramps and vagabonds of our own. Didn't they kill the pedlar for the sake of a bag of tobacco, and old Katiza for a couple of hens?"

"Why do you rake up things that happened twenty years ago?" cried another over the table. "You'd better tell us rather who killed Red Betty, and pulled Janos, the smith's farm hand, down into the swamp?"

"Yes, or who cut the bridge supports, when the brook was in flood, so that two good cows broke through and drowned?"

"Yes, indeed, if we only knew what band of robbers and villains it is that is ravaging our village."

"And they haven't stopped yet, evidently."

"This is the worst misfortune of all! What will our poor do now that they have murdered our good pastor, who cared for us all like a father?"

"He gave all he had to the poor, he kept nothing for himself."

"Yes, indeed, that's how it was. And now we can't even give this good man Christian burial."

"Shepherd Janci knew this morning early that we were going to have a new pastor," whispered the landlord in the notary's ear.

The latter looked up astonished. "Who said so?" he asked.

"My boy Ferenz, who went to fetch him about seven o'clock. One of my cows was sick."

Ferenz was sent for and told his story. The men listened with great interest, and the smith, a broad-shouldered elderly man, was particularly eager to hear, as he had always believed in the shepherd's power of second sight. The tailor, who was more modern-minded, laughed and made his jokes at this. But the smith laid one mighty hand on the other's shoulder, almost crushing the tailor's slight form under its weight, and said gravely: "Friend, do you be silent in this matter. You've come from other parts and you do not know of things that have happened here in days gone by. Janci can do more than take care of his sheep. One day, when my little girl was playing in the street, he said to me, 'Have a care of Maruschka, smith!' and three days later the child was dead. The evening before Red Betty was murdered he saw her in a vision lying in a coffin in front of her door. He told it to the sexton, whom he met in the fields; and next morning they found Betty dead. And there are many more things that I could tell you, but what's the use; when a man won't believe it's only lost talk to try to make him. But one thing you should know: when Janci stares ahead of him without seeing what's in front of him, then the whole village begins to wonder what's going to happen, for Janci knows far more than all the rest of us put together."

The smith's grave, deep voice filled the room and the others listened in a silence that gave assent to his words. He had scarcely finished speaking, however, when there was a noise of galloping hoofs and rapidly rolling wagon wheels. A tall brake drawn by four handsome horses dashed past in a whirlwind.

"It's the Count—the Count and the district judge," said the landlord in a tone of respect. The notary made a grab at his hat and umbrella and hurried from the room. "That shows how much they thought of our pastor," continued the landlord proudly. "For the Count himself has come and with four horses, too, to get here the more quickly. His Reverence was a great friend of the Countess."

"They didn't make so much fuss over the pedlar and Betty," murmured the cobbler, who suffered from a perpetual grouch. But he followed the others, who paid their scores hastily and went out into the streets that they might watch from a distance at least what was going on in the rectory. The landlord bustled about the inn to have everything in readiness in case the gentlemen should honour him by taking a meal, and perhaps even lodgings, at his house. At the gate of the rectory the coachman and the maid Liska stood to receive the newcomers, just as five o'clock was striking from the steeple.

It should have been still quite light, but it was already dusk, for the clouds hung heavy. The rain had ceased, but a heavy wind came up which tore the delicate petals of the blossoms from the fruit trees and strewed them like snow on the ground beneath. The Count, who was the head of one of the richest and most aristocratic families in Hungary, threw off his heavy fur coat and hastened up the stairs at the top of which his old friend and confidant, the venerable pastor, usually came to meet him. To-day it was only the local magistrate who stood there, bowing deeply.

"This is incredible, incredible!" exclaimed the Count.

"It is, indeed, sir," said the man, leading the magnate through the dining-room into the pastor's study, where, as far as could be seen, the murder had been committed. They were joined by the district judge, who had remained behind to give an order sending a carriage to the nearest railway station. The judge, too, was serious and deeply shocked, for he also had greatly admired and revered the old pastor. The stately rectory had been the scene of many a jovial gathering when the lord of the manor had made it a centre for a day's hunting with his friends. The bearers of some of the proudest names in all Hungary had gathered in the high-arched rooms to laugh with the venerable pastor and to sample the excellent wines in his cellar. These wines, which the gentlemen themselves would send in as presents to the master of the rectory, would be carefully preserved for their own enjoyment. Not a landed proprietor for many leagues around but knew and loved the old pastor, who had now so strangely disappeared under such terrifying circumstances.

"Well, we might as well begin our examination," remarked the Count. "Although if Dr. Orszay's sharp eyes did not find anything, I doubt very much if we will. You have asked the doctor to come here again, haven't you?"

"Yes, Your Grace! As soon as I saw you coming I sent the sexton to the asylum." Then the men went in again into the room which had been the scene of the mysterious crime. The wind rattled the open window and blew out its white curtains. It was already dark in the corners of the room, one could see but indistinctly the carvings of the wainscoting. The light backs of the books, or the gold letters on the darker bindings, made spots of brightness in the gloom. The hideous pool of blood in the centre of the floor was still plainly to be seen.

"Judging by the loss of blood, death must have come quickly."

"There was no struggle, evidently, for everything in the room was in perfect order when we entered it."

"There is not even a chair misplaced. His Bible is there on the desk, he may have been preparing for to-day's sermon."

"Yes, that is the case; because see, here are some notes in his handwriting."

The Count and Judge von Kormendy spoke these sentences at intervals as they made their examination of the room. The local magistrate was able to answer one or two simpler questions, but for the most part he could only shrug his shoulders in helplessness. Nothing had been seen or heard that was at all unusual during the night in the rectory. When the old housekeeper was called up she could say nothing more than this. Indeed, it was almost impossible for the old woman to say anything, her voice choked with sobs at every second word. None of the household force had noticed anything unusual, or could remember anything at all that would throw light on this mystery.

"Well, then, sir, we might just as well sit down and wait for the detective's arrival," said the judge.

"You are waiting for some one besides the doctor?" asked the local magistrate timidly.

"Yes, His Grace telegraphed to Budapest," answered the district judge, looking at his watch.

"And if the train is on time, the man we are waiting for ought to be here in an hour. You sent the carriage to the station, didn't you? Is the driver reliable?"

"Yes, sir, he is a dependable man," said the old housekeeper.

Dr. Orszay entered the room just then and the Count introduced him to the district judge, who was still a stranger to him.

"I fear, Count, that our eyes will serve but little in discovering the truth of this mystery," said the doctor.

The nobleman nodded. "I agree with you," he replied. "And I have sent for sharper eyes than either yours or mine."

The doctor looked his question, and the Count continued: "When the news came to me I telegraphed to Pest for a police detective, telling them that the case was peculiar and urgent. I received an answer as I stopped at the station on my way here. This is it: 'Detective Joseph Muller from Vienna in Budapest by chance. Have sent him to take your case.'"

"Muller?" exclaimed Dr. Orszay. "Can it be the celebrated Muller, the most famous detective of the Austrian police? That would indeed be a blessing."

"I hope and believe that it is," said the Count gravely. "I have heard of this man and we need such a one here that we may find the source of these many misfortunes which have overwhelmed our peaceful village for two years past. It is indeed a stroke of good luck that has led a man of such gifts into our neighbourhood at a time when he is so greatly needed. I believe personally that it is the same person or persons who have been the perpetrators of all these outrages and I intend once for all to put a stop to it, let it cost what it may."

"If any one can discover the truth it will be Muller," said the district judge. "It was I who told the Count how fortunate we were that this man, who is known to the police throughout Austria and far beyond the borders of our kingdom, should have chanced to be in Budapest and free to come to us when we called. You and I"—he turned with a smile to the local magistrate—"you and I can get away with the usual cases of local brutality hereabouts. But the cunning that is at the bottom of these crimes is one too many for us."

The men had taken their places around the great dining-table. The old housekeeper had crept out again, her terror making her forget her usual hospitality. And indeed it would not have occurred to the guests to ask or even to wish for any refreshment. The maid brought a lamp, which sent its weak rays scarcely beyond the edges of the big table. The four men sat in silence for some time.

"I suppose it would be useless to ask who has been coming and going from the rectory the last few days?" began the Count.

"Oh, yes, indeed, sir," said the district judge with a sigh. "For if this murderer is the same who committed the other crimes he must live here in or near the village, and therefore must be known to all and not likely to excite suspicion."

"I beg your pardon, sir," put in the doctor. "There must be at least two of them. One man alone could not have carried off the farm hand who was killed to the swamp where his body was found. Nor could one man alone have taken away the bloody body of the pastor. Our venerable friend was a man of size and weight, as you know, and one man alone could not have dragged his body from the room without leaving an easily seen trail."

The judge blushed, but he nodded in affirmation to the doctor's words. This thought had not occurred to him before. In fact, the judge was more notable for his good will and his love of justice rather than for his keen intelligence. He was as well aware of this as was any one else, and he was heartily glad that the Count had sent to the capital for reinforcements.

Some time more passed in deep silence. Each of the men was occupied with his own thoughts. A sigh broke the silence now and then, and a slight movement when one or the other drew out his watch or raised his head to look at the door. Finally, the sound of a carriage outside was heard. The men sprang up.

The driver's voice was heard, then steps which ascended the stairs lowly and lightly, audible only because the stillness was so great.

The door opened and a small, slight, smooth-shaven man with a gentle face and keen grey eyes stood on the threshold. "I am Joseph Muller," he said with a low, soft voice.

The four men in the room looked at him in astonishment.

"This simple-looking individual is the man that every one is afraid of?" thought the Count, as he walked forward and held out his hand to the stranger.

"I sent for you, Mr. Muller," said the magnate, conscious of his stately size and appearance, as well as of his importance in the presence of a personage who so little looked what his great fame might have led one to expect.

"Then you are Count ——?" answered Muller gently. "I was in Budapest, having just finished a difficult case which took me there. They told me that a mysterious crime had happened in your neighbourhood, and sent me here to take charge of it. You will pardon any ignorance I may show as a stranger to this locality. I will do my best and it may be possible that I can help you."

The Count introduced the other gentlemen in order and they sat down again at the table.

"And now what is it you want me for, Count?" asked Muller.

"There was a murder committed in this house," answered the Count.

"When?"

"Last night."

"Who is the victim?"

"Our pastor."

"How was he killed?"

"We do not know."

"You are not a physician, then?" asked Muller, turning to Orszay.

"Yes, I am," answered the latter.

"Well?"

"The body is missing," said Orszay, somewhat sharply.

"Missing?" Muller became greatly interested. "Will you please lead me to the scene of the crime?" he said, rising from his chair.

The others led him into the next room, the magistrate going ahead with a lamp. The judge called for more lights and the group stood around the pool of blood on the floor of the study. Muller's arms were crossed on his breast as he stood looking down at the hideous spot. There was no terror in his eyes, as in those of the others, but only a keen attention and a lively interest.

"Who has been in this room since the discovery?" he asked.

The doctor replied that only the servants of the immediate household, the notary, the magistrate, and himself, then later the Count and the district judge entered the room.

"You are quite certain that no one else has been in here?"

"No, no one else."

"Will you kindly send for the three servants?" The magistrate left the room.

"Who else lives in the house?"

"The sexton and the dairymaid."

"And no one else has left the house to-day or has entered it?"

"No one. The main door has been watched all day by a gendarme."

"Is there but one door out of this room?"

"No, there is a small door beside that bookcase."

"Where does it lead to?"

"It leads to a passageway at the end of which there is a stair down into the vestry."

Muller gave an exclamation of surprise.

"The vestry as well as the church have neither of them been opened on the side toward the street."

"The church or the vestry, you mean," corrected Muller. "How many doors have they on the street side?"

"One each."

"The locks on these doors were in good condition?"

"Yes, they were untouched."

"Was there anything stolen from the church?"

"No, nothing that we could see."

"Was the pastor rich?"

"No, he was almost a poor man, for he gave away all that he had."

"But you were his patron, Count."

"I was his friend. He was the confidential adviser of myself and family."

"This would mean rich presents now and then, would it not?"

"No, that is not the case. Our venerable pastor would take nothing for himself. He would accept no presents but gifts of money for his poor."

"Then you do not believe this to have been a murder for the sake of robbery?"

"No. There was nothing disturbed in any part of the house, no drawers or cupboards broken open at all."

Muller smiled. "I have heard it said that your romantic Hungarian bandits will often be satisfied with the small booty they may find in the pocket or on the person of their victim."

"You are right, Mr. Muller. But that is only when they can find nothing else."

"Or perhaps if it is a case of revenge."

"It cannot be revenge in this case!"

"The pastor was greatly loved?"

"He was loved and revered."

"By every one?"

"By every one!" the four men answered at once.

Muller was still a while. His eyes were veiled and his face thoughtful. Finally he raised his head.

"There has been nothing moved or changed in this room?"

"No—neither here nor anywhere else in the house or the church," answered the local magistrate.

"That is good. Now I would like to question the servants."

Muller had already started for the door, then he turned back into the room and pointing toward the second door he asked: "Is that door locked?"

"Yes," answered the Count. "I found it locked when I examined it myself a short time ago."

"It was locked on the inside?"

"Yes, locked on the inside."

"Very well. Then we have nothing more to do here for the time being. Let us go back into the dining-room."

The men returned to the dining-room, Muller last, for he stopped to lock the door of the study and put the key in his pocket. Then he began his examination of the servants.

The old housekeeper, who, as usual, was the first to rise in the household, had also, as usual, rung the bell to waken the other servants. Then when Liska came downstairs she had sent her up to the pastor's room. His bedroom was to the right of the dining-room. Liska had, as usual, knocked on the door exactly at seven o'clock and continued knocking for some few minutes without receiving any answer. Slightly alarmed, the girl had gone back and told the housekeeper that the pastor did not answer.

Then the old woman asked the coachman to go up and see if anything was the matter with the reverend gentleman. The man returned in a few moments, pale and trembling in every limb and apparently struck dumb by fright. He motioned the women to follow him, and all three crept up the stairs. The coachman led them first to the pastor's bed, which was untouched, and then to the pool of blood in his study. The sight of the latter frightened the servants so much that they did not notice at first that there was no sign of the pastor himself, whom they now knew must have been murdered. When they finally came to themselves sufficiently to take some action, the man hurried off to call the magistrate, and Liska ran to the asylum to fetch the old doctor; the pastor's intimate friend. The aged housekeeper, trembling in fear, crept back to her own room and sat there waiting the return of the others.

This was the story of the early morning as told by the three servants, who had already given their report in much the same words to the Count on his arrival and also to the magistrate. There was no reason to doubt the words of either the old housekeeper or of Janos, the coachman, who had served for more than twenty years in the rectory and whose fidelity was known. The girl Liska was scarcely eighteen, and her round childish face and big eyes dimmed with tears, corroborated her story. When they had told Muller all they knew, the detective sat stroking his chin, and looking thoughtfully at the floor. Then he raised his head and said, in a tone of calm friendliness: "Well, good friends, this will do for to-night. Now, if you will kindly give me a bite to eat and a glass of some light wine, I'd be very thankful. I have had no food since early this morning."

The housekeeper and the maid disappeared, and Janos went to the stable to harness the Count's trap.

The magnate turned to the detective. "I thank you once more that you have come to us. I appreciate it greatly that a stranger to our part of the country, like yourself, should give his time and strength to this problem of our obscure little village."

"There is nothing else calling me, sir," answered Muller. "And the Budapest police will explain to headquarters at Vienna if I do not return at once."

"Do you understand our tongue sufficiently to deal with these people here?"

"Oh, yes; there will be no difficulty about that. I have hunted criminals in Hungary before. And a case of this kind does not usually call for disguises in which any accent would betray one."

"It is a strange profession," said the doctor.

"One gets used to it—like everything else," answered Muller, with a gentle smile. "And now I have to thank you gentlemen for your confidence in me."

"Which I know you will justify," said the Count.

Muller shrugged his shoulders: "I haven't felt anything yet— but it will come—there's something in the air."

The Count smiled at his manner of expressing himself, but all four of the men had already begun to feel sympathy and respect for this quiet-mannered little person whose words were so few and whose voice was so gentle. Something in his grey eyes and in the quiet determination of his manner made them realise that he had won his fame honestly. With the enthusiasm of his race the Hungarian Count pressed the detective's hand in a warm grasp as he said: "I know that we can trust in you. You will avenge the death of my old friend and of those others who were killed here. The doctor and the magistrate will tell you about them to-morrow. We two will go home now. Telegraph us as soon as anything has happened. Every one in the village will be ready to help you and of course you can call on me for funds. Here is something to begin on." With these words the Count laid a silk purse full of gold pieces on the table. One more pressure of the hand and he was gone. The other men also left the room, following the Count's lead in a cordial farewell of the detective. They also shared the nobleman's feeling that now indeed, with this man to help them, could the cloud of horror that had hung over the village for two years, and had culminated in the present catastrophe, be lifted.

The excitement of the Count's departure had died away and the steps of the other men on their way to the village had faded in the distance. There was nothing now to be heard but the rustling of the leaves and the creaking of the boughs as the trees bent before the onrush of the wind. Muller stood alone, with folded arms, in the middle of the large room, letting his sharp eyes wander about the circle of light thrown by the lamps. He was glad to be alone—for only when he was alone could his brain do its best work. He took up one of the lamps and opened the door to the room in which, as far as could be known, the murder had been committed. He walked in carefully and, setting the lamp on the desk, examined the articles lying about on it. There was nothing of importance to be found there. An open Bible and a sheet of paper with notes for the day's sermon lay on top of the desk. In the drawers, none of which were locked, were official papers, books, manuscripts of former sermons, and a few unimportant personal notes.

The flame of the lamp flickered in the breeze that came from the open window. But Muller did not close the casement. He wanted to leave everything just as he had found it until daylight. When he saw that it was impossible to leave the lamp there he took it up again and left the room.

"What is the use of being impatient?" he said to himself. "If I move about in this poor light I will be sure to ruin some possible clue. For there must be some clue left here. It is impossible for even the most practiced criminal not to leave some trace of his presence."

The detective returned to the dining-room, locking the study door carefully behind him. The maid and the coachman returned, bringing in an abundant supper, and Muller sat down to do justice to the many good things on the tray. When the maid returned to take away the dishes she inquired whether she should put the guest chamber in order for the detective. He told her not to go to any trouble for his sake, that he would sleep in the bed in the neighbouring room.

"You going to sleep in there?" said the girl, horrified.

"Yes, my child, and I think I will sleep well to-night. I feel very tired."

Liska carried the things out, shaking her head in surprise at this thin little man who did not seem to know what it was to be afraid. Half an hour later the rectory was in darkness. Before he retired, Muller had made a careful examination of the pastor's bedroom. Nothing was disturbed anywhere, and it was evident that the priest had not made any preparations for the night, but was still at work at his desk in the study when death overtook him. When he came to this conclusion, the detective went to bed and soon fell asleep.

In his little hut near the asylum gates, shepherd Janci slept as sound as usual. But he was dreaming and he spoke in his sleep. There was no one to hear him, for his faithful Margit was snoring loudly. Snatches of sentences and broken words came from Janci's lips: "The hand—the big hand—I see it—at his throat—the face—the yellow face—it laughs—"

Next morning the children on their way to school crept past the rectory with wide eyes and open mouths. And the grown people spoke in lower tones when their work led them past the handsome old house. It had once been their pride, but now it was a place of horror to them. The old housekeeper had succumbed to her fright and was very ill. Liska went about her work silently, and the farm servants walked more heavily and chattered less than they had before. The hump-backed sexton, who had not been allowed to enter the church and therefore had nothing to do, made an early start for the inn, where he spent most of the day telling what little he knew to the many who made an excuse to follow him there.

The only calm and undisturbed person in the rectory household was Muller. He had made a thorough examination of the entire scene of the murder, but had not found anything at all. Of one thing alone was he certain: the murderer had come through the hidden passageway from the church. There were two reasons to believe this, one of which might possibly not be sufficient, but the other was conclusive.

The heavy armchair before the desk, the chair on which the pastor was presumably sitting when the murderer entered, was half turned around, turned in just such a way as it would have been had the man who was sitting there suddenly sprung up in excitement or surprise. The chair was pushed back a step from the desk and turned towards the entrance to the passageway. Those who had been in the room during the day had reported that they had not touched any one of the articles of furniture, therefore the position of the chair was the same that had been given it by the man who had sat in it, by the murdered pastor himself.

Of course there was always the possibility that some one had moved the chair without realising it. This clue, therefore, could not be looked upon as an absolutely certain one had it stood alone. But there was other evidence far more important. The great pool of blood was just half-way between the door of the passage and the armchair. It was here, therefore, that the attack had taken place. The pastor could not have turned in this direction in the hope of flight, for there was nothing here to give him shelter, no weapon that he could grasp, not even a cane. He must have turned in this direction to meet and greet the invader who had entered his room in this unusual manner. Turned to meet him as a brave man would, with no other weapon than the sacredness of his calling and his age.

But this had not been enough to protect the venerable priest. The murderer must have made his thrust at once and his victim had sunk down dying on the floor of the room in which he had spent so many hours of quiet study, in which he had brought comfort and given advice to so many anxious hearts; for dying he must have been—it would be impossible for a man to lose so much blood and live.

"The struggle," thought the detective, "but was there a struggle?" He looked about the room again, but could see nothing that showed disorder anywhere in its immaculate neatness. No, there could have been no struggle. It must have been a quick knife thrust and death at once. "Not a shot?" No, a shot would have been heard by the night watchman walking the streets near the church. The night was quiet, the window open. Some one in the village would have heard the noise of a shot. And it was not likely that the old housekeeper who slept in the room immediately below, slept the light sleep of the aged, would have failed to have heard the firing of a pistol.

Muller took a chair and sat down directly in front of the pool of blood, looking at it carefully. Suddenly he bowed his head deeper. He had caught sight of a fine thread of the red fluid which had been drawn out for about a foot or two in the direction towards the door to the dining-room. What did that mean? Did it mean that the murderer went out through that door, dragging something after him that made this delicate line? Muller bent down still deeper. The sun shone brightly on the floor, sending its clear rays obliquely through the window. The sharp eyes which now covered every inch of the yellow-painted floor discovered something else. They discovered that this red thread curved slightly and had a continuation in a fine scratch in the paint of the floor. Muller followed up this scratch and it led him over towards the window and then back again in wide curves, then out again under the desk and finally, growing weaker and weaker, it came back to the neighbour-hood of the pool of blood, but on the opposite side of it. Muller got down on his hands and knees to follow up the scratch. He did not notice the discomfort of his position, his eyes shone in excitement and a deep flush glowed in his cheeks. Also, he began to whistle softly.

Joseph Muller, the bloodhound of the Austrian police, had

found a clue, a clue that soon would bring him to the trail he was seeking. He did not know yet what he could do with his clue. But this much he knew; sooner or later this scratch in the floor would lead him to the murderer. The trail might be long and devious; but he would follow it and at its end would be success. He knew that this scratch had been made after the murder was committed; this was proved by the blood that marked its beginning. And it could not have been made by any of those who entered the room during the day because by that time the blood had dried. This strange streak in the floor, with its weird curves and spirals, could have been made only by the murderer. But how? With what instrument? There was the riddle which must be solved.

And now Muller, making another careful examination of the floor, found something else. It was something that might be utterly unimportant or might be of great value. It was a tiny bit of hardened lacquer which he found on the floor beside one of the legs of the desk. It was rounded out, with sharp edges, and coloured grey with a tiny zigzag of yellow on its surface. Muller lifted it carefully and looked at it keenly. This tiny bit of lacquer had evidently been knocked off from some convex object, but it was impossible to tell at the moment just what sort of an object it might have been. There are so many different things which are customarily covered with lacquer. However, further examination brought him down to a narrower range of subjects. For on the inside of the lacquer he found a shred of reddish wood fibre. It must have been a wooden object, therefore, from which the lacquer came, and the wood had been of reddish tinge.

Muller pondered the matter for a little while longer. Then he placed his discovery carefully in the pastor's emptied tobacco-box, and dropped the box in his own pocket. He closed the window and the door to the dining-room, lit a lamp, and entered the passageway leading to the vestry. It was a short passageway, scarcely more than a dozen paces long.

The walls were whitewashed, the floor tiled and the entire passage shone in neatness. Muller held the light of his lamp to every inch of it, but there was nothing to show that the criminal had gone through here with the body of his victim.

"The criminal"—Muller still thought of only one. His long experience had taught him that the most intricate crimes were usually committed by one man only. The strength necessary for such a crime as this did not deceive him either. He knew that in extraordinary moments extraordinary strength will come to the one who needs it.

He now passed down the steps leading into the vestry. There was no trace of any kind here either. The door into the vestry was not locked. It was seldom locked, they had told him, for the vestry itself was closed by a huge carved portal with a heavy ornamented iron lock that could be opened only with the greatest noise and trouble. This door was locked and closed as it had been since yesterday morning. Everything in the vestry was in perfect order; the priest's garments and the censers all in their places. Muller assured himself of this before he left the little room. He then opened the glass door that led down by a few steps into the church.

It was a beautiful old church, and it was a rich church also. It was built in the older Gothic style, and its heavy, broad-arched walls, its massive columns would have made it look cold and bare had not handsome tapestries, the gift of the lady of the manor, covered the walls. Fine old pictures hung here and there above the altars, and handsome stained glass windows broke the light that fell into the high vaulted interior. There were three great altars in the church, all of them richly decorated. The main altar stood isolated in the choir. In the open space behind it was the entrance to the crypt, now veiled in a mysterious twilight. Heavy silver candlesticks, three on a side, stood on the altar. The pale gold of the tabernacle door gleamed between them.

Muller walked through the silent church, in which even his light steps resounded uncannily. He looked into each of the pews, into the confessionals, he walked around all the columns, he climbed up into the pulpit, he did everything that the others had done before him yesterday. And as with them, he found nothing that would indicate that the murderer had spent any time in the church. Finally he turned back once more to the main altar on his way out. But he did not leave the church as he intended. His last look at the altar had showed him something that attracted his attention and he walked up the three steps to examine it more closely.

What he had seen was something unusual about one of the silver candlesticks. These candlesticks had three feet, and five of them were placed in such a way that the two front feet were turned toward the spectator. But on the end candlestick nearest Muller the single foot projected out to the front of the altar. This candlestick therefore had been set down hastily, not placed carefully in the order of things as were the others.

And not only this. The heavy wax candle which was in the candlestick was burned down about a finger's breadth more than the others, for these were all exactly of a height. Muller bent still nearer to the candlestick, but he saw that the dim light in the church was not sufficient. He went to one of the smaller side altars, took a candle from there, lit it with one of the matches that he found in his own pocket and returned with the burning candle to the main altar. The steps leading up to this altar were covered by a large rug with a white ground and a pattern of flowers. Looking carefully at it the detective saw a tiny brown spot, the mark of a burn, upon one of the white surfaces. Beside it lay a half used match.

Walking around this carefully, Muller approached the candlestick that interested him and holding up his light he examined every inch of its surface. He found what he was looking for. There were dark red spots between the rough edges of the silver ornamentation.

"Then the body is somewhere around here," thought the detective and came down from the steps, still holding the burning candle.

He walked slowly to the back of the altar. There was a little table there such as held the sacred dishes for the communion service, and the little carpet-covered steps which the sexton put out for the pastor when he took the monstrance from the high-built tabernacle. That was all that was to be seen in the dark corner behind the altar. Holding his candle close to the floor Muller discovered an iron ring fastened to one of the big stone flags. This must be the entrance to the crypt.

Muller tried to raise the flag and was astonished to find how easily it came up. It was a square of reddish marble, the same with which the entire floor of the church was tiled. This flag was very thin and could easily be raised and placed back against the wall. Muller took up his candle, too greatly excited to stop to get a stick for it. He felt assured that now he would soon be able to solve at least a part of the mystery. He climbed down the steps carefully and found that they led into the crypt as he supposed. They were kept spotlessly clean, as was the entire crypt as far as he could see it by the light of his flickering candle. He was not surprised to discover that the air was perfectly pure here. There must be windows or ventilators somewhere, this he knew from the way his candle behaved.

The ancient vault had a high arched ceiling and heavy massive pillars. It was a subterranean repetition of the church above. There had evidently been a convent attached to this church at one time; for here stood a row of simple wooden coffins all exactly alike, bearing each one upon its lid a roughly painted cross surrounded by a wreath. Thus were buried the monks of days long past.

Muller walked slowly through the rows of coffins looking eagerly to each side. Suddenly he stopped and stood still. His hand did not tremble but his thin face was pale—pale as that face which looked up at him out of one of the coffins. The lid of the coffin stood up against the wall and Muller saw that there were several other empty ones further on, waiting for their silent occupants.

The body in the open coffin before which Muller stood was the body of the man who had been missing since the day previous. He lay there quite peacefully, his hands crossed over his breast, his eyes closed, a line of pain about his lips. In the crossed fingers was a little bunch of dark yellow roses. At the first glance one might almost have thought that loving hands had laid the old pastor in his coffin. But the red stain on the white cloth about his throat, and the bloody disorder of his snow-white hair contrasted sadly with the look of peace on the dead face. Under his head was a white silk cushion, one of the cushions from the altar.

Muller stood looking down for some time at this poor victim of a strange crime, then he turned to go.

He wanted to know one thing more: how the murderer had left the crypt. The flame of his candle told him, for it nearly went out in a gust of wind that came down the opening right above him. This was a window about three or four feet from the floor, protected by rusty iron bars which had been sawed through, leaving the opening free. It was a small window, but it was large enough to allow a man of much greater size than Muller to pass through it. The detective blew out his candle and climbed up onto the window sill. He found himself outside, in a corner of the churchyard. A thicket of heavy bushes grown up over neglected graves completely hid the opening through which he had come. There were thorns on these bushes and also a few scattered roses, dark yellow roses.

Muller walked thoughtfully through the churchyard. The sexton sat huddled in an unhappy heap at the gate. He looked up in alarm as he saw the detective walking towards him. Something in the stranger's face told the little hunchback that he had made a discovery. The sexton sprang up, his lips did not dare utter the question that his eyes asked.

"I have found him," said the detective gravely.

The hunchback sexton staggered, then recovered himself, and hurried away to fetch the magistrate and the doctor.

An hour later the murdered pastor lay in state in the chief apartment of his home, surrounded by burning candles and high-heaped masses of flowers. But he still lay in the simple convent coffin and the little bunch of roses which his murderer had placed between his stiffening fingers had not been touched.

Two days later the pastor was buried. The Count and his family led the train of numerous mourners and among the last was Muller.

A day or two after the funeral the detective sauntered slowly through the main street of the village. He was not in a very good humour, his answer to the greeting of those who passed him was short. The children avoided him, for with the keenness of their kind they recognised the fact that this usually gentle little man was not in possession of his habitual calm temper.

One group of boys, playing with a top, did not notice his coming and Muller stopped behind them to look on. Suddenly a sharp whistle was heard and the boys looked up from their play, surprised at seeing the stranger behind them. His eyes were gleaming, and his cheeks were flushed, and a few bars of a merry tune came in a keen whistle from his lips as he watched the spirals made by the spinning top.

Before the boys could stop their play the detective had left the group and hastened onward to the little shop. He left it again in eager haste after having made his purchase, and hurried back to the rectory. The shop-keeper stood in the doorway looking in surprise at this grown man who came to buy a top. And at home in the rectory the old housekeeper listened in equal surprise to the humming noise over her head. She thought at first it might be a bee that had got in somehow. Then she realised that it was not quite the same noise, and having already concluded that it was of no use to be surprised at anything this strange guest might do, she continued reading her scriptures.

Upstairs in the pastor's study, Muller sat in the armchair attentively watching the gyrations of a spinning top. The little toy, started at a certain point, drew a line exactly parallel to the scratch on the floor that had excited his thoughts and absorbed them day and night.

"It was a top—a top," repeated the detective to himself again and again. "I don't see why I didn't think of that right away. Why, of course, nothing else could have drawn such a perfect curve around the room, unhindered by the legs of the desk. Only I don't see how a toy like that could have any connection with this cruel and purposeless murder. Why, only a fool—or a madman—"

Muller sprang up from his chair and again a sharp shrill whistle came from his lips. "A madman!—" he repeated, beating his own forehead. "It could only have been a madman who committed this murder! And the pastor was not the first, there were two other murders here within a comparatively short time. I think I will take advantage of Dr. Orszay's invitation."

Half an hour later Muller and the doctor sat together in a summer-house, from the windows of which one could see the park surrounding the asylum to almost its entire extent. The park was arranged with due regard to its purpose. The eye could sweep through it unhindered. There were no bushes except immediately along the high wall. Otherwise there were beautiful lawns, flower beds and groups of fine old trees with tall trunks.

As would be natural in visiting such a place Muller had induced the doctor to talk about his patients. Dr. Orszay was an excellent talker and possessed the power of painting a personality for his listeners. He was pleased and flattered by the evident interest with which the detective listened to his remarks.

"Then your patients are all quite harmless?" asked Muller thoughtfully, when the doctor came to a pause.

"Yes, all quite harmless. Of course, there is the man who strangely enough considers himself the reincarnation of the famous French murderer, the goldsmith Cardillac, who, as you remember, kept all Paris in a fervour of excitement by his crimes during the reign of Louis XIV. But in spite of his weird mania this man is the most good-natured of any. He has been shut up in his room for several days now. He was a mechanician by trade, living in Budapest, and an unsuccessful invention turned his mind."

"Is he a large, powerful man?" asked Muller.

Dr. Orszay looked a bit surprised. "Why do you ask that? He does happen to be a large man of considerable strength, but in spite of it I have no fear of him. I have an attendant who is invaluable to me, a man of such strength that even the fiercest of them cannot overcome him, and yet with a mind and a personal magnetism which they cannot resist. He can always master our patients mentally and physically—most of them are afraid of him and they know that they must do as he says. There is something in his very glance which has the power to paralyse even healthy nerves, for it shows the strength of will possessed by this man."

"And what is the name of this invaluable attendant?" asked Muller with a strange smile which the doctor took to be slightly ironical.

"Gyuri Kovacz. You are amused at my enthusiasm? But consider my position here. I am an old man and have never been a strong man. At my age I would not have strength enough to force that little woman there—she thinks herself possessed and is quite cranky at times—to go to her own room when she doesn't want to. And do you see that man over there in the blue blouse? He is an excellent gardener but he believes himself to be Napoleon, and when he has his acute attacks I would be helpless to control him were it not for Gyuri."

"And you are not afraid of Cardillac?" interrupted Muller.

"Not in the least. He is as good-natured as a child and as confiding. I can let him walk around here as much as he likes. If it were not for the absurd nonsense that he talks when he has one of his attacks, and which frightens those who do not understand him, I could let him go free altogether."

"Then you never let him leave the asylum grounds?"

"Oh, yes. I take him out with me very frequently. He is a man of considerable education and a very clever talker. It is quite a pleasure to be with him. That was the opinion of my poor friend also, my poor murdered friend."

"The pastor?"

"The pastor. He often invited Cardillac to come to the rectory with me."

"Indeed. Then Cardillac knew the inside of the rectory?"

"Yes. The pastor used to lend him books and let him choose them himself from the library shelves. The people in the village are very kind to my poor patients here. I have long since had the habit of taking some of the quieter ones with me down into the village and letting the people become acquainted with them. It is good for both parties. It gives the patients some little diversion, and it takes away the worst of the senseless fear these peasants had at first of the asylum and its inmates. Cardillac in particular is always welcome when he comes, for he brings the children all sorts of toys that he makes in his cell."

The detective had listened attentively and once his eyes flashed and his lips shut tight as if to keep in the betraying whistle. Then he asked calmly: "But the patients are only allowed to go out when you accompany them, I suppose?"

"Oh, no; the attendants take them out sometimes. I prefer,

however, to let them go only with Gyuri, for I can depend upon him more than upon any of the others."

"Then he and Cardillac have been out together occasionally?"

"Oh, yes, quite frequently. But—pardon me—this is almost like a cross-examination."

"I beg your pardon, doctor, it's a bad habit of mine. One gets so accustomed to it in my profession."

"What is it you want?" asked Doctor Orszay, turning to a fine-looking young man of superb build, who entered just then and stood by the door.

"I just wanted to announce, sir, that No. 302 is quiet again!"

"302 is Cardillac himself, Mr. Muller, or to give him his right name, Lajos Varna," explained the doctor turning to his guest. "He is the 302nd patient who has been received here in these twenty years. Then Cardillac is quiet again?" he asked, looking up at the young giant. "I am glad of that. You can announce our visit to him. This gentleman wants to inspect the asylum."

Muller realised that this was the attendant Gyuri, and he looked at him attentively. He was soon clear in his own mind that this remarkably handsome man did not please him, in fact awoke in him a feeling of repulsion. The attendant's quiet, almost cat-like movements were in strange contrast to the massivity of his superb frame, and his large round eyes, shaped for open, honest glances, were shifty and cunning. They seemed to be asking "Are you trying to discover anything about me?" coupled with a threat. "For your own sake you had better not do it."

When the young man had left the room Muller rose hastily and walked up and down several times.

His face was flushed and his lips tight set. Suddenly he exclaimed: "I do not like this Gyuri."

Dr. Orszay looked up astonished. "There are many others who do not like him—most of his fellow-warders for instance, and all of the patients. I think there must be something in the contrast of such quiet movements with such a big body that gets on people's nerves. But consider, Mr. Muller, that the man's work would naturally make him a little different from other people. I have known Gyuri for five years as a faithful and unassuming servant, always willing and ready for any duty, however difficult or dangerous. He has but one fault—if I may call it such—that is that he has a mistress who is known to be mercenary and hard-hearted. She lives in a neighbouring village."

"For five years, you say? And how long has Cardillac been here?"

"Cardillac? He has been here for almost three years."

"For almost three years, and is it not almost three years—" Muller interrupted himself. "Are we quite alone? Is no one listening?" The doctor nodded, greatly surprised, and the detective continued almost in a whisper, "and it is just about three years now that there have been committed, at intervals, three terrible crimes notable from the cleverness with which they were carried out, and from the utter impossibility, apparently, of discovering the perpetrator."

Orszay sprang up. His face flushed and then grew livid, and he put his hand to his forehead. Then he forced a smile and said in a voice that trembled in spite of himself: "Mr. Muller, your imagination is wonderful. And which of these two do you think it is that has committed these crimes—the perpetrator of which you have come here to find?"

"I will tell you that later. I must speak to No. 302 first, and I must speak to him in the presence of yourself and Gyuri."

The detective's deep gravity was contagious. Dr. Orszay had sufficiently controlled himself to remember what he had heard in former days, and just now recently from the district judge about this man's marvellous deeds. He realised that when Muller said a thing, no matter how extravagant it might sound, it was worth taking seriously. This realisation brought great uneasiness and grief to the doctor's heart, for he had grown fond of both of the men on whom terrible suspicion was cast by such an authority.

Muller himself was uneasy, but the gloom that had hung over him for the past day or two had vanished. The impenetrable darkness that had surrounded the mystery of the pastor's murder had gotten on his nerves. He was not accustomed

to work so long over a problem without getting some light on
it. But now, since the chance watching of the spinning top in
the street had given him his first inkling of the trail, he was following it up to a clear issue. The eagerness, the blissful vibrat-
ing of every nerve that he always felt at this stage of the game,
was on him again. He knew that from now on what was still
to be done would be easy. Hitherto his mind had been made up
on one point; that one man alone was concerned in the crime.
Now he understood the possibility that there might have been
two, the harmless mechanician who fancied himself a dangerous murderer, and the handsome young giant with the evil eyes.

The two men stood looking at each other in a silence that
was almost hostile. Had this stranger come to disturb the peace
of the refuge for the unfortunate and to prove that Dr. Orszay,
the friend of all the village, had unwittingly been giving shelter
to such criminals?

"Shall we go now?" asked the detective finally.

"If you wish it, sir," answered the doctor in a tone that was
decidedly cool.

Muller held out his hand. "Don't let us be foolish, doctor. If
you should find yourself terribly deceived, and I should have
been the means of proving it, promise me that you will not be
angry with me."

Orszay pressed the offered hand with a deep sigh. He realised the other's position and knew it was his duty to give him
every possible assistance. "What is there for me to do now?"
he asked sadly.

"You must see that all the patients are shut up in their cells
so that the other attendants are at our disposal if we need them.
Varna's room has barred windows, I suppose?"

"Yes."

"And I suppose also that it has but one door. I believe you
told me that your asylum was built on the cell system."

"Yes, there is but one door to the room."

"Let the four other attendants stand outside this door. Gyuri
will be inside with us. Tell the men outside that they are to seize
and hold whomever I shall designate to them. I will call them in
by a whistle. You can trust your people?"

"Yes, I think I can."

"Well, I have my revolver," said Muller calmly, "and now we can go."

They left the room together, and found Gyuri waiting for them a little further along the corridor.

"Aren't you well, sir?" the attendant asked the doctor, with an anxious note in his voice.

The man's anxiety was not feigned. He was really a faithful servant in his devotion to the old doctor, although Muller had not misjudged him when he decided that this young giant was capable of anything. Good and evil often lie so close together in the human heart.

The doctor's emotion prevented him from speaking, and the detective answered in his place. "It is a sudden indisposition," he said. "Lead me to No. 302, who is waiting for us, I suppose. The doctor wants to lie down a moment in his own room."

Gyuri glanced distrustfully at this man whom he had met for the first time to-day, but who was no stranger to him—for he had already learned the identity of the guest in the rectory. Then he turned his eyes on his master. The latter nodded and said: "Take the gentleman to Varna's room. I will follow shortly."

The cell to which they went was the first one at the head of the staircase. "Extremely convenient," thought Muller to himself. It was a large room, comfortably furnished and filled now with the red glow of the setting sun. A turning-lathe stood by the window and an elderly man was at work at it. Gyuri called to him and he turned and rose when he saw a stranger.

Lajos Varna was a tall, loose-jointed man with sallow skin and tired eyes. He gave only a hasty glance at his visitor, then looked at Gyuri. The expression in his eyes as he turned them on those of the warder was like the look in the eyes of a well-trained dog when it watches its master's face. Gyuri's brows were drawn close together and his mouth set tight to a narrow line. His eyes fairly bored themselves into the patient's eyes with an expression like that of a hypnotiser.

Muller knew now what he wanted to know. This young man understood how to bend the will of others, even the will of a sick mind, to his own desires. The little silent scene he had watched had lasted just the length of time it had taken the detective to walk through the room and hold out his hand to the patient.

"I don't want to disturb you, Mr. Varna," he said in a friendly tone, with a motion towards the bench from which the mechanician had just arisen. Varna sat down again, obedient as a child. He was not always so apparently, for Muller saw a red mark over the fingers of one hand that was evidently the mark of a blow. Gyuri was not very choice in the methods by which he controlled the patients confided to his care.

"May I sit down also?" asked Muller.

Varna pushed forward a chair. His movements were like those of an automaton.

"And now tell me how you like it here?" began the detective.

Varna answered with a low soft voice, "Oh, I like it very much, sir." As he spoke he looked up at Gyuri, whose eyes still bore their commanding expression.

"They treat you kindly here?"

"Oh, yes."

"The doctor is very good to you?"

"Ah, the doctor is so good!" Varna's dull eyes brightened.

"And the others are good to you also?"

"Oh, yes." The momentary gleam in the sad eye had vanished again.

"Where did you get this red scar?"

The patient became uneasy, he moved anxiously on his chair and looked up at Gyuri. It was evident that he realised there would be more red marks if he told the truth to this stranger.

Muller did not insist upon an answer. "You are uneasy and nervous sometimes, aren't you?"

"Yes, sir, I have been—nervous—lately."

"And they don't let you go out at such times?"

"Why, I—no, I may not go out at such times."

"But the doctor takes you with him sometimes—the doctor or Gyuri?" asked the detective.

"Yes."

"I haven't had him out with me for weeks," interrupted the

attendant. He seemed particularly anxious to have the "for weeks" clearly heard by this inconvenient questioner.

Muller dropped this subject and took up another. "They tell me you are very fond of children, and I can see that you are making toys for them here."

"Yes, I love children, and I am so glad they are not afraid of me." These words were spoken with more warmth and greater interest than anything the man had yet said.

"And they tell me that you take gifts with you for the children every time you go down to the village. This is pretty work here, and it must be a pleasant diversion for you." Muller had taken up a dainty little spinning-wheel which was almost completed. "Isn't it made from the wood of a red yew tree?"

"Yes, the doctor gave me a whole tree that had been cut down in the park."

"And that gave you wood for a long time?"

"Yes, indeed; I have been making toys from it for months." Varna had become quite eager and interested as he handed his visitor a number of pretty trifles. The two had risen from their chairs and were leaning over the wide window seat which served as a store-house for the wares turned out by the busy workman. They were toys, mostly, all sorts of little pots and plates, dolls' furniture, balls of various sizes, miniature bowling pins, and tops. Muller took up one of the latter.

"How very clever you are, and how industrious," he exclaimed, sitting down again and turning the top in his hands. It was covered with grey varnish with tiny little yellow stripes painted on it. Towards the lower point a little bit of the varnish had been broken off and the reddish wood underneath was visible. The top was much better constructed than the cheap toys sold in the village. It was hollow and contained in its interior a mechanism started by a pressure on the upper end. Once set in motion the little top spun about the room for some time.

"Oh, isn't that pretty! Is this mechanism your own invention?" asked Muller smiling. Gyuri watched the top with drawn brows and murmured something about "childish foolishness."

"Yes, it is my own invention," said the patient, flattered. He started out on an absolutely technical explanation of the mechanism of tops in general and of his own in particular, an explanation so lucid and so well put that no one would have believed the man who was speaking was not in possession of the full powers of his mind.

Muller listened very attentively with unfeigned interest.

"But you have made more important inventions than this, haven't you?" he asked when the other stopped talking. Varna's eyes flashed and his voice dropped to a tone of mystery as he answered: "Yes indeed I have. But I did not have time to finish them. For I had become some one else."

"Some one else?"

"Cardillac," whispered Varna, whose mania was now getting the best of him again.

"Cardillac? You mean the notorious goldsmith who lived in Paris 200 years ago? Why, he's dead."

Varna's pale lips curled in a superior smile. "Oh, yes—that's what people think, but it's a mistake. He is still alive—I am—I have—although of course there isn't much opportunity here—"

Gyuri cleared his throat with a rasping noise.

"What were you saying, friend Cardillac?" asked Muller with a great show of interest.

"I have done things here that nobody has found out. It gives me great pleasure to see the authorities so helpless over the riddles I have given them to solve. Oh, indeed, sir, you would never imagine how stupid they are here."

"In other words, friend Cardillac, you are too clever for the authorities here?"

"Yes, that's it," said the insane man greatly flattered. He raised his head proudly and smiled down at his guest. At this moment the doctor came into the room and Gyuri walked forward to the group at the window.

"You are making him nervous, sir," he said to Muller in a tone that was almost harsh.

"You can leave that to me," answered the detective calmly. "And you will please place yourself behind Mr. Varna's chair, not behind mine. It is your eyes that are making him uneasy."

The attendant was alarmed and lost control of himself for a moment. "Sir!" he exclaimed in an outburst.

"My name is Muller, in case you do not know it already, Joseph Muller, detective. Gyuri Kovacz, you will do what I tell you to! I am master here just now. Is it not so, doctor?"

"Yes, it is so," said the doctor.

"What does this mean?" murmured Gyuri, turning pale.

"It means that the best thing for you to do is to stand up against that wall and fold your arms on your breast," said Muller firmly. He took a revolver from his pocket and laid it beside him on the turning-lathe. The young giant, cowed by the sight of the weapon, obeyed the commands of this little man whom he could have easily crushed with a single blow.

Dr. Orszay sank down on the chair beside the door. Muller, now completely master of the situation, turned to the insane man who stood looking at him in a surprise which was mingled with admiration.

"And now, my dear Cardillac, you must tell us of your great deeds here," said the detective in a friendly tone.

The unfortunate man bent over him with shining eyes and whispered: "But you'll shoot him first, won't you?"

"Why should I shoot him?"

"Because he won't let me say a word without beating me. He is so cruel. He sticks pins into me if I don't do what he wants."

"Why didn't you tell the doctor?"

"Gyuri would have treated me worse than ever then. I am a coward, sir, I'm so afraid of pain and he knew that—he knew that I was afraid of being hurt and that I'd always do what he asked of me. And because I don't like to be hurt myself I always finished them off quickly."

"Finished who?"

"Why, there was Red Betty, he wanted her money."

"Who wanted it?"

"Gyuri."

The man at the wall moved when he heard this terrible accusation. But the detective took up his revolver again. "Be quiet there!" he called, with a look such as he might have thrown at an angry dog.

Gyuri stood quiet again but his eyes shot flames and great drops stood out on his forehead.

"Now go on, friend Cardillac," continued the detective. "We were talking about Red Betty."

"I strangled her. She did not even know she was dying. She was such a weak old woman, it really couldn't have hurt her."

"No, certainly not," said Muller soothingly, for he saw that the thought that his victim might have suffered was beginning to make the madman uneasy. "You needn't worry about that. Old Betty died a quiet death. But tell me, how did Gyuri know that she had money?"

"The whole village knew it. She laid cards for people and earned a lot of money that way. She was very stingy and saved every bit. Somebody saw her counting out her money once, she had it in a big stocking under her bed. People in the village talked about it. That's how Gyuri heard of it."

"And so he commanded you to kill Betty and steal her money?"

"Yes. He knew that I loved to give them riddles to guess, just as I did in Paris so long ago."

"Oh, yes, you're Cardillac, aren't you? And now tell us about the smith's swineherd."

"You mean Janos? Oh, he was a stupid lout," answered Varna scornfully. "He had cast an eye on the beautiful Julcsi, Gyuri's mistress, so of course I had to kill him."

"Did you do that alone?"

"No, Gyuri helped me."

"Why did you cut the bridge supports?"

"Because I enjoy giving people riddles, as I told you. But Gyuri forbade me to kill people uselessly. I liked the chance of getting out though. The doctor's so good to me and the others too. Gyuri is good to me when I have done what he wanted. But you see, Mr. Muller, I am like a prisoner here and that makes me angry. I made Gyuri let me out nights sometimes."

"You mean he let you out alone, all alone?"

"Yes, of course, for I threatened to tell the doctor everything if he didn't."

"You wouldn't have dared do that."

"No, that's true," smiled Varna slyly. "But Gyuri was afraid

I might do it, for he isn't always strong enough to frighten me with his eyes. Those were the hours when I could make him afraid—I liked those hours—"

"What did you do when you were out alone at night?"

"I just walked about. I set fire to a tree in the woods once, then the rain came and put it out. Once I killed a dog and another time I cut through the bridge supports. That took me several hours to do and made me very tired. But it was such fun to know that people would be worrying and fussing about who did it."

Varna rubbed his hands gleefully. He did not look the least bit malicious but only very much amused. The doctor groaned. Gyuri's great body trembled, his arms shook, but he did not make a single voluntary movement. He saw the revolver in Muller's hand and felt the keen grey eyes resting on him in pitiless calm.

"And now tell us about the pastor?" said the detective in a firm clear voice.

"Oh, he was a dear, good gentleman," said No. 302 with an expression of pitying sorrow on his face. "I owed him much gratitude; that's why I put the roses in his hand."

"Yes, but you murdered him first."

"Of course, Gyuri told me to."

"And why?"

"He hated the pastor, for the old gentleman had no confidence in him."

"Is this true?" Muller turned to the doctor.

"I did not notice it," said Orszay with a voice that showed deep sorrow.

"And you?" Muller's eyes bored themselves into the orbs of the young giant, now dulled with fear.

Gyuri started and shivered. "He looked at me sharply every now and then," he murmured.

"And that was why he was killed?"

The warder's head sank on his breast.

"No, not only for that reason," continued No. 302. "Gyuri needed money again. He ordered me to bring him the silver candlesticks off the altar."

"Murder and sacrilege," said the detective calmly.

"No, I did not rob the church. When I had buried the reverend gentleman I heard the cock crowing. I was afraid I might get home here too late and I forgot the candlesticks. I had to stop to wash my hands in the brook. While I was there I saw shepherd Janci coming along and I hid behind the willows. He almost discovered me once, but Janci's a dreamer, he sees things nobody else sees—and he doesn't see things that everybody else does see. I couldn't help laughing at his sleepy face. But I didn't laugh when I came back to the asylum. Gyuri was waiting for me at the door. When he saw that I hadn't brought the candlesticks he beat me and tortured me worse than he'd ever done before."

"And you didn't tell anyone?"

"Why, no; because I was afraid that if I told on him, I'd never be able to go out again."

"And you, quite alone, could carry the pastor's body out of his room?"

"I am very strong."

"How did you arrange it that there should be no traces of blood to betray you?"

"I waited until the body had stiffened, then I tied up the wound and carried him down into the crypt."

"Why did you do that?"

"I didn't want to leave him in that horrid pool of blood."

"You were sorry for him then?"

"Why, yes; it looked so horrid to see him lying there—and he had always been so good to me. He was so good to me that very evening when I entered his study."

"He recognised you?"

"Certainly. He sprang up from his chair when I came in through the passage from the church. I saw that he was startled, but he smiled at me and reached out his hand to me and said: 'What brings you here, my dear Cardillac?' And then I struck. I wanted him to die with that smile on his lips. It is beautiful to see a man die smiling, it shows that he has not been afraid of death. He was dead at once. I always kill that way—I know just how to strike and where. I killed more than a hundred people years ago in Paris, and I didn't leave one of them the time for even a sigh. I was renowned for that—I had a kind heart and a sure hand."

Muller interrupted the dreadful imaginings of the madman with a question. "You got into the house through the crypt?"

"Yes, through the crypt. I found the window one night when I was prowling around in the churchyard. When I knew that the pastor was to be the next, I cut through the window bars. Gyuri went into the church one day when nobody was there and found out that it was easy to lift the stone over the entrance to the crypt. He also learned that the doors from the church to the vestry were never locked. I knew how to find the passageway, because I had been through it several times on my visits to the rectory. But it was a mere chance that the door into the pastor's study was unlocked."

"A chance that cost the life of a worthy man," said the detective gravely.

Varna nodded sadly. "But he didn't suffer, he was dead at once."

"And now tell me what this top was doing there?"

No. 302 looked at the detective in great surprise, and then laid his hand on the latter's arm. "How did you know that I had the top there?" he asked with a show of interest.

"I found its traces in the room, and it was those traces that led me here to you," answered Muller.

"How strange!" remarked Varna. "Are you like shepherd Janci that you can see the things others don't see?"

"No, I have not Janci's gift. It would be a great comfort to me and a help to the others perhaps if I had. I can only see things after they have happened."

"But you can see more than others—the others did not see the traces of the top?"

"My business is to see more than others see," said Muller. "But you have not told me yet what the top was doing there. Why did you take a toy like that with you when you went out on such an errand?"

"It was in my pocket by chance. When I reached for my handkerchief to quench the flow of blood the top came out with it. I must have touched the spring without knowing it, for the top began to spin. I stood still and watched it, then I ran after it. It spun around the room and finally came back to the body. So did I. The pastor was quite still and dead by that time."

"You have heard everything, Dr. Orszay?" asked the detective, rising from his chair.

"Yes, I have heard everything," answered the venerable head of the asylum. He was utterly crushed by the realisation that all this tragedy and horror had gone out from his house.

Varna rose also. He understood perfectly that now Gyuri's power was at an end and he was as pleased as a child that has just received a present. "And now you're going to shoot him?" he asked, in the tone a boy would use if asking when the fireworks were to begin.

Muller shook his head. "No, my dear Cardillac," he replied gravely. "He will not be shot—that is a death for a brave soldier—but this man has deserved—" He did not finish the sentence, for the warder sank to the floor unconscious.

"What a coward!" murmured the detective scornfully, looking down at the giant frame that lay prostrate before him. Even in his wide experience he had known of no case of a man of such strength and such bestial cruelty, combined with such utter cowardice.

Varna also stood looking down at the unconscious warder. Then he glanced up with a cunning smile at the other two men who stood there. The doctor, pale and trembling with horror, covered his face with his hands. Muller turned to the door to call in the attendants waiting outside. During the moment's pause that ensued the madman bent over his worktable, seized a knife that lay there and dropped on one knee beside the prostrate form. His hand was raised to strike when a calm voice said: "Fie! Cardillac, for shame! Do not belittle yourself. This man here is not worthy of your knife, the hangman will look after him."

Varna raised his loose-jointed frame and looked about with glistening eyes and trembling lips. His mind was completely darkened once more. "I must kill him—I must have his blood—

there is no one to see me," he murmured. "I am a hangman too—he has made a hangman of me," and again he bent with uplifted hand over the man who had utilised his terrible misfortune to make a criminal of him. But two of the waiting attendants seized his arms and threw him back on the floor, while the other two carted Gyuri out. Both unfortunates were soon securely guarded.

"Do not be angry with me, doctor," said Muller gravely, as he walked through the garden accompanied by Orszay.

Doctor Orszay laughed bitterly. "Why should I be angry with you—you who have discovered my inexcusable credulity?"

"Inexcusable? Oh, no, doctor; it was quite natural that you should have believed a man who had himself so well in hand, and who knew so well how to play his part. When we come to think of it, we realise that most crimes have been made possible through some one's credulity, or over-confidence, a credulity which, in the light of subsequent events, seems quite incomprehensible. Do not reproach yourself and do not lose heart. Your only fault was that you did not recognise the heart of the beast of prey in this admirable human form."

"What course will the law take?" asked Orszay. "The poor unfortunate madman—whose knife took all these lives— cannot be held responsible, can he?"

"Oh, no; his misfortune protects him. But as for the other, though his hands bear no actual bloodstains, he is more truly a murderer than the unhappy man who was his tool. Hanging is too good for him. There are times when even I could wish that we were back in the Middle Ages, when it was possible to torture a prisoner."

"You do not look like that sort of a man," smiled the doctor through his sadness.

"No, I am the most good-natured of men usually, I think— the meekest anyway," answered Muller. "But a case like this—. However, as I said before, keep a stout heart, doctor, and do not waste time in unnecessary self-reproachings." The detective pressed the doctor's hand warmly and walked down the hill towards the village.

He went at once to the office of the magistrate and made his report, then returned to the rectory and packed his grip. He arranged for its transport to the railway station, as he himself preferred to walk the inconsiderable distance. He passed through the village and had just entered the open fields when he met Janci with his flock. The shepherd hastened his steps when he saw the detective approaching.

"You have found him, sir?" he exclaimed as he came up to Muller. The men had come to be friends by this time. The silent shepherd with the power of second sight had won Muller's interest at once.

"Yes, I found him. It is Gyuri, the warder at the asylum."

"No, sir, it is not Gyuri—Gyuri did not do it."

"But when I tell you that he did?"

"But I tell you, sir, that Gyuri did not do it. The man who did it—he has yellowish hands—I saw them—I saw big yellowish hands. Gyuri's hands are big, but they are brown."

"Janci, you are right. I was only trying to test you. Gyuri did not do it; that is, he did not do it with his own hands. The man who held the knife that struck down the pastor was Varna, the crazy mechanician."

Janci beat his forehead. "Oh, I am a foolish and useless dreamer!" he exclaimed; "of course it was Varna's hands that I saw. I have seen them a hundred times when he came down into the village, and yet when I saw them in the vision I did not recognise them."

"We're all dreamers, Janci—and our dreams are very useless generally."

"Yours are not useless, sir," said the shepherd. "If I had as much brains as you have, my dreams might be of some good."

Muller smiled. "And if I had your visions, Janci, it would be a powerful aid to me in my profession."

"I don't think you need them, sir. You can find out the hidden things without them. You are going to leave us?"

"Yes, Janci, I must go back to Budapest, and from there to Vienna. They need me on another case."

"It's a sad work, this bringing people to the gallows, isn't it?"

"Yes, Janci, it is sometimes. But it's a good thing to be able to avenge crime and bring justice to the injured. Good-bye, Janci."

"Good-bye, sir, and God speed you."

The shepherd stood looking after the small, slight figure of the man who walked on rapidly through the heather. "He's the right one for the work," murmured Janci as he turned slowly back towards the village.

An hour later Muller stood in the little waiting-room of the railway station writing a telegram. It was addressed to Count ——.

Do you know the shepherd Janci? It would be a good thing to make him the official detective for the village. He has high qualifications for the profession. If I had his gifts combined with my own, no one could escape me. I have found this one however. The guards are already taking him to you. My work here is done. If I should be needed again I can be found at Police Headquarters, Vienna.

Respectfully,

Joseph Muller

ANNA KATHARINE GREEN

(1846–1935)

Anna Katharine Green, one of the towering figures in the early days of the detective story, grew up in Brooklyn and Buffalo and set most of her three dozen books in New York City or elsewhere in the state. Her father was an attorney. As a young woman she became curious about his work and learned as much as possible about the legal profession. Beginning shortly after she completed college, she worked in secret for six years on a novel, scrawling in varicolored notebooks, before asking his opinion of it. He was impressed. In 1878, when *The Leavenworth Case* was published, she was dumbfounded when it became a bestseller. This charming and fast-paced first case for Ebenezer Gryce of the New York City Police Department even became required reading at Yale Law School, as an example of the risks of circumstantial evidence. You can find more about Green and her debut in my introduction to the Penguin Classics edition of *The Leavenworth Case*.

The tireless and sardonic Gryce, who deserves more attention than he receives nowadays, appeared in several other novels. Green also created two female detectives. Amelia Butterworth, an eagle-eyed elderly busybody, is a more nuanced and convincing character than Agatha Christie's Miss Marple, whom she surely helped inspire. Butterworth sometimes collaborates with Gryce and sometimes snoops on her own.

Violet Strange, the detective in the following story, appears in a single collection published by G. P. Putnam's Sons in 1915—*The Golden Slipper and Other Problems for Violet Strange*. Strange is a wealthy and moody young New York socialite, about as far away on several spectra from working-class policeman Gryce as it is possible to imagine, and quite some distance even from Amelia Butterworth. Strange appears in ten stories. Not until the final case, "Violet's Own," does Green reveal the reason behind Strange's sneaking around to investigate crimes while keeping such work secret from her social equals. It turns out that long ago her sister was unjustly disinherited and young Violet is trying to raise money for her education as a musician. Thus she manages to be adventurous and heroic through numerous cases, only to prove in the end to be doing so for acceptably noble and ladylike reasons.

Readers learn this motivation only when she ceases investigative work, when she marries and reveals to her husband the origin of her rather alarming need for money. She has been covertly working for a private detective agency. "An Intangible Clue," the third story in the series, opens with a lively conversation between her boss and his secret operative. She prefers cases of theft or identity, and must be convinced to look into a murder. The "mutual compact" she refers to, in trying to avoid the murder investigation, is the realization that she and her employer share that they are valuable to each other, and can maintain a mutually profitable relationship only if her investigations remain absolutely secret from her high-society friends.

AN INTANGIBLE CLUE

"Have you studied the case?"

"Not I."

"Not studied the case which for the last few days has provided the papers with such conspicuous headlines?"

"I do not read the papers. I have not looked at one in a whole week."

"Miss Strange, your social engagements must be of a very pressing nature just now?"

"They are."

"And your business sense in abeyance?"

"How so?"

"You would not ask if you had read the papers."

To this she made no reply save by a slight toss of her pretty head. If her employer felt nettled by this show of indifference, he did not betray it save by the rapidity of his tones as, without further preamble and possibly without real excuse, he proceeded to lay before her the case in question. "Last Tuesday night a woman was murdered in this city; an old woman, in a lonely house where she has lived for years. Perhaps you remember this house? It occupies a not inconspicuous site in Seventeenth Street—a house of the olden time?"

"No, I do not remember."

The extreme carelessness of Miss Strange's tone would have been fatal to her socially; but then, she would never have used it socially. This they both knew, yet he smiled with his customary indulgence.

"Then I will describe it."

She looked around for a chair and sank into it. He did the same.

"It has a fanlight over the front door."

She remained impassive.

"And two old-fashioned strips of parti-coloured glass on either side."

"And a knocker between its panels which may bring money some day."

"Oh, you do remember! I thought you would, Miss Strange."

"Yes. Fanlights over doors are becoming very rare in New York."

"Very well, then. That house was the scene of Tuesday's tragedy. The woman who has lived there in solitude for years was foully murdered. I have since heard that the people who knew her best have always anticipated some such violent end for her. She never allowed maid or friend to remain with her after five in the afternoon; yet she had money—some think a great deal—always in the house."

"I am interested in the house, not in her."

"Yet, she was a character—as full of whims and crotchets as a nut is of meat. Her death was horrible. She fought—her dress was torn from her body in rags. This happened, you see, before her hour for retiring; some think as early as six in the afternoon. And"—here he made a rapid gesture to catch Violet's wandering attention—"in spite of this struggle; in spite of the fact that she was dragged from room to room—that her person was searched—and everything in the house searched—that drawers were pulled out of bureaus—doors wrenched off of cupboards—china smashed upon the floor—whole shelves denuded and not a spot from cellar to garret left unransacked, no direct clue to the perpetrator has been found—nothing that gives any idea of his personality save his display of strength and great cupidity. The police have even deigned to consult me,—an unusual procedure—but I could find nothing, either. Evidences of fiendish purpose abound—of relentless search—but no clue to the man himself. It's uncommon, isn't it, not to have any clue?"

"I suppose so." Miss Strange hated murders and it was with difficulty she could be brought to discuss them. But she was not going to be let off; not this time.

"You see," he proceeded insistently, "it's not only mortifying to the police but disappointing to the press, especially as few reporters believe in the No-thoroughfare business. They say, and we cannot but agree with them, that no such struggle could take place and no such repeated goings to and fro through the house without some vestige being left by which to connect this crime with its daring perpetrator."

Still she stared down at her hands—those little hands so white and fluttering, so seemingly helpless under the weight of their many rings, and yet so slyly capable.

"She must have queer neighbours," came at last, from Miss Strange's reluctant lips. "Didn't they hear or see anything of all this?"

"She has no neighbours—that is, after half-past five o'clock. There's a printing establishment on one side of her, a deserted mansion on the other side, and nothing but warehouses back and front. There was no one to notice what took place in her small dwelling after the printing house was closed. She was the most courageous or the most foolish of women to remain there as she did. But nothing except death could budge her. She was born in the room where she died; was married in the one where she worked; saw husband, father, mother, and five sisters carried out in turn to their graves through the door with the fanlight over the top—and these memories held her."

"You are trying to interest me in the woman. Don't."

"No, I'm not trying to interest you in her, only trying to explain her. There was another reason for her remaining where she did so long after all residents had left the block. She had a business."

"Oh!"

"She embroidered monograms for fine ladies."

"She did? But you needn't look at me like that. She never embroidered any for me."

"No? She did first-class work. I saw some of it. Miss Strange, if I could get you into that house for ten minutes—not to see her but to pick up the loose intangible thread which I am sure is floating around in it somewhere—wouldn't you go?"

Violet slowly rose—a movement which he followed to the letter.

"Must I express in words the limit I have set for myself in our affair?" she asked. "When, for reasons I have never thought myself called upon to explain, I consented to help you a little now and then with some matter where a woman's tact and knowledge of the social world might tell without offence to herself or others, I never thought it would be necessary for me to state that temptation must stop with such cases, or that I should not be asked to touch the sordid or the bloody. But it seems I was mistaken, and that I must stoop to be explicit. The woman who was killed on Tuesday might have interested me greatly as an embroiderer, but as a victim, not at all. What do you see in me, or miss in me, that you should drag me into an atmosphere of low-down crime?"

"Nothing, Miss Strange. You are by nature, as well as by breeding, very far removed from everything of the kind. But you will allow me to suggest that no crime is low-down which makes imperative demand upon the intellect and intuitive sense of its investigator. Only the most delicate touch can feel and hold the thread I've just spoken of, and you have the most delicate touch I know."

"Do not attempt to flatter me. I have no fancy for handling befouled spider webs. Besides, if I had—if such elusive filaments fascinated me—how could I, well-known in person and name, enter upon such a scene without prejudice to our mutual compact?"

"Miss Strange"—she had reseated herself, but so far he had failed to follow her example (an ignoring of the subtle hint that her interest might yet be caught, which seemed to annoy her a trifle), "I should not even have suggested such a possibility had I not seen a way of introducing you there without risk to your position or mine. Among the boxes piled upon Mrs. Doolittle's table—boxes of finished work, most of them addressed and ready for delivery—was one on which could be seen the name of—shall I mention it?"

"Not mine? You don't mean mine? That would be too odd— too ridiculously odd. I should not understand a coincidence of that kind; no, I should not, notwithstanding the fact that I have lately sent out such work to be done."

"Yet it was your name, very clearly and precisely written— your whole name, Miss Strange. I saw and read it myself."

"But I gave the order to Madame Pirot on Fifth Avenue. How

came my things to be found in the house of this woman of whose horrible death we have been talking?"

"Did you suppose that Madame Pirot did such work with her own hands?—or even had it done in her own establishment? Mrs. Doolittle was universally employed. She worked for a dozen firms. You will find the biggest names on most of her packages. But on this one—I allude to the one addressed to you—there was more to be seen than the name. These words were written on it in another hand. Send without opening. This struck the police as suspicious; sufficiently so, at least, for them to desire your presence at the house as soon as you can make it convenient."

"To open the box?"

"Exactly."

The curl of Miss Strange's disdainful lip was a sight to see.

"You wrote those words yourself," she coolly observed. "While someone's back was turned, you whipped out your pencil and—"

"Resorted to a very pardonable subterfuge highly conducive to the public's good. But never mind that. Will you go?"

Miss Strange became suddenly demure.

"I suppose I must," she grudgingly conceded. "However obtained, a summons from the police cannot be ignored even by Peter Strange's daughter."

Another man might have displayed his triumph by smile or gesture; but this one had learned his role too well. He simply said:

"Very good. Shall it be at once? I have a taxi at the door."

But she failed to see the necessity of any such hurry. With sudden dignity she replied:

"That won't do. If I go to this house it must be under suitable conditions. I shall have to ask my brother to accompany me."

"Your brother!"

"Oh, he's safe. He—he knows."

"Your brother knows?" Her visitor, with less control than usual, betrayed very openly his uneasiness.

"He does and—approves. But that's not what interests us

now, only so far as it makes it possible for me to go with propriety to that dreadful house."

A formal bow from the other and the words:

"They may expect you, then. Can you say when?"

"Within the next hour. But it will be a useless concession on my part," she pettishly complained. "A place that has been gone over by a dozen detectives is apt to be brushed clean of its cobwebs, even if such ever existed."

"That's the difficulty," he acknowledged; and did not dare to add another word; she was at that particular moment so very much the great lady, and so little his confidential agent.

He might have been less impressed, however, by this sudden assumption of manner, had he been so fortunate as to have seen how she employed the three quarters of an hour's delay for which she had asked.

She read those neglected newspapers, especially the one containing the following highly coloured narration of this ghastly crime:

"A door ajar—an empty hall—a line of sinister looking blotches marking a guilty step diagonally across the flagging—silence—and an unmistakable odour repugnant to all humanity,—such were the indications which met the eyes of Officer O'Leary on his first round last night, and led to the discovery of a murder which will long thrill the city by its mystery and horror.

"Both the house and the victim are well known." Here followed a description of the same and of Mrs. Doolittle's manner of life in her ancient home, which Violet hurriedly passed over to come to the following:

"As far as one can judge from appearances, the crime happened in this wise: Mrs. Doolittle had been in her kitchen, as the tea-kettle found singing on the stove goes to prove, and was coming back through her bedroom, when the wretch, who had stolen in by the front door which, to save steps, she was unfortunately in the habit of leaving on the latch till all possibility of customers for the day was over, sprang upon her from behind and dealt her a swinging blow with the poker he had caught up from the hearthstone.

"Whether the struggle which ensued followed immediately upon this first attack or came later, it will take medical experts to determine. But, whenever it did occur, the fierceness of its character is shown by the grip taken upon her throat and the traces of blood which are to be seen all over the house. If the wretch had lugged her into her workroom and thence to the kitchen, and thence back to the spot of first assault, the evidences could not have been more ghastly. Bits of her clothing torn off by a ruthless hand, lay scattered over all these floors. In her bedroom, where she finally breathed her last, there could be seen mingled with these a number of large but worthless glass beads; and close against one of the base-boards, the string which had held them, as shown by the few remaining beads still clinging to it. If in pulling the string from her neck he had hoped to light upon some valuable booty, his fury at his disappointment is evident. You can almost see the frenzy with which he flung the would-be necklace at the wall, and kicked about and stamped upon its rapidly rolling beads.

"Booty! That was what he was after; to find and carry away the poor needlewoman's supposed hoardings. If the scene baffles description—if, as some believe, he dragged her yet living from spot to spot, demanding information as to her places of concealment under threat of repeated blows, and, finally baffled, dealt the finishing stroke and proceeded on the search alone, no greater devastation could have taken place in this poor woman's house or effects. Yet such was his precaution and care for himself that he left no finger-print behind him nor any other token which could lead to personal identification. Even though his footsteps could be traced in much the order I have mentioned, they were of so indeterminate and shapeless a character as to convey little to the intelligence of the investigator.

"That these smears (they could not be called footprints) not only crossed the hall but appeared in more than one place on the staircase proves that he did not confine his search to the lower storey; and perhaps one of the most interesting features of the case lies in the indications given by these marks of the raging course he took through these upper rooms. As the accompanying diagram will show [we omit the diagram] he went first into the large front chamber, thence to the rear where we find two rooms, one unfinished and filled with accumulated stuff most of which he left lying loose upon the floor, and the other plastered, and containing a window opening upon an alley-way at the side, but empty of all furniture and without even a carpet on the bare boards.

"Why he should have entered the latter place, and why, having entered he should have crossed to the window, will be plain to those who have studied the conditions. The front chamber windows were tightly shuttered, the attic ones cumbered with boxes and shielded from approach by old bureaus and discarded chairs. This one only was free and, although darkened by the proximity of the house neighbouring it across the alley, was the only spot on the storey where sufficient light could be had at this late hour for the examination of any object of whose value he was doubtful. That he had come across such an object and had brought it to this window for some such purpose is very satisfactorily demonstrated by the discovery of a worn out wallet of ancient make lying on the floor directly in front of this window—a proof of his cupidity but also proof of his ill-luck. For this wallet, when lifted and opened, was found to contain two hundred or more dollars in old bills, which, if not the full hoard of their industrious owner, was certainly worth the taking by one who had risked his neck for the sole purpose of theft.

"This wallet, and the flight of the murderer without it, give to this affair, otherwise simply brutal, a dramatic interest which will be appreciated not only by the very able detectives already hot upon the chase, but by all other inquiring minds anxious to solve a mystery of which so estimable a woman has been the unfortunate victim. A problem is presented to the police—"

There Violet stopped.

When, not long after, the superb limousine of Peter Strange stopped before the little house in Seventeenth Street, it caused a veritable sensation, not only in the curiosity-mongers lingering on the sidewalk, but to the two persons within—the officer on guard and a belated reporter.

Though dressed in her plainest suit, Violet Strange looked

much too fashionable and far too young and thoughtless to be observed, without emotion, entering a scene of hideous and brutal crime. Even the young man who accompanied her promised to bring a most incongruous element into this atmosphere of guilt and horror, and, as the detective on guard whispered to the man beside him, might much better have been left behind in the car.

But Violet was great for the proprieties and young Arthur followed her in.

Her entrance was a coup de theatre. She had lifted her veil in crossing the sidewalk and her interesting features and general air of timidity were very fetching. As the man holding open the door noted the impression made upon his companion, he muttered with sly facetiousness:

"You think you'll show her nothing; but I'm ready to bet a fiver that she'll want to see it all and that you'll show it to her."

The detective's grin was expressive, notwithstanding the shrug with which he tried to carry it off.

And Violet? The hall into which she now stepped from the most vivid sunlight had never been considered even in its palmiest days as possessing cheer even of the stately kind. The ghastly green light infused through it by the coloured glass on either side of the doorway seemed to promise yet more dismal things beyond.

"Must I go in there?" she asked, pointing, with an admirable simulation of nervous excitement, to a half-shut door at her left. "Is there where it happened? Arthur, do you suppose that there is where it happened?"

"No, no, Miss," the officer made haste to assure her. "If you are Miss Strange" (Violet bowed), "I need hardly say that the woman was struck in her bedroom. The door beside you leads into the parlour, or as she would have called it, her work-room. You needn't be afraid of going in there. You will see nothing but the disorder of her boxes. They were pretty well pulled about. Not all of them though," he added, watching her as closely as the dim light permitted. "There is one which gives no sign of having been tampered with. It was done up in wrapping paper and is addressed to you, which in itself would not have seemed worthy of our attention had not these lines been scribbled on it in a man's handwriting: 'Send without opening.'"

"How odd!" exclaimed the little minx with widely opened eyes and an air of guileless innocence. "Whatever can it mean? Nothing serious I am sure, for the woman did not even know me. She was employed to do this work by Madame Pirot."

"Didn't you know that it was to be done here?"

"No. I thought Madame Pirot's own girls did her embroidery for her."

"So that you were surprised—"

"Wasn't I!"

"To get our message."

"I didn't know what to make of it."

The earnest, half-injured look with which she uttered this disclaimer, did its appointed work. The detective accepted her for what she seemed and, oblivious to the reporter's satirical gesture, crossed to the work-room door, which he threw wide open with the remark:

"I should be glad to have you open that box in our presence. It is undoubtedly all right, but we wish to be sure. You know what the box should contain?"

"Oh, yes, indeed; pillow-cases and sheets, with a big S embroidered on them."

"Very well. Shall I undo the string for you?"

"I shall be much obliged," said she, her eye flashing quickly about the room before settling down upon the knot he was deftly loosening.

Her brother, gazing indifferently in from the doorway, hardly noticed this look; but the reporter at his back did, though he failed to detect its penetrating quality.

"Your name is on the other side," observed the detective as he drew away the string and turned the package over.

The smile which just lifted the corner of her lips was not in answer to this remark, but to her recognition of her employer's handwriting in the words under her name: Send without opening. She had not misjudged him.

"The cover you may like to take off yourself," suggested the officer, as he lifted the box out of its wrapper.

"Oh, I don't mind. There's nothing to be ashamed of in embroidered linen. Or perhaps that is not what you are looking for?"

No one answered. All were busy watching her whip off the lid and lift out the pile of sheets and pillow-cases with which the box was closely packed.

"Shall I unfold them?" she asked.

The detective nodded.

Taking out the topmost sheet, she shook it open. Then the next and the next till she reached the bottom of the box. Nothing of a criminating nature came to light. The box as well as its contents was without mystery of any kind. This was not an unexpected result of course, but the smile with which she began to refold the pieces and throw them back into the box, revealed one of her dimples which was almost as dangerous to the casual observer as when it revealed both.

"There," she exclaimed, "you see! Household linen exactly as I said. Now may I go home?"

"Certainly, Miss Strange."

The detective stole a sly glance at the reporter. She was not going in for the horrors then after all.

But the reporter abated nothing of his knowing air, for while she spoke of going, she made no move towards doing so, but continued to look about the room till her glances finally settled on a long dark curtain shutting off an adjoining room.

"There's where she lies, I suppose," she feelingly exclaimed. "And not one of you knows who killed her. Somehow, I cannot understand that. Why don't you know when that's what you're hired for?" The innocence with which she uttered this was astonishing. The detective began to look sheepish and the reporter turned aside to hide his smile. Whether in another moment either would have spoken no one can say, for, with a mock consciousness of having said something foolish, she caught up her parasol from the table and made a start for the door.

But of course she looked back.

"I was wondering," she recommenced, with a half wistful, half speculative air, "whether I should ask to have a peep at the place where it all happened."

The reporter chuckled behind the pencil-end he was chewing, but the officer maintained his solemn air, for which act of self-restraint he was undoubtedly grateful when in another minute she gave a quick impulsive shudder not altogether assumed, and vehemently added: "But I couldn't stand the sight; no, I couldn't! I'm an awful coward when it comes to things like that. Nothing in all the world would induce me to look at the woman or her room. But I should like—" here both her dimples came into play though she could not be said exactly to smile—"just one little look upstairs, where he went poking about so long without any fear it seems of being interrupted. Ever since I've read about it I have seen, in my mind, a picture of his wicked figure sneaking from room to room, tearing open drawers and flinging out the contents of closets just to find a little money—a little, little money! I shall not sleep to-night just for wondering how those high up attic rooms really look."

Who could dream that back of this display of mingled child-ishness and audacity there lay hidden purpose, intellect, and a keen knowledge of human nature. Not the two men who listened to this seemingly irresponsible chatter. To them she was a child to be humoured and humour her they did. The dainty feet which had already found their way to that gloomy stair-case were allowed to ascend, followed it is true by those of the officer who did not dare to smile back at the reporter because of the brother's watchful and none too conciliatory eye.

At the stair head she paused to look back.

"I don't see those horrible marks which the papers describe as running all along the lower hall and up these stairs."

"No, Miss Strange; they have gradually been rubbed out, but you will find some still showing on these upper floors."

"Oh! oh! where? You frighten me—frighten me horribly! But—but—if you don't mind, I should like to see."

Why should not a man on a tedious job amuse himself? Piloting her over to the small room in the rear, he pointed down at the boards. She gave one look and then stepped gingerly in.

"Just look!" she cried; "a whole string of marks going straight from door to window. They have no shape, have they,—just blotches? I wonder why one of them is so much larger than the rest?"

This was no new question. It was one which everybody who went into the room was sure to ask, there was such a difference in the size and appearance of the mark nearest the window.

The reason—well, minds were divided about that, and no one had a satisfactory theory. The detective therefore kept discreetly silent.

This did not seem to offend Miss Strange. On the contrary it gave her an opportunity to babble away to her heart's content.

"One, two, three, four, five, six," she counted, with a shudder at every count. "And one of them bigger than the others." She might have added, "It is the trail of one foot, and strangely, intermingled at that," but she did not, though we may be quite sure that she noted the fact. "And where, just where did the old wallet fall? Here? or here?"

She had moved as she spoke, so that in uttering the last "here," she stood directly before the window. The surprise she received there nearly made her forget the part she was playing. From the character of the light in the room, she had expected, on looking out, to confront a near-by wall, but not a window in that wall. Yet that was what she saw directly facing her from across the old-fashioned alley separating this house from its neighbour; twelve unshuttered and uncurtained panes through which she caught a darkened view of a room almost as forlorn and devoid of furniture as the one in which she then stood.

When quite sure of herself, she let a certain portion of her surprise appear.

"Why, look!" she cried, "if you can't see right in next door! What a lonesome-looking place! From its desolate appearance I should think the house quite empty."

"And it is. That's the old Shaffer homestead. It's been empty for a year."

"Oh, empty!" And she turned away, with the most inconsequent air in the world, crying out as her name rang up the stair, "There's Arthur calling. I suppose he thinks I've been here long enough. I'm sure I'm very much obliged to you, officer. I really shouldn't have slept a wink to-night, if I hadn't been given a peep at these rooms, which I had imagined so different." And with one additional glance over her shoulder, that seemed to penetrate both windows and the desolate space beyond, she ran quickly out and down in response to her brother's reiterated call.

"Drive quickly!—as quickly as the law allows, to Hiram Brown's office in Duane Street."

Arrived at the address named, she went in alone to see Mr. Brown. He was her father's lawyer and a family friend.

Hardly waiting for his affectionate greeting, she cried out quickly, "Tell me how I can learn anything about the old Shaffer house in Seventeenth Street. Now, don't look so surprised. I have very good reasons for my request and—and—I'm in an awful hurry."

"But—"

"I know, I know; there's been a dreadful tragedy next door to it; but it's about the Shaffer house itself I want some information. Has it an agent, a—"

"Of course it has an agent, and here is his name."

Mr. Brown presented her with a card on which he had hastily written both name and address.

She thanked him, dropped him a mocking curtsey full of charm, whispered "Don't tell father," and was gone.

Her manner to the man she next interviewed was very different. As soon as she saw him she subsided into her usual society manner. With just a touch of the conceit of the successful debutante, she announced herself as Miss Strange of Seventy-second Street. Her business with him was in regard to the possible renting of the Shaffer house. She had an old lady friend who was desirous of living downtown.

In passing through Seventeenth Street, she had noticed that the old Shaffer house was standing empty and had been immediately struck with the advantages it possessed for her elderly friend's occupancy. Could it be that the house was for rent? There was no sign on it to that effect, but—etc.

His answer left her nothing to hope for.

"It is going to be torn down," he said.

"Oh, what a pity!" she exclaimed. "Real colonial, isn't it! I wish I could see the rooms inside before it is disturbed. Such doors and such dear old-fashioned mantelpieces as it must have! I just dote on the Colonial. It brings up such pictures of the old days; weddings, you know, and parties;—all so different from ours and so much more interesting."

Is it the chance shot that tells? Sometimes. Violet had no especial intention in what she said save as a prelude to a pending request, but nothing could have served her purpose better than that one word, wedding. The agent laughed and giving her his first indulgent look, remarked genially:

"Romance is not confined to those ancient times. If you were to enter that house to-day you would come across evidences of a wedding as romantic as any which ever took place in all the seventy odd years of its existence. A man and a woman were married there day before yesterday who did their first courting under its roof forty years ago. He has been married twice and she once in the interval; but the old love held firm and now at the age of sixty and over they have come together to finish their days in peace and happiness. Or so we will hope."

"Married! married in that house and on the day that—"

She caught herself up in time. He did not notice the break.

"Yes, in memory of those old days of courtship, I suppose. They came here about five, got the keys, drove off, went through the ceremony in that empty house, returned the keys to me in my own apartment, took the steamer for Naples, and were on the sea before midnight. Do you not call that quick work as well as highly romantic?"

"Very." Miss Strange's cheek had paled. It was apt to when she was greatly excited. "But I don't understand," she added, the moment after. "How could they do this and nobody know about it? I should have thought it would have got into the papers."

"They are quiet people. I don't think they told their best friends. A simple announcement in the next day's journals testified to the fact of their marriage, but that was all. I would not have felt at liberty to mention the circumstances myself, if the parties were not well on their way to Europe."

"Oh, how glad I am that you did tell me! Such a story of constancy and the hold which old associations have upon sensitive minds! But—"

"Why, Miss? What's the matter? You look very much disturbed."

"Don't you remember? Haven't you thought? Something else happened that very day and almost at the same time on that block. Something very dreadful—"

"Mrs. Doolittle's murder?"

"Yes. It was as near as next door, wasn't it? Oh, if this happy couple had known—"

"But fortunately they didn't. Nor are they likely to, till they reach the other side. You needn't fear that their honeymoon will be spoiled that way."

"But they may have heard something or seen something before leaving the street. Did you notice how the gentleman looked when he returned you the keys?"

"I did, and there was no cloud on his satisfaction."

"Oh, how you relieve me!" One—two dimples made their appearance in Miss Strange's fresh, young cheeks. "Well! I wish them joy. Do you mind telling me their names? I cannot think of them as actual persons without knowing their names."

"The gentleman was Constantin Amidon; the lady, Marian Shaffer. You will have to think of them now as Mr. and Mrs. Amidon."

"And I will. Thank you, Mr. Hutton, thank you very much. Next to the pleasure of getting the house for my friend, is that of hearing this charming bit of news in its connection."

She held out her hand and, as he took it, remarked:

"They must have had a clergyman and witnesses."

"Undoubtedly."

"I wish I had been one of the witnesses," she sighed sentimentally.

"They were two old men."

"Oh, no! Don't tell me that."

"Fogies; nothing less."

"But the clergyman? He must have been young. Surely there was some one there capable of appreciating the situation?"

"I can't say about that; I did not see the clergyman."

"Oh, well! it doesn't matter." Miss Strange's manner was as nonchalant as it was charming. "We will think of him as being very young."

And with a merry toss of her head she flitted away.

But she sobered very rapidly upon entering her limousine.

"Hello!"

"Ah, is that you?"

"Yes, I want a Marconi sent."

"A Marconi?"

"Yes, to the *Cretic*, which left dock the very night in which we are so deeply interested."

"Good. Whom to? The Captain?"

"No, to a Mrs. Constantin Amidon. But first be sure there is such a passenger."

"Mrs.! What idea have you there?"

"Excuse my not stating over the telephone. The message is to be to this effect. Did she at any time immediately before or after her marriage to Mr. Amidon get a glimpse of any one in the adjoining house? No remarks, please. I use the telephone because I am not ready to explain myself. If she did, let her send a written description to you of that person as soon as she reaches the Azores."

"You surprise me. May I not call or hope for a line from you early to-morrow?"

"I shall be busy till you get your answer."

He hung up the receiver. He recognized the resolute tone.

But the time came when the pending explanation was fully given to him. An answer had been returned from the steamer, favourable to Violet's hopes. Mrs. Amidon had seen such a person and would send a full description of the same at the first opportunity. It was news to fill Violet's heart with pride; the filament of a clue which had led to this great result had been so nearly invisible and had felt so like nothing in her grasp.

To her employer she described it as follows:

"When I hear or read of a case which contains any baffling features, I am apt to feel some hidden chord in my nature thrill to one fact in it and not to any of the others. In this case the single fact which appealed to my imagination was the dropping of the stolen wallet in that upstairs room. Why did the guilty man drop it? and why, having dropped it, did he not pick it up again? but one answer seemed possible. He had heard or seen something at the spot where it fell which not only alarmed him but sent him in flight from the house."

"Very good; and did you settle to your own mind the nature of that sound or that sight?"

"I did." Her manner was strangely businesslike. No show of dimples now. "Satisfied that if any possibility remained of my ever doing this, it would have to be on the exact place of this occurrence or not at all, I embraced your suggestion and visited the house."

"And that room no doubt."

"And that room. Women, somehow, seem to manage such things."

"So I've noticed, Miss Strange. And what was the result of your visit? What did you discover there?"

"This: that one of the blood spots marking the criminal's steps through the room was decidedly more pronounced than the rest; and, what was even more important, that the window out of which I was looking had its counterpart in the house on the opposite side of the alley. In gazing through the one I was gazing through the other; and not only that, but into the darkened area of the room beyond. Instantly I saw how the latter fact might be made to explain the former one. But before I say how, let me ask if it is quite settled among you that the smears on the floor and stairs mark the passage of the criminal's footsteps!"

"Certainly; and very bloody feet they must have been too. His shoes—or rather his one shoe—for the proof is plain that only the right one left its mark—must have become thoroughly saturated to carry its traces so far."

"Do you think that any amount of saturation would have

done this? Or, if you are not ready to agree to that, that a shoe so covered with blood could have failed to leave behind it some hint of its shape, some imprint, however faint, of heel or toe? But nowhere did it do this. We see a smear—and that is all."

"You are right, Miss Strange; you are always right. And what do you gather from this?"

She looked to see how much he expected from her, and, meeting an eye not quite as free from ironic suggestion as his words had led her to expect, faltered a little as she proceeded to say:

"My opinion is a girl's opinion, but such as it is you have the right to have it. From the indications mentioned I could draw but this conclusion: that the blood which accompanied the criminal's footsteps was not carried through the house by his shoes;—he wore no shoes; he did not even wear stockings; probably he had none. For reasons which appealed to his judgment, he went about his wicked work barefoot; and it was the blood from his own veins and not from those of his victim which made the trail we have followed with so much interest. Do you forget those broken beads;—how he kicked them about and stamped upon them in his fury? One of them pierced the ball of his foot, and that so sharply that it not only spurted blood but kept on bleeding with every step he took. Otherwise, the trail would have been lost after his passage up the stairs."

"Fine!" There was no irony in the bureau-chief's eye now. "You are progressing, Miss Strange. Allow me, I pray, to kiss your hand. It is a liberty I have never taken, but one which would greatly relieve my present stress of feeling."

She lifted her hand toward him, but it was in gesture, not in recognition of his homage.

"Thank you," said she, "but I claim no monopoly on deductions so simple as these. I have not the least doubt that not only yourself but every member of the force has made the same. But there is a little matter which may have escaped the police, may even have escaped you. To that I would now call your attention since through it I have been enabled, after a little necessary groping, to reach the open. You remember the one large blotch on the upper floor where the man dropped the wallet? That blotch, more or less commingled with a fainter one, possessed great significance for me from the first moment I saw it. How came his foot to bleed so much more profusely at that one spot than at any other? There could be but one answer: because here a surprise met him—a surprise so startling to him in his present state of mind, that he gave a quick spring backward, with the result that his wounded foot came down suddenly and forcibly instead of easily as in his previous wary tread. And what was the surprise? I made it my business to find out, and now I can tell you that it was the sight of a woman's face staring upon him from the neighbouring house which he had probably been told was empty. The shock disturbed his judgment. He saw his crime discovered—his guilty secret read, and fled in unreasoning panic. He might better have held on to his wits. It was this display of fear which led me to search after its cause, and consequently to discover that at this especial hour more than one person had been in the Shaffer house; that, in fact, a marriage had been celebrated there under circumstances as romantic as any we read of in books, and that this marriage, privately carried out, had been followed by an immediate voyage of the happy couple on one of the White Star steamers. With the rest you are conversant. I do not need to say anything about what has followed the sending of that Marconi."

"But I am going to say something about your work in this matter, Miss Strange. The big detectives about here will have to look sharp if—"

"Don't, please! Not yet." A smile softened the asperity of this interruption. "The man has yet to be caught and identified. Till that is done I cannot enjoy any one's congratulations. And you will see that all this may not be so easy. If no one happened to meet the desperate wretch before he had an opportunity to retie his shoe-laces, there will be little for you or even for the police to go upon but his wounded foot, his undoubtedly carefully prepared alibi, and later, a woman's confused description of a face seen but for a moment only and that under a personal excitement precluding minute attention. I should not be surprised if the whole thing came to nothing."

But it did not. As soon as the description was received from

Mrs. Amidon (a description, by the way, which was unusually clear and precise, owing to the peculiar and contradictory features of the man), the police were able to recognize him among the many suspects always under their eye. Arrested, he pleaded, just as Miss Strange had foretold, an alibi of a seemingly unimpeachable character; but neither it, nor the plausible explanation with which he endeavoured to account for a freshly healed scar amid the callouses of his right foot, could stand before Mrs. Amidon's unequivocal testimony that he was the same man she had seen in Mrs. Doolittle's upper room on the afternoon of her own happiness and of that poor woman's murder.

The moment when, at his trial, the two faces again confronted each other across a space no wider than that which had separated them on the dread occasion in Seventeenth Street, is said to have been one of the most dramatic in the annals of that ancient court room.

Acknowledgments

My thanks to the gracious and patient Elda Rotor, vice president and publisher of Penguin Classics, who has been helping shape this book from concept to last edits, and to the talents and professionalism of the excellent Penguin team that it has been lucky enough to find—associate editor Elizabeth Vogt, senior director of production editorial Norina Frabotta, production editor Chelsea Cohen, eagle-eyed copyeditor Dave Cole, reader Jennifer Tait, and cover artist Jaya Miceli.

My thanks also to other editors and anthologists and scholars, invariably gracious colleagues such as Martin Edwards, Otto Penzler, Leslie Klinger, and Laurie King, and historians such as Lucy Sussex, David Brion Davis, Lucy Worsley, LeRoy Lad Panek, and especially the encyclopedic and elegant Judith Flanders.

And thanks especially to Mae Reale. We owe our entire friendship and romance to the lure of old books.

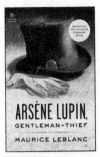